They Danced by the Light of the Moon

AN ANDY GAMMON MYSTERY

THEY DANCED BY THE LIGHT OF THE MOON

TEMPA PAGEL

FIVE STAR

A part of Gale, Cengage Learning

GALE
CENGAGE Learning

Detroit • New York • San Francisco • New Haven, Conn • Waterville, Maine • London

LIBRARY OF CONGRESS CATALOGING-IN-PUBLICATION DATA

Pagel, Tempa.
    They danced by the light of the moon : an Andy Gammon mystery / by Tempa Pagel. — First edition.
        pages cm
    ISBN 978-1-4328-2799-1 (hardcover) — ISBN 1-4328-2799-5 (hardcover)
    1. Murder—Investigation—Fiction. 2. Historic hotels—Fiction. 3. Family secrets—Fiction. 4. Women—Social conditions—Fiction. I. Title.
PS3616.A33765T48 2014
813'.6—dc23   2013038370

First Edition. First Printing: February 2014
Find us on Facebook– https://www.facebook.com/FiveStarCengage
Visit our website– http://www.gale.cengage.com/fivestar/
Contact Five Star™ Publishing at FiveStar@cengage.com

Printed in Mexico
1 2 3 4 5 6 7 18 17 16 15 14

For Tom

ACKNOWLEDGMENTS

Thank you to Jan Soupcoff, Margaret Ouzts, and Susan Oleksiw for suggestions, honesty, and continued support.

They dined on mince, and slices of quince,
    Which they ate with a runcible spoon;
And hand in hand, on the edge of the sand,
    They danced by the light of the moon,
            The moon,
            The moon,
    They danced by the light of the moon.

—*The Owl and the Pussycat,* Edward Lear, 1871

Grand Hotel of the Atlantic
New Hampshire Coastline
June Twenty-Third, 1901

Marguerite shuts the slim leather-bound book and sets it on top of the letters scattered on the desk. The cover doesn't fully close because the well-thumbed pages of the volume no longer lay flat. So many keepsakes—pressed flowers, dance cards, a hair ribbon—have been slipped between its pages over the years that now when something is removed, the binding, having stretched to accommodate the item, remembers it still and retains its shape.

She had been about to empty the book. For an instant she had poised it over the wicker wastebasket, ready to shake out its contents. A lone violet, faded gray and pressed paper-thin with a threadlike stem, had in fact slid out and landed atop a discarded envelope when—just as suddenly as she had thought to throw it all away—she had changed her mind. She had retrieved the flower and put it back in its place between two of her favorite poems.

Now she touches the smooth leather cover, but it is out of habit, without affection. For which birthday did she receive it from Timothy? Her fourteenth? Fifteenth? She wonders how it is that a single event, a chance meeting, an aberrant thought, can lead a person on a path that alters relationships with things beloved and familiar. How is it that her eyes can now glance over the objects of this room and see them as just that? Not as carefully chosen volumes of history or poetry; not as hats and dresses specially tailored in the latest style

11

with meticulous regard to her slender figure and rosy coloring; not as precious correspondence linking her to loved ones—Melinda, Bess, Mama and Papa, Timothy. And Timothy: Can she have so little feeling for her fiancé's letters? On this day they are all just objects: a jumble of papers on the desk, a crooked row of books on the fireplace mantel, clothing strewn over the chaise, the bed, the privacy screen. Is it possible to be one person for nineteen years, and then somebody entirely different?

Brisk footsteps sound in the hallway. Frantically, she scans the room. To outward appearances everything is the same; however, she feels that were anyone to enter the room just now, all would be told on her face.

The footsteps pass by her door, but the alarm has dashed away momentary doubts. She twists Timothy's grandmother's ring off her finger, slides it onto a hair ribbon, and knots it in the middle. She takes up the poetry book again and, without hesitation this time, dumps its contents straight into the wastebasket. She opens the book dead center where the pressed violet had been, and places the ring atop the third stanza of a sonnet by Emily Dickinson, opposite another oft-read poem, The Wanderer. *She smoothes out the ribbon so that its pink ends overhang both top and bottom of the book, and closes the pages over the diamond.*

Now where to leave it for Timothy? Not among her clothes in case someone other than Alice is given the task of packing. She considers and dismisses, in turn, windowsills, bed, bureau, wardrobe. In the end, she slides it back into its usual spot, alongside her other books. But the pink ribbon draws attention to itself, and the pages don't quite shut over the ring, causing the book to stand apart from the others. Impatient now, she plucks the book from its spot, pulls out the ring, and unties the ribbon. Inside a suitcase she finds a sheet of tissue paper, which had been used in packing to separate shoes from garments. She tears off a corner, twists the paper around the ring, and tucks it safely away until she can write to Melissa with instructions.

At last, Marguerite is ready. She turns the stem on the lamp on the wall, its low hiss falling to silence as light drains from the room. In one graceful movement she pulls the chiffon wrap off the back of the chair and swirls it around her shoulders. A corner catches and she yanks it free, upsetting the chair. As she stoops to right it, more footsteps sound in the hallway—ponderous, purposeful steps. Papa.

Leaving the chair, she grabs the drawstring bag that contains her journal, the one thing she cannot leave behind, and bolts for the window. The sash resists her efforts, although she has done this same thing before. Annoyed, she tears off the hampering wrap. The footsteps are just outside the door when the sash gives way and slides, then stops in its usual place, two-thirds of the way up. She pushes the screen window, whose lower hooks have already been unlatched in preparation for this moment, outward and squeezes through, crawling out onto the verandah roof.

Papa knocks on the door, calls her name. She slips off her shoes and stands, pressing herself against the wall just outside the window. This is foolish, she berates herself. She should have answered the door, spoken with him, gotten him to go away. Now he may become alarmed, enter her room, and understand right away what she is doing.

"Marguerite? Are you awake?" There is another soft knock, a hesitation, and then Papa's footsteps recede down the hall.

Marguerite moves now, sidling close to the wall toward the corner of the building, a hand trailing along the clapboards for assurance. Where the back porch roof forms a miter joint with the side roof, she bundles her skirt up around bag and shoes. She sits and slides inch by inch, feet acting as brakes, down the rough shingles to the gutter. Craning her neck, and avoiding a dizzying direct look downward, she scans the verandah below. She sees nobody, but then it is difficult to see into shadows behind the new strings of the bright electric bulbs that outline the hotel.

She listens to the distinct sounds of the night: a mild wind tickling leaves on the highest branches of a tree, the soprano solo of a cricket, the muffled drone of voices from a window that has not yet been closed against the night air. A breeze brings the briny tang of the sea whose unseen but constant pulsing presence is somewhere beyond the lawn. She tries to gauge the likelihood that someone could be sitting in the shadows or walking the grounds. Finally, because she can wait no longer, Marguerite tosses shoes and bag to the grass.

She listens a scant minute for a reaction from below—nothing— then wraps her skirt up around her hips, rolls onto her stomach, and slides over the roof edge. She reaches a foot downward, gaining hold in the notch of the V brace on the side of a column, then shimmies awkwardly, bunched skirt catching and dragging, to the porch floor. She throws a leg over the railing, straddling it as she grips the baluster, and pauses to judge the distance. It is greater at this end— more than a six-foot drop—but she can't risk being seen walking to the other end of the verandah. She flings the other leg over and jumps, landing softly in the grass, her skirt falling into place. A moment later, she has slipped on her satin shoes and is running across the lawn, the dampness of the dew already seeping through their thin soles.

CHAPTER ONE

From the passenger seat beside me came an audible intake of air. "Oh, would you look at that!" Mayta said.

As if stage curtains had been pulled aside, we'd emerged from the trees and were presented with a spectacular tableau. The Atlantic Ocean spread out to the east, the broad mouth of the Piscataqua River to the west, and center stage, on the highest point of land, the last of the sun spotlighting its white facade, stood the majestic Grand Hotel of the Atlantic.

"Wow," I said quietly.

"Hard to think anything bad could have happened in such a place, isn't it?" Mayta said. Driving along the winding coastal route north to New Hampshire, my mother-in-law had regaled me with stories of the Grand Hotel of the Atlantic, where she had once spent a weekend. While she'd continued on about its history and lore, my thoughts had wandered. Despite it being a splurge we couldn't really afford, Gus had understood my wanting to go with Mayta to the opening gala at the newly restored hotel, even insisting on having us pose, all dressed up, with the kids in front of the rose bushes. I smiled; it had kind of felt like prom night without the dates.

"Huh?" I said now, with a creeping feeling that a response to Mayta's rambling was expected. "Something bad happened there?"

"I was telling you about a girl who went missing from the hotel."

"Oh. Is this ancient history, too?"

"Didn't you hear anything I said? It was around 1900. She was from a wealthy Boston family and had come by herself to the hotel. One night she just disappeared."

"So what happened to her?"

"I can't remember the whole story," Mayta said. "Just that she left all her things in her room so they thought that she'd been kidnapped. I don't think they ever found her."

"Another romantic twist to the Grand Hotel saga."

"Yep." She glanced at me sideways.

"Why did you look at me that way?"

She shrugged. "Just thinking it would be an interesting project—finding out what happened to her."

"Hmm," I said. We crossed a small bridge onto the island and pulled up to the front porch where a smartly uniformed valet waited at the bottom of the red-carpeted stairs.

"You're always researching old records and things," Mayta said. "Tell me you haven't googled the Grand Hotel."

"Okay, I googled it. I like architecture and history. Your buildings out here are so much older than the ones I grew up with in the Midwest."

"I'm just saying it's an intriguing mystery," she said. "Especially with the interest right now in the hotel's reopening." We got out of the car and I handed the keys to the valet.

"I'm so excited!" Mayta squeezed my arm as we ascended the red-carpeted steps.

It was too early to be seated for dinner, so, after giving our names to the maitre'd at the door and ordering cocktails, we threaded through the other gala attendees gathering on the verandah, and managed to snag the last vacant wicker settee at the end.

"Mmm, you're right," I said to Mayta, after tasting my first Cosmopolitan. "It's yummy." We chatted with each other and those around us as the dropping sun smeared the sky a Crayola orange.

At one point, when Mayta turned to join a conversation, I closed my eyes and imagined myself transported back in time. The painted boards beneath my feet and the wicker arm support under my hand could easily have been the same as a century ago. A lull in the arrival of cars brought other sounds to my ear: the susurration of a breeze moving through trees; the low drone of conversation around me; one man's voice emerging as he described his tennis match to a woman whose soft response erupted several times in a tinkly laugh. In my imagination the man wore tennis whites, the woman a high-necked dress with a folded parasol at her side.

As I indulged in eavesdropping, more snippets of conversations bubbled to the surface. From my right: "We always go to Sebring BMW."

From my left: ". . . ran into Al Wright out on the course today."

Then the husky and now urgent voice of the tennis player: ". . . wearing a green dress." From the right again: "Chuck Miller is going to run for mayor."

The tennis player again, this time jarringly terse: ". . . follow her. Don't let her out of your sight."

I opened my eyes, wondering why the tennis player wanted someone—tinkly laughing lady?—to follow somebody else.

"Hey, Andy! Quit daydreaming!" It was Mayta's voice now in my ear.

I looked around. Everyone else was moving toward the door. I tried to match people with voices I'd heard, especially a couple in the modern-day equivalent of tennis whites and Victorian gown but, of course, could not.

"Come on," Mayta said. "Dinner time."

In the lobby, I just had time to take in its elegant woodwork and marble fireplace before we were escorted into the dining room where floor-to-ceiling windows framed magnificent river views. We were led to a round table for six, already occupied by a young couple who had their heads together conferring about something, and an older man wearing a dated but well-tailored three-piece suit.

The older man stood immediately and gave a small bow. "Chauncey Brown," he said warmly, his eyes dancing. With an open hand he gestured to the young couple. "And let me present our tablemates, the lovebirds Claudia and Daniel Dean." Claudia, pretty in her short gauzy dress and long brown hair, smiled in greeting while her male counterpart grimaced at the word "lovebirds." "They're newlyweds," Chauncey said.

"Oh! Congratulations!" I said, thinking that for a newlywed, Daniel looked pretty sour. After Mayta and I introduced ourselves and took our seats, Chauncey launched a friendly conversation, during which we learned that he was a retired lawyer from New York.

"I'm staying for the weekend," he said. "Since my wife died a few years ago, I do a bit of traveling on my own." I thought to offer condolences, but Chauncey did not look sad, and the reference to his wife had seemed matter-of-fact.

"We're only here for dinner," Mayta said, explaining that we lived not far away, in Newburyport.

"Oh, we live nearby too," Claudia said. "We just had to see the restored hotel. Or rather I did." She grinned at her husband, who smiled weakly in return. "Daniel is humoring me by coming." While Claudia talked excitedly about the hotel, Daniel's smile gelled. I wasn't impressed by his "humoring"; if I had asked Gus to come, he would have been gracious and a good sport even if it wasn't something he wanted to do.

"Did you see the restored fresco?" Claudia pointed overhead and we looked up at the delicate painting of cherubs and rose

18

garlands that decorated the domed ceiling.

"Isn't it beautiful!" Mayta exclaimed. As she and Claudia enthused about architectural details, a compact, fortyish woman in a business suit arrived at the table.

"Beverly Magill." She thrust her hand at Chauncey, who had stood. "Reporter for the *Portsmouth Daily Monitor.* I'm covering this event for the society page." She nodded to each of us as Chauncey made introductions, and then took the final seat between Chauncey and Mayta. "So," she said without wasting any time, "why are you all here?"

Mayta told about staying at the hotel as a young woman, adding, "Andy here likes history and architecture."

"I spent ten summers here with my parents; the hotel was an important part of my childhood," Chauncey said.

"It's so romantic!" Claudia said. "When I heard it had reopened, I just had to come!"

Beverly directed her next question to Chauncey. "Do you think it's been restored to its original grandeur, the way the brochure says?"

"Oh yes. In my opinion, it has," he said. "I've already had a chance to sample everything. The food is delicious, the service impeccable, and the accommodations comfortable, with every amenity one could want."

"Have you all toured the hotel?" Beverly looked around the table. When Mayta and I shook our heads, she lifted a hand as if she were hostess of the event, and the maitre d' came over. He took down our names, along with Claudia's, for the last tour, which would be after dinner.

"I've already gone twice," Claudia said, "but I can't resist another chance to snoop around."

Beverly turned to Daniel. "Don't you want to take the tour?"

"Nope, and I know nothing about the hotel, so I can't answer any questions," he said with a smug smile. There was an awkward moment during which Beverly opened her mouth to retort, and the rest of us buried our noses in the menus. But then the waitress came and Mayta quickly said we were ready to order.

I chose the Maine crab and lobster cake appetizer, the lobster bisque, a baby arugula salad, and the pan-seared Atlantic salmon. Mayta chose the same appetizer, soup, and salad, but the grilled beef tenderloin for an entree. We decided on wines to complement our various dinners and the bottles were decanted at the table. Chauncey Brown did the honors of tasting and approving the burgundy, and Beverly the Cotes du Rhône. From then on, our glasses were kept refilled.

While soft jazz played in the background, waiters glided efficiently around the dining room. Low cultured voices were punctuated by soft laughter or a ringing clink of silver on china. By the time we'd finished our main course, Beverly's questions had revealed that Claudia Dean's great-aunt had worked in the Grand Hotel's kitchen for many years. When the hotel closed its doors decades ago, her great-aunt had bought some of the old hotel dishes at the auction, and Claudia now had them.

"I guess I'm a Grand Hotel groupie," she said, flicking her long hair back over her shoulder. "Ever since I was little, I loved hearing stories from Great-Aunt Dennis—especially about the celebrities who came—and reading about the hotel's history. Sometimes I feel like I should've lived back then or something."

"I know what you mean," I said. "When I'm in a historical place it drives me nuts that I can't just pop back a hundred years or so and see what's going on."

"Have you seen *Forever After*?" Claudia asked. "The movie that was filmed here with Granger Moore and Lenore Lamot?"

Before I could answer, Mayta cut off her conversation with Beverly, swiveled in her seat, and leaned across my plate toward Claudia. "That's my favorite movie!"

"I've seen it six times," Claudia said.

"I've seen it at least a dozen!" Mayta said. Which launched the two of them into a scene-by-scene dissection containing numerous "do you remembers": when Lenore Lamot did something; what Lenore Lamot wore; what Granger Moore said. After a few minutes I tuned out.

Daniel, who looked like he was as interested in the subject of a sixty-year-old movie as I, had pushed away from the table and was leaning back in his chair, his long jeaned legs stretched out, his wine glass cradled in his lap. After my question about what he did for a living received a one-word answer—mechanic—I turned to Chauncey Brown and asked him about his memories of the hotel.

"Yes, tell us what it was like," Beverly urged, and took out a small notebook. Chauncey eagerly told about playing croquet on manicured lawns, tennis on clay courts, and swimming in the Olympic-sized pool. He remembered Gloria Swanson coming to stay one summer. "That was when the hotel was at its largest—about 300 rooms, I believe. And the service! We were treated like royalty."

As Chauncey's monologue continued, I began analyzing my tablemates. Chauncey had obviously come from money, yet his jacket sleeve was moth-eaten. Had he fallen on hard times or was he just one of those eccentric understated Yankees? Daniel tapped fingertips on the base of his empty wine glass, occasionally responding with a tight smile to something humorous, but was otherwise detached from the group. He was ill-mannered and self-centered, I decided, but I couldn't fault him entirely; it must be difficult to deal with his wife's obsession with Grand Hotel of the Atlantic. And I found Beverly's relentless questions, jotting down of notes, and periodic interrupting to clarify a detail annoying, too. Couldn't she just relax and enjoy the atmosphere?

Mayta, who had for the moment exhausted the subject of Lenore Lamot, interrupted Chauncey to add her own memories. I could tell from her animation that the group's idiosyncrasies weren't marring *her* experience.

When the waitress returned, all but Daniel ordered coffee and decadent desserts. "None for me," he said. "I have to go." He stood abruptly and took his jacket from the back of his chair.

"Not yet, Daniel, please," Claudia said. "Can't you wait?"

He flashed her an angry look and said in a low voice, "I'm due back. You knew that from the beginning." To the rest of us, he flung over his shoulder, "It was nice meeting you all."

Claudia, her cheeks flushed, watched Daniel disappear into the lobby. "Sometimes men can be so pigheaded," she said with a wry twist of her mouth.

"Oh, I'd agree with that," Mayta said in an easy tone, and I mumbled in accordance, while thinking there had to be something more going on between Claudia and Daniel than his not wanting to be here. Beverly glared after him, but Chauncey remarked on the mildness of the evening as if nothing were amiss. Then, thankfully, our desserts came and we attacked them, relieved to have something to attend to.

Halfway through her molten chocolate cake, Claudia checked her watch, picked up her oversized designer bag, and excused herself to find the ladies' room. I glanced at the grandfather clock, visible from the lobby. Nine o'clock already. The evening had gone by quickly.

Claudia had not returned when, fifteen minutes later, the final tour of the evening was announced. As Mayta and I rose, Beverly said she had a call to make first and would catch up with us. Chauncey stood also and announced he was out onto the verandah to catch the reflection of the moon on the river before retiring to his room, so we said our goodbyes to him.

"I wonder what happened to Claudia," Mayta said. "She wanted to take the tour."

"Maybe she went after Daniel."

While the group gathered in the lobby we looked at a display of enlarged black-and-white photographs from the hotel's heyday. About ten minutes later, when the guide began her talk about the restoration process, I noticed that neither Beverly nor Claudia had joined the group.

We were led through the old ballrooms updated now to serve as convention rooms, day rooms, and sun rooms, all beautifully appointed with understated elegance in soothing seascape colors. As we passed the spa, the guide said, "Our services include massages, body mudpacks, facials, manicures, pedicures, full hair salon, and makeup application."

"Remind me to come here for a tune-up in the near future," Mayta quipped in my ear. "I'm sure it's reasonable—a few grand or so."

"At least!" I laughed, picturing my no-nonsense mother-in-law in a body mudpack.

"We have three outdoor swimming pools." The guide paused at a window that looked out onto tennis courts. "And beyond that tree line is the marina."

"Is it possible to see anything from a window that is less than spectacular?" I said, half in jest.

She thought a moment, then said seriously, "No. On every side of the building there is the harbor, river, or ocean, so I would say it's impossible not to have a good view."

It took two trips to deliver all of us to the second floor where we were to see a restored guest room in the oldest section of the hotel. At the end of the hallway, the guide slipped a card into a lock, and opened the door. "First, I'll show you one of our singles," she said. "Then we'll go up one floor to see a suite."

The room was decorated in restful gradients of blue and

green, continuing the theme of water and sky, but was not as immaculate as I would have expected, for I noticed some small dark spots on the carpet by the bureau. Our guide listed the numerous amenities of the room and waved a hand in the direction of the bathroom. "Take a look. You'll find complimentary products from The Spa downstairs: Soothing Sea Kelp shampoo and conditioner and Ultra Care body lotion."

As Mayta and several others moved toward the bathroom, I wandered over to inspect the spots on the floor, wondering how a maid could have missed them in her cleaning. At that moment, a shriek from behind me streaked up my spine.

I whirled to see a woman, who had poked her head into the bathroom, press both hands to her cheeks and step backward hard onto Mayta's foot. Mayta yelped and in two strides I was at her side. She and I and a couple of others pushed past the woman and crowded the doorway, craning our necks to take in and make sense of the sight before us.

Inside the shell-pink bathtub at the opposite end of its shining chrome spigot lay a woman on her back, arms folded on her chest, legs bent, knees together, resting against one side as if somebody had gently set her there. She was fully clothed, down to her high-heeled shoes and the large handbag that lay next to her. A sweep of long hair covered her face and chest, the long strands parting where a short silver-handled knife was inserted into her chest. Blood seeped from the wound, staining the ends of her brown hair and her pale green gauzy dress.

"Oh my! It's Claudia!" Mayta exclaimed at the same moment the truth dawned on me.

"Get help!" I yelled. "She's bleeding!"

CHAPTER TWO

Claudia was indeed bleeding, as in present tense. Appalling as the wound was, she was still alive. Her mouth, under a wisp of hair, was moving, emitting a gargled sound as if from under water. Involuntarily, I stepped into the bathroom and leaned closer to hear. "Ma . . . mahg . . ." she said, then nothing more.

I felt jostling behind me and turned to find the rest of the tour group pushing forward to see. "Move back!" I spread out my arms to stem the surge. "You!" I jabbed a finger in the air at the guide across the room. "Call somebody quick! We need an ambulance!" She gave me a blank look, but snatched up the room phone. "Everybody else, out!" I began shooing them like geese toward the door, waving my hands over my head.

And then Beverly appeared, taking up the cry, "Out! Out!" Along with Mayta, the three of us had moved everyone into the hallway when a distinguished-looking man appeared at the door. The tour guide, who had timidly approached the bathroom to peek in, backed away as soon as the man entered.

"I'm the manager here—" he began, looking at us questioningly.

"Shut the door behind you," I said.

He obeyed, and then turned to the guide, who looked shell-shocked. "What's going on?" Without waiting for a reply, he brushed past us and hurried to the bathroom. Stopping at the doorway, he peered in and blurted an expletive.

"Have you called nine-one-one?" I said.

25

"Yes, of course." He frowned at me. "An ambulance and the police are on their way. What happened here?"

"There's been a murder," Beverly said. "Anyone can see that!"

An attempt at one, anyway. The manager ran his fingers nervously through his short gray-streaked hair while the guide, who had found her voice, explained, somewhat unnecessarily, that a woman—a dinner guest—had been stabbed.

"I wish we could do something for her." At my side, Mayta was wringing her hands, twisting one within the other.

"You can't do CPR or anything with that knife in her," Beverly said.

"Where is the ambulance?" I turned to the manager. "Are you sure somebody's coming?"

The elevator bell dinged then. Paramedics barged into the room with a gurney, and we were sent out into the hallway to stand with everyone else. A few moments later, the Portsmouth police arrived. Two officers went into the room with the manager, while one moved our group further down the hall and gave instructions for us not to leave. After about ten minutes, the group began to get antsy. Low horrified murmurs turned to louder excited tones.

"Such a horrible thing!" Mayta said. "Whatever could have happened?"

"This isn't good," I said. "Why aren't they bringing her out?"

"Nobody could survive a wound like that," Beverly said.

The elevator bell sounded again. A man with a black bag stepped off the elevator, crossed the hallway in a steady but unhurried gait, and entered the room.

"Medical examiner," Beverly said.

"How do you know?" Mayta said.

"I've seen him before in the course of my work." She gave an apologetic shrug.

"By the way," I said, "when did you get here?"

"Just in time, apparently. I followed the scream." I looked at her closely, noting an excited glimmer in her eyes. Would her society piece now turn into a front-page news story?

The door of the room opened and the chatter died. Our worst fears were confirmed; the body of Claudia Dean, covered in a white sheet, was whisked across the hall and into the elevator. Another policeman came over then and instructed us to go downstairs. In the lobby we joined others who were milling around looking like a herd of terrified steer at a stockyard. Chauncey caught sight of us and came over. Everyone in the rooms had been told to come to the lobby, he said, but he didn't know why. When we told him about finding Claudia dead, he shook his head in disbelief.

An officer quieted us then and announced to everyone that a woman had been found dead and that, due to the circumstances surrounding the incident, we would all need to be questioned before we could leave. Since the victim had sat at our table, a young policewoman spoke first with Mayta, Beverly, Chauncey, and me, then requested that we remain at the hotel while the others were questioned.

Afterward, we compared notes on what we had said, which was pretty much the same: that Claudia had been with us during dinner, had gone to the ladies' room during dessert and hadn't returned, that she had planned on taking the last tour but hadn't shown up. Now, with the glamour of the evening diminished, the four of us gathered around the marble fireplace in the lobby, bright lights showing the rumples in our clothes and faded makeup on our faces. Our coaches had turned to pumpkins, our white horses to mice.

Mayta, Chauncey, and I settled into the cushy chairs, but Beverly turned her back to us, tapping the toe of her low-heeled black pump on the parquet floor while speaking in low tones into her cell phone. I nodded in her direction. "The busy reporter," I said under my breath to Mayta.

"What a terrible thing to happen to that young couple." Chauncey sank back into his chair.

Mayta sighed. "Poor Daniel. I wonder if they've told him yet."

"I guess Claudia didn't catch up to him after all," I said.

At some point, after replaying in my mind the horrific picture of Claudia lying in the tub, crumpled and bleeding, two voices rose to the surface of my thoughts: "wearing a green dress," and the response, "follow her"—the exchange between the tennis player and his soft-spoken partner on the verandah before dinner.

And now it occurred to me that Claudia's trendy little dress was green. There had to be more than one woman here wearing green—if the speakers were even talking about somebody here. Still, it seemed a bit of a coincidence that I overheard those words just a few hours before a woman who wore a dress loosely fitting the description was stabbed. Had the couple been talking about Claudia? Had one of them followed her? Stabbed her? And why in that particular room?

Suddenly I was tired of hanging around doing nothing. Since we were free to move about the open area of the first floor, I told Mayta I needed to stretch my legs and headed for the dining room. Most of the guests were congregated at the cleared tables or in clusters standing around. As I sauntered through, I tallied the women's outfits that could be considered green: one emerald gown, a tailored mint-colored suit, and three shorter dresses. I discounted the suit because you wouldn't call it a dress, and a short teal dress, deciding it was too blue. That left three possibilities other than Claudia's: the emerald gown encasing an overweight middle-aged woman and two short dresses, both worn by young women—a forest green one and a silky pale one that was similar in hue (pale) and in style (loose and flowy) to Claudia's. I paused at the edge of the dining room to watch this last woman. Could the murder have been a case of mistaken identity? But other than her dress and age, this woman bore no resemblance to Claudia, and I was sure a murderer looking for his target would have had more to go on than the color of her clothing.

I meandered back through the dining room again, this time listening among the excited conversations for that soft voice with its tinkly laugh, and looking for a stylish couple, one of whom would be a tennis player (whatever that might look like, since he wouldn't be wearing tennis whites). Almost immediately, I spotted an attractive couple standing apart at the end of the dining room. She appeared to be in her thirties, tall and slender with medium-length brown hair that was complemented by the yellow of her clingy gown. Her companion, about ten years older, had an athletic build and a deep tan. Their backs to the restless crowd, they were in conversation, faces just inches from each other, their body language discouraging outsiders. I moved in their direction. Halfway there, however, someone touched my elbow.

"How are you holding up?" Chauncey spoke around an unlit pipe in the corner of his mouth.

"All right," I said, a little annoyed at being waylaid. "It's hard just waiting around."

He nodded and removed the pipe. "It's understandable that the police have to interview everyone, given the circumstances, but you're right: it's tedious." He gestured with the pipe stem to the glass door. "I'm told I may light this out on the verandah. Would you care to join me?"

"I was going—" I glanced toward the end of the room, then scanned the entire dining area. The couple was gone. "Uh, sure."

Outside, Chauncey turned his back to the mild breeze,

cupped his hands around the pipe's bowl, and lit a match to it. He drew air through the stem a couple of times before turning to me. "I'm sorry. I didn't ask if this would bother you."

"No, not at all." In fact, the mild fruity tobacco scented the air in a surprisingly pleasant way. We leaned our elbows on the rail and looked out. Moonlight skimmed the river's ruffled surface, its illumination not reaching to the banks beyond or the other small islands. It was a reminder of just how out of proportion water was to land at this spot, the crux of two mighty waterways: the Piscataqua spreading wide around our little dot of earth to converge with the Atlantic on the other side. The night was mild; still, feeling suddenly vulnerable, I shivered.

"Hard to believe a lovely night like this could yield such horror," Chauncey commented just as someone below us spoke.

"Hmm," I intoned softly, hoping to discourage conversation. Chauncey took the cue and was silent while I cocked an ear toward sounds from under the verandah. Cautiously, I peeked over the rail, but could see nothing in the dark. Then someone spoke again from below.

"You can't leave," came a whispery voice, a woman's.

A man said something low that was difficult to decipher. Then in a louder, rushed tone, ". . . talk to you tomorrow." There was a brief warbled protest on the part of the woman, followed by a swish of feet moving through grass. I rushed to the end of the verandah and looked around the corner of the building. Silhouetted in the moonlight was a figure—a man, I determined from his gait—running toward the bridge we'd driven over. Then he was gone. In vain, I peered into the shadows alongside the building for his partner.

"What is it?" Chauncey was at my side.

"There were people down there—just two, I think. Did you hear them?"

"No. What did they say?"

30

"Something about leaving, then the man ran off."

"Nobody's supposed to leave." Chauncey took the pipe out of his mouth. "We'll have to tell the police." He turned to go but I hesitated, listening for sounds below. Was the woman still there? Had she and her companion been the couple I'd heard earlier on the verandah? She had sounded familiar, but it was hard to compare voices in regular conversation with ones mumbled and whispered.

By the time I reentered the dining room, Chauncey was already speaking to a policeman. Instead of joining them, I went to the other end where I'd seen the attractive couple earlier. I exited the room and paused. Right would lead me back to the lobby; I could see Mayta's back as she talked to Beverly. Left led to the bathrooms. Just as I turned in that direction, the women's restroom door opened and out came one half of the couple I sought: the woman in the yellow gown. She had her head down and wasn't paying attention, so I moved into her path.

"Oh! Excuse me." She pulled up just short of banging into me, and brought her startled blue eyes up to meet my gaze.

"Not at all. My fault," I said, then faked a double take. "Carol? Carol Thomas?"

She frowned, gave a short shake of her head, and said softly, "No. Sorry." She ducked her head again, circumvented me, and hurried toward the dining room. I pivoted and followed, thinking it likely that hers was the voice I'd heard earlier on the verandah, and maybe even the one I'd just heard outside. But could she and her companion have gone from dining room to under the verandah in the time it took Chauncey and I to step out onto it? What about her getting back inside to the second floor and then ducking in and out of the bathroom before I bumped into her?

At the entrance to the dining room I got stuck behind a

throng of four women talking and gesticulating excitedly. By the time I squeezed past them, the woman in the yellow gown was nowhere to be seen. I scanned the crowded room, then backtracked down the hallway, this time passing the bathrooms and the small gift shop until I reached a junction I remembered from the tour. To the right lay the spa area. To the left was a door marked *Fire Exit*.

I looked around to make sure nobody was watching and then turned the knob, fervently hoping it wouldn't set off an alarm. A soft click of the door's mechanism echoed on the other side as I slipped through it. The stairwell light was dim, but my eyes adjusted quickly. I ran down the stairs, thinking I'd be hard-pressed for an explanation if I got caught leaving the assigned area.

At the bottom, I pushed open a heavy automatic door designed to close and lock on its own and, holding it ajar with one hand, stepped outside. I was under the back verandah, but corners jutting out along the building made it impossible to see to the end where Chauncey and I had stood above. Still, based on the door's proximity to the hallway, this was likely where the pair I'd heard talking had exited, and where the one who remained had reentered alone. Moreover, I decided, it wouldn't have taken more than a few minutes for them to get from the dining room to here, and likewise for the woman in the yellow gown to skip back up a flight of stairs and visit the ladies' room before our encounter. I pulled back into the stairwell, letting the door shut with a solid thunk, and immediately fell backward over an obstacle, landing on my rear end.

"Crap!" I struggled to my feet and pulled the hem of my dress from the leg of an upended dining room chair. Since there was no other apparent reason it would be there, I surmised it must have been used to prop open the door.

Back up in the dining room, I searched without success for

the woman in the yellow gown before joining Mayta out in the lobby.

"Where've you been?" Her suspicious eyes took in my dragging hem.

"Oh, just meandering about." I looked at my watch. "It's almost midnight! I should call Gus to tell him what's going on, and that we'll be late." I took out my phone and saw that I had three missed calls. In the commotion of the evening, I hadn't heard it ring.

Gus picked up at once. "I've been trying to reach you. On the eleven o'clock news they said a woman was killed up there."

I reassured him that we were fine, and then told him about Claudia.

"They said police were looking for her husband," he said. "Sounds like he's a suspect."

"Really? He was with us at dinner, but he left early."

"That's probably why he's a suspect. Where'd he go?"

"He didn't say—just that he was 'due back' somewhere. I think he expected Claudia to leave with him, but she didn't. At least not then." I paused, musing. "It was odd the way she looked at her watch as if she needed to be somewhere at a certain time, then excused herself to go to the ladies' room. Maybe she didn't go there at all. Maybe she went to find Daniel and when she did, he killed her."

"Don't go poking around."

"But why would she look at her watch first?"

"Andy," Gus warned, "just tell the police what you observed and leave it there."

"Oh, I will."

"I mean it, Andy. Be careful. I know you—" The reception started breaking up then, and I hurriedly promised to call when we were free to leave.

Mayta, who'd been listening to our conversation, nodded.

She repeated what Gus had said: The police were looking for Daniel Dean, who hadn't been seen since dinner.

Beverly, Mayta, Chauncey, and I were called into the manager's office to speak to the policewoman a second time. When it was my turn, I told her again about Daniel's abrupt departure, and then Claudia's, this time adding the part about Claudia looking at her watch first.

"About what time was that?" she asked.

"Nine o'clock, exactly."

The policewoman looked up from her notes, eyebrows raised.

"I do that sometimes. When someone looks at his watch, I have a tendency to do the same—look to see what time it is." She nodded and I continued. "It was like Claudia had to be somewhere at that time and used the restroom as an excuse to leave." I went on to tell about hearing a man and a woman talking outside and then seeing somebody—the man, I thought— run off toward the bridge. I gave my lame-sounding opinion that they might have been a couple I'd seen before in the dining room. "She's attractive, thin, brown hair, wearing a long yellow dress. He's tanned, athletically built. Have you talked with them?"

"Doesn't ring a bell," she said neutrally. "They were probably interviewed by another officer."

After debating with myself, I mentioned the conversation concerning the green dress that I'd overheard earlier, but since it had been fragmented and I hadn't seen the speakers, it sounded even weaker than my suspicions concerning the couple in the dining room. The policewoman took notes, asked a few questions, but I couldn't tell if she took my observations seriously.

"Do you have any idea where Claudia's husband might have gone?" she asked. "Did he say anything that would indicate his plans?"

I said no, Daniel Dean had said very little all evening. Then I asked a question of my own. "Do you have any clues as to who stabbed her? She must have been stabbed in the bedroom because I noticed drops of blood over by the bureau. And the knife looked different—not like a serious weapon."

"Not at this point." She addressed the question, not the comments. "Anything else you think might help us?"

"One more thing: When we found her, Claudia mumbled something."

She looked up from her pad. "What did she mumble?"

"She said, 'ma' or 'mahg,' something like that."

"Ma?" She jotted it down. "Is that all?"

"And mahg; she said both."

Mayta was alone when I met her in the lobby; everyone else had been allowed to go. She gave a wry smile. "I went to pay our dinner bill and guess who forgot to settle his account."

"Daniel Dean, I expect."

"No, actually he paid his and Claudia's when he left. It was our distinguished elder member who stiffed the waitress."

"Chauncey Brown? He probably just expected her to put it on his room tab."

"There is no room," Mayta said. "He's not staying here."

"Well, isn't that interesting."

CHAPTER THREE

Claudia Dean, if that was who she really was, for there was no identification on her, was a mystery woman. According to the television news reporter, nobody knew anything about her other than the name she'd given for her dinner reservation at the hotel. Since the man she'd introduced as her husband, Daniel Dean, couldn't be found, the police were looking for someone who could positively identify the murdered woman—they were calling it that now, a murder.

"Well, what else were they going to call it?" I said. "It's not likely she'd have stumbled into the knife or stabbed herself in the heart."

"Shhh," Gus said.

"And what's with no ID? She had one of those huge designer bags; there was no ID in it?"

Gus shushed me again, louder this time, as the reporter continued. The weapon, according to police, was a hotel logo-emblazoned letter opener, provided on the desktops in all of the rooms.

"Aha!" I said. "I knew it wasn't a regular knife! And did they find the blood on the carpet?"

Mayta arrived then. Glued to the TV, I mumbled a greeting, but Gus lifted his head to sniff the air appreciatively. "Hmm!"

She set down a bag of still-warm bagels on the coffee table, alongside a tub of whipped cream cheese and a stack of napkins. As the moist doughy aroma hit me, I came to life, emerging from my corner of the sofa to peer into the bag.

"Ooh! Thank you! Go grab yourself a cup of coffee or some orange juice." I waved her toward the kitchen, and plucked out a sesame seed–covered bagel.

She shook her head. "Already had enough to float a boat. Been up since four."

"Couldn't sleep, huh?" I said, thinking of the restless hours I'd spent between strange vivid dreams. "Sit down. Have you seen the news?"

"Yeah, I've been watching it."

"Here, Ma." Gus leaped up and cleared strewn sections of the *Sunday Globe* from an armchair before heading for the kitchen.

"Thanks." Mayta dropped into the chair.

On the TV a picture of our dining table at the hotel suddenly filled the screen. Beverly, Mayta, and Chauncey were smiling at the camera, Daniel's face was a little blurry as if he'd moved the moment the shot was snapped, and Claudia and I were engaged in conversation, our profiles to the camera.

"Oh, my God!" I stopped in mid-action, a piece of bagel hovering above the cream cheese. "That's us. Who took that picture? And when did the skin under my chin begin to sag?"

"It was Beverly, remember?" Mayta said. "She had the waiter take it."

The TV camera zoomed in on Claudia, her expression animated, head inclined toward me, hair falling to the linen tablecloth. Then there was a close-up of Daniel warily watching the camera. Caught in the act of turning away, his features were unclear but recognizable, his face angular with its high cheekbones and square chin. The reporter asked for anyone recognizing either person to contact the Portsmouth police.

"That picture sure brings the evening back, doesn't it?" I swiped the piece of bagel across the top of the cream cheese and stuffed it into my mouth.

"Yeah," Mayta sighed. "At that point it was like a fairy tale."

"You know," I said, "I don't think I told the police that Claudia's aunt worked for the Grand Hotel. Maybe they could trace her that way."

"She lied about who she was," Gus said, entering from the kitchen, "so everything else she said was probably false, too."

"I don't know. Daniel wasn't into the whole fancy-shmancy thing, didn't even want to be there, but Claudia—there was something about her that rang true."

"I liked her," Mayta said.

"I wonder what she had in that big bag if she didn't carry identification," I said.

Gus crossed the room and set a butter knife on the rim of the cream cheese tub. He frowned at its contents, which now had sesame seeds mixed in the top layer. "So, who do you think killed her?"

"Daniel," Mayta said. "First he argues with her, then he walks out, and she's found stabbed a little while later—pretty suspicious."

"Maybe, but there were other suspicious people around." I told Mayta and Gus about the two conversations I'd overheard, and the couple in the dining room. "I suppose it could have been Daniel beneath the verandah talking with someone—the woman in the yellow gown, perhaps—before running off. But why kill her in that room?" I shook my head. "It doesn't make sense."

"It's not your job to make sense of it," Gus said. "It's up to the police now."

"Another thing: Claudia was surprised when Daniel left suddenly. She had planned on meeting someone because she looked at her watch, but it wasn't Daniel," I said. "Besides, how could he have gotten into a room where he wasn't staying?"

"Well, I say there was something fishy about Daniel," Mayta said. "First of all, he was bored all night. Who could be bored with such a dinner at such a beautiful place?"

"Oh, yes, that sounds very fishy," Gus said mildly. I narrowed my eyes at him in warning.

"And second, where'd he go after dinner?" she continued. "Why can't he be found?"

"Maybe he hired someone else to do it. He was probably the guy under the porch paying off a hit man." Gus was beginning to enjoy himself so I shot him a dirty look. But Mayta nodded thoughtfully.

"That would make sense," she said, "him leaving before the murder like he knew it was going to happen."

"Daniel Dean wasn't the only one unaccounted for during the time Claudia was killed," I said. "Chauncey, who by the way lied to us about staying at the hotel, left the table first and wasn't seen until afterward in the lobby. And Beverly missed the whole tour, showing up at the very end when we found Claudia."

"Oh pooh!" Mayta said. "Chauncey wouldn't hurt a fly. And Beverly is a reporter!"

"Do you remember Beverly's last name?" When Mayta shook her head I said, "Magill. Think about Claudia's last words: 'ma' and 'mahg.' Maybe she was trying to say the murderer's name: Magill."

Mayta's face paled. "Claudia said something?"

"You were there. I thought you heard her." I shuddered, remembering the words and thinking for the first time that it might have been blood causing that gurgling sound in her throat.

Mayta winced and set down the bagel she'd been about to bite into. Gus was watching me, all seriousness now. The news was over and a Sunday morning talk show had begun. I clicked off the TV and we rose. Gus crammed the last bite of his bagel into his mouth, grabbed the bag and cream cheese, and we drifted toward the kitchen.

"I think I'll go home and try to get in a nap," Mayta said.

Then the somber mood was dispelled by Moose thundering down the stairs followed by Max and Molly, both clad in Disney-themed pjs, and tousle-headed—his brown hair sticking up from several cowlicks, and hers pillow-rubbed into a big blonde tangle on the back of her head.

"Grandma! Grandma!" Mayta was tackled from both sides, two sets of short arms wrapped tight around her middle, while Moose wove in and out whacking everyone with his long feathery tail. It took a few moments for Mayta to disentangle herself, give hugs and kisses around, and make her escape with a promise to call later.

I went into mommy mode: getting breakfast, clarifying plans, and dictating appropriate clothing for the day. Two hours later, with the kitchen cleaned up, Gus outside doing yard work, Max delivered to a friend's house to play, and Molly awaiting the arrival of a playmate, I sat down at the computer. I looked up the Grand Hotel of the Atlantic, and spent the next hour browsing through advertising brochures from the 1890s that boasted listings of special features (like centrally located "toilet-rooms" on each floor) and floor plans.

Switching eras, I came across a listing of employees from the 1970s and skimmed through the names, realizing the impossibility of figuring out which of the more than one hundred women listed would have been Claudia's great-aunt, if the fact that she had worked at the Grand Hotel were even true. Then I found a newspaper article from June 1901 titled, "Woman Missing from Hotel." Recognizing it as the story Mayta had told me about, I began reading.

Marguerite Miller, a nineteen-year-old guest, had disappeared from the Grand Hotel after spending a week there with a companion, recuperating from some undisclosed malady. She had apparently left unobserved sometime during the evening and never returned, leaving behind all of her belongings in Room Thirty-three. The only clue was a tipped-over chair, indicating a hasty departure, perhaps a kidnapping. Individuals connected with the hotel and a circus that had camped nearby had been questioned with no results. Although it was assumed something untoward had happened to Marguerite Miller, nothing indicating foul play was found. Her mother suffered a breakdown, her fiancé was heartbroken, and her father offered rewards for information.

Mayta was right; it was a compelling story. Wondering if Marguerite Miller was ever found, I searched subsequent news articles, but found no more mention of her. On a whim I clicked back on the 1890s brochure that showed the hotel floor plans, and noticed something curious. Rooms were numbered consecutively in the main building, and floors were labeled ground floor, first, second, and third, which meant room number thirty-three at the rear south end of the hotel's first floor was actually one story up.

I grabbed the phone and punched in Mayta's number. "Oh, sorry," I apologized when she answered in a weary voice. "I forgot you were going to take a nap."

"That's okay. Couldn't sleep anyway. What's up?"

"I was wondering if you knew the number of the room where we found Claudia."

Mayta answered right away. "One-thirteen."

"Are you sure? I mean, how do you remember that?"

"I kept staring at the door there in the hallway, waiting for it to open, dreading it. But no, I'm not sure. It could've been one thirty-three or one thirty-one. I just remember thinking, unlucky thirteen."

"It was the end back room on the second floor, wasn't it?"

"Yeah, I think so. Why?"

41

"I think it's the same room that Marguerite Miller stayed in."

"Who?"

"The girl who disappeared from the hotel way back when—you told me about her, remember? I think she disappeared from the same room that Claudia was murdered in."

"Really? Do you suppose it's haunted?"

I guffawed. "By bad luck, maybe. Or bad coincidence."

"Well, how many guest rooms are there? One hundred and fifty or so? It's some coincidence that out of all those rooms something tragic happened twice in the same one."

"Over a hundred-year span," I pointed out.

"Yeah, even over a hundred-year span." She pronounced it "ovah."

"Wait a minute. Say her name."

"Whose name?"

"The girl who went missing," I said. "Indulge me; say her name."

"Marguerite—I forget the rest." She pronounced it "Mahguerite."

"That word Claudia was trying to say—'mahg'—could it have been 'Marguerite'? The way you guys talk around here, softening and leaving out your 'r's, it could be the beginning of her name." I repeated it. "Mahg."

There was a moment's pause on the other end of the line. "Well, now, it does sound like it, doesn't it?" Mayta said.

Monday started the last week of school before summer vacation. Gus left early to work on final grades and the kids were excited about field day. After I saw them off, marching up the street with lunch bags swinging, I took stock of the time: two hours to myself before I was due at school as a spectator. I went online and looked up the hotel again. Through the years, a lot of energy had been put into convincing the public to save it.

Articles extolling the Grand Hotel of the Atlantic's historical importance had been written by architectural experts as well as the Joe Shmoes—the neighbor down the street or somebody whose great-uncle's sister had once stayed there. I found some of these articles now, reprinted online with sidebars of hotel facts and figures.

But it was the images of a bygone era that captivated me: a steamboat pulling into a pier, sailboats in the harbor, a Victorian gazebo perched on the rocks. All populated with men in suits and women in long white dresses and wide-brimmed hats. I scrutinized the women, imagining each as Marguerite Miller. What had happened to her? Could there be a connection between her and Claudia? Had Claudia been killed in the same room Marguerite disappeared from? Had Claudia been trying to say, "Marguerite" when she died? I looked up at the clock a few minutes later and blinked in disbelief. I'd whiled away an hour and a half!

I took a quick shower and threw on clothes—yesterday's jeans and a rumpled tee-shirt pulled out of the dryer. I ran fingers through my wet hair, decided to forgo any attempt at makeup, shoved my feet into flip-flops, and jumped into the car. It was a textbook beauty of a day with a brilliant sun in an azure sky and a temperature in the eighties for the first time this season. I regretted not having time to follow my original plan to walk the short distance to the Kelley School.

Hurrying up the walk, I was met by a frowning Max, the first-born worrywart, who fell in beside me and matched my stride while chastising me for being late. Molly, the easygoing child, jumped up and down, smiling and waving from the kindergarten line.

"Sorry, sweet cakes, I got tied up with work," I fibbed, "but I'm here now. And I didn't miss anything, right?" Then his teacher called him back into line and I was spared additional admonitions. I joined Mayta and the other parents to cheer on the wheelbarrow race, sack race, three-legged race, and egg-on-a-spoon race.

Between events I told Mayta what I'd found online. "I'd like to find out if Claudia's story about her great-aunt was true. She called her Great-Aunt something. Do you remember?"

"It was like her own name—Dean. Another man's name that started with a D."

"Dean, David, Dale," I rattled off. "Dennis, Donald—"

But Mayta shook her head. "I can't recall."

Gus, who had scooted out of school, arrived then. He greeted his mother and planted a quick kiss on my cheek. "Molly said I missed her event."

"Well, you're in time for the first-grade race. And if you think missing Molly's event is a tug on the guilt strings, believe me when I say missing Max's race would be a major drag across burning coals. I got reprimanded for being thirteen minutes late—exactly, because the kid can tell time to the minute now—and that was before anything had started."

"Why were you late?" Gus said. Leave it to him to follow that thread.

"Just got caught up in stuff. Look! The race is beginning."

Almost immediately, a small group that included Max pulled ahead of the other first graders, and we went wild, yelling and cheering. Max passed by us, eyes squinty and focused, mouth pinched in a tight seam, and crossed the finish line in second place. *Determined little bugger,* I thought proudly. After congratulations and hugs, Gus headed back to school, and I walked Mayta to her car where we lingered a moment, chatting.

"Dennis," she said suddenly. "That's what Claudia called her—Great Aunt Dennis."

"Yes, that's it! You're fantastic, Mayta! Call you later."

I went home, back to my computer, this time with an agenda.

I found about twenty-five Dennises around the Portland area in the online white pages directory. After six nonproductive calls (two were machines, one was disconnected, one didn't answer, and the other two didn't have relatives who had ever worked at the Grand Hotel) I got a reaction. An elderly woman demanded to know who I was. I repeated my name, and then politely told her I'd met Claudia Dean and had been intrigued by her story of an aunt who had worked at the Grand Hotel. The woman paused a few seconds, just long enough to make suspicious her denial: "She's not my niece."

"Do you know who—" I said to the dial tone. I took down her name—D. S. Dennis—the telephone number and the address.

I called Mayta. "I think I found Claudia's great-aunt. Do you recall anything else Claudia said about her?"

She thought a moment. "She was a baker. She told me about the special popovers her great-aunt was known for."

"Wait a minute. I think there was a picture of the kitchen crew. Maybe I can find out who the bakers were." Cradling the phone between my ear and shoulder, I tapped on the keyboard, bringing up the article on the hotel closing in 1987, and then the page that showed the kitchen employees—a group picture of fifty-odd women and men who worked there that final year. None were labeled according to a specific job, but underneath was a list of names alongside the number of years of service. I found her in the fourth row, third person in: Dorothy Dennis, twenty years' service. "Eureka! I feel a trip back to Portsmouth coming on."

"Count me in," Mayta said.

By Wednesday, the police had identifed Claudia Dean. Her real name was Claudia Harrison, and although originally from New Hampshire, she had most recently lived in Newark, New Jersey.

45

The item on the evening news rated only a few seconds, so after dinner I put on my sneakers and power-walked downtown to Fowles, which has the best selection of newspapers in the area. I bought the *Portsmouth Daily Monitor,* tucked it under my arm, and power-walked back home. Gus raised eyebrows above the *Daily News* he held, but said nothing when I plopped down on the couch, put my feet up on the coffee table, and opened the paper.

As I'd hoped, the *Monitor* provided more details. Claudia Harrison, aged twenty-eight, had been a waitress at a popular restaurant in Newark that catered to upscale, young, single business types who liked to linger at its martini bar. She'd been at the restaurant since its inception three years ago, but had just quit the week before her death. The report said that she had lived by herself in the same apartment in a rather shabby section of the city for the past four years. Neighbors described her as a pleasant woman whom they saw on her way to and from her apartment, often late at night, probably coming home from work.

Coworkers, likewise, had little to say about Claudia; she was friendly, but since she was older, hadn't socialized with them outside of work. Somebody thought that she might have had a boyfriend. The manager of the restaurant had been surprised at the suddenness of her decision to leave, but then that was the restaurant business. He'd assumed she'd left for another job. The man who called himself Daniel Dean still could not be found, and there was no record of him as the husband of Claudia Harrison. Relatives of Claudia's were being sought.

"Curiouser and curiouser." I noted the familiar name of the reporter: Beverly Magill. Maybe I'd give her a call.

"Don't even think about it," Gus said from behind the sports section.

"What?" I said, all innocence.

"It's a murder investigation, so don't get involved. And next time my mother calls with some interesting tidbit concerning Claudia Dean, I'll hang up on her."

"Harrison. Her name was Harrison."

He shook his paper to smooth it out and bent his head to another article.

CHAPTER FOUR

The leading lady swooned. The hero—Granger Moore—caught her and, uttering sappy endearments, lowered her to the floor where her silky gown somehow managed to artfully drape itself over his tuxedo-clad knees. I stifled an impulse to snort in disgust as yet another close-up of Lenore Lamot—her dark hair held back with a ribbon and fluffed flatteringly around her pale heart-shaped face—obliterated the background.

"I used to be completely absorbed by the whole Hollywood scene," Mayta said, eyes glued to the television, "back when I was a teenager."

I cut my eyes sideways at her. "Used to be?" Since Gus and I had given her the new thirty-two-inch television and DVD player that dominated her comfortably shabby living room, Mayta was always renting and buying movies to watch—a number of them old black-and-white classics, giving rise to the suspicion that she would have been content with her thirty-year-old black-and-white model had we just added a DVD player.

She ignored my tone. "I followed all the movie stars in the newspapers and magazines—Garbo, Hepburn, Bacall—but Lenore Lamot was my favorite. Wasn't she beautiful?"

I grunted in reluctant agreement, miffed that thus far—forty minutes into the movie—I'd caught only a glimpse of the setting, which was the carrot Mayta had dangled to get me to sit through this maudlin specimen of 1940s Hollywood.

48

It was almost a week after the benefit at the Grand Hotel of the Atlantic, and the disturbing murder had receded from the headlines. Claudia Harrison's funeral and burial had taken place in a small New Jersey town where her parents lived. When located, her mother insisted that Claudia wasn't married and didn't even have a boyfriend. She'd never heard of Daniel Dean, who was still missing and whose identity remained a mystery.

Still, Mayta and I conferred almost daily on some new bit of information learned or remembered. And once the horror of the experience had faded a bit, the romance of the evening up to the moment of the murder returned, and we talked about that, too. Mayta enthused over the elegance of the hotel and again brought up her favorite movie, *Forever After,* which had been filmed there.

Then, when she heard that it was Gus's annual poker night with the guys, she invited the kids and me out to her cottage for "a classic movie-fest sleepover." It was the perfect opportunity for me to watch *Forever After,* and see what the original Grand Hotel of the Atlantic had looked like. I agreed on the conditions that she let me bring dinner, and that she not regale me with movie star trivia. She agreed to the first.

So here we were, camped out in Mayta's tiny living room, now resembling a tableau of the last moments of Pompeii, the floor littered with bodies, empty pizza boxes, and soda cans. Max and Molly had made it through one and a half Disney films before zonking out on top of their sleeping bags, legs and arms flung out, frozen in whatever positions they'd been in when sleep caught them.

"Lenore Lamot was so classy." Mayta dug a hand into the popcorn bowl. "Everybody used to imitate her style but nobody looked like she did with her tiny waist and long legs. She had this fragile, ethereal quality. And her eyes were so blue they were almost purple."

"How do you know? The movie's in black and white."

Two kernels of popcorn sprung out from between Mayta's fingers as she waved her full fist dismissively in the air. "I don't know. Read it somewhere."

"Well, I wish the camera would pan out so I could see the room. Where are they?"

"Ballroom," she mumbled around a mouthful. "First floor, back wing."

"So it's not there anymore."

"Nope. Tore both back wings down." She leaned forward and pulled her cotton floral robe down over her knees so that the hemline skimmed the top of the Bugs Bunny slippers the kids had gotten her for her birthday last year. "Okay, now, this is where he declares his love but she won't listen."

Even from a distance of some sixty-odd years, I could appreciate Lenore Lamot's appeal. She knew exactly how to play to the camera, using her wide eyes for dramatic effect, and tossing her dark curls as she paced back and forth talking a mile a minute to her leading man. But it wasn't the snappy repartee that got my attention. The scene had changed and the background—the elegant wide verandah that ran the entire length of the Grand Hotel of the Atlantic—was finally visible. While the characters parried, I scrutinized the architectural details behind them. Crisp white clapboarding and large windows flanked by wicker chairs and tall potted ferns telescoped as far into the background distance as the movie camera could capture. "Wow, that was some porch," I said as the background changed back to a Hollywood set.

"Yep. Not the same now since they tore down so much of the building." Mayta bumped my hand as we both scrabbled for kernels at the bottom of the bowl wedged between us. "Pause the movie and I'll make more popcorn." She made a movement to rise.

"No, keep it going," I said quickly as the scene changed to another setting off the hotel grounds. "I'll make it. I can watch from the kitchen."

"You sure?" Mayta said halfheartedly as she settled back into the couch cushions, already absorbed again.

The kitchen was an open attachment to the living room, so while I poured popcorn into the bottom of the saucepan and set it on the stove to cook the old-fashioned way, I could easily watch the movie at the same time had I wanted to. Instead, I gazed out the picture window to the beach and the ocean at dusk. It seemed a shame to be ignoring the spectacular view outside—the vastness of sea and sky, matched in serenity and color at this time of evening, joined in a smudgy gray-blue line on the horizon.

"How's it coming?" Mayta said, beside me.

Startled, I jumped and grabbed the panhandle. "Slow. But I think we're finally developing a serious sizzle. Why'd you stop the movie?"

"I didn't want you to miss anything."

"That's okay. Those movies always turn out the same: the heroine comes to her senses and realizes all she ever wanted out of life was to be in love."

"I guess it's pretty corny by today's standards." She sounded a little dejected, and I felt sorry about my comment.

"But this was a great idea," I said. "The kids had a ball eating pizza and falling asleep on the floor. And I loved seeing what the Grand Hotel used to look like—the porch, anyway." There were a couple of pops just then and I shook the pan with renewed energy.

"Yeah, I never noticed how little you could see of the hotel." She sat down at the kitchen table and fiddled with the fringe on a placemat. "I was going out with Augustus when that movie came out."

51

A couple more kernels pinged and I bent over the pan to examine the others. I'd forgotten what agonizingly slow work popping corn the old-fashioned way was. I shook the pan some more and made a mental note to talk to Gus about getting Mayta a microwave for Christmas. "Gus's dad liked movies, too, didn't he?"

She chuckled and flapped a hand at the air beside her ear. "Aw heck, I don't really know. I think he just indulged me."

More kernels popped. I sprang back, but not before a speck of oil zapped me in the face. At arm's length I slapped the lid onto the pot as a thousand tiny explosions went off simultaneously with volcanic intensity.

"The poor man sat through *Forever After* three times in a row at the Strand Theater," Mayta said above the popping. "That was when they ran shows continuously. If you wanted to see a movie again, you just stayed in your seat."

I dumped the popcorn into the bowl, then set the pan in the sink and ran water over the burnt layer encrusted on the bottom. Yes, Mayta could definitely use a microwave.

"Hey," I said. "That porch went around the hotel, right?"

"Yeah, I believe so."

"It just occurred to me that Room Thirty-three would've had windows opening out onto the porch roof," I said. "If nobody saw Marguerite Miller leave, maybe it was because she went out the window onto the roof, and then somehow got down onto the porch. Maybe somebody was there with a ladder."

"You think she eloped?"

"Or ran away. Would a proper young Victorian lady have done something like that?"

Mayta shrugged. "Proper young ladies have done all sorts of wild things throughout history."

I handed her the popcorn bowl. "Ready to get back to the movie?"

"We don't have to finish it."

"No, really," I said as brightly as I could, "I'd like to see the rest."

"Yeah?" She perked up a bit and I was glad I'd insisted. "Are we still on for tomorrow? Go up and see the hotel again? Have a drink on the verandah?"

"You bet," I said as we picked our way back over the littered living room floor. "We could check out Room Thirty-three—or whatever it is now—from the outside, see how high up the window is. I'd like to stop at the library up there, too, to do a little research. Maybe even drive by D. S. Dennis's house."

"Great!" Mayta pressed the play button and we settled down to watch the remainder of the movie.

"I wish they'd show more of the hotel."

"Shhh," she said. "Watch this part. This is where she leaves him because she knows his parents will never accept her."

"Why do I need to watch if you tell me everything that happens before it happens?"

"Shhh!"

Portsmouth newspapers from the turn of the century devoted whole pages to whatever new remodeling or landscaping was taking place at the Grand Hotel. Sporting tournaments, orchestras that played, toasts and speeches made, sightings of the rich and famous and what they wore, even menus and decorations were newsworthy.

In 1901, the summer had begun as usual. Employees—many coming from as far away as North Carolina—arrived first to prepare for the two hundred guests expected at the onset of the season. Regular patrons, set to stay until September, arrived by steamship and rail next with their trunks, hatboxes, parasols, golf clubs, and rackets. They were followed by a convention of insurance men on a working holiday. Rounding out the guest list were the itinerant tourists who would come and go throughout the summer.

The hotel, which was outlined by hundreds of light bulbs, was fully electrified from its own power plant, and water was provided through the hotel's own private spring. Guests crossed over a new bridge constructed specially to accommodate horseless carriages, which were becoming more common. The golf course had been expanded, and there was excitement over the upcoming lawn tennis season that would draw leading players from across the country for exhibition matches. And if golf, tennis, croquet, billiards, boating, swimming, bicycling, and horseback riding (with stables housing forty thoroughbreds) weren't enough to anticipate, a circus was coming to town. Ah, to be alive and rich and vacationing at the Grand Hotel of the Atlantic in 1901!

While I sifted through a century's worth of hotel news at the Portsmouth Library, with some vague thought of finding a connection between Marguerite Miller and Claudia Harrison, Mayta was on a mission to hunt up a new store she'd heard about that sold homemade pastas down by the waterfront. In an hour she was to meet me back at the library.

The first article I found on Marguerite Miller was right after she disappeared on June twenty-third, 1901, and featured a grainy picture of a slender young woman, face shaded by a wide-brimmed hat, standing next to a formidable middle-aged man with a bushy mustache: Marguerite and her father. Archibald Miller was described as a prominent Boston doctor who "dabbled in new medicines and theories, including psychology." He had met Sigmund Freud, whose book, *Interpretation of Dreams,* published the year before, had set the medical field on its ear for its controversial theories.

It had been Dr. Miller's idea for his daughter to spend therapeutic time at the hotel. Toward the end of her stay there,

Dr. Miller, along with Marguerite's fiancé, Timothy Farley, had come up from Boston, and the three of them had enjoyed dinner together the night before she went missing. Farley said that this last conversation with Marguerite was happy; they had spoken of wedding plans and his future with his father's company.

Dr. Miller was devastated, blaming himself for sending his daughter to the hotel in her delicate condition. Marguerite's mother, who had stayed in Boston, had collapsed upon hearing of her disappearance, and was in the care of her younger daughter. This being the first tragedy of its kind at the hotel, the manager was beside himself with concern for the family who had been longtime seasonal guests.

The investigation had begun with the hotel, its grounds, and the rest of New Island, altogether about one square mile in area. The search was then extended into Portsmouth and beyond that, across the Piscataqua River to Kittery, Maine. Leads were followed: a worker at a circus camped nearby had been seen speaking with Marguerite before she disappeared; a woman had acted jealous of her husband's attentions to Marguerite one night at dinner. Police spoke with her maid, and her fiancé when it was learned that Marguerite had second thoughts about marrying him.

Among the staff, it was known that the young woman liked to walk alone in the woods and along the beach early in the morning and in the evening, so all doormen, waiters, cooks, porters, bellboys, and tray boys were questioned. Every lead ended in frustration. By mid-July news concerning the hotel returned to lighthearted social events.

I made copies of a few of the articles and then took everything back to the archives. I was organizing papers into a manila folder when Mayta entered the room. She raised her eyebrows in question, and I nodded: yes, I had found something of worth.

CHAPTER FIVE

"Mostly trivia," I said when we were in the car. "But it paints a picture of sorts. Young girl, about to get married, gets cold feet, develops a 'nervous condition,' so Daddy sends her off to the country with a nursemaid in hopes she'll come to her senses. Only instead of it ending the way it should, she runs away or is abducted."

"My guess is that while she was on one of her night walks, she came to harm," Mayta said. "Maybe she fell into the ocean."

"Hmm. Could be," I said. "News reports said she was close to her family so it seems unlikely she'd just run off. And her fiancé said they discussed wedding plans the night she disappeared, so it sounds like she'd gotten over her marriage jitters."

We drove out of the city along the winding Piscataqua River, Mayta following a map that would take us by Farrell Road, where D. S. Dennis lived.

"There it is," she said. "Next right. Are you sure we should do this? We don't even know that she's Claudia's great-aunt. She could call the police on us for harassment."

"It's not harassment to drive down a street." I made a right turn and headed up away from the river. "Okay, now, look for number fifty-two."

Mayta scrutinized the squatty colonial houses huddled together in the oldest section of town. "Thirty-six, thirty-eight, oops, didn't get that one . . . forty-four. Wait—slow down. I think that was fifty-two. Came up pretty quick."

I turned around in one of the few driveways on the street and crept back down the narrow road.

"That's it." Mayta pointed. "Fifty-two."

I stopped across the street from a mustard-yellow clapboard house, which displayed a small plaque painted with the date 1798. The house was positioned sideways, the end facing the street barely wide enough for the small-paned windows—two on each story—that were set into it. A patch of browning lawn separated house from sidewalk, and an uneven brick walk flanked by colorful perennials led up alongside the house. I pulled the car over as close to the curb as I could, put the shift in park, and opened the door.

"What are you doing? I thought we were just going to look."

"Now, what good would that do?" I slid out before Mayta could object.

Resigned, she scooted out on the other side. "What are we going to say?"

"I don't know yet."

We followed the path to a green door with a granite slab below it. Mayta hung back as I stepped onto the slab, raised the brass scallop shell doorknocker, and let it fall. The sound echoed inside the house with no response. I peeked in the sidelight and saw a staircase straight ahead, and two doorways off the entrance: one to the back of the house and the other to the living room at the front. A doily on a small table and a dowdy black coat on a wooden peg against the staircase wall gave the feel of an elderly person living there. Was it Claudia's great-aunt's house? I knocked two more times, waited, and then we returned to the car.

"Whoever lives there probably has no connection with Claudia Harrison, anyhow," Mayta said.

"Yeah, probably." But I wasn't convinced. The person I'd

talked to on the telephone had been too fast in her denial of knowing Claudia. Moreover, she had sounded wary, almost scared. As I put the key in the ignition, a woman approached from down the street. When she stepped onto the brick path, I jumped out of the car. I caught up to her as she was unlocking the door.

"Mrs. Dennis?"

The woman turned abruptly, and I saw that she couldn't be Dorothy Dennis, for she was no more than forty-five years old. "What do you want with Mrs. Dennis?"

"This is her house, isn't it?"

"I'm her companion. What can I do for you?"

"My name is Andy Gammon. I'm . . . an acquaintance of her niece, Claudia."

"Are you a reporter? Mrs. Dennis is frail and can't be upset."

"No, I was with Claudia the night she died and I thought maybe Mrs. Dennis would want to hear—"

"I'm sorry, but she isn't home, and she won't speak with you, anyway." She pushed open the door just wide enough to shove herself through, and then shut it firmly behind her.

I related the exchange to Mayta. "D. S. Dennis has to be Dorothy Dennis, Claudia's great-aunt. That rude woman didn't deny it."

"She's just protecting Mrs. Dennis," Mayta said.

"Yeah, I probably wasn't as tactful as I could have been. Still, I want to talk to Dorothy Dennis." We drove back along the river and crossed onto New Island, arriving at our third destination for the afternoon: the Grand Hotel of the Atlantic.

After parking in the side lot, we walked around the back of the hotel. This part of the building was original, and it resembled the old drawings and photographs I'd just been looking at. Right away I was able to locate the room from which Marguerite had disappeared in 1901, and where Claudia had been found, confirming my suspicion that the room's two windows overlooked the original porch roof.

I pointed them out to Mayta. "If someone were determined to do it, she could climb out a window onto the porch roof, and then figure a way to get down."

"That's a good two stories high."

"Yeah, but it's possible. I'd like to see that room again."

"How do you plan on doing that?"

"I'll have to think on it. Let's go get those drinks."

We settled in the same corner of the front verandah as last time, but as it was early for the dinner crowd, there were fewer customers.

"Sitting here reminds me of the conversation I overheard," I said after a sip of my white wine. "He said something about 'the woman in the green dress' and 'follow her,' then something about 'after dinner'."

"And Claudia was wearing a green dress."

"Yeah, although I counted five other green dresses."

"I remember one spectacular dress with a swath of pearl beads and sequins across the front of it." Mayta made a swipe back and forth across her bosom to illustrate.

"Hmm. Make it six. I missed that one."

"On second thought, it was probably more yellow than green."

"Well, one I counted was a suit and another was too bluish, so I guess that still leaves only three dresses that were truly green besides Claudia's."

"But you think that conversation had to do with Claudia?"

"Yeah. I think somebody was after her." I stood up and set down my glass. "I'm going to the ladies' room. Want to come?"

Mayta cocked her head, but didn't put words to her question. "Okay." She followed me into the lobby and down the hall past the restrooms. At the end I slipped through the door to the fire exit stairwell. We climbed up one flight and stopped at a door.

"Now," Mayta said, slightly out of breath, "even though I have a pretty good idea, I'm going to ask what we're doing."

"I want to see that room again. There's got to be some connection between Claudia's death there and Marguerite's disappearance."

"But it'll be locked, whether somebody's staying there or not."

"Let's just go in that direction and see what happens."

We walked down the hallway as if we belonged there, past a housekeeper pushing a cart piled with clean linens and cleaning supplies who didn't even look at us. We passed the elevators and crossed into the other half of the building. When I saw another housekeeping cart parked in front of the open door of a room, I had an idea. I doubled back down the corridor, motioning for Mayta to follow, and ducked into an alcove. We stood out of sight while the second housekeeper made up the room and then moved on to the next room, the second to last one on this side. The last room was where we'd found Claudia and where Marguerite had disappeared from: formerly room number thirty-three, now number one-thirteen, as Mayta had correctly remembered.

"Just a little longer," I whispered in answer to Mayta's raised eyebrows.

After about ten minutes, I heard the cart move again and a door open. I peeked out; the housekeeper was entering one-thirteen.

"Come on." I led the way back down the hall, pausing in front of the open door to Room One-thirteen. "Excuse me," I said to the woman who was pulling sheets off the queen-sized bed. "I think I left something in the bathroom. Do you mind if I check?"

"No, go ahead." She turned back to the bed, no doubt in her mind that we were the legitimate occupants.

I headed for the bathroom while Mayta dawdled in the bedroom, smiling guiltily at the housekeeper. I had to forcibly expel the picture of Claudia with the knife in her chest that came to mind in order to look around the room with new eyes. I guess I hoped to find some relationship between Claudia's murder and Marguerite's disappearance, but there were no clues from either time period. Other than rumpled towels on the floor, it was clean as a whistle, and since rooms in Marguerite's day didn't have private baths, there wasn't a single atom of 1901 originality in it.

The housekeeper stepped out into the hall with a bundle of soiled sheets in her arms, so I walked around the bedroom. My eyes went to the carpet in front of the bureau, and I noticed that the spots were gone. Had the section been replaced or merely cleaned? A new letter opener with the hotel crest sat innocently on the desk. I picked it up, walked to the bureau, and measured thirteen steps to the bathtub.

"Stop that!" Mayta hissed.

"Claudia was stabbed in front of the bureau and she ended up in the bathtub," I whispered. Mayta was eyeing the duplicate of the weapon in my hand, so I set it down, but continued pantomiming the actions. "The murderer grabbed up the letter opener and stabbed her. Or perhaps he was waiting for her over there," I pointed to a space between the door to the hall and the bathroom door, "and he jumped out when she entered. Then he either carried or dragged her to the tub. Why put her in the bathtub?"

"To hide her? Or tidy up?" Mayta suggested. "So blood wouldn't get all over?"

"Reason to think it may have been a woman," I agreed. "Of course, it's possible Claudia was killed elsewhere, then brought here. But I don't think so—too much movement in the hallways with the gala downstairs, tours, and all. And the blood on the carpet suggests it happened there."

Mayta looked nervously toward the door. "We should leave."

"Yes," I said, but crossed to one of the windows. I looked out, noting how easy it would be to step out onto the roof of the verandah and walk along its gentle slope. I fixed this spot with two references—the place where the back porch roof joined the side porch roof, and a large shrub below, thus verifying that the two windows I'd identified from below did belong to this room. The verandah roof, however, seemed even higher than two stories from this vantage point. Could an agile killer descend safely from the roof? Or—I rewound my thoughts one hundred years—could a girl who wanted to run away have done it? Had the same escape route been taken in both instances?

I looked around again and compared the present room with the brochure pictures taken around the time Marguerite had vanished. Virtually everything was different: new windows, although they still occupied the same places, and ceiling, flooring, and walls.

Except the fireplace, which was authentic to that period. I gazed into the oval mirror set in the paneling above the carved mantle and gave free rein to my imagination. I superimposed the Victorian-era pictures on the scene, refurnishing the reflected room with an iron bedstead, tall mahogany wardrobe, low armless chair beside the hearth. Then I added details: small feminine belongings—ribbons, combs, hair pins—on the mantle; articles of clothing—a cloak and straw hat—on the chair; and satin shoes with squat flared heels jumbled on the floor.

And then the girl was there in a long white dress, wavy dark hair framing a pensive expression, gazing into the mirror, hairbrush in hand.

"Did you find what you left behind?" From over an armful of

fluffy white folded towels, the housekeeper scowled at me. Beyond her, Mayta beckoned urgently from the doorway.

"Uh, I must have packed it, after all." I sidled out of the room under her suspicious eye. But the scene was still there in my mind as I hurried down the hallway behind Mayta.

Grand Hotel of the Atlantic
June Seventeenth, 1901

The face in the mirror is placid, belying the anxiety that is her constant now. She cannot sit for longer than minutes at a time, and even then looks up often from her book as if expecting somebody. Thoughts twist and tangle into such confusion that she must take up her pen and unravel them onto paper. Being on her own—save for Alice, of course, who makes sure she takes her tonic in the morning and before dinner each day, and otherwise pretty much lets her be— has been intoxicating, but after four days of freedom she is unsatisfied. Papa was only partly right; this respite is what she needs, but it has not, thus far, made her "right as rain."

She can readily mark the onset of this unease—the visit to the fortuneteller—but wonders whether it manifested itself whole on that day or sprouted from some furtive seed dormant inside her. She had believed herself to be content until the day she and Bess, her closest confidant, went to a fair on Boston Common.

They had toured the consumer tents, admiring the latest in household gadgetry and the newest models of kitchen stoves and sewing machines, Marguerite with more enthusiasm because she would soon be furnishing a home of her own. Then they strolled along the midway, sharing a cone of cotton candy, and Marguerite purchased tickets for the Ferris wheel, daring Bess to come with her. Eyes squeezed shut, hands clutching the bar, they shrieked in terror and delight at every jerk and sway. They stood in line for the hot-air bal-

loon, but at the last minute decided against it when Bess spotted the fortuneteller's tent. On a lark, they entered it.

Sitting on caned chairs in front of a small round table draped with a black cloth, Bess had her palm read while Marguerite watched. The cheerless sharp-faced old woman predicted a long life with a devoted husband and three children. Bess pushed coins discreetly across the table, her cheeks pink, Marguerite knew, with the thought of John Morse, although John had thus far paid Bess scant attention. The fortuneteller shoved the money into a fold of her layered bodice, then reached for Marguerite's hand. But Marguerite pulled away, got to her feet, and backed out of the tent.

"Why didn't you have your fortune told?" Bess said when she caught up to Marguerite. "Were you afraid?"

Marguerite had no answer. Surely, it wasn't fear that drove her from the tent. Her fortune undoubtedly would have been delivered in the same uninspired voice, its content much like Bess's: a handsome husband in the future, two or three children, and a long life. If not fear, then what? Days later, still at a loss to explain her actions to herself, and her general malaise to those around her, Marguerite finally told her parents that she was nervous about the wedding, and that she had qualms about marrying Timothy. Once spoken, the answer seemed the right one.

Papa's response was an unexpected and pleasant solution: time away from the flurry of nuptial preparations. Since nobody in the family could leave his or her responsibilities at this time—Papa his medical practice, Melinda her lessons, and Mama the care of Papa, Melinda, and the house—Marguerite was to go with only Alice, a chambermaid, to accompany her.

Papa prevailed upon the manager of the Grand Hotel of the Atlantic near Portsmouth, New Hampshire, where the family were seasonal regulars, but had not, because of the impending wedding, planned to go this year. Marguerite and Alice were given simple rooms adjacent to each other, the family's usual suite not being avail-

able. In addition to rest, Papa prescribed a restorative tonic to be taken twice daily, proclaiming, "This and the salt air will soon have you right as rain."

On the day of her arrival at the hotel, a young stylish Boston couple, Ernest and Josephine Carter, befriended Marguerite and it is with them that she sits for meals. Like Marguerite, Ernest spent childhood vacations at the Grand Hotel, and is now introducing the hotel to his new wife. The threesome talk of Boston society, of Scott Joplin's ragtime jazz, which both Marguerite and Josephine enjoy, and of other popular topics, like the wonders of new inventions that are making their way into everyday life: the aspirin (A marvel! *Josephine exclaims.* Two little pills and a headache is gone!); *the telephone, which the Carters plan on installing in their home within the year; and the Duryea brothers' horseless carriage, which Ernest saw exhibited at Barnum & Bailey's before the circus left for its year-long European tour, and which he describes in excessive detail for the women.*

"The automobile will be the next household necessity," predicts Ernest, while Josephine shakes her head in mock horror.

Although she enjoys their company, Marguerite does not seek out the Carters at times other than meals, for she enjoys the indulgence of being spontaneous, and of being by herself, both of which she is rarely able to do at home. One afternoon she joins a family in a game of croquet on the terraced lawn; on another she takes out a rowboat by herself, lies down across both seats, and drifts on the calm harbor under a wide sky. Sometimes she goes down to the small sand beach and wades.

At first, she spent a good portion of her time on the verandah, sitting and reading her poetry and European history book, watching new arrivals laden with steamer trunks, or just gazing at the breathtaking view before her: harbor, islands, and Atlantic Ocean beyond. More and more, though, she is drawn away from the hotel, toward the water or the trees.

Her favorite place has become the stand of pines beyond the trimmed landscape, where she sits with her journal on a needle-carpeted bluff overlooking the bay. Here, unseen by all, save those who happen to look up from sailboats or canoes, she allows feelings of longing, dissatisfaction, and frustration to announce themselves in sharp slashing script. It feels dangerous to put such intense thoughts in ink on a page, and often, she thinks she must stop. But neither can she curb the urge to write, or destroy what has been born of that urge, so she hides the journal.

Now, as she gazes beyond the books, the toiletry bottles, and a small vase with six daisies, at the expressionless face that looks back at her from the mirror above the fireplace, she wonders if the turmoil within her is visible to anyone else. She picks up the pins with trembling fingers. By the time her hair is dressed, her hands are calm again, and she is ready to present herself for dinner.

A small cluster of hotel guests has gathered around the display board in the lobby. Marguerite moves close enough to see what has drawn their attention. Tacked up is a colorful poster depicting parading elephants, snarling lions and tigers, trapeze artists, and a grinning ringleader in top hat and mustache:

The Alfred Snelling Show
Will exhibit at Portsmouth, New Hampshire!
On Wednesday, afternoon and evening!
The largest and best 25-cent show on Earth!
A respectable show based on its merits! No fakirs, no thieves
    tolerated!

"Oh! A circus! How lovely," says Josephine Carter, who has come up behind her. "It's not the Barnum & Bailey, but a good substitute since they're still in Europe. We must get together a group to watch them set up!" Voices around them rise in excited agreement.

"Set up?" Marguerite asks.

"Oh, yes! It's fascinating! If you've never seen a circus set up, you

67

must come!" Josephine insists.

An outing to Portsmouth is arranged for early the next morning. Pooh-poohing Alice's concerns about tiring herself, Marguerite joins Ernest and Josephine Carter and a number of other hotel guests on a caravan of carriages to Portsmouth. In the end, Alice, taken ill with a headache, allows Marguerite to go without her. The hotel coaches line up along the riverfront park, where they let off their passengers. Marguerite, Josephine, and Ernest weave through an eager crowd that has gathered along the main street. Upon hearing drums and cymbals, Ernest shoulders his way between two men and ushers Marguerite and Josephine into a perfect viewing spot on the curb, just in time to catch the end of the band and the beginning of the elephants—eight of them lumbering two by two in perfect unison, indifferent to the excitement around them, although an occasional large languid eye roves over the crowd.

"Ooh!" squeals a little girl as she dances up and down beside her father. Marguerite can barely contain herself either, having only one other time seen the monstrous creatures outside of picture books. She leans out to look past Josephine at the long winding spectacle that stretches up the road to the city limits. Beyond the elephants are elegant high-stepping show horses with plumed headdresses, paired by color—black or white—followed by gilded wagons carrying bears, lions, and tigers, each pulled by its own team of stately white horses.

Then advances the most amazing assemblage of humans Marguerite has ever seen: patchwork clowns, jugglers hurtling balls and pins in the air, beautiful sequined and spangled girls, a dwarf trotting alongside a giant man triple his height, Egyptian dancing girls with rotating hips, a strongman with bulging bare torso, two Africans in exotic dress, and a snake charmer with turbaned head and covered basket. There are others whom she suspects are just workers, but are no less fascinating: a number of muscled and sun-darkened men, and a group of olive-toned men, women, and children in vivid clothing and showy gold jewelry.

Gaudy wagons advertise a man with no arms, a woman with a beard, and a dog-faced boy, along with confections, peanuts, popcorn, and lemonade. Some wagons are more utilitarian, no advertising on their sides, but still decorative in their red or blue paint, trimmed in gold.

The entire parade takes half an hour at least, maybe longer. In the crush of farmers and dignitaries, the elderly and children, falling in after the last wagon, Marguerite becomes separated from her companions. She is carried along with the jovial crowd down the street, over a bridge, and out of town, back the way the carriages had brought her from the hotel. She arrives at a large field where rustic work wagons loaded with hay, oats, straw, wood, and coal, having arrived earlier, are standing at the ready. With the others, she watches from the roadside.

In an amazingly short time, the caravans and wagons arrange themselves in groupings, and workmen lay out a plan for the main tent: some two hundred iron rods with little fluttering blue and red flags are stuck into the ground. Other workmen take over, replacing the rods with four-foot stakes, raising heavy sledgehammers, striking in a unison beat: one, two, THREE, four, until every stake is driven into the ground. Then, a leader shouts directives; men pull on heavy ropes, and the poles for the center of the big top soar into the air.

"Pull her . . . slack her . . . hold it," the leader cries, and one team exerts all its might on pulley lines, raising the huge white canvases, which, as they clear the ground, are roped together by another team of workers.

Marguerite wanders around the periphery of the vast area, absorbed by the frenetic but organized activity. Besides the big top there is the mushrooming of many lesser tents, and dozens of circus people of every description darting in and out of caravans, and over and under cables being drawn tightly around stakes in the ground. There is the arranging of the bandwagon, the calliope, as well as the ticket, sideshow, and water—"sprinkler," somebody calls them—

wagons. There are the cook wagons: a butcher with cleaver in hand hacking at a side of beef; a cook connecting steam pipes to a boiler; men building table after table from ten-foot planks and sawhorses.

She spots the Carters across the way, but doesn't join them. Instead, she follows a group of boys to the staked elephants, which shift from side to side and eye their audience warily. The boys move on, Marguerite with them, to the horses, aristocratic show breeds and their peasant counterparts, the heavy draft horses, segregated into two groups as they await completion of their respective tents.

Off by itself at the edge of the field, closest to the water's edge, stands a small tent. Intrigued, Marguerite heads in that direction, skirting the crowded work area, wading through long, thin weeds. As she approaches, she sees a fortuneteller's sign. Heart quickening, she walks by slowly, peering sideways through the slit in the tent flaps. The woman inside looks up and Marguerite's first impulse is to shake her head and hurry on. Then, before allowing a second thought, she enters and seats herself opposite the woman.

The interior is deceptively spacious. Blankets draped over ropes are strung around the periphery so that parts of the tent are obscured. Behind a tiny round table sits a younger, thinner version of the Boston fortuneteller. She is dressed similarly in blouse and long skirt in bright conflicting patterns, with a scarf set back on her head, revealing a neat part in her black hair. A multitude of thin gold bangles jingles as she takes Marguerite's hand and tilts its palm to the light of the oil lamp in the center of the table.

A slight movement behind the woman draws Marguerite's attention to a split between the blankets where a flash of scarlet cloth is visible for an instant. The woman's eyes follow Marguerite's gaze over her shoulder and she utters a harsh indecipherable syllable. From behind the blankets a man's voice answers, ". . . dya."

When the woman turns back to Marguerite, there is a stern set to her mouth. Her eyes are so black there is no delineation between irises and pupils. "We begin," she says in a low hoarse voice. She holds

Marguerite's wrist, resting her thumb on its pulse; with the other hand she traces a line down each of Marguerite's fingers with her forefinger. In an unvarying voice she tells her that she will fall in love and marry and have two children. She tells her that she must follow her heart and that she should not listen to those who would dissuade her from her destiny. As the woman drones on, Marguerite finds herself paying more attention to the background. She is sure that the man who spoke is watching her from behind the blankets. There— they part a fraction and she catches a glimpse of a face. Boldly, she meets his gaze for an instant. Then the blankets fall back together.

"Life is destiny. You must follow your heart's desire." The fortune-teller squeezes her wrist.

Marguerite puts coins on the table and leaves the tent. She hurries back through the long grass, yanking her skirts away from prickly weeds that catch at them. She is perspiring from the heat and breath-ing heavily from exertion. She passes a team of workmen taking a break, leaning on sledgehammers, their bare muscled torsos shiny with sweat. Several watch her out of the corners of their eyes. One gives a low whistle, one makes a remark in another language loud enough for only her ears. She hurries by, stumbles over a mislaid stake, and hears laughter behind her.

Most of the onlookers have streamed back to town or their farms. Scanning those who remain scattered about, she doesn't see the Car-ters or others from the hotel so she walks back into town alone. The coaches stand waiting, but since it is too early to board, Marguerite walks through the park. She sits on a bench overlooking the Piscat-aqua River, thinking about what the fortuneteller said. Not the part about love, marriage, children, delivered by rote and probably told to every young single woman who enters her tent, but about the last thing the woman said: "Life is destiny. You must follow your heart." Told as if it was an admonition. But of what? Does following your heart mean you will fulfill your destiny? And how, she asks herself with some irritation, does one know one's destiny beforehand? Then she thinks about the eyes behind the curtain. To whom do they belong?

It is nearly noon and she is hungry, but she continues to watch people pass in front of her, and boats go by on the river. Maybe if she sits here long enough, destiny will find her. And then she realizes that somebody else is sitting on the bench. She hasn't heard or seen him arrive, only feels the sensation she had in the fortuneteller's tent seep into her consciousness. For a few moments she barely breathes. Her stomach is clenched, her gaze frozen straight ahead, her heart hammering. In fear? In anticipation?

Finally, she darts a look at him. He is leaning back, elbows propped up on the back of the bench on either side of him, one leg bent with ankle resting on the other knee. He is gazing at the river, chin high, offering his profile as if giving her a chance to inspect him, which she does discreetly, sideways from under lowered eyelids. His clothes are loose and casual, almost ragged. His complexion is like dark honey; his hair falls long and free, wavy and almost black. He is not much older than her, which is surprising because the eyes that had peered from the blankets conveyed an ageless worldly quality. She feels fear, not of this man who has singled her out for scrutiny and then followed her, but of herself, of what she is doing, of what she might do.

He turns his gaze to her and smiles in a flash of white teeth. His head moves in a quick little vertical jerk that affirms something—what, Marguerite doesn't know, only that by not looking away she has given him permission to affirm it.

"Marguerite," she whispers to an unspoken question, feeling foolish.

He nods. "Marguerite. A flower. It is a nice name." He has a foreign accent with a soft melodic cadence. He doesn't tell her his name in return, but she has the odd thought that she might already know it. It doesn't come to her as a word, but as a form, as something murmured, something that can be uttered in a single syllable, something she might have heard in a whisper or a dream.

"It is a beautiful day, is it not?"

"*Yes.*" *Marguerite smiles stiffly and looks away. If anyone were watching, they would think her only polite for answering. She should discourage further conversation; she should stand up and leave. She watches a family pass, two children bouncing and tugging on the father's sleeves, remembering a time as a child, walking through the Boston Public Gardens with her own father, holding onto his arm for protection against beggars who looked at them beseechingly.*

The man appears to understand her desire for propriety and says nothing further until the family has passed, and then, "I am Emil."

Two syllables, but yes, something she might have heard before in a dream. Could she be sleeping even now?

"Did you enjoy seeing the circus set-up?"

"Yes." A sailboat tacks close to the shoreline, and she thinks that surely she is awake.

"Will you come to the show tonight?"

She shakes her head.

"No?" His voice rises in surprise or perhaps mockery. "But it is the best show on the American continent now." They pull back into their separate selves as an elderly couple passes. Then he asks, "Did you have your fortune told?"

"You know that I did because you were there."

"Ah, you are right," he says. "But I did not hear it. What were you told?"

"That I will marry and have two children," Marguerite says in an even tone.

"So it was not what you wanted to hear." Again, the low, musical voice she feels compelled to answer.

Suddenly she is angry with him, at herself, and at Timothy, whose disapproval of this respite was evident in his impatience at the train station when he saw her off. She turns to him. "It is none of your business but I will tell you that it was *what I wanted to hear." With that, she rises and hurries down the path to the carriages.*

"Be sure to come to the circus tonight." The soft words float after

her, as if coming from the rustling leaves of the trees overhead or the gentle breeze off the river. "It is the best show on the continent."

"To whom were you talking?" Josephine has a quizzical look when she meets Marguerite at the street.

"Nobody." She looks back at the bench, and there is, indeed, nobody there now.

CHAPTER SIX

What harm would come in trying to reach D.S. Dennis? As I put in the numbers I hoped I wouldn't get the grumpy woman who'd identified herself as Dorothy's companion, and luck was with me; it was Mrs. Dennis herself who answered.

I spoke quickly before she could hang up. "My name is Andy Gammon. I was on the tour that found Claudia Harrison that night. I'm very sorry for your loss, and I'm sorry for bothering you, but I was hoping that maybe you would talk to me." She hadn't hung up so I continued, "Claudia seemed very nice. We talked about the hotel, and she told me about her great-aunt—you, I believe. She said you were a baker at the Grand Hotel for many years." I paused then, holding my breath.

"Who did you say you were?"

I gave my name again, reiterating that I'd met Claudia at the hotel's grand opening gala. Then I waited for the line to disconnect.

"Huh!" she said, "First that reporter woman, then you. It's time to straighten things out. Do you know where I live?"

I hesitated, not wanting to admit I'd already staked out her place, and she gave me directions. We set up a time for the following day, and I thanked her.

I looked at my watch. Mayta was coming a little before ten to go to the kids' last day award assembly. Deciding I had a little time to play with, I dug out the copies I'd run off about Marguerite Miller's father. There was something in the newspaper account that niggled at my memory, and now I skimmed the information again. Dr. Miller was a general practitioner, yet was described as having an interest in psychiatry; in fact, the article stated that he had once met Sigmund Freud.

Having only a vague idea of Freud, I googled him and found, not surprisingly, a wealth of information. *The Interpretation of Dreams,* an analysis of the unconscious mind, was considered at the time of its publication in 1900 to be his masterpiece, at least by Freud himself. Coming in the middle of the rigid Victorian Age, Freud's ideas—that dreams feature uniform symbols, that they are often sexually spawned, and that they are fulfillments of wishes or the result of repression—were predictably controversial, and were the substance of debates and popular conversation among the general public, as well as professionals in the fields of medicine and psychology.

Finding it interesting that Freud had been mentioned in an article about a man whose daughter was missing in New Hampshire, I looked up Archibald Miller and the year, 1901. You never know what obscure old records might have found their way onto the Internet; if Miller had had enough clout to be introduced to the father of psychiatry, what other connections might he have made?

After weeding out a number of references, I found one that was promising. An article in a fairly recent medical periodical on the history of a Boston-area hospital—Danvers State—ran lists of trustees, administrators, and doctors affiliated with the institution from its inception in 1874 until its closing in 1992. A Dr. Archibald Miller, one of the original doctors appointed to select the design and location of the new asylum, and who then served as trustee until 1902, could be the one I was seeking. How many Dr. Archibald Millers interested in psychiatry could there have been in Boston during those years?

"Mommy! We have to go!" Max yelled up from the first floor.

"Did you brush your teeth?" I yelled back, tapping keys quickly. "Is Molly ready?" Another page came up—pictures of the then-new state asylum—and I paused, caught by surprise. Although there's nothing that says institutions for the mentally ill at the turn of the century had to be somber or spooky-looking, I'd never imagined the opposite to be true. Gothic, it was; but Danvers State was far from creepy.

The brick buildings, with their myriad of airy turrets and spires with windows like fancy cutwork cloth, rose magnificently into the sky, and were made even more impressive by their situation atop a hill. Towers and wings radiating out from the main building were reminiscent of a European castle. In every observable respect, including the groomed lawns and geometrical flowerbeds, these were dwellings worthy of royalty.

"Mo-om! We're going to be late!" Max yelled again. "Grandma's here!"

"Coming!" I bookmarked the page, put the computer to sleep, and shoved my feet into sandals as I dashed for the stairs. Okay, so Miller was interested, perhaps even involved, in psychiatry—at least in the building and maintaining of a fancy psychiatric asylum. What did that tell me about his daughter, Marguerite, and why or how she disappeared? It was something to ponder, but it would have to wait because there were now three voices bellowing at me from the first floor.

Mayta had a wrapped plate of brownies in one hand. With the other she'd corralled both kids and was herding them out the kitchen door, her big black handbag swinging from the crook of her elbow dangerously close to Molly's head. She opened her mouth to say something, but I didn't give her a chance.

"I know. We're late." I grabbed a container of deli macaroni salad out of the fridge, my pocketbook and keys, and dashed out after them.

"You guys buckled in?" I looked over my shoulder as I slid behind the wheel. "Good. We're off."

"Max touched me!"

"Did not!"

"Did so!"

I backed out of the driveway, pointed the nose of the car up the street, and took note of the time. Four minutes, we'd be there; seven minutes, we'd be parked. I'd let them off first, and then park.

"Did not!"

"Did so!"

"Where's Gus?" Mayta asked.

"He can't make it. He'll meet us at the picnic."

"Molly touched me!"

"Did not!"

"Did so!"

I pulled up to the school. "Get out! Hurry! You're late!" They scrambled out, one after the other. Once she'd gained her feet on the sidewalk, Molly whirled around, tucked her head down and rammed it into Max's stomach. Max cried out, but recovered quickly, landing a wallop on the side of Molly's head. Wailing, she tore up the front stairs after her brother.

"Molly! Max!" I screamed threateningly out the car window, but the school had already swallowed them up. Mayta and I exchanged murderous looks.

The awards assembly lasted forty-five minutes. Max was presented with a Good Citizen Award for being especially helpful to others in his class, and Molly proudly accepted a Good Neighbor Award for going out of her way to be kind and understanding. Mayta and I exchanged looks again, this time rolling our eyes.

Immediately afterward was the all-school picnic at Moseley Pines, a wooded park on the edge of town. While Max and

Molly, now all lightness and cheer, ran with friends from climbing structure to swings to monkey bars, Mayta and I helped line up picnic tables on the covered pavilion and set up the food buffet-style. I picked the price sticker off the side of the tub and plunked down my macaroni salad next to a cheerful array of Tupperware holding all manners of obviously homemade potato, pasta, lettuce, and fruit salads.

"You know," I rationalized to Mayta, "someday, when I can equal the supermarket's deli in creating a decent side dish, I will gladly put in the effort."

She looked at me in mild disgust. "You're just lazy."

"Yep," I agreed cheerfully, trailing behind as she carried her plate to the dessert end. Then I told her about the conversation I'd had with Dorothy Dennis.

"She talked to you? She's really Claudia's great-aunt?"

"Didn't deny it. She said she needed to straighten things out, though, whatever that means. And she said that a woman reporter has been calling her." I slid my hand under the plastic wrap and took a brownie off the plate. "What do you want to bet it's Beverly Magill?"

"Probably. That woman has a nose like a bloodhound."

"Anyway, she actually invited me to her house, so I'm going back up to Portsmouth tomorrow. Want to come?" I stuffed the brownie into my mouth.

"Sure! That should be interesting."

We went to claim a spot for our blanket near a circle of other families. The kids all ran around, shrieking delightedly, until the parents reined them in and herded them into the food lines. The four of us had loaded our plates and were seated, ready to dig in, when Gus arrived in shorts and sandals, signifying the official end to his school year.

"Happy summer!" I strained up to receive his kiss as he bent down.

"Indeed!" he responded, and went to get food.

"That girl, Claudia, wasn't any relative of mine," Dorothy Dennis said as soon as Mayta and I were seated in matching faded floral armchairs in her living room. "I have no brothers or sisters. My husband died fifty years ago, and he had no living relatives left. And we never had children of our own."

After instructing us to call her Dorothy, and offering coffee, which both of us declined, she lowered herself opposite us onto a pale blue velveteen loveseat. She was at least eighty years old, and tall for an elderly woman—about five foot eight. While she moved stiffly, she otherwise appeared vigorous, not frail, as her companion had said. Her short gray hair was styled in waves close to her head, and she wore a neat small-print dress in shades of blue and lavender that matched her living room. Her favorite colors, I guessed.

"She came to see me a couple of months ago, claiming she was the great-granddaughter of my mother's sister," Dorothy continued.

"Why would she say that if it weren't true?" I asked.

"Who knows why she would make up a cockamamie story like that! Still, I thought she was nice. Didn't like her husband much, though. Too moody." She indicated a plate of cookies on the coffee table. "Please help yourselves."

"Claudia came here with Daniel?"

Dorothy nodded. "I think they'd been arguing. He just slumped in that chair over there and brooded about something. She did all the talking."

"What did she want?" Mayta reached for a cookie.

"To sell me on the story of her as my long-lost relative." She snorted in disgust. "She pulled out some papers, supposedly

80

proof of her claim, but it was hogwash. My aunt died young and she didn't have any children."

"Your aunt?" I said.

"My mother's older sister. The girl, Claudia, tried to convince me that there had been a child born to my aunt, and that her great-grandmother was this child. Then she asked about the engagement ring and that's when I'd had enough and asked them to leave."

"What engagement ring?" Mayta said.

She sighed impatiently. "There's an old rumor that my aunt hid her diamond ring, purportedly worth a lot of money, somewhere at the Grand Hotel. It's not true; the ring was not that valuable and it was lost or stolen over a century ago. But people love treasure stories."

"So Claudia and Daniel came here looking for a ring?" I was confused.

"I guess so. They must have made up that story of her being related to me, thinking I'd help them find Marguerite's lost ring."

I exchanged glances with Mayta. "Your aunt—your mother's sister—was Marguerite Miller?"

"That's right. Melinda Miller was my mother, and Marguerite was her older sister." Dorothy narrowed her eyes at me. "How do you know about Marguerite?"

Briefly, I explained our interest in the history of the hotel. "I thought Marguerite disappeared."

"Oh, she did, but she was found a year later. Then she became ill and died in a hospital."

It took a moment for this to soak in. "But . . . I thought she was never seen again. It wasn't in the newspapers that she was found."

Dorothy sighed again. "There was no foul play. She'd left on her own accord. It was a disgraceful situation, a young woman running off like that." Sitting ramrod straight in the center of the loveseat, chin held high and unwavering, Dorothy presented some of the starch that I surmised had been passed down from her formidable ancestors.

"The Millers were influential enough to be able to keep it quiet at the time," she said. "They made a small statement without details, saying that she'd been found, and the hotel owners, who'd had their share of adverse publicity, were happy to let the whole thing die down. Besides, a year had passed, so it wasn't big news anymore."

"Why did Marguerite run away? And where did she go?" Mayta said.

"I don't know." Dorothy hesitated. "But I think it was to be married to somebody other than her fiancé. Whatever happened, in the end there was no husband and she came home."

"You said she died in a hospital," I prompted.

"Not long after she was found, her parents—my grand-parents—were killed in a car accident, and then Marguerite became ill and died also. My mother, who was only sixteen at the time, went to live with her aunt in New York. It was a very difficult time for my mother; even in her later years she never liked to talk about it." Dorothy pressed her lips together. "Imagine losing your entire family within a few months."

Mayta and I made sympathetic sounds. After a respectful moment I asked, "Where was Marguerite during the year she was missing?"

"If my mother knew, she never said. I don't think she even knew where her sister was buried—she's not in the family plot in Boston."

After a few moments, Mayta said, "What a coincidence that you went to work at the same place your aunt disappeared from."

"Yes, I suppose it seems that way." Dorothy understood the implication about the family's declined fortune, but wasn't insulted. "The family was well-to-do back then and could afford to vacation at the Grand Hotel of the Atlantic. But they lost almost everything during the stock market crash. Years later, when my husband died, I needed to find employment. I liked to bake and the hotel was hiring. That's all."

My mind buzzed with so many questions I didn't know where to start. Finally, I said, "Why would Claudia think she was the great-granddaughter of Marguerite Miller? You said she showed you papers?"

"Yes." Dorothy tilted her head to one side, remembering. "One looked like the page of a hospital record from some place in Massachusetts. Her name, Marguerite Miller, was typed on it, and there was a date of admittance—1902, I remember thinking the year fit. But Marguerite Miller wouldn't have been an unusual name back then, and I thought that either the file was fake or it was some other girl.

"The other paper she showed me was a torn piece of letter with a picture drawn on it. She claimed it was from my mother to Marguerite, but I didn't look at it very carefully. I was angry at that point and just wanted them gone."

"How did Claudia get these papers?" I asked.

Her brow crinkled in thought. "She said they came down through her great-grandmother to her grandmother, who then gave them to her before she died."

"The great-grandmother being Marguerite's daughter."

"So she claimed," Dorothy said.

The doorknob rattled then, and a couple, one of whom was the woman I'd met outside Dorothy's on my first visit, entered the house. She gave Dorothy a questioning glance as she set the mail down on the little table next to the door.

"Hello Ellen, Walter," Dorothy called out. "Come join us."

Ellen looked the opposite of her feminine, floral-loving employer. Neat and spare, she was of average height and large-boned, though not overweight. Her dark hair was cropped short and she wore her chinos, boat shoes, and white crew neck tee like a uniform. She moved to Dorothy's side, eyes regarding us from behind her tortoise-shell glasses.

The man remained in the entry. Something about him reminded me vaguely of an actor, but I couldn't think of which one. He was the same height as Ellen, but thinner, and looked younger despite touches of gray in his dark hair. He was also dressed in chinos with boat shoes, but wore them in more of a dressed-down careless but stylish sort of way.

"This is my home health aide and companion, Ellen Timmons." Dorothy smiled up at Ellen. "For ten years now she's been my secretary, bill payer, nurse, and friend all rolled up in one. I don't know what I'd do without her. And this is her brother, Walter, who's visiting from Rhode Island."

"How do you do," Ellen said formally. Walter smiled and raised a hand in greeting from the doorway.

"Hi. I'm Andy and this is my mother-in-law, Mayta." I thought about giving some reason for being there, but Ellen had already turned to her employer.

"You're tired," she said. "And it's almost time for lunch."

"Oh, I'm sorry." I rose, taking the hint, and Mayta followed suit. "We were just leaving."

Dorothy shook her head in irritation. "Oh, Ellen, stop fussing! I'm fine, really."

Ellen rolled her eyes at her brother on her way to the kitchen. Walter shrugged in commiseration—what can you do?—but when he turned to us, his eyes were crinkled in amusement, indicating that he didn't take his sister too seriously.

"Nice meeting you all." He dipped his head. "Goodbye, Dorothy. I'm going as well."

"Goodbye, Walter. Are you off to the track, then?"

The slight disapproval in Dorothy's voice didn't appear to

faze Walter, who paused at the door long enough to respond in a cheerful tone, "Yes, ma'am. See you sometime tomorrow."

"One last question, if you don't mind, Dorothy." I decided to take advantage of Ellen being out of the room. "Did Claudia ever contact you again?"

"Yes. She called and wanted to stop by to show me some other proof that her great-grandmother was Marguerite's daughter."

"What was it?"

"I don't know because that's when . . . she died." Dorothy's voice turned wistful. "Even though I didn't believe her story, I wish I'd had the chance to talk to her again."

"Did you tell the police about her visit?"

She looked surprised. "What would I tell them? That this stranger visited me, claiming she was a long-lost relative?"

I shrugged. "You were one of the last persons she spoke with. The police are looking for anything to help them find her killer."

"Dorothy, there's a chair in the middle of the kitchen." Ellen had returned and was standing at the entrance to the room, hands on her hips, openly exasperated with her employer. "Did you climb up on it again?"

"The pull for the fan was tangled and I couldn't reach it." Dorothy raised her chin an inch, as if attempting defiance, but she didn't meet Ellen's eyes. "I was careful."

"Well, that is a very dangerous thing to do! You could have fallen." Her disapproving gaze slid to us and she said pointedly, "Mrs. Dennis is tired."

I apologized again and Mayta thanked Dorothy for seeing us. After writing down my phone number for Dorothy, we made haste for the door.

"A bit overprotective, that Ellen," I said when we reached the car.

"She probably has to be that way for Dorothy's sake," Mayta

said. "Sounds like Dorothy takes risks."

We were on the expressway heading home before we spoke again.

"So," I said, "there *was* a connection between Claudia and Marguerite Miller."

"And now we know what happened to Marguerite," Mayta said. "She ran off, got sick, and died in a hospital."

"Why did she run off? Where was she during that year? What did she die of? And where did she die?"

"You're right; it's still a mystery." Mayta smiled. "Guess you're hooked now, huh?"

"Did she have a baby," I continued, "and if so, who was the father?"

CHAPTER SEVEN

"Chauncey Brown here, calling for Mrs. Andy Gammon." His refined voice took me back to that elegant table: china, damask tablecloth, glassware glinting by candlelight. And back, also, to some questions I had for him.

"Hi, Chauncey. How are you?"

"Fine, thank you. I was calling to inquire about your well-being. That was an unnerving event at the Grand Hotel, especially for you and your mother-in-law, being the ones to come across Claudia like that."

"Hmm, yes," I said. "How did you get this number?"

"You're listed in the phone book."

"Yes, but why are you calling?"

He cleared his throat. "From my experience as a lawyer, I know that sometimes the shock of an event like that doesn't have its full impact until days later. If I can be of help in any way, as a sounding board or anything—"

At this point, I'd had enough of his charm. "Chauncey, just who are you? You talk a big game—telling us about spending summers at the Grand Hotel and all—but it turns out that you lied about staying there that night, and even skipped out on paying for your dinner."

It was some seconds before he responded. "Well, ah, I guess I got carried away. Please forgive me. And I must have forgotten about the bill. I will take care of it."

"How much of what you told us was true?"

"Why, all of it except the part about staying at the hotel. And spending summers there."

"And traveling since your wife died? Pretending to be wealthy?"

"Oh yes, I do travel, but, alas, I never had a wife. As for being wealthy, I had a spate of hard times some years back, but I don't think I pretend . . ."

"Did you know Claudia and Daniel before that night?" I decided to push further. "Where did you go when you left the table?"

There was silence on the other end. Then he said, "I may not be all that I purport, but I am no murderer, if that's what you're implying. When I left the table, I took a walk around the grounds."

I sighed. "Okay, so tell me why you're calling."

"Yes, well, your mother-in-law said you like to solve mysteries." While he paused, I put "Scream at Mayta" on my list of things to do that day. "And since the police haven't found Claudia's killer, and I am also a curious person, I thought we could pool our resources—"

"No. That is the job of the police, not mine or yours."

"Hmm, yes, you're right, but how about I give you my number anyway, in case you think of some way I can be of assistance?"

I took down his number, mainly to get rid of him, and said goodbye.

"By the way," he said as I was about to hang up, "I really was a lawyer in New York."

Before I could move from the phone, it rang again. This time it was Beverly Magill, another person I had a question for.

"I read your story on Claudia," I said.

"Yeah, I'm covering it since I was there. In fact, that's why I called. I heard you've gotten chummy with Dorothy Dennis.

Since I went through a lot of trouble to locate the great-aunt Claudia told us about, I'm curious as to how *you* found her. Did Claudia tell you something she didn't tell me?"

"Not really. I just did a little detective work."

"Well, I couldn't get the old girl to talk to me, so how did you manage it?"

"Who said she talked to me?"

"My source down at the station said Dorothy Dennis called and volunteered information because you'd advised her to."

"Oh, good," I said, mildly surprised that Dorothy had followed through.

"So I called her today, and she still refused to talk to me. Says she doesn't trust the press."

I laughed. "She's kind of a tough cookie."

"Think you can put in a good word for me?"

"Sure, but I can't guarantee anything."

"Thanks. In the meantime, can you tell me why I can't find anything that says she's related to Claudia?"

"Because she probably isn't."

"Who is she, then?"

"Just a nice elderly lady who used to work at the Grand Hotel."

"So does Claudia have any family in Portsmouth?"

"Not as far as I know," I said. "Hey, you never said why you missed the tour the night Claudia was killed."

"I think I said I had to make a phone call."

"That was a long call."

"Yes. Listen," she said, suddenly in a rush, "if you find out anything new that I could use in a story on Claudia Dean, give me a ring." She rattled off her cell number and I wrote it below Chauncey Brown's. "And don't forget to mention me to Mrs. Dennis. I still think there's some connection there."

★ ★ ★ ★ ★

After dinner that night, with the kids finally in bed, Gus and I plunked down in front of the television to catch the ten o'clock news. In order to steal a little time for ourselves we were trying, mostly without success, to keep the kids on a schedule. For the first half of the news there were sounds of feet scampering from one room to the other, then down the hall to the bathroom. After a few yells up the stairs, it finally began to quiet down. I'd rounded the corner to the living room, after having called upstairs for the last time, when an item on television caught my eye: a woman talking in front of what looked like a Gothic castle.

"What building is that?" I asked Gus.

"It's part of Danvers State."

"The mental hospital?"

"Yeah, the one you see up on the hill off Route 1. It's going to be torn down."

I sat on the couch and listened to the last few moments of the interview. The woman was an advocate from an organization that wanted to save the hospital buildings because of their historical and architectural significance. She was lamenting the decision, made by developers, to demolish the long-deserted structures. Her group was hoping that at least the Kirkbride building, which was behind her, could be saved, given the fact it was listed on the National Register of Historic Places.

"Why so interested?" Gus asked during the station break.

"The doctor whose daughter ran away from the Grand Hotel in 1901 was on the board that founded Danvers State Hospital. Only it wasn't called that back then; it was the State Lunatic Hospital, or something like that."

"I knew some kids in college who worked there as attendants on the wards," Gus said. "They used to tell some pretty interesting stories. And not just about the patients, either; some who'd worked there for a long time were as crazy as the residents."

"Wait a minute," I said. "I wonder if Marguerite was hospitalized because she was mentally ill, not physically ill. Her father was connected to the hospital, and if she ran away because she was—"

Gus had held up a hand. It's acceptable to talk during the news and occasionally during sports, but never during what the kids say is their father's favorite program: Weather, with a capital W, like it's part of the nightly lineup of sitcoms and dramas. After we were assured there were no imminent natural disasters, and were informed precisely of the temperature and amount of humidity in the air for the following morning, midday, and evening hours, Gus turned his attention back to me.

"—pregnant," I finished, raising my voice over a commercial that came on. "If she was pregnant out of wedlock, her father might have had her committed. They did things like that back then."

"That would've been like sentencing her to death." Gus reached over and hit the off button on the TV remote.

"Not really. I was just reading about it a few days ago. The turn of the century was the golden age of psychiatry. They had progressive ideas of treatment, and money to fund programs." I warmed to my subject, reciting what I'd learned. "Institutions were built on the belief that good light, ventilation, and aesthetic surroundings would cure the mentally ill. They were beautiful buildings with landscaped grounds. That one on the news—the Kirkbride building—is on the National Register of Historic Places."

"Funny, you only hear how horrible those places were."

"Yeah, they *were* horrible, but that was later, when they got overcrowded and rundown. When new, the Victorian asylums were almost like country clubs."

"So what makes you think that girl ended up at Danvers?"

"Well, Marguerite died in a hospital in Massachusetts—Dorothy Dennis was sure of that, although she couldn't recall the name on the paper Claudia had. And her father was on the governing board of Danvers at the time, so he obviously had confidence in the asylum's programs, and might have sent his daughter there with the best intentions."

"Those are pretty slim connections."

"Yeah, probably. Still, I'd like to ask Dorothy about it. She saw the record that Claudia had. If I mentioned the name of the hospital, she might remember it." I looked at the mantle clock: ten forty-five. "I'll call her in the morning."

"Hey," Gus said, "I think Mike Murray used to work at Danvers."

"Shannon's husband?" Shannon's youngest, Sarah, takes ballet lessons with Molly, so we often chat over coffee. Gus and Mike, a school psychologist, know each other through Shannon and me, and generally only get together at kid events or when one of us women arranges an outing that includes them.

"Yeah. I'm sure he said he did some work there when he was in grad school."

"That's interesting. Maybe I'll talk to him."

I made two phone calls the next morning. The first was to Dorothy, who told me that the police had called her back, and that Ellen was taking her down to the station later in the day to make a statement. She also told me about her perennial garden—at its seasonal best right now—which I took as a subtle invitation to visit again. When I brought up the reason for my call, her memory was triggered by the name of the city, Danvers, which she thought was on the hospital record Claudia showed her. But when I gave the original name of the hospital, the State Lunatic Hospital at Danvers (I'd looked it up), she became insulted that I would think her aunt had been committed to an insane asylum. By the time I hung up, I thought that I might *not* be invited to visit her perennial garden any time soon.

The second call was to Mayta to see if she wanted to go tramping around the deserted Danvers State Hospital grounds, but she had a luncheon date with the mayor, Ben Barrett.

"Oh?" I put raised eyebrows in my voice.

"Yeah," she said offhandedly. "He's been pestering me to go for lunch since last year when we all went out and he gave us the lowdown on his crooked ancestor."

"Yes, I remember. He was flirting with you, and you were flattered. In fact, I'm surprised the two of you haven't gotten together before this."

"Well, we've talked a couple of times."

"Really?"

"Now, you can just stop with that tone. There's nothing going on. When he gets tired of dealing with political muckedy-mucks, he calls and I give him an earful of practical advice."

"I see. You're an advisor of sorts."

"I guess. Listen, I gotta go now."

"Wow," I said, unable to resist, "this must be some date if you have to start getting ready two hours beforehand."

"Listen, Miss Smarty-pants, I am not getting ready for lunch yet. I happen to have some errands to do before I meet Ben."

"Uh-huh, and is one of those errands a visit to the Clip 'n' Curl?" As she began to sputter, I said goodbye, adding quickly, "I expect details tomorrow."

Gus had been promising Max and Molly a trip to Chuck E. Cheese, and since it was a cool, cloudy day, not good for the beach, he broke down under their combined pressure. When he tried to include me in the plans, I demurred, reminding him of how many Chuck E. Cheese birthday parties I had endured—or rather, enjoyed—when he had been otherwise (conveniently) occupied, and that now it was his turn.

Then I told him about Dorothy recognizing the name Danvers as being on the hospital record Claudia had shown her. "Marguerite Miller. Danvers. The slim connections are becoming less slim," I said.

"So, while I am enjoying the maniacal fun house of a giant fake mouse, you will be . . . ?"

"Tramping around fields and abandoned buildings." I shook my head regretfully. "Very unsafe places for children."

"If you're talking about Danvers, I don't think they just let you tramp around their fields and go through their buildings."

"Actually, I went onto Beth Ann Roy's website—she's the one who was on the news last night. Her group, *Save Danvers State*, is giving tours in an effort to get community support. And there's one today, so I'm going." Then, feeling a little guilty, I said, "Hey, how about a real date tonight? We could go out to a movie, maybe even dinner."

He considered. "That'd be fun. Do you want to see what the Murrays are doing? Maybe Mike will tell you about Danvers."

"Great idea! A double date." I called right away and was able to get our favorite babysitter for the night. Then I left a message on Shannon and Mike's home phone.

Having planned the night, and therefore feeling a little less like a heel for ditching the kids with Gus, I jumped in the car and headed south on I-95. About twenty minutes later, I took the exit for Route One and within a few moments arrived at the gate for Danvers State Hospital, at the bottom of the hill.

Beth Ann Roy stood in front of a green mini-van, waving in the dozen or so people milling around wearing raincoats or carrying umbrellas. The weatherman had promised that the rain was ending, but after a glance at the threatening sky, I grabbed my umbrella also. Beth Ann, who was tall, thin, and stylish in a swing coat and narrow black slacks, was introducing herself as I joined the group.

"The State Lunatic Hospital at Danvers was begun in 1874 and completed in 1878," she said. "It was a state-of-the-art facility, its design influenced by a psychiatrist, Thomas Story Kirkbride, superintendent of the Pennsylvania Hospital for the Insane. Kirkbride believed that the best possible conditions were necessary to cure the insane. I'll tell you more about his plan when we get up to the top."

We followed Beth Ann up the drive, her cape-like coat swaying in the mild wind, the soles of her shoes crunching in loose gravel on the deteriorating tarmac. When the brush and trees on either side of the road opened out onto a field, she swept an arm out, explaining that this area had once been elaborate formal gardens, open to the public. But our eyes were drawn to the fortress-like brick building, now in complete view, rising regally in Gothic-styled towers, turrets, and spires, and telescoping out and back in a number of wings.

There was one "Wow" among the awe-inspired murmurs.

"Will we be able to go in?" I asked as we stopped in front of the grand structure.

Beth's look pinned me. "Absolutely not," she said in a clipped tone. "It would be dangerous. Security guards will arrest anyone who tries to enter."

Feeling chastised, I nodded as if the idea was dashed from my mind. At the same time, though, I began planning how I might do exactly that—sneak into this incredible building.

Beth Ann gestured at the imposing facade. "This is Thomas Kirkbride's signature building. His plan called for the buildings to be arranged in a specific order with the tallest, central administration, at the center. Spreading from its hub are two wings to either side that step back to two more wings that go off in opposing angles, then back to yet another set of wings so that there are six wings spreading out in a kind of curving design. Like a large bird with outstretched wings."

"Yeah, like a vulture," said a middle-aged man in a blue shirt.

"I was thinking of an eagle," Beth Ann said in disapproval. "The benefit of this design is that each ward has windows on all four sides. Kirkbride believed that an asylum should be built in a secluded place, that there be good soil for vegetables and flowers, and that the building should have nice views, fresh air, and good light. He felt that, given the proper treatment and a pleasant environment, eighty percent of the asylum's population could be cured."

There was a small ripple of murmurs through the group. "Questions?" Beth Ann asked.

"More of an observation," I said. "I'm guessing this place must have been very expensive to build, even by nineteenth-century standards."

"Yes, it was. Kirkbride believed that state hospitals should be good enough for the highest-class citizens. Materials used were of the best quality: rich red Danvers brick, granite, slate for the roof, copper trim, and iron crestings." We looked up at the roof-line with some of its delicate metal edgings visible and an occasional remaining finial atop a spire.

"Unfortunately, the buildings are no longer safe," her eyes darted in my direction, "but if we were allowed inside, you would see what's left of the mahogany and oak woodwork, marble mantels, brass hardware, and stained glass." She paused, giving us time to appreciate her words.

"It's true," said the man in the blue shirt, turning to the woman next to him. "I been in there. It's got all this dark wood and tall, spooky windows."

"When did you tour the inside?" Beth Ann said.

"Oh, it wasn't any tour. I was ghost hunting. We sneaked in."

"That's dangerous! Besides the fact you could get injured, a lot of damage has been caused to the buildings as a result of trespassers."

The man shrugged. "The chick who led us does it regularly." He turned to his neighbor again. "It was real spooky. One of the guys saw a ghost and we all felt real cold at the same time. A place like this with all its history has a lot of bad karma."

Beth Ann frowned and turned to the rest of us, "As I was saying, nothing was spared in the building. It cost about one and a half million, an exorbitant amount for the times. But this was during an era of strong morality and social commitment, and Dorothea Dix, the famous advocate for the mentally ill, personally lobbied for its funding."

We continued around the side of the building, admiring the intricate structure, the ivy-covered towers, the deep red brick that almost glowed in the overcast day. The windows on the lower level were boarded, and trees sprouted in broken sections of the tarmac, but recalling the old photographs I'd found online, I could picture its original grandeur. I thought of the inspired doctors, architects, and engineers who worked together to create this extraordinary set of buildings, sparing neither expense nor effort. How excited they must have been when Danvers opened to receive its first patients. Dr. Archibald Miller would have been proud of his affiliation with such a facility. But would he have sent his daughter here if he thought she was mentally ill?

We descended the side of the hill and walked along a dirt road, people talking among themselves in groups of twos and threes. I caught snatches of conversation; most commenting on the architecture or the facility's history. One woman, who identified herself as a paranormal researcher, began talking about haunted events at Danvers that had been reported over the years.

"There's a woman who appears in the hallways of the Kirkbride," she said. "She dresses in white and has long white hair."

"That's her! I think that's who we saw," the man in the blue shirt said excitedly, and went on to embellish the story he'd mentioned earlier.

Another man, a fan of a horror movie filmed at the hospital, was pointing out sections of the building he recognized from the movie to his companion.

Beth Ann stepped off the road into an area that was cleared of brush and had been mowed. She stopped about fifteen feet in and waited for us to walk through the wet grass. Behind her, set into the ground at regularly spaced intervals, were brick-sized granite pavers engraved with numbers.

"This is one of two cemeteries on the grounds," she said. "Several years ago a memorial group was formed to restore these cemeteries, which were completely overgrown with weeds and briars."

"But where are the headstones?" someone asked.

"There aren't any. The numbers on these markers refer to inmates of the hospital."

"That's it?" a man said. "They just buried them with a number?"

"It was considered confidential to not put names on the markers," Beth Ann explained. "It had to do with the stigma of mental illness at the time."

"But didn't they have a funeral or anything?" a woman said.

"Sometimes not. If there was no family, there'd be no service, just a quick burial," Beth Ann said. "Anyway, the memorial group got publicity when a TV news reporter came out. There was lobbying, and eventually there was enough support to clean up the sites and begin research to identify the people buried here by matching numbers with names."

"How do they do that—" I said, "—identify the buried?"

"Good question. There are some hospital records, but many of them have been lost. Committee members have spent hours researching records at the town hall, matching numbers with names."

"So the patients who died here are listed at Danvers Town Hall?" I said.

"Not all. Some would be in their hometown records, depending on who claimed them."

Of course. If Marguerite had been here, her family would have claimed her body when she died. But, if she wasn't in the family plot as Dorothy claimed, where was she?

"Eventually, they hope to have proper markers with names," Beth Ann said. "That fight was won at the state level. The privacy argument has been thrown out; it's now been determined that it's disrespectful to be buried with no name." She softened her voice for the first time. "All these lives plucked from the mainstream, put on hold, and then never even acknowledged in death; it's a tragedy, don't you think?"

Her comment silenced us as we looked out over the modest little numbered squares of granite. Number four: a middle-aged woman with depression? Number five: an elderly man with dementia? Number seven: a young woman in disgrace with an unborn child? Whatever misfortune or illness had befallen them, they were owed more for their lives than a block with a chiseled number on it.

One of the women up front asked a question I couldn't hear, and Beth Ann shook her head. "To my knowledge they have never allowed séances inside the buildings. There's been a lot of interest in Danvers, especially since it closed, from history buffs, paranormal groups, horror film followers—a horror movie was filmed here some years back—and teens. Somebody is always trying to sneak in. But the place is well guarded by police and private security, and not many get away with it anymore. Usually, it's kids looking for thrills who are arrested. Anyway, that's partly why we're now offering two tours a month—to satisfy the public's curiosity so that, hopefully, we don't have people sneaking into unsafe areas and getting injured."

I thought that the reverse could be true. My curiosity had been fanned by the tour. I now had an almost overwhelming desire to see the interior of the Danvers State Hospital.

We headed back down the road. As I passed the last of the markers, I thought about Marguerite Miller. She had run away, was found some time later, became ill, and went into a hospital. Then her parents had died and her sister Melinda had gone to live with her aunt. The aunt, then, would presumably have been Marguerite's guardian at the time of her death, which meant she would have made her funeral arrangements. So where did she have Marguerite buried? Had the aunt felt disgraced, the way Beth Ann said many family members had, and wanted the fact that her niece had been in an asylum kept private? Did she have her buried at the hospital?

I hurried to the front of the group. "Beth Ann, how far have the researchers gotten in identifying the graves?"

"Not very far on hospital death records from 1878 to 1920 because they were lost and have to be searched for in the town records. But they've made good headway on those buried since 1920."

"How could I find out if a certain person was buried here in 1902 or 1903?"

She thought a minute. "Well, I suppose you could start with Sandy Parker. She's doing a lot of the research for the memorial movement. I can give you her number."

Portsmouth, New Hampshire
June Eighteenth, 1901

Had Alice been feeling well, had she not retired to her room after giving approval for the trip, she might have noticed the high color on Marguerite's cheeks or a certain shine to her eyes when she departed once more for Portsmouth that night (for although Marguerite had told the strange man in the park she would not attend the circus, she had every intention of doing just that). And if the others in her carriage—a family with two adolescent girls, the Carters, and another young couple, the Flannerys—don't notice the expectation Marguerite feels is conspicuous in her manner, it is because they are distracted by their own excitement, chatting animatedly for the entire ride. A circus, after all, is not a common event.

At the park the passengers disembark and the drivers stipulate a time to return. Marguerite's group moves off toward the circus grounds. Once inside the big top, however, the family is absorbed into a surge toward the front, the Carters sidle down an aisle, and Marguerite loses sight of the Flannerys. Good, she thinks; the family will think I'm with one of the couples and each couple will think that I am with the other, and I will be accountable to nobody.

She takes a seat in the rear of the tent. It is an exciting show, but she finds it difficult to sit still. At the end of the third act she slips away from the rapt audience. Outside, the night is soft and warm, and the mist has begun to gather over the Piscataqua River. Feeling deliciously daring, a small knot of anticipation in her stomach,

Marguerite saunters among the deserted tents. She has not ventured far before the man, Emil, emerges from the shadows. His appearance does not startle her. He greets her with a smile—a flash of the very white teeth—and a slight jaunty jerk of his head as he falls into step with her. She quickens her pace to match his, admiring (from beneath lowered eyelids) his proud carriage, his sure gait.

Beyond the circus encampment, at the river's edge, he jumps down from the grass bank onto the sand, wet from the receding tide. Marguerite hesitates, thinking of the new satin shoes she is wearing, their soles the thinnest of leather. When he offers his hand, she bends and quickly removes the shoes and her stockings, leaving them at the edge of the grass. A moment's hesitation, then she accepts his hand, which is strong and calloused, yet gentle in touch. After helping her down, he does not release her and she does not pull away.

Fog swirls around her knees, obscuring her feet. If it were not for sinking into the cold wet sand, Marguerite could believe she is floating in the sky through a field of clouds. They walk under a wharf, where barnacles, mussels, and seaweed cling to the massive pilings close to where the river pulls from land and then rushes forth. Here, Emil turns to her, takes hold of her shoulders, his touch light yet electric, a charge that courses into her center and makes her feel slightly ill. The moon, which has risen above the mist, backlights him and, although she cannot see his eyes, she feels them upon her.

"We know each other," he says. She nods. She does feel that she knows him. And maybe that is why she begins to talk about Timothy. She tells Emil about how intertwined are her family, the Millers, and Timothy's family, the Farleys. She tells how the mothers have been fast friends since they were classmates at school, and how the fathers share views on politics and are successful in their respective fields of medicine and law. She talks of the elegantly appointed townhouses the Millers and Farleys own within a block of each other in one of the best neighborhoods of Boston, where their children (two each) were born within a four-year period, the youngest Farley (Elizabeth,

called Bess) within a month of the oldest Miller (Marguerite). She tells of the many family gatherings at each other's homes: parlor parties, garden luncheons, Christmas get-togethers, and birthday celebrations. She tells how Timothy Farley, as eldest, is protector of the four while Melinda Miller, the youngest, is the pampered one. How Bess and Marguerite are inseparable friends who sat next to each other at school, took painting lessons together, and shared diaries. How even now, out of school, they exchange confidences while packing Christmas baskets side by side at church, or practicing needlecraft at each other's houses. How, since her earliest remembrances, it has been expected that she and Timothy would marry. Finally, she says that she has come to the hotel to think over her future. That she does not think she can marry Timothy.

At least, she believes that she told him all of these things; later she isn't sure what she actually said and what she thought she said. Nor can she remember all he told her, although he spoke of the circus and the traveling life. After a while, Emil bends and touches his lips to her forehead. She closes her eyes, breathing in his smell, which reminds her of woods and earth with something spicy, smoky, and exotic mixed in. He puts a finger on the spot where his lips had touched her and says, "I will come for you."

When she opens her eyes, Emil is gone. Clouds obscure the moon, and it is so dark she cannot see the shoreline or the water, which now swirls up around her calves, the tide pulling heavy at the bottom of her dress. Disoriented, she turns round and round to determine the direction of the shore.

"What are you doing down there?" comes a disembodied voice, and in relief, Marguerite splashes toward it. A bloated ruddy visage emerges from the gloom. A clown, face scrubbed raw of makeup, but still in partial costume—red suspenders dangling over yellow and green block-patterned pants stretched across his paunch—leans over the bank. "Do you need help?"

"No, thank you." She clambers up onto the grass, ignoring his

outstretched hand. She wrings out her hem and then searches for her shoes, having lost all sense of where she left them.

"Did you lose something?" The clown trails behind her on unsteady feet.

"No! Don't follow me!" Barefoot, she picks her way back through tents now bustling with post-show activity, dodging performers and workers who move aside and watch her pass with open curiosity. The circus has ended; has she been gone that long? How did the audience dissipate so quickly?

"Missy, are you lost?" A short fat woman touches her arm. "Missy?"

Marguerite jumps, but upon pulling away, finds herself in a knot of circus workers. She is touched again, a hand on her back. She shrieks and pushes her way through a sea of skin slippery with sweat and clothing damp and pungent with body odor. Finally, on the other side of the encampment, she breaks into a run, crossing the field to the road.

Keeping to the grassy edge, she encounters nobody save two men leaning against a split-rail fence, their eyes above the glow of lighted pipes following her as she passes. Shivering from cold, she reaches the park to find none of her group, no waiting coaches. She gives a soft cry of despair; how will she get back? The distance—some eight miles down the coast—is too great to walk even if it were daylight and she had her shoes.

In desperation she has started to walk, wincing as she steps on pebbles, when miraculously, a carriage with the hotel's crest on its side appears. She waves and, when it stops, scrambles aboard before the driver can dismount to open the door. If it has been sent for somebody else, she hopes the driver will not realize it until they arrive back at the hotel. She tucks herself into a corner, pulling feet up under her, grateful to be hidden as the carriage rolls through the foggy streets.

At the hotel, a cross Alice confronts her. "Where have you been?

Why didn't you come back with the others?"

Marguerite says that she left her reticule at the circus and went back to retrieve it, thereby missing the carriage. Alice's face darkens in suspicion, her eyes taking in the wet dress, the bare feet. Marguerite blushes and tells a half-truth this time: she waded in the water and when she came back for her shoes, found them stolen. Alice sets her jaw, thinking it another prank like those that Marguerite and Bess used to play on her. The difference being that this time there is no Bess.

"Thank you for sending the carriage." Marguerite shifts the focus.

"You can thank Josephine Carter," Alice says. "When they arrived back, she saw that you weren't in either carriage, and sent one back for you."

"Please don't say anything to Mama and Papa," Marguerite pleads.

Alice leaves without promises, but Marguerite is confident she will not tell on her. She turns off the lights and lies fully dressed upon the bed, staring up at the ceiling. She thinks about the pranks she and Bess pulled when they were children: sneaking off on Alice, leading her on wild goose chases while they hid behind bushes in the Public Gardens, sticking out tongues at passersby, and stealing chestnuts from the vendor while he wasn't looking, only letting Alice find them when they tired of their game. As a rule, Alice didn't tell on them, feeling, most likely, that it would reflect poorly on her supervisory skills, but sometimes she would be so irate that she did tell and then there would be punishments when they got home. Bess always got it worse at her house than did Marguerite, whose father was more apt to be amused at these sparks of independence from his eldest daughter. But punishments never deterred the girls from trying some new prank planned to provide themselves a few moments of exhilarating freedom while provoking Alice.

Although those days are long behind her, that desire to be wild and free, which Marguerite had attributed to childishness, had flared to life today. This time there is a disturbing new twist; Marguerite cannot deny that she is attracted to that man, Emil. Is it because he represents something forbidden like making faces at strangers and stealing chestnuts once did? She wishes Bess were here to talk to, but then, on second thought, takes it back. Bess is now proper in all respects, and besides, she is bound by loyalty to her brother Timothy, and would not empathize with Marguerite's indiscretion.

She closes her eyes, remembering Emil's touch. Given the chance, would she meet him again? She must not be given that chance. Then she remembers his words, I will come for you. *Did he say that or did she imagine it? She sits up. What if he comes to the hotel? Did she tell him where she was staying? If he does, it is a big hotel and they don't let strangers just walk in. She relaxes somewhat then, and plans how to spend her last week: walking along the shore, reading on the bluff. Alice's faith in her will be restored before they return to Boston, and Mama and Papa need never know she had been anything but circumspect in every action.*

Two days pass. It is almost as if the dreamlike night of the circus hadn't happened. Alice ceases hovering over her and the Carters, skeptical of her story about getting lost that night, stop commenting on her "unfortunate incident." Marguerite is a model of propriety. She reads on the porch, takes morning tea and toast in her room, and lunch and dinner in the dining room. Setting aside her journal, she writes shallow, chatty letters that detail the weather and daily happenings to her sister, mother and father, Bess, and Timothy. Letters that she puts into envelopes and stacks in a pile on her desk.

The turmoil inside her has not diminished. She realizes now that she does not want to marry Timothy, but it does not set her mind at ease. Feeling betrayed, he will be hurt and angry when she breaks the engagement, and her friends—Timothy's friends, as well—will disapprove of, maybe even scorn, her. And there is the disappointment she will bring to her family and to the Farleys. Can she return to her life in Boston when all of her friends and her parents' friends are

106

linked in some way to Timothy? Can she live in her parents' house, disdained by all, perhaps even by Mama, Papa, and Melinda? Might it be better not to go back?

On Saturday evening, the Carters invite Marguerite to accompany them to the theater in town. She declines, but Alice, in a rare outgoing mood, accepts. After dinner, Marguerite settles in the chair by the unlit fireplace in her room. But, as soon as she opens her poetry book, she feels restless; stanzas that usually provide solace fail her. It is the same with her Eastern European history; she closes the book on a section that had absorbed her the day before, slavery in Romania prior to the 1850s. She is seized by the thought that she has read more about events, adventure, pain, and joy than she has experienced, that she has spent her life thus far receiving information through a historian's recording of them, or emotions filtered through a poet's interpretation.

Marguerite goes to the window. A full moon lights the expanse of lawn to the line of trees bordering it. While she watches, a shadow separates itself from a tree, and is silhouetted in the moonlight. She recognizes the cant of his head, the proud stance. In panic, she draws the curtains. What to do? Wait in the dark until Alice comes back? And then tell her what? That a man she met in town came for her? Alice would notify the hotel manager, the police, and her parents.

She will say nothing. In the morning she will wire her parents that she is coming home early. Or she will plead illness and hide in her room for the remaining days.

No. She is not ready to go home. And she will not hide in her room. She glances at the window. If she ignores him, he will go away. He might already be gone. She puts her eye to the part in the curtains. There, he is gone. Scanning the lawn, she feels a strange mix of relief and disappointment.

She falls asleep in the chair, wakened later by Alice's knock letting her know she's returned, and asking if she needs anything. Marguerite thanks her, adding that she will be going to bed soon. She listens for

Alice's door to shut, then goes to the window. Something in the shadows by the edge of the lawn wavers; Emil is there again. Her pulse racing with the excitement of a sudden decision made, she lets herself out into the hallway.

The lobby is empty when Marguerite passes through. She pauses at the back entrance, then slips outside. She walks the length of the verandah, passing a couple with heads together and an elderly lady rocking in a chair. At the end where the lights don't reach and the shadows are darkest, she stops at the rail.

Emil appears against the shrubbery below, beckoning. Behind her, the couple is absorbed in themselves and the old woman has dozed off. Marguerite bundles up her skirt and flings one leg over the rail, then the other. Poised on the edge, she crouches and accepts his help as she leaps to the ground. Then they are running, his firm handclasp steering her along the shadows of the building, then across open lawn to the trees, and through the trees onto the strip of sand along the river. They run faster, her skirt billowing in the breeze coming off the water, her hair whipping across her face. She has a silly thought that if they run fast enough they will become airborne and fly above the river, out over the sea.

They enter trees again, and veer away from the river. Here they adapt their pace to the rougher terrain but still move quickly, tree-filtered moonlight illuminating the way. There doesn't appear to be a path now, yet Emil doesn't falter, knowing where to step around trees and bushes, over roots and rocks. Marguerite darts this way and that, sometimes bounding over obstacles as deftly as does her companion, exhilarated as much by her skill in matching his pace as by her own outrageous behavior. She thinks it would be a fine thing if they never reach a final destination, if they just keep running.

But Emil does stop, abruptly. He leads her around a large outcropping of rock onto sand on the other side, and they are next to the river again. They duck under a slab of granite that juts out from the bank, forming a shelter over a fire ring, which glows with a few embers. Emil kneels to stir the coals with a stick, feed them twigs, and put on a log. When a small steady flame is attained, he sits back, feet crossed, elbows resting on raised knees, hands dangling. Seated cross-legged opposite him, the fire between them, Marguerite stretches her hands to the warmth, dipping her head so that she can regard her companion discreetly.

His clothes are shabby, but of good fabric: the pants once part of a suit, the loose shirt cut from fine linen, the vest a tapestry of blue, red, and gold in an intricate design. She tries to imagine the places his boots, well scuffed, soles worn through in places, have traveled. In the opening of his shirt, a gold necklace glints against his dark skin. When she raises her eyes to his face, she sees that he has been unabashedly observing her as well. His eyes, almond-shaped and black, catch the firelight and sparkle with a hint of amusement. Other than the prominent nose, his features are balanced, with thick eyebrows over wide-set eyes and high cheekbones. She thinks it a nice face until he flashes his quick broad smile and then she thinks it a handsome face.

"See?" He cocks his head. "You know it, too."

"Know what?"

"About us." His hand moves in a graceful gesture that indicates first her, then himself. "Te sorthene."

"Why . . ." she falters. Why are you here? Why did you come for me? She thinks these things, but says only, ". . . me? Why me?"

"It is bart."

She shakes her head, confused.

"It is the way things are. You and I have always known each other." Again that trace of somewhere else—Europe?—in the lilt of his voice. His gaze drops to the fire. "And always I find you." His tone is low, reassuring, and, while she knows she shouldn't be here, she is not fearful.

Emil scoots to her side of the fire. He plucks something from a handkerchief in his hand, leans over, and puts it to her lips. She takes *a small bite of something sweet—a date. He pops the rest of it into his mouth and grins. He holds another out to her. She takes a larger bite this time, and again he finishes it. In this way, they eat half a dozen dates. She closes her eyes and lets his presence wrap around her like a warm cocoon. There are things she wants to ask him: Where is he from? How does he know her? How did he find her at the hotel? But she doesn't think of these questions until later when she is back in her room, amazed at what she has done.*

What she does ask, Emil answers, at least in part. He acknowledges that the woman at the tent is his mother, but that the rest of his family is "pfft"—he waves a hand and a hardness comes over his face— "gone" and doesn't elaborate. Then he shrugs, smiles, and changes the subject. He would rather talk about nature, of which he is very knowledgeable. He tells her about the cycles of the moon and identifies various animal sounds.

"That one," she says after a call pierces the night.

"Fox."

"And that," she says to a muffled warbled sound.

"A dove."

"I know this one." Her voice is triumphant. "An owl." But he bows his head. "What's wrong?"

"It is bibart. *Very bad luck. The owl's cry means death."*

"Death? Do you mean someone will die?" They are quiet for a while after that.

Much of what she remembers afterward is not the words but the timbre and cadence of his voice, and the way he anticipates her needs before she utters them: warmth, food, touch. When she thinks she must leave, he rises before she mentions it. He leads her back the way they came, saying goodbye to her at the corner of the hotel. Like the first time, he touches his lips to her forehead, and then melts into the shadows.

Luck is with her as she scoots across the lobby—the grandfather clock bonging three a.m.—up the stairs and down hallways without meeting a single person. She lets herself into her room and leans against the door, savoring the warm thrill that flows through her. She smiles; tonight she began experiencing life.

CHAPTER EIGHT

We were lucky enough to get a table at Michael's Riverside Restaurant outside on the deck, an excellent place for viewing Newburyport's active waterfront. During tourist season, working trawlers and fully rigged fishing boats share space with every kind of pleasure craft, from kayaks and small motorboats to world-traveling yachts and replicas of yesteryear's tall ships. All against an ever-changing backdrop of sky—ranging from electric blue to icy to black thunderheads rolling in from the ocean. And water, with the Merrimack's current perceptible only by a dinghy's gentle turning on anchor, or raging with a strength fierce enough to carry uprooted trees. On this particular night, a mild offshore breeze brought a delightful salty tang, the fading sky was smeared low with peach and purple, and the river lay like a wide navy satin ribbon.

We ordered summer drinks: Gus and Mike, Coronas with lime; Shannon a strawberry daiquiri; and a margarita rimmed with salt for me. Euphorically, we toasted the onset of summer with its expansive promise. Then Gus mentioned my visit to Danvers State that day, and I told Mike and Shannon about the tour.

At once interested, Mike said, "I interned there."

"Really?" I said, as if it wasn't part of the reason we'd set up this date.

"Yeah, I spent a whole summer at Danvers. They never had enough help on the wards so they'd use us interns to fill in."

"When was that?" Gus's nonchalance matched my own.

"Oh, back about twenty years ago when I was in college." Mike poked the wedge of lime further down the neck of his bottle with his finger. "Sometimes it got a little scary. I remember one ward that housed a severe population—harmless for the most part, although a few could get violent. Looking back, they were probably only in their thirties and forties, but they seemed much older." He took a sip and set the bottle back on the small paper napkin. "I was more or less a nurse's aide, caring for their physical needs and making sure they didn't harm themselves."

"Could they communicate?" I asked.

"Not much. Most couldn't—or wouldn't—talk; those who did mumbled to themselves. They'd pace back and forth or bang heads against the floor or walls. We had to be careful because some were always picking up things off the floor and putting them in their mouths. One time a ward attendant and I spent an entire morning at a local hospital after this woman swallowed a watch." He laughed ruefully at our surprised reactions. "Really, she did! I remember it was a Timex. Apparently, she'd been there a lot because the hospital administration reamed us out about not watching her close enough, and said not to bring her there again."

Shannon was indignant. "They can't refuse treatment, can they?"

Mike shrugged.

"Were the residents you worked with more emotionally disturbed or more mentally handicapped?" I said.

"You know, I used to wonder about that. They were definitely both, but it was difficult to tell where one left off and the other began."

"Like which came first: the chicken or the egg," Gus said.

"Right. Were they mentally impaired, and then became

emotionally disturbed after spending all those years in the institution? Or were they emotionally disturbed, and then became mentally impaired from lack of stimulation and appropriate peer modeling? I came to the conclusion that the question was moot because in the end they were both and that's what you had to deal with."

"Working there must have been a real eye-opener," I commented as Shannon opened her mouth to—I sensed—change the subject.

"Oh, it was." Mike traced the trail of a drip down the side of his beer bottle, hesitating as if deciding how far to carry the topic. Then he leaned forward confidentially. "There we were, these young college kids straight from the classroom, each of us assigned eight to ten scary-looking individuals. We were supposed to walk them over to the gym, try to play basketball or do something with them. Of course, we figured out eventually that they were pretty harmless. They wouldn't have put us with the really dangerous inmates. Still, it was a pretty depressing introduction to the field of psychology.

"It could be spooky, too." Warming to his subject, Mike needed no further prompting. "One time I worked late. As I was walking to my car in the dark there came these sudden shrieks that echoed off the buildings all around me. I looked back at those Gothic towers up on the hill silhouetted against a moonlit sky, then took off, running like a scared little kid all the way to the parking lot."

"Sounds like a good setting for a horror movie." Shannon wrinkled her nose as she bent to her frothy pink drink.

"It certainly had that feel, all right."

"Actually, they did make a horror film up there a few years ago," Gus said. "I never saw it, and now I've forgotten the title."

"I remember that," Shannon said. "What was the name of that movie?"

"What were the wards like?" I interjected before the conversation could take a turn.

"There were at least thirty beds all jammed close together." Mike gazed out over the river, seeing a picture the rest of us could only imagine. "I was on a locked men's unit and we carried keys strung on shoelaces around our necks. No matter how clean it seemed to be, it always stank." His attention came back to the table. "I'd be at home, showered and changed, and still I'd smell urine and feces. It was like it got into your pores or your olfactory memory or something and you couldn't get rid of it."

"Pleasant dinner conversation," Shannon said.

"Sorry! Didn't mean to get carried away." Mike smiled apologetically at the waitress who, having arrived with our entrees, looked askance at him.

"No, it's interesting, really," I reassured him, ignoring my shrimp scampi for the moment. "It just seems so tragic the way Danvers ended up. I read how it was state of the art when it was built and that its programs were progressive. I'm talking about late 1800s, of course."

"Yeah, I'm sure it was very different then." Mike picked up his fork and held it in attack position. "Even when I was there, there was good leadership and some really dedicated staff. There were better wards, where the higher functioning lived, where nurses and attendants were more nurturing and were able to make headway despite the conditions. To fix up that facility and run programs the right way, though, would've taken exorbitant amounts of money." He dug into his pasta dish and for a few minutes we were all busy with the plates in front of us.

"Our guide said that many inmates were sad when Danvers was shut down and they had to leave," I said. "They thought of it as their home."

"Mmhm." Mike nodded, then swallowed. "I believe that."

"So why did things deteriorate so drastically over the years?" Gus asked.

"One reason is that until the 1950s most of the institutions were working communities, with the residents taking care of the grounds, tending crops, and caring for farm animals," I said. "The residents had jobs and a purpose and were tired at night. Then the farming program was terminated, and they had nothing to do but sit around all day."

"By that time, also, the state institutions were grossly overcrowded, understaffed, and underfunded," Mike said. "They'd become dumping grounds for all societal problems. Besides the mentally ill, you now had the mentally retarded, vagrants who didn't speak English, elderly Alzheimer's patients, and kids who couldn't be controlled by their parents. With the expectation, of course, that administrators could perform miracles with minimal money for programs and maintenance."

"Boy, doesn't that sound familiar," Gus said. The waitress came to light the small oil lamp on the table and to take orders for coffee, and our conversation moved on to schools—another place where there's always minimal money and high expectations—and from there it drifted to our kids, as it usually does at some point. It was dark, with lights twinkling on the bridge and boats on the river, by the time we got up to leave. We walked the few blocks up into town to our little local arts theater, where we got the last four seats together just as the movie, an Italian comedy with subtitles, was beginning.

On Monday morning, as soon as decently acceptable, I made a call to the woman whose number Beth Ann had given me. Sandy Parker talked in a chirpy voice that curled up at the ends of her sentences, making them sound like questions. I told her I was helping an elderly friend track down an aunt who may have died at Danvers State Hospital, and wondered if she could help me.

"Sure, honey," she said over the phone. "But why don't you come on over? I got lots of files, and you could help me look up the name?" There was a momentary pause, during which she might have been checking a calendar. "Can you come today?"

"Well, okay." Realizing it had probably been, unreasonable to expect a quick answer in a phone call. "How is mid-afternoon?"

"Sure, honey. Any time. I'm always here."

I asked where "here" was and got detailed directions from downtown Danvers.

Two hours later, with both kids involved in sandbox architecture while Gus mowed the lawn, I had turned off the expressway, cut over to Danvers, and followed Sandy's directions on small streets that led through the outskirts of Peabody. Peabody? I glanced down again at the instructions I'd scrawled on the back of an envelope. I'd followed them exactly; Sandy lived in Peabody. So why did she give Danvers as a point of reference?

I was still scratching my head over that when I pulled up in front of a faded green triple-decker within sight of the Salem Bridge. Now, everybody knows where the bridge into Salem is; had Sandy said she lived within a stone's throw of it, I'd have had her pinpointed and could have bypassed Danvers, saving myself at least ten minutes. As I climbed the sagging steps to the small porch, I guessed that maybe Sandy's world centered on Danvers, included Peabody where she lived, but ended at the Salem Bridge.

I scanned the row of six mailboxes, found S. Parker and an apartment number, then stepped into a hallway with grungy gray-white walls and a cobweb condominium stretched across one entire corner of the ceiling. Old varnish-darkened hardwood floors were worn clean (and a few shades lighter) in pathways down the middle, but dirt, dust rolls, even a few decaying leaves from the previous fall, had built up in corners, under an ornate rusty radiator and on the edges of the stairs I now started up.

A door was flung open on the second floor, and a short, round, sixtyish woman in an oversized floral shirt that tented down over pink leggings appeared. "Hi! I'm up here!"

I climbed the stairs, introduced myself, and crossed the threshold into Sandy's apartment, leaving the squalor of the hallway behind. Although shabby—sagging couch and thread-bare armchair—and cluttered with about a thousand small china and blown glass figurines atop every other flat surface, her home was immaculate.

"This is my headquarters." She ushered me into her tiny kitchen. Here, also, every surface was taken up: the top of the refrigerator with baskets, the stove with gleaming pots and pans, the counter with canisters, decorative tins, and jars. "Tea? Coffee? Tang?" Her hand hovered over a cluster of glass containers.

"Oh, tea would be very nice."

"I spent most of my life at Danvers?" She looked at me over her shoulder as she held the kettle under the faucet. I nodded because her curious way of ending sentences seemed to require answers. "See, I was a holy terror as a child? Gave everybody a hard time—the teachers, my mom and dad?" She gave a short laugh. "I was always fighting with other kids, so finally they had enough and dropped me off up at Danvers."

While she chuckled in amusement, I tried not to gasp aloud in horror as I realized she meant the institution, not the town. "Your parents left you at Danvers State Hospital? How old were you, Sandy?"

"Oh, I guess nine or ten? I think ten?"

"How long were you there?"

She frowned in thought. "About thirty years? Yeah, I was forty when I left."

"Your family waited that long to get you out?" I asked,

incredulous.

"Oh, no. They didn't get me out." Sandy reached up into a cupboard and took down two pink and yellow polka-dotted mugs. "See, my dad had taken off? And my mom visited some at the beginning? But she had all these other kids and since I was already being taken care of she didn't have to worry about me?" She talked matter-of-factly as she put tea bags in the mugs. "They were phasing out the hospital, that's how I got out."

As she moved between stove, refrigerator, and counter, Sandy told about living at the institution in its last years before the state closed it down, depositing its charges out onto the street, bolstered by the theory that new medications and community programs could take the place of around-the-clock care. They hadn't been enough for Sandy. She'd lost her home—Danvers State—and for years she searched for another place to belong to, moving in with one relative after another until none would take her in. One summer she lived on the streets in an abandoned building with others in similar circumstances.

Gradually, somehow, Sandy got things together. Sure, she had had a counselor, coming out of the institution, and she'd been given several work opportunities, but it wasn't until she got herself in hand, she said, that things began to go her way.

"I had some bad habits in those days, you know?" I nodded as she shook her head in regret. "But when I finally decided to shape up, I quit drinking and hanging around with no-goods, started getting along with people, and I got me a good job." The kettle whistle had begun to wheeze and Sandy went to stand over it until it built into a full-blown shriek. Then she poured boiling water in the mugs and waved me over to fix my tea. She'd put out spoons, napkins, sugar and milk in a matching pink-flowered bowl and pitcher, and a plate of cookies. After I'd put milk into my tea and helped myself to a cookie, she continued.

"I work full time at Esmenson's Bakery, you know?" she said with pride. "I been there eight years now? And Ben says I'm their best employee." She picked up a cookie and waggled it in the air. "This came from there—good, isn't it?"

I took a quick bite and *hmhm*ed in agreement.

"I got a good life now, and my own apartment, but sometimes I still miss Danvers. We were like family, looking out for each other, you know?" I followed her back into the living room, where she paused to pat a big yellow-striped cat curled up in an armchair. "This is Tommy." Then she pointed to a framed picture on the wall of herself with two other women. "I keep in touch with a few from back then. Some haven't done so good as me, you know?"

It was while she was walking around the old site one day, reminiscing, she said, that she came across the cemetery and found out about the Memorial Committee. "They'd started working to save it, you know, writing to their congressman and such? Anyway, it got me thinking how important it was for somebody to clean it up, put names on the graves, give these people respect? Who knows? If I'd died while I was there and nobody in my family claimed me, it could be me lying there under those weeds with nothing but a number on top. Heck! Don't everyone deserve a resting place with their name on it?"

"They certainly do." I followed her across the room where she took a seat on the swivel chair behind a dinged-up metal desk with neat piles of papers and file folders. "Do you ever go back to visit?"

"Oh, sure. I used to before it closed."

"How about since then?"

"It's against the law to enter any of them buildings now." She pulled a stack of folders over in front of her.

"It sounds like people do it anyway."

"I been back a time or two." She opened the top folder and leafed through some papers, suddenly businesslike. "What name were you looking for?"

"Marguerite Miller. It would have been 1902 or 1903."

She closed the folder. "Sorry, can't help you. Those records between 1878 and 1920? They're lost, you know? You can look up the death records at the Danvers Town Hall, but you can't match them with a gravestone number."

"If I found her in the death records," I said, "I'd at least know if she was at Danvers when she died; I just wouldn't know where she was buried, right?"

"Right. It'd be on the death certificate if she was at the hospital. Also, next of kin and that kind of stuff? If you want, I could take you there? You know, help you find it?"

"That would be great!" I said. Then she stood up, and I realized she meant to go right then.

CHAPTER NINE

Sandy locked up and we went out to my car. I turned down a side street to reverse direction, and headed back toward the town of Danvers.

"It's spooky up there now." Sandy looked out the windshield in the general direction of the old hospital, which was too far away to be seen. "All gone, but somehow you can still feel them, you know? I swear sometimes I can hear Miss Mabel talking, telling us to get off our duffs and come to dinner. Or Jolene who whined a lot, but was real generous with what she got from the outside—candy and stuff."

"How many times have you been back since it closed?"

"Probably six or seven times." She looked sideways at me again, and I had the feeling I was being sized up. "I lived there for thirty years. I know ways in that most don't."

I parked in front of the Danvers Town Hall and followed Sandy inside where she yelled "Hi" to a clerk at a desk. She filled out a request form, and in no time we were admitted to the files that held death records. She went through those for 1902 and I went through those for 1903.

"Bingo!" I exclaimed not ten minutes later. Sandy looked over my shoulder as I read, "Marguerite Elise Miller, age twenty. Date of death: March fourteenth, 1903."

"Look." Sandy pointed. "Residence: State Lunatic Hospital at Danvers. She was there, all right, huh?"

I skimmed the page. "Cause of death was influenza. Funny

how a disease that's routine nowadays was so lethal back then. Different strains, I guess."

"Parents deceased. Next of kin was Ada—Adel—" Sandy frowned as she read.

"Adelaide C. Miller—her aunt in New York. That would be right. Her parents died in an accident while she was hospitalized and her father's sister became guardian of Marguerite and her sister."

Sandy took the paper out of my hand and peered close at the faded writing. "Hey, looky this. Auntie refused to collect the body."

I read the line she pointed to, halfway down the page. "Why would she refuse it?"

Sandy sighed. "It's the stigma, you know? The embarrassment of having somebody in the family who's mentally ill? Easier to just let the institution take care of it? Cheaper, too."

"That's despicable!" The clerk at the desk raised her eyes from her work, and I said more quietly, "How could they get away with that?"

"Dunno, but they did." Sandy made a copy on the machine against the wall, and deposited fifteen cents on the counter. Then she slipped the original back into the file.

"That means, then, that she's buried in one of the Danvers State Hospital's cemeteries."

"Probably. Wish I could say we could find her. But without those hospital records? Just about impossible, you know? Leastways we can put her name on a monument the way we're doing with others we can't find?" She handed the copy to me.

"No child," I said, looking over the paper again.

"What?" Sandy had her arms crossed, the toe of one pink Nike tapping the floor. With the file no longer in her hand she was anxious to get moving.

"There was no mention of a child. I thought maybe she gave

birth at Danvers."

"Well, she could've. But if she did, it'd be on her hospital records, not her death record." Sandy slapped the top of the file box with the palm of her hand and waved at the clerk. "Thanks, Jesse, see ya!"

I followed her outside. "And those records are lost."

At the car, Sandy turned to face me over the roof. "They aren't lost."

"But you said—"

"The hospital's cemetery records between 1878 and 1920 are lost. The hospital records—admission, treatment, and all that? They're with the state department now. A family member can petition to get them."

I thought of Dorothy. "I have to tell her niece."

"She's got a niece still alive?"

"Yes, that's who I'm doing this for. Dorothy is the only daughter of Marguerite's younger sister, and she should read her aunt's files."

Sandy smiled, full of pride and purpose. "That's why we're doing this. It's only right for people to learn where a family member was buried, you know?"

And if that family member had a child, I added to myself. We got in the car then, and while I drove, Sandy chatted on about the cemetery project, the AA meetings she attended, and her medications. She'd just started telling me about the church she belonged to when we arrived at her apartment building.

"About Danvers—" I was going to ask about her years inside the asylum but she interrupted me.

"You want to get inside, don't you?" She lowered her voice even though we were still in the car and nobody could hear us. "Some people just got to get in there to see it for themselves."

I wanted to deny it but, taken by surprise, I didn't. "Well, uh, it would be interesting."

"I'm leading a group in to do some paranormal research next week?" she said. "I'll give you a call?"

"I don't know," Dorothy said in clipped tones. "What good would looking up old records do?" She was perturbed that I would think her great-aunt had ended up in an asylum. Sandy was right: the stigma surrounding mental illness remained strong.

We were in her living room. Gus and the kids had come with me as far as the Portsmouth Children's Museum, where I'd dropped them off before scooting down a few streets to Dorothy's.

"Could it be some other Marguerite Miller?" she asked.

I had already shown her the copy of the death certificate, so I didn't point out that the information matched Marguerite's background—her address, her age, the aunt as guardian. "She ran away," I began gently. "For whatever reason: she didn't want to get married; she wanted an adventure; she was meeting a lover; she was pregnant—" At this last suggestion, Dorothy, who grew up in an era when pregnancy out of wedlock was a scandal, looked out the window at her garden. I continued, "Then she was found a year later, you said. Do you know the circumstances?"

Dorothy shook her head once. I went on, "Shortly after that, she entered a hospital where she died some months later. Her father, Dr. Miller, was on the board at Danvers—it was called the State Lunatic Hospital at Danvers then—and I think he might have taken his daughter there for treatment. He probably only planned on keeping her there for a short time, but then he died in the accident . . ."

"Yes, the car accident." Dorothy smiled weakly. "My grandfather had just bought an automobile—few people had them at the time—and he took my grandmother out for her first ride.

They were thrilled, traveling at the then unheard-of speed of thirty-five miles an hour."

"How did it happen?"

"Didn't I tell you? The car stalled going across the railroad tracks just as a train was coming. I imagine in his inexperience with cars, my grandfather panicked. Maybe he tried to crank it instead of just getting the two of them to safety. Anyway, it was quite horrible, as you can imagine."

I *could* imagine it: the horn blaring, the powerful locomotive crushing the car like a tin toy, scattering its pieces the entire length of the train's screeching, skidding stop. Two lives snuffed out in the middle of an exhilarating ride. A daughter at home left an orphan. A daughter in an asylum left a prisoner. I thought about that: committed to an asylum, suddenly losing both parents, one of whom—your father—being the only person who could procure your freedom.

Dorothy shuddered. "Oh, it's all so awful." I guessed that, besides the accident, she was also thinking about having an aunt who had been institutionalized.

"The hospital was only about twenty years old," I said. "It was still a model facility in the world of psychiatry, a place your grandfather—Dr. Miller—was proud to be affiliated with. Otherwise, he wouldn't have been on its board."

She sighed. "I suppose so. But Marguerite's been dead for all these years, so what does all of this matter now?"

"If Claudia's story is true, Marguerite's granddaughter—Claudia's mother—is still alive. She could be your . . . let me see . . . second cousin?" It wasn't a very close relationship but I figured if there was nobody left in your family, a newly found second cousin could be exciting. When Dorothy didn't respond, I changed topics and asked about Adelaide Miller, the woman who had taken her mother in after the accident.

"Adelaide never married," Dorothy said. "She was domineering, and disapproved of the man my mother wanted to marry—my father. She died when I was quite young and I only remember her vaguely."

"So, not taking into account Claudia's claim, you are the last of the family?"

"Yes."

I looked around the room at the antique furniture, understated solid pieces in mahogany and cherry, upholstered chairs and sofa covered in faded brocades and velvets, a marble-topped table. "That's a lovely table," I commented.

"It was my great aunt's—Adelaide's. Most of this furniture came to me from her, through my mother, of course, who had inherited them." Dorothy smiled with benevolent tolerance as if the pieces were idiosyncratic family members. "They aren't exactly my taste, but what could I do? You can't just sell family heirlooms."

I had the sense that the heirlooms somehow substituted for the family she didn't have. "Do you think Claudia was trying to insinuate herself in the hope of becoming an heir?"

Dorothy was taken aback. "I wouldn't have fallen for that. Besides, it's a ridiculous idea. I have only my house and a very modest bank account. Whatever Miller inheritance there was has dissipated over the years."

"There are the antiques," I suggested. "And Claudia believed there was a ring—"

"There's no ring. I told her that. And what would a young person do with a house full of musty old furniture? Anyway, it's all settled. The contents go to the historical society when I die, and I'm leaving the house to Ellen—it's been her home all these years." She rose stiffly from her seat and crossed the room to a built-in bookcase. "If you're interested in Marguerite Miller, I have two of her books." She pulled down two volumes and set them on a small table. "She was quite a reader, apparently. She loved history and poetry."

I went over and picked up a slim blue book with a broken spine, titled *Modern Verse*. On the inside cover was written "For M. Love, T" in fading brown script. I flipped through it, then set it down and chose the thicker volume, *A History of Eastern Europe*. I turned a few pages, noticing several places where a paragraph was bracketed or had a check next to it. I paused to read one of the marked passages.

"You may borrow those, if you like."

"Oh, I couldn't. They're old and valuable." Then longing overcame a sense of propriety, and I said, "Maybe just this one, if it's really okay."

"Certainly. Come, I'll show you my garden." Dorothy replaced the other book on the shelf, and we went outside.

As she pointed out the boxwood she'd planted thirty years before, and her blooming peonies, I realized that Dorothy lived with her ancestors inside the house, but that it was outside, in her garden, that her true personality was revealed.

The gardens ran along one entire side and the back of the house, parceled out among gravel walks, some bordered by box hedges. They were formal arrangements, yet casual in their upkeep and attitude, with weeds sprouting throughout and, here and there in the mix, touches of whimsical cement statuary—a frog, a rabbit, a pixie. A clematis vine wound around an intricate old iron headboard staked in one bed. A small corner garden contained herbs, and Dorothy plied me with fragrant clippings of parsley, rosemary, and spearmint, which she tied together with bits of string pulled from the pocket of her dress. When we sat down on a cement bench in the midst of it all, it was Dorothy who brought up the subject again.

"I did rather like her—Claudia, I mean."

"Do you think she really believed she was Marguerite Miller's great-granddaughter?"

"Maybe. But why would she be interested in an old woman just because she might be a relation?"

I offered no ideas, and we were silent for a few moments, taking in the peaceful surroundings. Then Dorothy said, "What would a person who was raised in an insane asylum be like when she got out?"

I thought of Sandy, of what she'd accomplished, her pride in her work, her neat albeit cluttered apartment. "I think many former patients lead normal, fulfilled lives."

Dorothy didn't respond, and after a moment I continued, "I've been reading about mental institutions during the first half of the twentieth century. People—especially women—were institutionalized for all kinds of reasons, some trivial: for vagrancy, Alzheimer's, postpartum depression, not doing housework, misbehaving as children, or just acting a little strange. It was easy for a parent to have a child committed, or a husband his wife. And once committed, almost impossible for the patient to get herself released." I decided to push my point home. "What I'm saying is that Marguerite's only sin might have been pregnancy, and Claudia's great-grandmother's, being born in an asylum."

Dorothy stood and walked away from me, down the gravel path that bisected her garden. She bent over a lavender iris, gently cupped it in her hand, released it, and then reached beyond it to pull out a tall spindly weed by its stalk. She continued on, plucking here and there, choosing weeds or dead leaves she could reach without bending too far. When she had a small collection of undesirable vegetation in her hand, she returned and dropped it onto a wilting refuse heap next to the bench.

"Besides the hospital record with Marguerite's name on it, you said Claudia showed you another paper," I said when she sat down again.

"Yes. It was the bottom part of a letter, signed by a Melinda—no last name. Under the signature was a childish stick drawing of two girls with big smiles and arms around each other labeled 'you' and 'me.' Claudia said it was from my mother to Marguerite, and that her grandmother had it when she died."

"Did the letter look authentic?"

Dorothy shrugged. "It was little more than a scrap. How could I tell?"

"What did it say?"

"There was only the end of it, which said, 'I miss you. Can't wait for Papa to bring you home.' Something to that effect. It was immature writing, obviously from a young girl. My mother's script wasn't like that, but then handwriting changes with age. I have letters that she wrote to my father during World War I that I could have compared it to, but I didn't think of it at the time."

"And Claudia said she had something else that proved her claim?"

"Yes, she said that she would bring it to show me next time she came. Then, of course, she didn't come again."

Dorothy stood again and moved down the other side of the path, plucking out a weed here and there. I watched, knowing that she was mulling things over. When she returned to deposit her handful of weeds, she said, "Maybe I should request Marguerite's records from the state. It couldn't hurt to read them."

Grand Hotel of the Atlantic
June Nineteenth, 1901

When Alice's knock comes in the morning, Marguerite begs more sleep. She falls back into a fitful slumber, disturbed by snatches of dreams that she doesn't remember when she awakens a second time at ten o'clock. Still tired, she dresses and sits at the window, thinking about the previous night. She has never been willfully disobedient— not since childhood, anyway—and here she is defying all her parents' rules. It is hard to reconcile her conscience with her behavior and yet she is reluctant to make vows not to repeat her actions. In fact, however much she determines to do the proper thing, she knows that she will go with Emil again, and has already begun planning how to keep Alice from becoming suspicious.

That night, she stays downstairs, socializing until most of the guests have retired, leaving only herself, the Carters, and a few others. Ernest Carter has been drinking and pays Marguerite too much attention, complimenting her, leaning in close, teasing her about her fiancé. Since the day of the circus he has acted differently toward her. Annoyed, Josephine first snaps at, then ignores her husband. Marguerite finally excuses herself and retreats to her room.

While she waits at the window, she takes up where she left off in her history book. Half of her is reading about the freed slaves of Romania who fled into Europe in the 1850s, the other half is deciding whether she will stay in tonight or sneak out should Emil come. But it is a game she plays with herself, a token of resistance necessary to the rhythm of the night, for when she looks up from her book and sees Emil out beyond the lawn, all pretense drops away. At once she is in motion, as if every step has been planned. She changes into a simple dark dress seldom worn, chosen so it can be hidden if damaged, and not missed by Alice. She turns out the light and lets herself out the door.

The hallway is clear. A few minutes later she is at the bottom of the stairs, waiting until the clerk in the lobby turns to the mail cubbies behind his desk. She crosses the room on soundless soles and slips outside. She meets Emil at the corner where he left her the night before. He grasps her hand and they take off as if chased but, in fact, running for no reason other than the exuberance of it. Like one being, they bolt through the trees on the wide needle-carpeted path, across the beach, kicking up grains of sand that fly up under Marguerite's skirt and sting her legs, and then back into the trees again. When they are far from the hotel, beating arms against twigs that reach for them and dodging briars that grab and catch, a sound bubbles up and escapes from Marguerite: a half-laugh, half-exclamation. Emil answers immediately with a whoop as he leaps a large rock that Marguerite dodges. And then laughter erupts from them both, ringing out into the night.

When they reach the outcropping by the river, Emil pulls her to him, hugging her hard and quick, and then releases her before she can respond. Between jubilant outbursts, they gasp for breath and collapse against the largest slanted stone. The moon glows soft in a starless sky, its pale beam draping them like fragile netting. The pervasive calm of the river is soothing, and their breathing quiets enough to hear the night sounds.

"Tell me about Emil." Marguerite's voice is playful. "Where is he from?"

Emil sweeps an arm, fingers spread, through the air in front of him. "From the earth, the sky." He adopts her light tone. "His father was a fox, his mother an eagle."

132

Marguerite raises her hand, within which his is clasped, and bites his knuckle.

"Ow!" He howls in mock pain and she laughs.

"I mean it. I want to know about you." Then she stops laughing so he will know she is serious. "Where do you come from?"

He looks out over the river and shrugs. "Before now does not matter." But after a few moments he says, "My family comes from across the world—on the other side of the ocean, and then far east of there. For many years we have been seeds blown here and there by the wind. Just once, as a child, was I in one place for a while: a village in France."

"Why did you leave?"

He hesitates. "The gadje—the other villagers—burned our houses."

"But that's awful! Why did they do it?"

"Because they hate my people." Emil sits up and pulls his hand away. "Because we are who we are." He raises his face to the moon, talking to the night, weaving words together as if reciting poetry. No longer reticent, his voice takes on a lighter entertaining quality that contrasts with the content of his story. Emil's little brother was killed in the fire. They buried him with only a crude stick to mark the grave. His family—mother, father, two older sisters, and himself—left with the rest of their band, never to return, never to settle anywhere after that. They had a few horses to pull the wagons, but everyone walked, the men leading the way, the women and children following. They traveled the French countryside, sometimes risking encampment near a big city where opportunities were better to make money. Everyone had a skill—metalworking, storytelling, playing an instrument, or singing. Emil's father, a tinsmith, made pots and pans to sell while his mother told fortunes. It was his father's dream to save enough to take them all to America.

He is quiet for a few moments and Marguerite observes his rugged profile, thinking how different he is from anyone she has ever known. Then he turns to her, his face shadowed, and begins again, talking directly to her now, a harsh edge replacing the musical lilt.

It took many long hard years, during which his two sisters married and left to enter the households of their mothers-in-law, but finally the family had enough money for three tickets to America. Then, as they were camped outside Lyons one night, the gens d'armes came and arrested all the men. Some were released but others, among them Emil's father, were taken away. Nothing could be learned about them until weeks later, when one of the women found out that the men had been tried, found guilty of vagrancy and not having work permits, and sentenced to five years in prison. While imprisoned, Emil's father died. "The others said he was beaten," he says bitterly.

"I'm sorry," she whispers.

"My mother and I came to New York. We found work with the circus. That is all." He pushes himself away from the rock. "Do you hear that?" His head cocked, he is engaged now in the present. "It is a loon calling to his mate."

Marguerite stands also. As she reaches out to touch his arm he turns to her. "When I leave, will you come with me?"

She draws back, startled. How can she do that? But even as she asks the one thing, she is thinking the other: isn't it what she has wished for? She shoves the idea away, not ready to explore it just yet.

It is even later than the previous night when Marguerite returns to her room. She undresses by moonlight, and it is when she bends down to remove her stockings that she finds the note on the floor by the door. Alice's terseness is conveyed in her writing: She knocked but could not rouse Marguerite. Would Marguerite please come see her immediately upon rising in the morning?

Distressed, Marguerite looks for evidence that Alice had entered her room. Then she calms herself. Had Alice done so, she would have left the note on the table instead of sliding it under the door.

She sleeps fitfully and is therefore awake when the rap on her door comes early the next morning. "It was barely ten o'clock when I came to your room last night." Alice says, her eyes scanning the room, catching at the sight of the dress draped over the chair. "I knocked loudly." She is a small, compact person, quick and concise, with no waste of movement. She crosses to the chair, picks up the frock, and begins smoothing out wrinkles with a thwacking motion.

Marguerite had thought of several excuses to give her for not answering the door the night before, but in the end has no good one. "I was so tired I fell asleep early. I didn't hear you." She tries to put more apology than irritation in her voice. "Did you need something?"

Alice holds up the dress that Marguerite had meant to hide away, and inspects the smears of dirt and grass on its hem; it will have to be washed. She says, "I received a telegram from your father."

"What is it?" At once Marguerite is alarmed. "Is it mother? Has something happened to Melinda?"

"No." Alice's eyes barely meet Marguerite's before darting away again. She bends to pick up a stocking. "Everyone is well."

"Then what?" Marguerite stands rooted in the center of the room, watching Alice move between chair, wardrobe, and bureau, smoothing, shaking, folding, and putting away. "Alice, what is it?"

"Dr. Miller and Mr. Farley are coming to Portsmouth."

"Father? Timothy? They're coming here?" Marguerite tries to keep the rising panic out of her voice. "Why?"

"To see you." Alice closes a drawer and turns to look fully at Marguerite for the first time. Her face is placid, telling nothing.

"But I have five more days." Marguerite's voice is tight. "Why now? Did Papa wire you? Why you instead of me?"

Alice shrugs. "They departed this morning. Dr. Miller has a business stop to make. They will arrive tomorrow morning."

"You wired Papa first, didn't you?"

Alice averts her gaze from Marguerite to the wallpaper where entwining stems curl and twist between plate-sized leaves and droopy flower heads. Her hands, now still at her sides, are clenched.

"Why did you wire him?" A flutter of dread moves in Marguerite's chest. "What did you tell him?"

135

Alice's attention snaps back to Marguerite, her expression righteous and cold. "Only what I felt bound to tell him as your chaperone." She bites out the words. "I told him that you have been sneaking out of your room in the evening. I told him that you have been behaving improperly for a young lady."

CHAPTER TEN

"By the way," I said casually, "how was the date with Ben Barrett?" I accepted the mug of tea Mayta handed to me and set it down on the wide arm of my Adirondack chair.

"Wasn't a date. Just dinner." Mayta settled into the mate of my chair and propped her feet up on the lower rail between posts. She had invited us out to the beach in celebration of July Fourth, and now she and I were on her porch, enjoying the waning of a picture-perfect summer day. Nobody had gone into the water, which is still frigid in early July, but we'd played chicken with the waves, walked the beach, and collected shells at the tide line.

When no details on her dinner with the mayor were forthcoming, I changed the subject to something that continued to bother me. "Why would Claudia's last word be the name of a woman who disappeared more than a century earlier? Sure, she claimed Marguerite was her great-grandmother, but what was she trying to communicate by saying her name?"

"Maybe it only sounded like 'Marguerite.' "

"I thought maybe she was trying to say Magill, Beverly's last name, but I can't find a connection between them, other than dining at the same table that night. Mahg—what else could it mean?" I took a sip of my steaming tea.

Mayta looked out over the ocean. "I keep seeing her."

"Me, too," I said and, as if bidden, the picture of Claudia's bleeding body in the bathtub flashed onto the screen in my mind. We sat in somber silence for a few minutes.

Below Mayta's feet, a row of moon snails in diminishing sizes lined the edge of the porch, the painstaking work of Molly who, at this moment, was off with Gus on a mission to choose dinner out of the big tanks at a nearby lobster pound. Beyond the porch, halfway to the shoreline, Max was constructing a fort out of driftwood, a project started hours earlier that absorbed him to the point that he had declined his father's invitation. Periodically seized by inspiration, he darted off down the beach to return with a sea-crafted tree limb, twisty, gnarly, and washed silvery clean, or a handful of shells, or a long banner of kelp. Mayta and I watched him now, stretching on tiptoe to loop the rope of a faded blue and red Styrofoam buoy over a protruding log.

"It could just be a coincidence and we're making too much of it," Mayta said. "Maybe what you heard was just a sigh, like they say the dying do."

"No, she was trying to say something. I think it's a clue to her murderer."

"Hunh." Mayta took a foot off the rail and nudged a shell into alignment with her big toe.

"Maybe she was murdered to stop her from doing something or from asking questions about Marguerite."

Mayta iterated her doubt with another grunt.

"Maybe Daniel Dean ran away because he's in danger, too." I sat forward with a sudden thought. "Maybe somebody didn't want him and Claudia to pursue this idea that Claudia was Marguerite's great-granddaughter. Somebody who stood to lose something."

"But you said Dorothy has no living relatives—no children, nieces, nephews—who would inherit from her."

"Yeah. She says the family money is long gone, and she's leaving her house to Ellen and giving the family antiques to the historical society." I heard the low growl of a car engine and the crunch of tires on stones in the driveway.

"Okay. So what did Claudia want from Dorothy?" Mayta said.

"She asked about Marguerite's diamond ring; maybe she thought she could find it. Or perhaps it was something as simple as wanting to connect with a long-lost family member."

The slap of the old wooden screen door at the front of the cottage signaled the return of Gus and Molly, and the end of our conversation. There were footfalls through the house, the rustle of paper bags being deposited on the kitchen table, and then Molly pushed open the porch door, letting that one slap shut behind her also.

"Grandma, we got pound and a quarters!" she announced, bounding onto Mayta's lap.

"Molly! Be careful!"

"Oh, she's okay." Mayta wrapped her arms around Molly and squeezed her. "So, pound and a quarters, eh? We'll have to have big appetites, won't we?"

Gus came out onto the porch. "Good deal today so I couldn't resist. Got steamers, too."

"Well, I guess we better get going on dinner." I got to my feet.

In the kitchen, conversation was light, with bantering between Gus and Molly. Max was finally coaxed in from the beach to view the lobsters set out on the counter. He picked up one, its banded claws waving helplessly in the air, while Molly bent down eye level with another one. "What happens to his eyes when we boil 'em?" she asked.

I flinched, letting Gus offer a doubtful explanation of a lobster's quick and painless demise in a pot of boiling water. Probably because I'm a Midwesterner, I'm squeamish on the topic. I prefer not to see my main course crawling around just before dinner, but I've learned to hide it when among New Englanders who, in my opinion, sometimes seem a bit hard-boiled themselves. I pulled out lettuce and veggies from Mayta's fridge and got busy making a salad at the opposite end of the counter.

We put on sweatshirts and ate outside. The sun was going down and Mayta lit the citronella torches that were stuck in the sand around the picnic table. Along with the lobsters and steamers, we had salad, corn on the cob (not local, yet), Mayta's baked beans made with three different kinds of beans, and crusty rolls with real butter. I always manage to overcome my squeamishness at the dinner table.

In an amazingly short time we had two large mixing bowls heaped high with exoskeletons and empty shells. Mayta and I were groaning in satisfaction, Gus chewing and sucking on his last lobster leg, and the kids were back out on the beach playing, when Mayta's telephone rang.

She waved it off. "Oh, ignore that."

So we did, through no less than ten rings before it finally stopped. Then, two minutes later, it started again. "I turned off the answering machine," Mayta said in answer to Gus's questioning look. "Guess I should get it." She got up and trudged through the sand. We heard her answer on the sixth ring, and then make an exclamation. Gus and I jumped to our feet and raced up the steps to the porch.

"What's wrong?" I said in alarm, pushing open the screen door.

"Nothing. Just come in quick and watch this." She was in front of the television, which had been turned on. "That was Ben who called. The police have apprehended Daniel Dean."

There was a commercial break, so Gus returned outside to check on the kids. When the news came back on, Daniel Dean was the first story. Captured in Virginia, he was shown being escorted out of a house, identified as belonging to a friend, with handcuffs on. He looked scruffier than I'd last seen him, sitting across a formal dining table. His hair was mussed; he had the beginnings of a beard and was wearing faded jeans and a tight black tee-shirt. The only information given was that he was being held for questioning in the stabbing death of Claudia Harrison at the Grand Hotel of the Atlantic, that he had her wallet on him, and that he denied having any involvement in her murder. And that Dean wasn't his real name.

"Another alias," I said. "Surprise, surprise."

Gus came in as the news reporter segued to another story. "What's up?"

"Dean turned himself in," Mayta said. "Only that's not really his name. He's been hiding out at a friend's house in Virginia, and he says he's innocent."

"I wonder why he had her wallet," I said.

"After he stabbed her, he stole it for get-away money," Gus said.

I shook my head. "Why would they have gone upstairs to an empty hotel room?"

"Mommy! Mommy!" Molly ran into the room then, arms waving in the air. "The fireworks are starting. Hurry!" She grabbed my hand and pulled me toward the back door. Mayta shut off the television and we followed Molly out onto the beach, where the first in a series of small displays that would erupt throughout the island that night had begun.

The next morning I left a message at the *Portsmouth Daily Monitor* for Beverly Magill, casually mentioning that I had spoken with Dorothy. Daniel's arrest had brought the murder back to the forefront of the news, and Beverly got back to me pronto, no doubt in hopes I had something for her. When it became evident I had questions instead of information, she lost her enthusiasm. She said she'd just finished writing up a piece on Daniel, and that she should make me wait to read it in print.

"Daniel Shropsgrove, alias Dean, grew up in New Jersey where he was in trouble with the law during his teens—petty thievery, stole a car once, took it for a joy ride," Beverly said rapid-fire. "Then he got arrested for selling drugs, spent time in prison, and seemed to wise up some when he got out. Got a job as a mechanic, paid his bills, stayed away from the old cronies, met regularly with his probation officer." She paused. "So, do you think Dorothy has warmed up to the press yet?"

"That would be a definite maybe," I hedged. "She does seem more talkative. When I call her today I'll mention you again. What else did you find out about Daniel?"

"He met Claudia at a bar and became involved with her. They'd dated only about a month when she asked him to take her to New Hampshire to see 'some hotel.' He agreed, even though it would be against probation rules for him to travel out of state. While there, she dragged him off to meet 'a relative'—again, his words—and she introduced them as a married couple, using the name Dean. He didn't know why she did that or why she dragged him with her to meet Dorothy in the first place.

"They drove all the way up from New Jersey one day, and back the next day in order for him to make his check-in with his probation officer. Then, a couple of weeks later, Claudia wanted to go up to New Hampshire again, to some fancy event at the Grand Hotel—that was the big opening, of course. Reluctantly, he agreed to go, and then got angry because, once there, she wanted to stay the whole weekend, which meant he could miss his check-in with his probation officer first thing Monday."

"No wonder he was out of sorts."

"Yes. Then at the dinner, Claudia told him she had to meet with some woman, to show her something important—this was pretty vague. He didn't know what the important thing was, just that it was in a folder she had with her, that she'd taken to Dorothy's house."

"A folder? Is that what was in that oversized designer bag of hers?"

"I guess, but if there really was a folder, it's missing," Beverly said. "Anyway, Daniel said that was the last straw. He left Claudia at the Grand Hotel, picked up his things at the motel where they were staying down the road, and took off for home. He figured she could find her own way back—bus, plane, whatever. He didn't hear the news that she'd been killed until he was out of the state, at which time he panicked and went into hiding." Beverly took a breath. "Oh, and he claims he had Claudia's wallet because she asked him to hold it and then he forgot he had it."

"He said Claudia was going to meet a woman that night?"

"That's what he said. Convenient, isn't it? Must have been this mysterious woman who killed her for some mysterious valuable papers."

"It could be true. Claudia did have papers with her at Dorothy's."

"Yeah, maybe. Listen, I'm under deadline and I've got a few things to finish up."

I thanked her for talking to me, and encouraged her to call Dorothy.

CHAPTER ELEVEN

Following Romania's abolishment of slavery in 1856, gypsies, or Roma as they were sometimes called, emigrated to Western Europe and America on a large scale. They were refused entry at the German border and many were turned away at Ellis Island because of the strict U.S. immigration policy of the 1880s.

A History of Eastern Europe, Marguerite Miller's book that Dorothy had loaned me, was a dull accounting of historical events without a single picture to liven it up. Even the passages that had been bracketed in Marguerite's pen held little interest for me. I skimmed through the rest of the book, stopping to read more sections that had been marked, gaining little insight into the serious young woman who found this stuff entertaining.

I put the book down and called the kids in for a cookie-making session. Mayta stopped by on her way to do errands downtown, and caught me in the kitchen cleaning up the aftermath. She eyed the baking sheets in the dish rack, the containers of sugar and flour still out, and sat down at the table without comment. She picked up Marguerite's book, which I'd placed on top of the toaster oven to keep out of harm's way. "What's this?"

"It's a history book that belonged to Marguerite Miller. Dorothy had it."

She leafed through it and set it back on the toaster oven, even less interested in it than I'd been. "What's new?"

I launched into what I'd learned from Beverly as I wiped down the counter and made a fresh pot of coffee. "It makes sense; I can see Daniel being worried about violating his probation and getting so disgusted with Claudia, who was trying to trick him into staying another night, that he just left her." I prepared a heterogeneous grouping of cookies in varying lumpy shapes and sizes on a plate and shoved it toward her.

"So you buy his story?" Mayta chose a chocolate chip cookie and took a nibble.

I shrugged. "Beverly said that most of what he told the police has checked out, including his appointment with the probation officer."

"This is good," Mayta commented in surprise, after a second more hearty bite. "Who made these?"

"Max and Molly," I said, adding with pride, "under my supervision."

"Well, I guess there's hope for you yet."

"What—as a mother or a cook?"

"A cook, of course. I'd never challenge your mothering skills."

"Thanks," I said dryly. I poured us mugs of coffee and sat down across from her. "I'm inclined to believe Daniel."

"But he used an alias," Mayta said. "And he left Claudia high and dry, without a car, never even checking to see if she made it back to the hotel safely. Then, when he heard she was killed, he ran off and hid."

"It was Claudia who introduced them using Dean instead of their real names," I said. "I'm not saying he's an upright kind of guy; I'm just saying I don't think he's the murderer."

"Why not?"

I broke off a piece of sugar cookie, dunked it into my coffee, and stuck it in my mouth while I pulled together my thoughts, trying to sort out what didn't fit. "Okay," I said finally, "tell me this. Why would Daniel accompany Claudia to dinner, wait for her to leave the table, follow her up to that room, and then stab her? If he was going to murder her, why not do it at the motel where they stayed or someplace where she wouldn't be found immediately?"

"Because he didn't plan it."

"Exactly my point. A murderer wouldn't have planned to use a letter opener; he would have brought his own weapon."

Mayta snorted in impatience. "Right. It was a crime of passion."

"Well, that's where I have a problem with Daniel as a suspect. He was ticked off at Claudia, not hotheaded angry, not pick-up-something-and-stab-you kind of angry."

"Couldn't he have followed her, got into an argument, got 'hotheaded angry,' and then picked up the letter opener and stabbed her?"

I shook my head. "This is what I think happened: Daniel said that Claudia was going to meet a woman to show her something important. Either Claudia was blackmailing this woman, or this woman was blackmailing Claudia. Anyhow, they met up, something happened, and the woman grabbed the letter opener and stabbed Claudia."

"But why would she meet Claudia there—at the hotel in that room?"

"Crazy as it seems, I'm thinking it had something to do with Marguerite Miller. Daniel said Claudia had the same folder that she'd taken to Dorothy's house, which, according to Dorothy, had papers concerning Marguerite. Claudia could have easily carried a folder filled with papers in that big bag of hers. Which, incidentally, was empty when she was found."

"Humph," Mayta uttered doubtfully.

"And don't forget Claudia's last words. They sounded like the beginning of the name Marguerite." Then I had an idea. "I'm going to call Chauncey."

"Who?"

"Chauncey Brown. Remember? The retired lawyer we sat with at the Grand Hotel gala?"

"Didn't he take off without paying his bill?"

"Yeah, and he told lies about who he was, but he did practice as a lawyer in New York, where Marguerite's and Dorothy's aunt lived—at least I believe he did—so maybe he has connections. He called the other day, suggesting that we 'pool our resources' in 'solving the mystery.' " I gave her a pointed look. "Apparently, you gave him the impression that I do that on a regular basis."

"I don't remember saying that."

I reached for my bag and scrabbled around in the bottom of it. "I'd like to learn something about this aunt who wouldn't even claim the body of her niece." Among an assortment of gum wrappers and receipts, I found a crinkled bit of paper with numbers scribbled on it. "Aha! Knew I'd kept it."

When I got through to Chauncey, Mayta listened for a minute and then let herself out the back door where Max and Molly were playing.

Chauncey seemed unsurprised and even moderately pleased that I'd called. After I answered his inquiries after my and Mayta's health, I told him about Dorothy, her connection to Claudia, both of their connections to Marguerite, and my suspicions that those connections had something to do with Claudia's murder. Before I got too long-winded I spiraled back to Dorothy, explaining that I wanted to know if her aunt had had any other heirs.

"You think the motive for Claudia's murder had something to do with inheritance?"

"Well, it's not likely," I admitted. "Still, Claudia seemed anxious to make a family connection, so it makes me wonder if there might be some other unknown relation out there."

"Someone who saw Claudia as a threat?"

"I guess it sounds far-fetched, but yeah, something like that."

Chauncey asked, "Is Dorothy well off?"

"She says not, but she might not know her own worth. She has all these antiques, and then there's the house itself—modest, but real estate being what it is in Portsmouth . . ."

Chauncey mulled this over, then said, "I can check some old city records to see if there might be other heirs. When did the aunt die?"

I gave him Adelaide's full name, the address that had been listed on the death certificate, and a range of years during which she might have died, based on an estimation of Dorothy's age and her comment that she was "quite young" when her aunt died.

"I think I have a friend who might be of assistance," he said, his enthusiasm building. "This should be interesting. Brings back memories of my days as a trial lawyer."

I thanked him, and then asked if, after settling his bill, he was back in good graces with the restaurant at the Grand Hotel.

"Oh, thank you for reminding me," he said. "I am going to do that today!"

"Chauncey, you do that often, don't you—walk out without paying a bill?"

He laughed but gave no answer.

"Just what kind of lawyer were you? Never mind, I don't want to know. If you get some info on Adelaide Miller, I'll appreciate it."

While Mayta was entertaining the troops, I made another call. The phone rang six times before Dorothy picked up. She'd been in the garden, she said breathlessly.

I apologized for bothering her, and asked if she'd heard about Daniel's arrest.

"Who?"

"The young man who was with Claudia. He called himself Daniel Dean." I told her most of what Beverly had told me about Daniel Shropsgrove.

"That's the woman reporter who called me, isn't it?"

I said that it was. "When I've asked her for information, she's been very helpful. She might be calling you again." There, I'd given Beverly the best endorsement I felt I could. I asked Dorothy if she'd contacted the state department to request records on her aunt.

"Yes, I did," she surprised me by saying. "They should be here in a week or so." I told her I thought that was the right thing to do, then rang off.

I joined Mayta and the kids in the backyard. She looked up questioningly from her perch on the side of the sandbox.

"Chauncey said he'd look into some things," I said.

She nodded. "He seemed like a nice man, however dishonest he might be."

"And Dorothy has requested records on her aunt Marguerite from the state."

"It seems that you are not only a woman of cooking talents, but a persuasive one, as well."

I smiled prettily at her.

After Mayta left, I woke up the computer and googled images for Danvers State Hospital. Surprised to find a number of thumbnail pictures, I clicked on one with spires against an eerie cloud-streaked night sky and found that it was part of a whole series of shots that had been taken fairly recently. I followed the back arrow to a website that proclaimed, *Explore At Your Own Risk!*

The site belonged to Turk, a self-described urban explorer—someone, I learned, who is fascinated with derelict buildings, who equips himself with dark clothes, sneakers, flashlights, cameras, and whatever other tools are needed to (often illegally) access dilapidated, decaying structures. Someone whose noble objective is "to experience the abandonment of something that was once so functional, so filled with life; to record a splendid piece of architecture before it is razed; to be a single lonely being within a massive dying, archaic structure whispering its secrets."

Apparently, there were many wannabe urban explorers, because Turk's home page issued a dire warning of the dangers one could face: armed police; structures ready to collapse; lead, tetanus, and toxic molds; and sketchy people, including crackheads, who frequent such places. Which made me question my sanity in even entertaining the idea of taking Sandy up on her offer to sneak into Danvers.

Turk had photographed abandoned buildings from across the United States and Europe, some unnamed to "protect their integrity." I entered the Danvers State Hospital portal and was presented with spectacular photographs taken from outside, inside, and atop the various abandoned buildings of the hospital. Turk excelled at highlighting architectural lines and artistic details using only a flashlight and the moon as illumination. Some of the more impressive shots: peaks, spires, roof slants, and angles taken from a rooftop looking down; a stairwell descending Escher-like in telescopic concentric squares; and old paint erupting from a wall in scaly patches above a row of smooth porcelain sinks.

Most poignant were the empty spaces with a hint of former occupants: a teal-colored door with a peeling dried strip of masking tape bearing a patient's name written in marker; floral curtains left hanging in a window; a stretcher in a hallway; old curling and rotting magazine clippings taped to a wall; a June 1979 calendar.

After I had browsed through the online pictures, I went back and read the comments in the attached blog, written by visitors to the website. Most, I surmised from their slang, were around the age of the urban explorer himself—in their early to mid-twenties. There were the few expected comments about ghosts or spirits, but overwhelmingly the responses were about the beauty of the architecture, the talent of the photographer in conveying feelings and artistry, or the sad fate of these buildings: "It's a tragedy people don't see the beauty in them . . ." lamented Tracey; "Awesome shot! It breaks my heart to think they will demolish these . . ." from Sarah; and from another, "I've dreamed about this place . . ."

The phone sounded and thinking it was Gus, I picked up without checking the caller ID. I hadn't expected Chauncey to get back to me for a day or two, so I was surprised to hear his voice.

"Adelaide Claire Miller never married and had no offspring," he said. "She died in 1927, her sole heir being her niece Melinda Miller, daughter of Adelaide's deceased brother, Dr. Archibald Miller."

"Well, that's that. No mention of a child from her other niece, Marguerite. So that means Claudia wasn't who she claimed to be—Marguerite's great-granddaughter."

"Not necessarily. It only means Adelaide chose not to list anyone else as heir, or did not know of one. I'd say Claudia's claims are unlikely, but we can't rule them out yet. Listen," he said, his voice charged with an undercurrent of excitement, "how about I look further into Miss Miller? Maybe I can find out something about Claudia Harrison as well."

"Sure."

Gus did call then. He said he was on his way back from the dump and was there anything we needed from the grocery store. I checked the fridge, then the time—twelve o'clock—and said no, but could he come straight home because I wanted to go up to Portsmouth for a few hours. There was some hesitation, during which I heard him thinking, *again*? But all he said was, "Okay."

With Chauncey working the Adelaide Miller and Claudia Harrison connection, it was time for me to get back to Marguerite.

CHAPTER TWELVE

The New Hampshire Seacoast Historical Research Library (NHSHR for short) was just off the town square, but I walked past it twice before I saw the unobtrusive lettering below the larger and more prominent *Portsmouth Monitor* sign. The private library occupied the top floor of the newspaper building. I briefly considered stopping in to see Beverly, and then thought better of it. I'd already pushed my luck with her. Besides, I needed to just get on with it.

I'd put off this visit since Mayta and I snooped around at the Grand Hotel. I'd realized then that in order to visualize what might have happened to Marguerite, I needed to see the layout of the area surrounding the hotel in 1901, which I hadn't been able to find online or at the public library. There were other things I wanted to learn also—exactly what I couldn't say, other than that I would know them when they presented themselves to me. I decided that the New Hampshire Seacoast Historical Research Library—one of the sources cited in a foreword to a book I'd read on the hotel—might have what I sought.

Being a private library, I figured that it was probably the kind of place where you'd have to make an appointment or ring a bell and explain yourself, which made it just daunting enough to delay an impromptu visit. But now, I decided it was time. The website for the NHSHR—even *that* was a mouthful—listed days and hours open to the public and a phone number. I called and found out that, although I didn't need an appointment, I *would* have to ring a bell—in this case, a buzzer—to announce my arrival.

A narrow windowless stairwell led to a small landing with a single door. I pressed the buzzer next to the door and a young man opened it promptly. I entered a busy room, lighted front and back by rows of small paned windows, which overlooked different sections of the city. While I couldn't see any people actually researching, there were at least five men and women who crossed back and forth carrying large covered cardboard cartons. They talked with each other, having no compunction about being quiet, like one would in a regular library.

Behind a gleaming mahogany desk, a portly woman with gray hair piled elaborately atop her head looked up from the only computer in sight to regard me over tiny half glasses perched on her nose. "Can I help you?" she asked in clipped tones.

I explained that I had come to look up information on the Grand Hotel of the Atlantic.

"Have you read *Grand Hotel of the Atlantic* by Elwin Dodge?" she said, almost before I'd finished speaking.

When I assured her that I had, her eyes slid back to the computer screen. "Then you have read just about everything there is on the hotel. Elwin was very thorough in his research."

"I want to look at the firsthand sources that he used," I said.

"Why would you want to do that?" Her eyes were still on the screen.

Here it was; I was being asked to explain myself, to justify why I should be allowed access to the inner sanctum of this august place. I fell back on what comes naturally to me in tense circumstances: fabrication.

"My great-grandfather worked at the hotel from 1900 until 1905. In fact, he was there during the Russo-Japanese Peace Conference, which was very exciting for him," I lied glibly. "He told my father stories about the hotel and I'd like to look through the pictures of that time, just to see what it looked like. Who knows? I might even find a picture of Great-Granddad."

Her Miss Nibs raised her eyes (and eyebrows) this time, but waved me to a counter that ran along the wall below book-shelves, which I took as permission that I might remain. "Put everything down there. Take a pencil from the box on the table and a form to fill out. You may not write with pen—only pencil—and you may have nothing on you but a pad of paper. Everything else is to be put on the counter. Go through those card catalogues"—here she pointed to the other side of the room—"then tell me what you want. I'll have somebody get it." She caught a glimpse of something on the other side of the room, and I was dismissed with the raising of her hand.

"Helen, you'll have to move," she called out peevishly to an elderly woman in a plaid kilt sitting next to the card file. "You can't spread out those papers there. You know that table is to be kept clear."

After I set my things down on the counter, I took up one of the sharpened and uniformly half-sized pencils and a small request form and tiptoed over to the card file, exchanging timid smiles with poor Helen, who was shuffling her papers together. Before long, I found some promising files, and fifteen minutes later, I presented Her Miss Nibs with a list of sources.

"Oh, no, no, nooo," she said. "You haven't written them down right. Look, you put the number there, and then the call letters here. There's a box number also." She pointed with her pencil to a line I'd left blank.

Sheepishly, I returned to the catalog. Helen looked up and gave me an empathetic smile. I noticed that she hadn't moved herself or her papers and I took heart. Perhaps Her Miss Nibs was more bark than bite. I was sent back one more time before my form was finally accepted with a smile of grudging approval. I took a seat at a long empty table between the bookcases and waited. Presently, one of the scurrying-back-and-forth people brought me a container box, and I set to work.

An hour and a half later, I had some brochures of the hotel in 1902, a map of the grounds, and various articles about the hotel, including ones on the disappearance of Marguerite Miller. I also had some other information that I had culled just because it interested me.

I read the articles on Marguerite first, most of them the same as I'd seen at the Portsmouth Library. There was little I didn't already know about her disappearance, but I did find out that she wasn't discovered missing until ten o'clock the following morning when her traveling companion—the family maid— knocked on her door. Depending on when she'd left during the night, Marguerite could have had many hours to get far away.

I studied a grainy newspaper picture of the nineteen-year-old. She stood in a formal garden, possibly at her parents' house in Boston, wearing a long white dress, her dark hair pulled up under a wide-brimmed hat. I couldn't see her eyes, which were shaded by the brim, but her smile was crooked, an amused, wry sort of smile that hinted at playfulness toward the photographer. I deduced that whoever took the picture was someone she knew well, like her father or fiancé. I could see in that smile and in her assured stance that this had been a young woman with spirit.

I turned my attention to the 1902 pictorial map, which encompassed all of New Island. Most likely an advertising piece of artwork, the map wasn't drawn to scale because it depicted the Grand Hotel and its surroundings prominently in the foreground, with the rest of the island receding from it.

Now that I'd proven I could handle myself with the catalogue forms, I was paid no attention and given free rein of the library, which included the copy machine. I enlarged the pictorial map so that it comprised four pages. And as it appeared that Helen—who was still putzing away with her papers on the forbidden table—and I were the only researchers present, I utilized my space to spread out my papers.

Alongside the map pieces I had historical articles, most falling into the "interesting, but not pertinent" category, of which I made copies nonetheless, and then whiled away half an hour or so perusing them. Among the historical tidbits I learned was that New Island, the area at the mouth of the Piscataqua River, was settled in 1623 by the British just three years after Plimouth Plantation in Massachusetts. The settlers eventually moved further inland along the river, first calling their settlement Strawbery Banke and later, Portsmouth.

The base for the early fishing industry, however, lay seven miles off the coast, on the Isles of Shoals. Discovered by explorer John Smith in 1614, they were reputedly visited by pirates (Captain Kidd and Blackbeard among them) during the 1700s. In the nineteenth century, the islands became a cultural center for leading artists, writers, musicians, and thinkers. Around this time also, small hotels popped up on a couple of the larger islands, and the Isles of Shoals became a vacation destination.

There was a harshness that came with living on small treeless islands far enough out to sea to be lost to sight from the mainland at the first hint of a haze. Islanders developed their own dialect and culture. During the windy and severe winters, they lived for weeks at a time sealed up in tiny cottages. The Isles of Shoals were the setting for one of New Hampshire's most heinous crimes—the ax murders of two women in 1873—as well as one of the state's worst tragedies, the 1902 capsizing of a boat and subsequent drownings of a headwaiter and twelve young waitresses from the Oceanic Hotel on Star Island. I paused over the latter, reading an account of local fishermen who came with their dories from the various islands to help with the rescue, putting themselves in great danger in the tumultuous waters.

But enough self-indulgence; none of this had to do with Marguerite's disappearance. I pushed aside the pamphlets and articles and went back to the map. Other than the Grand Hotel and the development right around it at the southern end of New Island, I guessed that the layout at the turn of the twentieth century had not changed remarkably since the 1700s. At the opposite end of New Island was (and still is) a tiny village. Between village and hotel were a winding road, trees, marsh, and the occasional farmhouse.

So, Marguerite, where did you hide that night? Where did you hide for a year? I ran a finger from the back of the hotel, across the lawn, and through trees to the Piscataqua River. Unless she took a boat or tramped through fields, she would have traveled by the only through road on the island: One B. After a moment's finger-tapping indecision, I traced Route One B south over the bridge into a sparsely settled area. How far might she have gone and still have it be considered "in the area" where, according to Dorothy, she had been found a year later? I went back to the hotel, plunked my finger there again, and followed the same road north to New Island village, and then across the bridges into Portsmouth proper.

She must have left on foot since nobody came forward to say she'd hired a carriage. But if she headed toward Portsmouth, would she have walked the five or so miles by herself at night? Of course, if she'd run away with somebody, other possibilities presented themselves. That person might have had a horse and carriage, a boat—even a car, I thought, remembering that her parents were killed just months later in an automobile accident. Maybe she went further away, and then was found upon her return to the Portsmouth area.

The formidable woman behind the computer cleared her throat, then gestured with a pencil to the clock on the wall: four o'clock, closing time. I made a few last copies, returned the papers to their box and my pencil to its container. I must have proven my trustworthiness because when I thanked her, I received a genuine smile from Her Miss Nibs, and an invitation to return. Actually, her exact words were, "Now you will know what to do on your next visit."

I checked my watch and decided that I had enough time to drop in on Dorothy before heading back. But first, I took Route One B out of town, across the two skipping-stone islands to New Island, and followed the winding way to the Grand Hotel at the south end, where I pulled into the parking lot.

I sat for a moment, looking up at the window of the room from which I believed Marguerite had left. Then I set my mileage counter, and headed back to Portsmouth the way I'd just come. As I drove along slowly, pulling off twice to let other cars pass, I tried to put myself in Marguerite's shoes. The terrain was hilly and rocky in spots; if she had taken off on foot at night, I was sure she wouldn't have traversed the island any other way but on the only road that went across it.

So, in which direction did she go? North toward a city or south into the country? It made better sense to hide in the country, but I doubted a well-bred Boston girl would be comfortable doing that. My bet was that if she was walking by herself, she headed toward civilization—toward Portsmouth.

Grand Hotel of the Atlantic
June Twenty-Second, 1901

Sitting at her desk, Marguerite thumbs through her journal, thinking, planning. When Papa and Timothy arrive, she will explain that her evening walks were because she couldn't sleep, and that she didn't ignore Timothy's letters; she just hadn't gotten around to mailing her responses. But their arrival is not all that agitates her. Until now she has avoided thinking about going back to Boston, to a future laid out like a patterned brick walk. When she came to the hotel she had only wanted a respite from the momentum of her life. Now, she wants more, perhaps too much. She wants choices. She wants to choose when—and if—she will return to Boston; she wants to choose what to do with her time and with whom to spend it. She snaps the journal shut, restlessness driving her to her feet. She paces the floor, her steps keeping time with her rapidly developing thoughts. She wants freedom: from Alice watching over her, from Papa's expectations, from her engagement to Timothy.

She thinks about staying in Portsmouth. She is well schooled; she could work as a tutor or a governess. Both are respectable positions that should satisfy her father's sense of propriety, and there's bound to be a family in the area in need of one or the other. She will convince Papa of the practicality of her obtaining such a position in Portsmouth. Then she will tell Timothy of her change of heart, apologize profusely, and leave him to his pouting, if he must.

Because her disquiet cannot be contained in her room, Marguerite goes down to supper early. At one of the few occupied tables in the dining room sit Ernest and Josephine Carter. Marguerite isn't in the mood to listen to their bickering or Ernest's teasing, which, she has learned, intensifies with the quantity of liquor he consumes, but before she can back out of the doorway Ernest sees her and waves. It would be impolite to do anything else, so Marguerite reluctantly joins them.

"Well, if it isn't our partner in crime," Ernest says heartily, running the words together. He waves a short fat glass in the air and liquid sloshes over its side. "Coming to find relief from this heat in libation?" Ernest beckons with his other hand to a waiter. Josephine smiles wanly. Her glass, filled with liquid of the same amber color, looks untouched, condensation seeping into the white damask tablecloth around its base.

"Yes, it certainly is hot." Marguerite tries to inject enthusiasm into her response. "I'll have an iced tea, please," she says to the waiter, shaking her head at the menu.

"How have you been keeping yourself busy?" Ernest leans forward, his loosened tie almost touching his half-eaten mashed potatoes. "Haven't seen you around today, have we, Jo?"

Josephine pushes a small piece of meat around her plate with her fork.

"I went for a walk along the beach this morning," Marguerite says, "and since then, I've been resting in my room."

Josephine looks up then, makes eye contact with Marguerite. "That is what I would like to do," she says. "I think I'll go rest after dinner."

"Yes. You do that." Ernest drains his glass, the ice knocking together, and then lifts it in the direction of the waiter. His voice is tired, his eyes flat and dull. At that moment Marguerite feels as sorry for Ernest as she does for his wife, thinking that he is no less trapped in his social set with its masked manners, its ridiculous rigidity. If she and Timothy married, would they be like this someday?

Ernest raises his voice in a forced jolly timbre. "Your little maid there—the grim one. Now, there's somebody who's been bustling around. I've run into her at every turn." He pauses for a response from Marguerite. When there is none, he presses, "Why do you suppose she's so busy?"

The waiter sets a fresh drink on the table and backs away but Ernest beckons him forward again. "Here! Take this away. It's too damned hot to eat."

"Yes, sir." The waiter picks up his plate and the butter knife slides off onto the table. Ernest snatches it up and thrusts it at the waiter, who jumps back involuntarily. Josephine cries out.

"For God's sake, I'm only fooling." Ernest hands the knife to the waiter, who takes it warily. "Sorry, old·man, didn't mean to scare you."

"Ernest, really—" Josephine begins after the waiter has left.

"Oh, for God's sake, Josephine, your holier-than-thou attitude is getting tiresome."

"Please, Ernest, lower your—"

"Don't tell me to lower my voice, because I will say what I damned well please!" Several heads turn their way as Ernest continues even more loudly, "Why don't you loosen up a bit, Josephine? Take Marguerite, here." He sweeps his arm in her direction. "She knows how to enjoy herself, out pussyfooting every night. What do you suppose she does out there in the moonlight?"

Marguerite springs up from her chair. "Excuse me."

"See here, I am sorry—" Ernest begins, struggling to get to his feet, but Marguerite cuts him off.

"It really is unbearably hot," she says, mustering some dignity. "I'm going to my room now."

Ears ringing and face burning, she rushes by tables where people don't turn their heads, but follow her out of the corners of their eyes. How many of them, like Ernest and Josephine, have watched her from their windows?

Back in her room, she cools her flushed cheeks with a wet cloth and thinks about Ernest's words: What do you suppose she does out there in the moonlight? *Does he know about Emil? No, she decides. If he did, he would be brazen enough to say so.*

Although it is still daylight, she begins a vigil at the window. She is certain that Emil will come tonight. And an hour later, just as day dims to dusk, she sees him leaning against a tree just beyond the lawn. Relieved, she opens the door to the hallway with no clear thought of what she will do. She taps on Alice's door.

Instantly, Alice's face, its features sharp, is there in the space between door and jamb.

"I'm going to get a book from downstairs," she says and then feels Alice's eyes follow her down the hallway.

The clerk at the desk in the lobby looks up and smiles. Instead of exiting to the porch, Marguerite enters the sitting room where she told Alice she was going. What had she been thinking? Just stepping outside to signal him would be foolhardy. Someone—Josephine and Ernest or Alice or any of the other hotel guests who have been or are now aware of her movements—would see. She grabs a book from one of the shelves and returns to her room.

She stands by the window until dark. When Alice knocks on her door, Marguerite bids her goodnight and turns out the light, but doesn't change into her nightdress. She paces the floor, thinking, still clutching the book, smacking its binding on the palm of her other hand.

She peers out the window again. Though she cannot see him, she knows Emil is still there. She drops the book, reaches down, and unfastens the lower hooks of the window screen. She pushes it outward and climbs through, the bottom of the wooden frame scraping against her back. The porch roof slopes gently away from the building, and it is not difficult to crawl over it. Still, Marguerite keeps close to the wall until she reaches the corner of the building. Then she looks out beyond the roof, to the lawn below, to where Emil has stepped out of the shadows. The height is enough to be dizzying, to frighten her into retreating, but knowing that he is there, waiting, encourages her.

She shortens her sight to the roof below her feet and sits, knees pulled up, at the point where the back and side roofs meet. After two deep breaths, she moves down the seam in a series of short slides, checking herself with the soles of her shoes against its surface. At the bottom, she peeks over, heart racing with fear. Emil is below, beckoning.

She could not climb back up the roof now, even if she wanted to, so she rolls over onto her stomach and lowers herself over the edge, reaching a foot for the crossed piece alongside the column. Then it is an easy matter to wrap arms and legs around the column and slide down to the rail, climb over it, and leap into Emil's arms.

Away they fly over the lawn to the shelter of trees and brush. When they reach the river, they sit facing each other, cross-legged, knees touching, and converse in low voices as the moonlight spills over their laps, bleaching out the hues of their clothes. Marguerite watches Emil's face, all planes of shadow and light, as she tells him about Alice's betrayal, and about her father and Timothy who are on their way to the hotel.

"This Timothy," Emil says, "you are promised to him?"

"Yes, but I will not marry him," she says, wondering how she had never before recognized that Timothy had inspired in her the affection of a sister, not a wife. Thinking that before Emil, she hadn't realized this.

"You can go back on your promise?"

"Yes," she says with growing certainty. "Papa won't expect me to marry someone I don't want to, and Timothy will respect my decision."

Emil looks out to the river, his eyes focused on something distant though Marguerite sees nothing but moonlight glinting off water. His rugged profile with its prominent nose and high cheekbones seems at once foreign and familiar to her. Should she say more? Can she explain something she doesn't fully understand herself, this decision to choose someone she has known only a few days over all that has come before—her home, family, Timothy? And if she can find the words, can she cross the barrier of propriety, of upbringing, to utter them?

But before she can try, he says, "You and I are meant to be together; it is bart. But you must make this right with Timothy and your father."

"I will," she promises.

"When I leave, will you come with me?" When she hesitates, he adds, "You must make a choice."

"But . . . how?" She is unable to put voice to ideas of engagement, marriage, elopement.

He shrugs as if it were simple. "We go on the night breeze, and then you and I will be together." And Marguerite begins to understand that Emil deals in the universal, not the particular. His announcement needs no details to define it, no reasoning to justify it, no date and time to confirm it; he says they will be together and Marguerite finds that she accepts this.

"There is your mother and . . . others?" she asks, partly to step back and take time to think about what she has learned about Emil. And what she has learned about herself, for a scene has appeared in her mind of escaping out a window, dashing over the lawn taking nothing but what she is wearing.

"Ha!" Emil tosses back his head, his loose hair gleaming as the moonlight catches it. Marguerite resists an urge to thrust her hands into it and feel its silky length slide through her fingers. "There are many in my familia.*"*

When she asks how many, he flicks the fingers of both hands, a quick graceful gesture. "There is the shena *to which we belong and the* kumpa'nia *to which our shena belongs. You will see when you come with us." He leans forward, takes her hands and squeezes them. "There are many, but not all live together all the time."*

"Where do they—you live?" Another thing she had considered

only in the abstract. She summons a thought of circus tents, occupies them with faceless people, and then tries to put Emil and herself into the picture.

"We live here, for now. Soon, though, we go south."

"South? To Boston?" Her thoughts are still on the tents: Will they live in a tent?

He shakes his head; she has asked him for particulars. "No big cities or cold places in the winter. And we do not always work with the circus."

"Will your people like me?" Marguerite thinks of Emil's mother, the grim fortuneteller with the jangling bracelets.

He brings her hand to his lips. "You are my vestacha, *my beloved." His breath is warm upon her fingertips. "Whom I love, they will also love. They will look inside and see the you that I see."*

"Who is the me that you see?" It is an effort not to be distracted by his touch, but she must know who it is he says he loves, who it is she might be.

His brow wrinkles in thought. "It is your spirit. I could see it right away."

"What is it about my spirit?"

"Why, it is old," he says as if she should already know it. "It is a good thing. You have a knowing, an understanding, a way of seeing life that others do not. You are my . . . te sorthene." He releases each syllable separately so they float among other subdued sounds of the night.

Marguerite rolls the strange magical-sounding words on her tongue, trying to grasp their meaning.

"Long ago your spirit and mine became bonded," he says. "We have known each other before and we will know each other again. Throughout time our paths will cross and we will meet as friends, sometimes as lovers. It is bart. Do you not feel it?"

A week ago she would have thought the idea ridiculous, even blasphemous. But now she considers it. There is a physical connection between them, she will admit that—but it is something else, too. Perhaps it is as Emil says, that their spirits are bonded. "Yes, I do feel it," she says.

CHAPTER THIRTEEN

I crossed over the last waterway and reentered Portsmouth proper. The large thundercloud off to the north that I had been ignoring suddenly moved overhead, plunging the city into near darkness. I turned on my car lights and continued on to Dorothy's.

A few moments later I pulled up in front of her house. I waited a moment, scanning the sky to see if all of heaven was going to open up on me the minute I opened the door. Deciding to chance it, I jumped out and hurried toward the house. As I lifted the doorknocker, I heard a loud, dull thump from inside. I let the knocker fall and then pounded on the door with my fist, calling Dorothy's name. I tried the door but it was locked. Peering in the sidelight, I heard footsteps behind me. Ellen Timmons, head bent against the first fat drops of rain, was hurrying up the walk.

"Oh, Ellen, I heard something inside, like somebody falling. Is Dorothy home?"

Ellen's eyes shot wide, her mouth dropped open, and she looked so stricken I was momentarily worried she'd had a heart attack. Her hand trembled as she stuck her key into the lock and pushed the door open, calling, "Dorothy? Are you all right?" She dashed down the hallway toward the back of the house and I followed on her heels.

"Oh, no!" Ellen sank to her knees in the middle of the kitchen floor where, next to a chair tipped over on its side, Dorothy lay spread out on her back. In the pale light coming from the kitchen window, I watched her feel for Dorothy's pulse and touch the back of her hand to her forehead. "Turn the light on," she commanded.

I flipped up the switch next to the door, but nothing happened.

"Someone's turned it off by the cord," she said. "There's one above the sink."

I crossed the room and found another wall switch on the backsplash. A rectangular fluorescent fixture above the sink flickered on, sending weak illumination across the floor. It was enough to see that Dorothy was conscious but dazed, her eyes glassy and fixed on the combination ceiling light and fan above her.

"Call nine-one-one! Tell them she has a rapid heartbeat, cold clammy skin, large pupils; she's likely concussed."

I reached for my cell, and then remembered I'd left it in the car. I raced back down the hallway to the little table in the entry where I'd seen a telephone next to a pile of mail. I told the woman who answered that Dorothy Dennis had taken a fall, and repeated what Ellen had told me, adding when asked that yes, she was conscious. When I returned to the kitchen, Dorothy was mumbling about the chair sliding out from under her. Some color had come back to her face, and she was attempting to sit up.

"Just rest." Ellen gently restrained her, then looked up at me.

"They're sending an ambulance," I said.

"No, no," Dorothy moaned. "I don't want an ambulance. Such fuss!"

"Lie still," Ellen said. "We're going to get you checked out, that's all. Everything is fine, but we need to play it safe." She sounded relieved, her voice back to normal, and I realized she had expected the worst when she'd entered the kitchen.

Having let loose only a splattering of raindrops, the thunder-cloud moved away as quickly as it had come, and the sky was again bright when, within minutes, medics appeared at the door. After they determined that the still protesting Dorothy was stable, they rolled her out to the waiting ambulance. I gave Ellen my cell number, and she promised to call me later in the day. Then she jumped into her car and followed the ambulance to the hospital. I stood for a moment, watching them leave before returning to make sure the house was secured. With all the commotion, I wasn't surprised to find the door not only unlocked, but also ajar. I slid the little button to release the lock, and then stopped just short of pulling the door closed.

I went back inside to the kitchen. The room was bright with late afternoon sunlight, so I turned off the fluorescent light. The chair still lay on its side on the black-and-white checkerboard-patterned linoleum floor, its vinyl padded seat a few feet away. What had Dorothy been doing with the chair in the middle of the room? The others were neatly pushed under a table that abutted the window.

I looked up at the combination ceiling fan and lamp fixture overhead. The cord that turned on the light was looped up over one of the fan blades, making it unreachable. Had Dorothy tried to stand on the chair to untangle it? Then I remembered, one of the first times I'd visited, Ellen admonishing Dorothy for doing exactly that.

I walked around the kitchen. I opened the door to the pantry, its narrow side shelves filled with canned goods and deep shelves at the back displaying crockery. No step stool. I shook my head. It was reckless of Dorothy to try to stand on a chair to reach the cord, but I had no doubt that was what she had done. I could see her wanting to take care of something like that herself.

I up-righted the chair, fitted the padded seat back into its frame, and pushed it to its spot at the table. I tested the other three chairs, finding their seats firmly attached. It seemed that Dorothy had chosen the sole rickety chair on which to stand. Still, I wasn't going to trust any of the chairs, so I went down into the basement, where I found a small stepladder. After I climbed up and fixed the cord, I took the stepladder back to the basement, along with the loose-seated chair.

On my way out of the house, I straightened the telephone I'd pulled askew in my haste to call nine-one-one. Then I noticed the mail stacked next to the telephone. The top envelope was addressed to Walter Timmons, care of Ellen Timmons. I picked up the stack and thumbed through bills and circulars addressed to Dorothy or to occupant. No other mail for Ellen or her brother. I looked at the top envelope again. The lettering was compact and tight and in all capitals, as if the writer didn't want his hand identified, and there was no return address. When she'd introduced her brother to me, Ellen had said Walter was just visiting, so why would he be getting mail here? Had he decided to stay on? I put the mail back as I'd found it and let myself out, locking the door again.

Ellen called that night and reassured me that Dorothy was fine. She had a minor concussion, but was released into Ellen's care with directions to keep watch on her. I thanked her for calling and then told her about the chair. Ellen said she'd have it repaired right away. In fact, she said, her brother was supposed to have reglued all the kitchen chairs while he was there, but hadn't gotten to it.

"He's gone, then?" I asked. "I thought he might be staying for a while."

"He visits now and then, and helps with maintenance around the house," Ellen said, which didn't explain why his mail would be sent in care of her, but I couldn't very well ask her about that. I told her to give me a call if anything changed with

Dorothy's health and also if I could help out. She thanked me, but said they'd be fine.

During the next two days I didn't bother Dorothy, figuring she needed rest. On Sunday afternoon Mayta came over to give me some ideas for regenerating the perennial bed along the driveway. Seeing Dorothy's gardens had given me new resolve to cultivate a green thumb, so I took down notes on how to care for lilies and peonies and roses, and accepted Mayta's offer to help me weed the area.

We had an early dinner—burgers on the grill by Chef Gus—and then I shooed Mayta out of the kitchen and into her car when she mentioned being tired. "Get some rest! You've been running around doing too much. I'll call you tomorrow."

Gus left for a run and the kids went upstairs to the toy room while I finished cleaning up. I was thinking of Dorothy, wondering if she was ready for company, when a loud bleating on the counter interrupted my thoughts. I picked up the telephone receiver.

"Hi, Andy?"

"Yes."

"This is Sandy? You know, from Danvers State? I took you to the town hall to look up records for your friend?"

"Oh, yes." I snapped out of my reverie. "How are you, Sandy?"

"I'm good. Remember I said I was taking a group of paranormal investigators into the hospital?"

"Yes?"

"Well, it's going to be tonight. We decided to do it sooner, you know, because of increased police activity up there and how it's only going to get worse?"

I bit back another *yes,* hoping she'd get to the point sooner.

"Anyway, I said I'd let you know about it?" She paused a

second. "Do you want to go?"

"You mean, like a séance?"

"No, just a group of ghost hunters."

"I thought they didn't allow anybody inside."

"They don't on account of some of the buildings are dangerous, and since that horror movie was filmed there everybody
wants to get in. So, we're going to sneak in?"

At my audible intake of breath, she said, "It's okay. I'm leading them in? I know how to do it so's nobody gets caught. And
we only go where it's safe, you know?"

"But isn't it still breaking the law?"

"Yeah, but I lived there for ten years? I've snuck in like a million times and never got caught?"

I wondered what percent of captured criminals had told
themselves that. "I don't know, Sandy."

"I thought you wanted to get inside? Get a feel for the
hospital, pick up on some spirits that still linger there, maybe
even your friend's ancestor's spirit?"

I waited for her giggle, but the spirit remark was serious. I
told myself that it was a ridiculous idea even as I began figuring
out how I might finagle it. Gus would be back in ten or fifteen
minutes, the kids would be going down to bed soon after that.
"What time?"

"We're meeting at ten in the Cinnabar Lounge parking lot?
Just off Route One?"

I checked the clock; it was already eight-thirty. I'd have to
hurry, but it could be done. "Okay, I'll meet you there at ten."

I ran upstairs. At the toy room doorway I was stopped by a
floor covered with every manner of building block imaginable—
wood, cardboard, Lincoln Logs, and Legos. Even the wooden
trains and tracks were spread out, ready to be incorporated into
some major construction plan. In two separate small clearings
sat Max and Molly, each occupied with projects that were part

of the same larger layout. So absorbed were they that I had arrived unobserved. I backed out, deciding not to issue the order to put things away and get ready for bed.

I changed quickly into jeans, a black pullover sweatshirt, and dark sneakers. I took a flashlight off the shelf in the basement and was coming back up the stairs when Gus arrived home from his run.

"Moratorium on bedtime," I announced. It's one of the things we do occasionally. When everything is exactly right—motivation, cooperation, creativity—we suspend rules like calling bedtime and allow what is taking place naturally to continue for as long as it works.

"Really?" Gus looked pleased. We hadn't had a moratorium on bedtime in a while because Max and Molly had been in a rather uncooperative phase.

"Yeah. They're heavy into a building mode. Working very well together, also."

"Okay. Who stays up?"

"You, until I get home. If they're still going at it, I'll take over at twelve-thirty."

He noticed my clothes then and narrowed his eyes. "Where are you going?"

"For a night tour. No time for questions. Tell you all about it tomorrow." He started to protest, but I held my ground. "Tomorrow. I'll be back by one at the latest." I air-kissed his cheek and ran out the door.

CHAPTER FOURTEEN

I pulled into the parking lot of the Cinnabar Lounge ten minutes early, my nervousness no doubt pushing the needle on the speedometer. I parked in the darkest corner, which, I soon realized from glances I got from people on their way into the bar, made me more, rather than less, conspicuous. So I moved the car over in line with the others, hoping that somehow Sandy would find me.

I kept a close eye on both entryways into the lot, following each vehicle that entered and parked, watching the people who disembarked until they entered the lounge. Ten o'clock came and went. Five more minutes passed, then ten. The parking lot was almost full now. My anxiety abated somewhat, I decided to wait another ten minutes, after which I felt I could, in good conscience, leave. I was rehearsing what I'd say to Sandy—*I waited twenty-five minutes*— when an old full-sized station wagon, riding low on its carriage, crept into the lot. Sandy. My heart sank and started jumping at the same time.

The station wagon parked at the end of the row in front of me. Nobody got out so I waited. When its lights flashed on and off, I took that as my sign. I creaked open the door and slid out, easing it shut with as little noise as possible. Then I remembered my flashlight and had to unlock the door and go through the whole process again. Finally ready, I kept to the shadows and started toward the station wagon. A streetlight silhouetted at least five people in its front and back seats.

Then a head emerged from the driver's-side window and Sandy shouted, "Hey, Andy!" So much for discretion. I reached the car as everyone started spilling out. "This is Carmine." Sandy waved a hand at a thin, attractive African-American woman with very short hair. "She's a paranormal investigator."

"How do you do." There was an island lilt to Carmine's voice, and a glimpse of a wide smile before she pulled a colorful caftan up over her head. Underneath, she wore what the rest of us wore: jeans, a dark top, and sneakers. "This is a good night for what we are doing," she said, emerging from under the hem. She rolled the caftan into a ball and threw it into the car. "An ascending full moon is a good time for restless souls."

Quickly, Sandy introduced me to the other members of the group: Mitch, Carmine's somber female assistant who was strapped down with equipment—a video camera, tape recorder, and a couple of other machines I couldn't identify; Amber and Suellen, both barely out of their teens, chattering between themselves excitedly; and the lone male, Dave, whom I recognized but couldn't place. Amber, Suellen, and Dave, Carmine explained, were aspiring paranormal investigators, on this trip to gain experience.

"Hey!" Dave's face lit up in recognition. "Remember me from the legit tour? That lady—Beth Ann—took us around?"

Ah, yes: the annoying middle-aged man who had bragged about sneaking into Danvers with ghost hunters. I smiled politely, but without encouragement.

"This is my first time with Carmine's group. She's supposed to be the best," he said in an aside to me. "Are you in training to join the team, too?"

"No. I'm just along for the ride."

Dave fell into step with me as we followed Sandy and Carmine across the parking lot. "Carmine isn't your average ghost hunter. A paranormal investigator takes pictures and makes thermal readings and EMF readings—that's electromagnetic field activity. It's all very scientific." He thrust a small dark box toward me. "This is a thermal scanner. I'm using it for the first time tonight."

"Oh," I said with mild interest, and he proceeded to demonstrate how the knobs and dials worked.

"This meter indicates a change in temperature. A drop can mean there's a presence, you see?"

"Oh, yes," I said, then edged away to join Sandy and Carmine who were drawing everybody together on a patch of grass next to the street.

Carmine spoke first. "I have not visited this place before. Those who work with me know I like to visit during the day to make baseline readings, but under the circumstances it was not possible." She giggled, and I chimed in with polite laughter alongside the others, not sure where the humor lay.

"However," she continued, using her long graceful fingers to accentuate her words, "I know what we might find. In this place horrible things happened to people. They were given shocks, they had lobotomies, their bodies were autopsied for research, there was abuse, neglect." Sandy made a guttural sound and Carmine acknowledged her with a bob of her head and a wave. "You were one of the lucky ones who called this place home. It was refuge for you. Mitch, you give that girl a hug!" Mitch, who was standing next to Sandy, dutifully put an arm around her, crushing her against the contraptions strapped across her body.

Carmine shook her head and wagged a finger back and forth. "But it wasn't so for others. Many here suffered. From dementia, alcoholism, drug addiction. There cannot help but be much bad energy from tortured souls in a place like this, and we will feel those negative vibrations." There were murmurings among the group, and Carmine raised her voice. "Yes, we will feel that because the brain's electromagnetic field survives physical death.

"But," she held up her long thin arm with a finger pointing skyward, "because we are professional we will not rely only on our feelings. Mitch will be taking readings on the EMF detector, which will tell us when there is a spirit near." I looked over at the detector hanging by a strap around Mitch's neck. Carmine continued, "And Dave will take readings." Dave smiled, holding up his nifty machine with pride. "Then we film and record sounds in areas that show activity, for analyzing afterward. Sometimes what we can't detect with our eyes or ears, we will see or hear after on film or tape.

"Suellen and Amber, you have your cameras?" They nodded, blond ponytails bobbing in unison. "Good. Don't waste efforts until we are inside, okay?" Again they nodded. "Okay. Now, we listen to Sandy because she is the one who gets us in, right?" Carmine smiled at Sandy, who drew her short plump body up a little taller.

"Listen up." Sandy raised a hand for attention. "We got to be careful, you know? There's security on patrol twenty-four/seven? Over a hundred people been arrested the past four years, meaning they had to go to court, pay fines and court fees, or spend three months in jail." She paused to let this sink in.

I understood now why Carmine hadn't chanced casing the joint earlier in the day. I *didn't* understand why I was doing this. Was getting inside this place worth the risk? Did I really need to see where a girl who bore no relation to me spent her last few months over a century ago? If I got caught, how would I justify my arrest to Gus? And, if all that wasn't enough deterrence, how would I like a criminal record?

"We're going to follow along the edge of the road a little ways?" Sandy was saying. "Then, we go up through the field? Soon's we start down that road, though, everybody's got to be real quiet? No whispers, no stepping on sticks, nothing? And no flashlights 'til I say so. If you hear a car, hide or duck down. Got that?"

We all nodded, a few voicing assents.

"Okay then, let's go." This was my last chance to back out. Instead, I followed the others across the street. When we turned onto the dirt road that led to the hospital, Sandy tapped a finger to her mouth and we fell silent. I stayed close behind her and Carmine, thinking I'd have the advantage of reacting quickly if either gave warning. Along the edge of the road, there was tall grass and brush into which I planned to dive, thorns or not, if the need arose.

Overhead branches allowed only a filtering of moonlight, so we moved with slow caution, passing a few houses set back from the road. Most were dark, but a couple still had lights on. The rush of Route One traffic dulled as we moved further from it. Soon there were no more houses, and it became darker.

By now, my eyes had adjusted and I could see pretty well. I'd relaxed enough to make comparisons between our leaders: Carmine's tall sleek silhouette to Sandy's short squat one; Sandy's purposeful, almost military gait to Carmine's smooth athletic strides. I was wondering what Carmine did for a day job when Sandy touched Carmine's arm and they suddenly veered off the road. Without hesitation, the rest of us followed.

We waded through several yards of high grass before coming out onto a path that led uphill through trees, several of which had what looked like "No Trespassing" signs nailed on them. Dave grunted, then one of the younger girls—Amber, I think— whispered something to the other one. Sandy turned around. We couldn't see her face in the dark, but we knew it wore a stern expression. There were no more sounds. Shortly after that, the path forked, and we went left.

Because it was dark and I was concentrating on where I stepped on the uneven path, I lost all sense of direction. It seemed to me that this new path wound around the hill, not straight up. At one point, I thought we walked by one of the cemeteries, but I couldn't see clearly enough to tell. We passed an old mattress, whitewashed by the moon, looking like some shipwrecked raft in a sea of weeds.

Then the path disappeared. Sandy ducked down in the grass and drew us together. Without speaking she pointed the way, and we all froze, crouched in the weeds, faces turned uphill to the crest where the moon, which had been playing peek-a-boo with the clouds, had emerged full and bright, backlighting the Kirkbride building, showcasing its gables, peaks, and angles to full advantage. It was an eerie sight.

"Whoa," Amber whispered.

"Shhh!" Sandy hissed.

Hunching low, we circled around the side of the hill, away from the front of the building, aware that there was little to hide us now. So far we'd seen no security guards or policemen. I hoped that Sandy was as good as her boast, and that she would deliver us into, and especially out of, the building safely.

At the back of one of the wings we bent down and darted single file across an open space to the shadowed wall of the Kirkbride, then alongside it until halted by Sandy. We watched as she shoved through some low bushes, got down on her hands and knees, and pushed against a board, which groaned on resistant nails before obliging, opening inward eight or so inches. Still on all fours, Sandy turned around and squeezed herself backward through the space. When just her upper body was protruding, she paused. "There's a table below. Feel for it with your feet," she instructed in a low voice just before her head and shoulders disappeared into a black abyss.

Carmine went next. She rolled over onto her stomach and slid lithely, feet first, through the opening. The rest of us followed, one by one, some with more grace than others. I was last, antsy while I waited, sure the strong arm of the law was about to clamp onto my shoulder. I sat and stuck my legs through what I now saw was a casement window, the glass removed from its frame and replaced by a plywood covering. I turned over onto my front, stretched one tentative leg down and found the table with the ball of my foot. It felt solid so I shifted my weight onto it and pulled the rest of my body through. Sandy instructed me to push the window covering back into place to hide our entry. Then I jumped down to join the others.

"Now we can use our flashlights," Sandy said, and at once six circles of light punctured the dark. "The windows are boarded up, so nobody can see from outside, but we need to be quiet, okay? Don't step on anything that makes sounds."

We murmured in agreement. From behind, I heard the sound of fingers moving on plastic knobs—Dave fussing with his machine. "Not yet," Carmine whispered, her staccato t's hanging in the air. "Wait to feel something."

We moved down a hallway, stepping over and around broken plaster that had fallen from walls and ceiling. I concentrated on placing my feet within the circle of my flashlight, trying not to think of what might lie ahead. We passed tunnels, some sealed by concrete, but most gaping black holes that were better not considered while scurrying by.

"Down there's the shock treatment room?" Sandy said softly as we passed one of these dark tunnels. "They'd strap you to a slab, still handcuffed to an attendant, put you out, you know, and turn on the juice? You'd watch it happening to the others—convulsing and all—until it was your turn."

"Did you have shock treatments?" I asked, but Sandy had moved ahead. Shock therapy hadn't been around at the turn of the century; it was one thing, at least, Marguerite Miller hadn't been subjected to.

Next to me, Dave said, "Do you feel that? I thought I felt a cold spot."

We followed Sandy up a set of stairs, arriving on a landing at the bottom of another stairwell, this one wide and elegantly paneled in mahogany. Sandy continued upward, moving quickly despite her weight and short legs. I was winded by the time we halted, two flights up.

"Wards is on this floor," she said as we huddled together in the middle of the hallway. "There's windows up ahead with boards off so we can see better up here? 'Course, that also means light can get out, so keep flashlights down. We don't want anybody outside getting suspicious, you know?" Turning, she added over her shoulder, "The hallway is safe but don't go into the rooms."

With the improved lighting and the flooring underfoot relatively clear of debris, I could raise my eyes and take in my surroundings. The sections of the plaster walls that weren't water-stained were crumbling or shedding huge reptilian-like patches of paint. At the intersection of the hallways sat an old metal desk, its vinyl padded chair pushed back as if the occupant had just gotten up to see about something on one of the wards and would return shortly. Here, water had buckled the tile and it was uneven under my feet. I pivoted in all four directions, noting tall windows at the ends of each corridor that had once allowed sunlight to flood in from all angles, a few of which now admitted the meager light that guided us. Sandy skirted the furniture and led us to the other side, to another ward.

I was picturing Marguerite Miller of the Boston picture— dark pinned-up hair and long white dress—here in the hallway, wondering if she'd lived on this floor, when Sandy abruptly turned to the left. She slipped through a door that stood ajar, and the rest of us followed. Then Suellen, who was the first behind Sandy, shrieked, and Carmine, next in line, gave a soft cry and crossed herself. I peered around her and gasped, prickles creeping down my arms.

A sliver of moonlight sliced through a window, falling on an upholstered chair where sat a person, back to us, wearing a preposterous coned hat on his head.

Chapter Fifteen

"Shhh! It's okay," Sandy reassured us. "I shoulda warned you. It's been here a while. Somebody found old patient clothing, is all."

As we came closer, we saw that it had been staged. A chair had been pulled into the middle of the room, and a dummy created out of clothing with a stuffed paper bag for a head—gaping eye sockets and mouth colored in with magic marker—and a dunce hat stuck atop.

"Somebody's idea of a joke," Sandy said. But the sight had put us on edge. Amber giggled nervously and we gave the display wide berth. I recognized the room from a picture on the urban explorer's website. It held a freestanding footed bathtub in an alcove, four lidless toilets along one wall, and, lining the opposite wall, a row of porcelain sinks filled with sheets of paint that had peeled off the wall above.

"One of the bathrooms," Sandy said needlessly. We kept a wary eye on the realistic figure in the chair as we sidled back around it and out to the hallway.

Most rooms we peeked into were empty of furniture, but here and there we came upon relics that reminded us of those who had once resided here: floral curtains hanging in a window; an Easter-type basket on the floor; a wheeled stretcher shoved at an angle against the wall, its leather restraining straps hanging unbuckled off the sides. We passed a stairwell that was wire-caged, then another stairway that was open, which we descended. At one point, Carmine and Mitch stopped to confer with each other, but said nothing to the rest of us, and Sandy led on.

We entered an auditorium with rows and rows of folding chairs facing an empty stage. Here, no outside light aided us, and we relied on flashlights, crisscrossing the widespread area with our beams, highlighting lively murals of graffiti—a reminder of a more recent generation who frequented the building—that covered every inch of wall from floor to as high as an artistic hand could reach.

Back in a hallway, now disoriented, I followed in blind faith. I no longer had any idea where in this huge building we were, much less how to exit it. We entered a patient's room still decorated with molding pictures cut from magazines and taped to the walls, which I also remembered seeing on the urban explorer's website. Looking closely, I saw the clippings were of celebrities: sports and movie stars from fifty-odd years ago. How did Marguerite decorate her room, if she was allowed? With pictures of her family?

We continued on. Before an open doorway, Sandy stopped. "Examination room," she said in a tight dull tone, and moved past. Carmine and Mitch followed her, but Amber, Suellen, and I stepped inside, with Dave behind us. It was a small room with no furnishings except a large industrial-looking light that hung from the middle of the ceiling. Here, damage was minimal. There was no noticeable peeling or crumbling or buckling, which, for some reason, made it uncannier than the rooms we'd seen thus far. Maybe because it was easier to visualize it being used: an examining table centered below the light; the fear a patient—Marguerite? Sandy?—lying on it might have.

"I think I feel something," Dave said. For a moment I thought I did also. Then I shook it off, sure I was being unduly influenced by the live beings around me.

A soft call drew us out of the examination room before Dave had a chance to fiddle with his dials. We caught up with the others about twenty feet down the hall, facing a closed door, Carmine and Sandy hunched over one of the machines that Mitch held.

"Some electromagnetic activity here." Mitch held her EMF detector closer to the door. We squeezed around to watch the needle move upward to three, four, then hover around five before dipping back down. Carmine tried the doorknob, but found it locked. She took out her camera and methodically filmed first the door, then the hallway in both directions. I shivered—from damp and cold or from something else?

"I felt something!" Dave had turned his machine on and was fumbling with the dials. Suellen and Amber began clicking pictures on their digital cameras, shooting the same area Carmine had just filmed. I wondered if it was overkill, but decided I had no idea what anyone was doing anyway. Sandy and I waited idly while the others scurried around us. After a few moments, when Mitch's detector needle lay still, Dave still hadn't detected any thermal change, and everyone had thoroughly documented the space, they moved away, and I went close to inspect the door that had caused so much excitement. It was painted blue; though faded, it clearly had once been vibrant, standing out among the other bland colors on this floor.

"Look!" Amber said, pointing to the middle of the door. On a strip of masking tape, its edges dried out and stiff with age, were scrawled two words in faded ink.

"What does it say?" Suellen asked.

Amber craned her neck and squinted. "I think it's a name."

I brought my flashlight beam closer to it and peered at the barely legible writing. "Jerry, I think. Yeah, that's a J. 'Jerry Smith' or 'South,' or something like that."

"I wonder why he had a private room." Suellen took another

shot of the door.

"Maybe that's why." I trained my flashlight about a foot above the masking tape. In faint block lettering were stenciled the words, "Extreme Precautions."

"Oh," Amber said quietly, then, "poor Jerry."

"Hey, look." Dave pushed his way between Suellen and me. "The jamb is broken." He rammed his shoulder against the blue door and it gave way about six inches, along with the entire jamb, before blockage on the other side halted it. Dave stuck his flashlight through the gap. Intrigued, the four of us crowded in to look. The walls were a dismal green, the floor a dirty gray or tan, but the space beyond whatever blocked the door was devoid of everything, even trash. The air that exited the room was clammy and foul.

"Phew!" Amber backed away. "Smells like something died in there!"

"So, Dave," I said, "is anything registering on your thermal scanner now?"

"Oh, I forgot to look!" The beam from his flashlight danced around, bouncing off walls, floor, and ceiling, as he fidgeted with his machine. I offered to hold the flashlight for him, but he declined. A moment later he announced in disappointment, "Nothing."

"We better catch up with the others," Amber said. Sandy, Carmine, and Mitch had gone on and were well ahead of us now, so we hurried after them.

"Do you hear that?" Dave's call halted us. We turned to see that he hadn't moved away from the blue door. He stood wide-eyed, mouth open, his scanner forgotten. "Do you hear it?"

"What?" Suellen asked.

"There's mumbling; they're saying something," he insisted. "Can't you hear them?" He put both hands to his ears, the machine dangling from its strap around his neck.

From the other end of the hall, Mitch turned and rushed back, Carmine and Sandy following. Holding up a small microphone, Mitch walked slowly around Dave who was now frozen in fear. Meanwhile, Carmine began filming with lights, and Suellen snapped nervous random pictures with her digital camera: Flash! Flash! She didn't appear to be focusing on anything. Amber had retreated backward down the hall, her fists clenched at her mouth, her camera forgotten.

I stood rooted in the middle of the hall, wanting desperately to leave, but not knowing where to go. There was a prickling at the back of my neck, likely brought on by the physical anxiety around me, but undeniable all the same. And then, suddenly, I did feel something—a strong thick feeling of dread, of sadness weighing down on me. With it came an eerie sensation that there were beings just outside of my vision; that if I peered hard into the dark I would see them.

I don't disbelieve those who claim to have seen ghosts, but I'm not a believer myself, and if there ever was a time I would choose to become a believer, it was not at that moment. When Amber shrieked, I'd had enough. Dave took off down the hall the way we'd come, and I followed him.

Amber was beside me as we hit the stairwell, and I heard the others in back of her. No care given now to restraint, we thundered down the steps like a herd of heavy beasts. I prayed I wouldn't trip and get trampled to death. At the landing we were brought up short behind Dave, who blocked the way. Over his shoulder I saw something that frightened me even more than the experience I'd just had. People—real live people—at the end of the hallway. There may or may not have been ghosts upstairs, but there were definitely beings in the flesh down here, with flashlights and badges that glinted in the dark, and they were out to arrest us.

"Shit! Guards!" Dave did an about-face. Then Sandy, who'd

brought up the rear, took back the leadership. She beckoned for us to follow, and we fell in line behind her, depending on her to be our savior. It was like the action scene in a B movie with the guards behind yelling, "Stop!" and all of us sprinting down hallways. I had the bizarre proud thought that I must be in pretty good shape to be outdistancing my pursuers.

Sandy pulled open a door and we entered a wire-caged staircase littered ankle deep with reams of eight and a half by eleven copy-sized sheets of paper. Our descent was muffled and slowed as we shuffled through the paper as if it were piles of leaves, slipping on it, kicking it aside.

On the third flight down, I looked up to see if we were still being chased. Nobody was in the stairwell, but there was a sight that gave me pause: a large crude drawing of three angels on one wall. Black spray paint had outlined circles for heads, ovals for bodies, small wings protruding from their backs, and haloes above. The angels were ascending the stairs, faces tilted upward, with dots for eyes and inverted U's for mouths. Poor sad angels climbing. To heaven?

A shout, a scuffle of feet, and two guards above hit the stairs to descend. I exited the door at the bottom and found myself in the basement, where I recognized a hallway we'd been in before, but didn't see or hear where the others had gone. Crap! Not only was I being chased by guards—and probably also police at this point—I was now lost from my group.

Thinking that Sandy must be leading us back to the window where we'd entered, I ran in that direction. I was one hallway away from our entry point, priding myself on being able to retrace my steps, when I sensed movement up ahead. Instinct told me it wasn't anyone from our group, so I ducked into one of the tunnels we'd passed earlier, one that disappeared into the inky underground.

Much as I didn't relish the thought of following a pitch-black tunnel under a deserted, potentially haunted insane asylum in the dead of the night, I plunged downward. In the close quarters my breathing was audible. When the dark swallowed me up I paused, listened for sounds behind, heard none, then dared to turn on my flashlight. It illuminated about ten feet ahead, which was a small comfort, and I took in my surroundings. The plaster on the walls and ceiling of the tunnel was buckled and mildewed. Underfoot, the cement flooring was littered with broken pieces of plaster and other indiscriminate rubble, but was otherwise pretty clear, which gave me hope that it led somewhere. About fifteen feet further, however, it bisected another tunnel. I decided to stay on the original path, but within a short distance the rubble became larger, more difficult to navigate, before suddenly ending in a dirt wall.

With a cry of frustration, I whirled around and scrabbled back over chunks of cement that scraped my hands and turned an ankle. What if all of these tunnels ended? What if I got lost down here? A verse of "Charlie on the MTA" played in my head and I restrained a hysterical impulse to laugh. When I regained the tunnel crossroads, I paused, took some deep breaths, and reined in the panic. I took stock of my choices: return the way I'd come, down the tunnel the opposite way back to an open area where I'd probably run into a guard, or push on, hoping to exit somewhere without getting arrested.

I had read that some tunnels ran between the buildings so I decided to continue on, trusting that I would eventually come up out of this nightmare. I shined my flashlight both ways. To the left looked decidedly clearer—more traveled, I wanted to think—so I chose it.

Not far down, I saw a door. Crying out in relief, I fell upon the knob and twisted it. Locked. I ran on, and another door appeared. Again I attacked the knob, and again that knob didn't give. I banged on the door in sudden panic, no longer caring who might be on the other side. Indeed, at this point had an angry policeman opened that door I'd have kissed him before holding out my wrists for the handcuffs. But nobody opened the door, and I ran on, dry sobbing, sucking in stale dusty air, desperation to get above ground now driving me more than escape from authorities.

I tried to remember what Sandy had told us about the tunnels. One, I recalled her saying, led to the shock treatment room. Great: something else to stimulate my already overactive imagination. Two more times I found doors that were locked, but now I saw a pattern: one came every certain number of yards. This, in addition to the fact that the tunnel continued to be somewhat clear of debris, gave me hope that it had been traveled regularly. Which meant it must lead somewhere. Which meant one of these doors had to open.

As soon as I calmed a little, I saw a door that was cracked open a few inches. In joy, I ran to it and burst through, exiting the hated tunnel, but entering an equally black space. Weak with a mixture of expended effort and relief, I leaned against a wall and shined my light around. I was in the basement of a different building, one that was in rougher shape than the Kirkbride, judging from the wreckage and trash.

Wasting no time, I scrambled over mounds of fallen plaster, broken chairs, and old mattresses, looking for an exit. When I came to a set of unsteady stairs, I took them, ascending along the outside edge of each tread where it looked the most secure, holding tight to the rail in case the wood underfoot gave way.

Gradually, I realized that I was breathing fresh air, which had to be coming from open or broken windows or doors. The gloom receded as I climbed, bypassing the first floor, which was blocked with wreckage, and continuing up to the second floor, where I saw light at the end of a hallway. Even though this floor was the least trashed of the three, and looked pretty stable, I played it safe and stayed close to the wall as I headed toward the light. Then a shadow separated itself from the wall just ahead of me, and I let loose a sharp cry.

"Shhh!"

The shrill directive was music to my ears. I stumbled forward into Sandy's arms.

"God, girl!" she whispered, pushing me off of her. "Where you been? We been waiting for you? Thought you were right behind us?"

"I . . ." I glanced back at the way I'd just come.

"You went through the tunnels?" Carmine asked in awe, and I noticed then that the rest of the group waited in the shadows.

"Wow! That musta been scary," Dave said.

"Isn't that how you guys got here?"

"No way . . . guards by the window we entered . . . upstairs . . . down there . . . kept looking for you . . ." Five excited voices tried to answer at once.

"Quiet!" Sandy said. "Never mind that now. We got to figure a way out of here!" She motioned for us to stay put, then picked her way down the hall through the rubble, testing each step with the ball of her foot before shifting weight onto it. At the end of the hall, she peeked out a broken window, then turned and came back in the same fashion. "It's clear, but follow me closely, okay?"

We crept along in a line behind her, keeping to the wall. Once, I flashed my light into a room we passed and saw that its entire floor was gone, caved into the room below it. A wrong step and one could potentially fall two stories. At the end, Sandy sidled past the window, pointing down in warning at broken glass on the floor, and then pushed open the emergency exit door. After a quick survey, she started down a rusty iron fire escape, and the rest of us followed. In retrospect, I should have worried if the metal was strong enough to hold our combined weight, but at that point I had implicit faith in Sandy's leadership and would have followed her through a raging fire.

Once on the ground, Sandy again scoped out our surroundings. After determining that all activity was on the other side of the building, she led us across an open area into the field. We came down the hill on a different side, which meant we had to circle around to meet up with the road. But we got out of there, and I promised whatever spirit, heavenly or not, that allowed me to emerge unscathed and unshackled, that I would never do such a foolish thing again.

Grand Hotel of the Atlantic
June Twenty-Third, 1901

Just before dawn Marguerite slips through a side door into the hotel, tiptoes down deserted hallways, and gains her room without encountering another person. Unable to sleep and still fully dressed, she rests on her bed until the sun rises. She has washed, changed clothes, straightened the mussed but still made bed, and is waiting when Alice knocks on her door to let her know that her father has arrived, and that she is to meet him for breakfast in half an hour.

Archibald Miller is seated alone at a small table by the window when she enters the dining room. In the moment before he notices her, Marguerite takes stock of her father as if he were a stranger. He is an attractive middle-aged man who looks trim in a three-piece suit. There is no gray in his thick brown hair or in his mustache; the only telltale signs of age are fine lines at the corners of his eyes and his mouth, evidence of the frequent smiles he bestows on patients. He is standing when she reaches the table and gives her a dry kiss on the cheek.

"You look very pretty today." He is watching her closely. Does he see how different she is from the Marguerite of a week ago?

"Thank you," she murmurs. She sits opposite him and busies herself with opening her napkin and placing it in her lap. "How are you, Papa? And Mama and Melinda?"

"We are all well and busy," he answers in his robust doctor-to-

patient voice. "*This new strain of influenza kept me running house to house all last week but it finally appears to be abating. Your mother has begun baking for the annual church fair.*"

"*Oh, I'd forgotten about the fair,*" *Marguerite says with some guilt.* "*I've always helped Mama with the baking.*"

"*She's managing fine.*" *His fingers lift from the table in a dismissive gesture.* "*You know how your mother thrives on activity. But Melinda . . .*" *He sighs as he shakes out the napkin and drapes it across his lap.* "*She's talking about not returning to the Girls Lyceum in the fall. She wishes to complete her studies at home with a tutor.*" *He indicates the pot between them.* "*Tea?*"

"*Yes, please.*" *Marguerite holds her cup and saucer as he pours, recalling early morning breakfasts alone with her father, the two of them sharing a pot of tea as they discussed matters of the world as comfortably as matters of the family. She thinks that she will be able to tell him about her change of heart concerning Timothy, about her desire to be independent.*

"*Don't worry, Papa,*" *she says now.* "*Melinda is fretting about her teacher for next year. If she'd just give her a chance, she'll find Miss Sim strict but fair. I'll talk to her again about it.*"

"*That should do it—a little sisterly advice.*" *Her father smiles.* "*Now, how about some breakfast?*"

As they eat, Marguerite waits for him to bring up the reason for his visit, the topic that hangs heavy and silent in the air between them. Finally, he lays fork and knife across his plate, and leans back in his chair. "*Alice is concerned about you,*" *he begins.*

Marguerite pushes away her plate with its half-eaten eggs, eager to have the subject broached. "*Oh, Papa,*" *she says with feeling,* "*I've not been myself lately. Or rather, I've been more myself, perhaps.*"

"*Are you unwell?*" *Concern is on his face.*

"*No. I feel fine. What I'm trying to say,*" *she proceeds with caution,* "*is that I've changed, and I'm afraid Alice has had to bear the brunt of my restlessness.*"

"What do you mean?" He tucks his napkin under the lip of his plate and signals the waiter.

"I don't know exactly," she begins. "It means I want things I didn't want before and I don't want things that I wanted before."

"It sounds as if you're growing up."

"Yes, Papa," Marguerite says, pleased with his answer. "I think that is it."

"That's perfectly normal, considering your upcoming wedding." He smiles his reassurance, slipping a hand into his jacket pocket to finger his pipe. "You must watch your actions, however, for they sometimes upset Alice."

"I didn't mean to upset her."

"She thinks you have been leaving your room at night." His eyes crinkle in amusement and Marguerite realizes that he is skeptical of Alice's allegation. Maybe if she denies it, her father will believe her over Alice. But then she thinks of the desk clerk who saw her leave and Ernest Carter who insinuated that he knew about Emil. It is best to be honest, at least partially.

"That's true, Papa. I go walking because I haven't been sleeping well." Her eyes shift to her lap as she tells the half-lie.

Her father regards her over the cup of tea at his lips. "It would have been more prudent to read in your room if you couldn't sleep."

"Yes, Papa." Then because she cannot stand to delay it any longer, Marguerite looks directly at her father and says, "I have decided that I cannot marry Timothy."

At first his expression is unreadable. Not shocked as she had expected, but not compassionate as she had dared hope. It's almost as if he anticipated her announcement. As he reaches over to pat her hand, though, his eyes soften. "It's natural to have some anxiousness."

"It's not that, Papa. I don't feel toward him as a wife should feel toward her husband."

"But Timothy and you are good friends. Surely that—"

"No." She jerks away her hand. "I cannot marry him."

Her father stiffens and draws back. "Well," he says, his voice even, the heartiness gone, "perhaps you can tell me what calamitous event has caused this sudden change of mind."

"There was no event, and it isn't sudden. I've been reconsidering for some time."

"What is 'some time'? A week? Two weeks?"

"Yes," she says. Then, "No. I mean longer than that."

Her father's voice is stern. "Marguerite, you cannot run away from important decisions just because they are difficult to make."

"I am not running away from this decision," she says. "I am making the decision not to marry Timothy." She has never before spoken in this manner to her father and her eyes drop to her lap, knowing she has overstepped her bounds. In the tense silence that follows, the waiter comes and deftly removes the remaining china and silver from the table.

"It is too late," her father says when he is gone. "You've given your word."

"Timothy would release me from my promise if . . . I asked him to. I thought maybe I could stay here . . ." She hears her voice take on a tentative edge.

"Here? What do you mean, here?"

"In Portsmouth. If I had some time to myself, maybe later—" What is she about to say? That she might some day reconsider marrying Timothy? It is difficult not to say things just to appease Papa.

"That was what this past week and a half was for—to give you time to yourself," her father says with a trace of exasperation.

Marguerite twists the napkin in her lap. Now is when she must come out with what she really means to say. She summons up the vestiges of her courage and says quickly, "Papa, I was thinking that maybe I could take a position as a tutor or a governess." She watches her father's mouth tighten. "Perhaps here, in Portsmouth."

"Have you been offered such a position?"

"No. I have only thought of it today."

He is silent for a moment. Then he exclaims, "Pah!" and abruptly pushes his chair away from the table, turning it at an angle as if he can no longer stand to face her. "You are not being sensible, Marguerite. You will come back to Boston."

"But, Papa—"

"No, Marguerite. I have been too lenient with you. I have allowed you to spend hours locked up in your room reading and writing poetry and that has not been good. You have become too fanciful in your ideas." He looks at her as if something has just occurred to him. "Is there another reason you wish to stay in Portsmouth? Does it have to do with a friendship you have developed here?"

"No!"

"Do you meet someone when you go out on your walks at night?" His gaze is hard.

She feels her face color. If she mentions Emil, she will have to be prepared to tell of his background and she cannot do that. Furthermore, her father will want to know where she met him, who introduced them, if he is a guest here at the hotel, and why Alice hasn't met him. Earlier thoughts of confiding in her father suddenly seem impossible. "No, of course not," she says, but the hesitation has cost her her father's trust.

"Marguerite, you have had little experience in life." His voice sounds weary, as if explaining something repeatedly to a dense child. "There are many dangers in the world at large, and people who would take advantage of your innocence in order to benefit themselves. I shouldn't have allowed you to come here on your own."

"No, Papa! It isn't like that, really it isn't."

"I will listen to no more nonsense," he says. "You will leave with us first thing tomorrow. In the meantime, you will apologize to Timothy for ignoring his letters, and you will say nothing to him about breaking off the engagement." He holds up a hand to stop her protest. "If, after enough time has passed for you to think this thing out properly, *you are still unwilling to proceed with the marriage, then it will be your decision to make."*

"How long is enough time?"

"I should think three months," he says after a short consideration. "If by November you still feel this way, you may call off the engagement." He sighs, and then says, "The Farleys are good friends and your mother and I think of Timothy as a son. It would be a great disappointment if you did not marry, but the decision will be yours in the end, Marguerite, for it is your future at stake here." He is fingering his pipe again. The conversation is at an end. "Do you understand?"

"Yes, Papa." She understands that to do what is proper, to protect her reputation, and consequently the family's, is foremost in her father's mind. Her happiness is secondary, ready to be sacrificed to ensure that social mores are followed. At least she was spared having to explain about Emil. Instead of feeling relieved, however, it makes her angrier.

"You must smooth things out with Timothy." Her father rises from his chair, his gaze averted from her face and the indignation it wears. He is relishing his after-breakfast smoke, thinking that he has settled things with his wayward daughter.

"Yes, Papa," She will talk with Timothy, but will not return home to Boston. She rises and, turning her back on him, proceeds down the middle aisle of the restaurant, past the now-occupied tables. Halfway up the stairs, she pauses and watches her father enter the smoking parlor. Then she turns and comes back down into the lobby. She easily blends into the fray of milling guests who chat in high octaves about the day's itinerary as they await partners with whom to play golf or tennis or embark upon excursions to Portsmouth. No mind is paid to the young woman as she weaves through them and exits the hotel.

Skipping down the verandah stairs, Marguerite is almost gleeful with a decision that now seems simple and clear to her: Tonight she will be freed of her father's expectations. Tonight she will leave with Emil. It will need careful planning, though. She crosses the lawn to the gazebo where she can sit undisturbed for the time it will take to figure out the details.

It is easy to act repentant. Marguerite seeks out Timothy, finding him in the lobby. She apologizes for her inattentiveness in not responding to his letters. He is sulky at first but easily won over. While she tells no untruths, Marguerite doesn't correct his impression that all is as before, that the engagement is still intact, that there was never reason for things to be other than they were. She accepts his invitation for a carriage ride into Portsmouth and is in high spirits the whole time. In fact, she has to repress some of the excitement that bubbles up inside her, thinking at this time tomorrow she will be gone. Thinking at this time tomorrow she will be with Emil.

They walk through town, stopping for lunch at a restaurant close to the harbor. Afterward, they stroll through the waterfront park where Marguerite first met Emil, along the path she walked with Emil, past the spot she took off her shoes and Emil helped her down onto the sand. She recalls that night: the mist casting magic on the scene, the briny smell of the water, the sensation of her feet sinking into the cold wet sand, Emil's touch. Thinking about it, her heart quickens and her face warms. She steals a sideways look at Timothy, who notices nothing and continues to talk. When they enter the formal gardens, beyond the places that remind her of Emil, Marguerite finds it easier to pay attention to Timothy.

"We passed some beggars on the way here last night," he says. "The man and woman were ragged and the children, filthy. I'm surprised a resort area like this would allow such riffraff around."

"They were begging in the street?"

"Not at the time." He tears a leaf from a hydrangea bush and twirls its stem between his finger and thumb. "They were heading toward town, so I assumed that's what their intention was. They were

obviously homeless, carrying bags with them."

"They could be going to seek jobs or going to visit family or moving to a new place. You shouldn't judge people by the way they look, Timothy."

He drops the leaf and gives her a tolerant smile. With his wavy dark hair neatly combed and oiled, his tanned face that speaks of leisurely weekends at his family's cottage in Gloucester, and his impeccable stylish suit, Timothy is very handsome. But he has become complacent. How different Emil is, compassionate and knowledgeable in ways that Timothy is not, appreciative of simple things, and nonjudgmental about people.

"Don't be condescending," she says, but her tone is mild, tempered by the reminder of Emil, and of her plans.

When they return to the hotel, she claims fatigue and leaves Timothy. She has the rest of the afternoon to herself for Alice isn't speaking to her and Father is giving her time and space in which to make things right with Timothy. She moves about her room, calm now, resolved in her decision to leave. She touches her items, deciding which are most important to her, which she will want in her new life. Her new life: What will it be like? What sights will she see? Who will she meet? Where will she live? That she cannot know the answers to these questions heightens the excitement.

Now, what to take? Everything must fit into one bag so she must decide carefully. Her books and her journal will come, of course, and her jewelry, brushes, and lotions. Clothes are the last consideration; when she thinks about it, she's never cared much for the fussiness of fashion, so it will be a relief to travel with only a few practical dresses. After some deliberation, however, she decides to take one special item: a sheer mauve tea dress. She chooses accessories to go with it, and packs them in the top of the bag. It is a shame to fold the dress, but there is no other way.

After that, it is merely a matter of waiting. Dinner passes uneventfully. Timothy, self-important because he thinks he has straightened things out with her, talks about his work most of the night, making inferences to his bright future with his father's business, several times including Marguerite ("We will buy a home close to the company") or even speaking for her ("Marguerite will continue her charity work with the hospital").

And Father, believing that all has been resolved between them, and that his daughter has come to her senses, nods in encouragement of Timothy. Marguerite smiles, thinking that they are both stupid for assuming so much about her while expecting so little from her. She smiles through the aperitifs, the fruit salad, roast duck, and, finally, ice cream with fresh strawberries. As they rise, she even kisses each of the men on the cheek as they leave for the smoking parlor. She has a headache, she tells them, and will be retiring early. She makes it clear that she does not want to be disturbed.

In the end, she has no plan for getting the sizable bag out the window, across the porch roof, and down to the ground, so she decides to take only what she can carry in a drawstring purse. She can't picture much of these things in her new life, anyway; even the books do not fit with the vague idea she has of her future (she intends to do things, rather than read and write about them). Besides, her original urge to flee without luggage has become irresistible.

She unpacks the bag and puts everything away, except the sheer dress, lightweight wrap, and matching shoes, which she puts on. Although impractical, the dress seems somehow right for this evening. Into the drawstring purse go only the basic necessities. She picks up the leather-bound journal, her closest confidant these last months. She cannot leave her innermost thoughts behind to be read. It is the last thing she tucks into the purse.

Footfalls in the hallway cause a moment's distress. Has Alice come to check on her? But they pass by her door. Set in motion, she takes the ring off her finger and, after deliberation, hides it where Melinda will be able to find, and then deliver, it to Timothy. One last time, she looks around the room at the belongings she might never see again, at reminders that it will be a long time before she sees her father, mother, or Melinda again.

But she must think only of right now. However the future turns out, it will be dealt with then. She smiles as she reaches up to extinguish the gaslight. Already, her outlook is more like Emil's.

CHAPTER SIXTEEN

Although I remembered no dream clearly, I woke as if coming out from under a dreadful weight: tired, but relieved. It was similar to the feeling I'd had the night before, after finally escaping the tunnel. I was not yet a believer in ghosts, but I couldn't deny the oppressive atmosphere I'd felt inside the buildings at Danvers, and had then relived in my dreams. One can sense tension or sorrow upon entering a room with live people, why can't those sensations linger after the people have left?

I still believed that the state hospitals were constructed at the turn of the century in the best possible interests of their charges. I believed that they were progressive places, which administered care and therapy humanely, and fostered beauty in architecture and gardening, and healthy living in farming. Yet, to be held indefinitely against your will, no matter how pleasant the circumstances, is sad at the least, frustrating and tragic at the worst. The experience of the night before had highlighted this for me. How had Beth Ann put it? *The tragedy of lives plucked from the mainstream and put on hold.* Marguerite had been a patient during an era of social commitment to and moral treatment of the mentally ill; still, it was sad that her brief life should have ended, incarcerated in a hospital for the insane, away from family and friends. What had she done, or what had been done to her, that landed her there?

I lay, looking up at my bedroom ceiling, postponing the impending confrontation with Gus, who had woken up briefly when I got into bed to ask what time it was—two o'clock in the morning—then had fallen back asleep, and was now no doubt waiting downstairs for a full accounting. My musings moved on to Sandy. I'd taken her at her word that Danvers had been her home, her "refuge" as Carmine had put it, but there were clues that her life there hadn't been without trauma. There was her reaction to the examination room—avoidance, possibly fear. Had she just disliked examinations, or had something happened to her in that room? And her knowing comments about shock therapy that told me she'd either experienced or witnessed it.

The Danvers State Hospital of Sandy's years—rundown, overcrowded, understaffed, accused of being abusive and neglectful—was at the opposite spectrum of the State Lunatic Hospital at Danvers of Marguerite's years—a grand, light, and airy model for humane treatment. Yet, Sandy remembered her time there fondly, or said she did. Was it denial? Or were there patients who had truly thrived there, even during the worst of times? Was one woman's hell another woman's heaven? And which—hell or heaven—had it been for Marguerite?

I heaved a sigh, sprang up from the bed, and headed downstairs to face my due.

Gus was at the table, lying in wait behind the sports section of yesterday's *Sunday Globe*. Knowing it would be a waste of time to soft-pedal my actions, I told him straight out that I'd sneaked into Danvers State Hospital with a former resident and a bunch of ghost hunters, and then settled back to wait for the fallout.

"You did what?" He stared at me as if I'd sprouted antlers.

"Guilty of stupidity to the nth degree," I said, beating him to the punch. "I almost got arrested, and I could have gotten injured. I thought about all of that beforehand, and went ahead anyway with brazen disregard of the risks involved."

"Do you realize how dangerous that was?"

"I just said that I did."

"I would have been worried if I'd known that was what you were doing!"

"Which is why I didn't tell you. I would have hated to have you worry."

"And, besides that, it's against the law!" He was almost sputtering.

"Yes, it is and I promise I will never do anything so stupid again."

"Well . . ." I watched his mouth moving, forming several different ways to say what had been said by me already, finally choosing, "At least you're repentant."

"Yes, I'm repentant." I waited a beat, gave him one more chance to get his licks in, then I grinned and blurted out, "But not sorry. What an incredible piece of architecture! They're going to tear it down in a few months and I got to see it!"

He let his mouth drop in exaggerated amazement. "You're incorrigible."

"Do you want to hear about it?"

"I better not, because then I'd have to turn you in."

I continued to grin, remembering the haunting beauty of the Kirkbride combined with the adrenaline rush of doing something forbidden and dangerous. Gus cleared his dishes, and then said something that wrenched me back to Earth. "I start my computer class today, remember?"

"No! I forgot. It's this week, then?"

"Yep." It was his turn to grin. "Have fun with the kids." He gave me a quick kiss and was out the door before I could respond.

Grounded. *Well, okay,* I said to myself, *it's time I got something done around here, anyway.* Housecleaning came to mind, since none had been done in recent history . . . two? Three weeks? Surely, it hadn't been that long! I looked down and determined it was entirely possible that, other than a run-through with a Quick Vac a time or two, the kitchen floor hadn't been touched in weeks. I would mend my slovenly ways and give the house a thorough cleaning, starting with the kitchen. Since the kids had been up late, I could count on them sleeping in.

But first, I decided enough time had passed that I could call Dorothy. Ellen answered and said that while Dorothy was recovering, she still felt woozy. Then I heard Dorothy's insistent voice in the background, and Ellen handed the phone to her.

"I shouldn't have gotten up on that chair," Dorothy lamented, her voice wavering. "I know better than that, but I've done it before and I'm always very careful. That string gets tangled up sometimes and you have to climb up there."

"But it has a loose seat. Nobody should even sit on it until it gets repaired."

"That's the funny thing," she said. "I keep that chair at the other end of the table, by the window, where it doesn't get used. Usually, there's just Ellen and me, and we use the two outside ones. So, when I pulled out a chair to use, I didn't realize it was the broken one until it gave way. It was in the wrong place at the table."

"Maybe it got moved when the floor was mopped."

"Yes, that's probably what happened." Dorothy agreed readily as if she'd thought of it, too. "Rebecca came to clean the other day."

"Well, I put it in the basement, so you won't sit on it by mistake."

"That was a good idea." She sounded tired, the volume of her voice tapering off. I wished her a quick recovery and said I'd visit soon.

I put on water for tea. Then I gave Mayta a ring. Her answering machine picked up. "If you want to hear about the exciting adventure I had last night, call me!" I said after the beep.

I dragged out the vacuum cleaner, but the water was ready, so I made my tea and sat down at the counter, expecting Mayta to call back any minute. I ruminated over what Dorothy had told me about her life. She'd been an only child, and her father had died when she was only five. Dorothy's husband had died relatively young and there had been no children. Then she'd gone to work at the Grand Hotel because she needed money. I wondered about her current financial situation. Other than Social Security, she probably didn't receive much, if any, retirement money. How did she afford Ellen, a full-time companion?

But now, I really needed to start cleaning. I plugged in the vacuum cleaner, attached the wand, and was ready to snap on the switch, when Max appeared, bleary-eyed and pajama-clad, in the doorway. Behind him was Molly. They'd gone to bed at midnight and here they were up by eight o'clock.

"Morning, you guys!" I said with a cheerfulness I didn't feel.

"I want breakfast," Max demanded. "Not cereal. Pancakes."

"Me, too," Molly said. "With blueberries on top."

"We don't have blueberries."

"But I want blueberries," she whined, while he mumbled something darkly.

Great. To bed late, up early, tired and grumpy, Gus gone. It was going to be a long day and I was going to get my come-uppance. "Okay, listen up, guys. I'll make pancakes, but it'll have to be without blueberries. How about sliced bananas on top?"

"Euww!" Max said, wrinkling his nose.

"Okay," Molly said begrudgingly.

"Bananas it is for Molly then, and none for Max. Anyway, it's a beautiful day—sunny, temperature going up into the eighties. Maybe Grandma would like some company out at the beach."

"Go to Grandma's?" Max instantly brightened. "Yay!"

"Okay," cautiously from Molly, reluctant to abandon the mood.

"Good. That's settled." I shoved the vacuum cleaner out of the way and got busy making up a batch of pancakes. While the first round was cooking on the griddle, I called Mayta again and left a second message, saying we wanted to come out. Where was she? After I'd promised the beach, I'd have to deliver.

Molly sliced the bananas, and Max decided that, after all, he'd have some on his pancakes, too. After pouring on syrup, I topped each stack with a dollop of Cool Whip and chocolate jimmies, which was just enough to nudge even Molly into the good mood category. As we were eating (I couldn't resist a second breakfast), Mayta finally called, saying she'd been walking the beach, and urged us to come out right away. The tide was going down and it was good starfish and shell hunting.

"Hurry!" I urged, and we stuffed last bites into our mouths. Dishes were piled in the sink, the vacuum relegated back to the closet, and we dashed for swimsuits and towels.

Mayta was waiting in the driveway with two plastic pails, which she handed to Max and Molly. We rounded the cottage toward the ocean and set off, walking for at least a mile down the beach, culling treasures—as many shells, small pieces of driftwood, and beach glass as would fit in the pails. When the sun was hot and high overhead, we returned and dumped our treasures on the sand in front of Mayta's cottage. Since the water was too cold to go swimming, we waded and chased waves with an occasional quick dip. Then the kids got involved in castle building, using much of their booty for architectural interest, and Mayta and I settled into beach chairs a short distance away.

That's when I told Mayta about my adventure with Sandy and the ghost hunters. She looked at me askance. "You did what?"

I backed up and explained about Sandy. "I got her name from the tour I took of Danvers, remember? The day you were busy with your boyfriend there, the mayor."

The look turned dark; she was not appreciative of my humor.

"Anyway, Sandy is on this committee to restore the Danvers cemetery. She helped me find Marguerite's death certificate." I was trying to establish Sandy's legitimacy.

"You broke into Danvers State?" There was no beating around the bush with Mayta.

"No, nothing like that. It wasn't locked." Not the window we went through, anyway.

"That's still breaking in."

"Yeah, I know, but it was okay." I felt like a teenager justifying herself. "Sandy used to live there, and she knows how to get people in and out safely."

"And what would you have done if you'd gotten arrested?"

"Listen, I know it was foolish, but I don't need another lecture. I've already gone through this with Gus." For a few minutes we watched the kids embellish their respective architectural creations with shells, beach glass, and crab claws. Then, feeling guilty for being snappish, I said, "Why are you so angry, anyway?"

"I'm not angry." She looked down at her toes as she dug them in the sand. "I understand why you did it."

"Oh ho!" I crowed. "That's it! You're envious!"

She gave it about thirty seconds before turning to me, curiosity seeping through every pore in her body. "Yeah, okay, so I am. Tell me about it."

I related the whole experience then, from beginning to end, and even though there was no practical way she could have crawled through windows, climbed over mounds of debris, or run downstairs, I knew she was performing those feats in her mind as I described them, reliving them with me.

"Do you believe in spirits? Not ghosts so much, but leftover feelings in a place where there's been a lot of anguish?"

She thought for a minute. "I think so. I've been places—like a battlefield or a historical building—where I felt something I couldn't explain."

"Well, that was what it was like, only stronger." I sat forward in my beach chair. "Here were these people using ghost detector machines and thermal scanners and taking digital pictures of nothing you could see, and I was thinking they're all pretty strange. Then, suddenly, I was overcome by these strong sensations—grief and other feelings I couldn't identify. Maybe it was just being in that spooky building, thinking about Marguerite being there, that got to me."

"I suppose there's a certain energy that stays around such a place." Mayta was thoughtful. "I don't know how else to explain it. It's hard to feel cheerful in a cemetery, or anything but humble in a grand cathedral. Sure, the architecture has a lot to do with it, but I think sometimes people's feelings over a span of years in particular places make an imprint." We were silent for a while. Then she said, "So, what did you get out of it? Going through all that?"

I thought a minute, and then tried to put it into words. "Probably nothing practical. Just a sense of how awful it must have been for anyone—Marguerite, Sandy, whoever—to have been just dropped off, like being let off at a bus stop, only this stop lets you out of your life. You step off, leaving everything—your rights as a citizen, as a free person—and enter another world where others command you totally and your only hope of rescue is somebody who cares about you from the outside. And the punch line is that you're probably in there because nobody from the outside cares."

CHAPTER SEVENTEEN

Daniel Dean, or rather Shropsgrove, was released from police custody on Tuesday. I got a quick call from Beverly who told me that Daniel's story had checked out. The desk clerk at the motel saw him pull into the parking lot, load up his car, and then leave it idling outside the motel office while he came in to pay the bill. Daniel told him he had to leave, but that his girlfriend would be staying the night. The clerk was sure these events all took place just before nine o'clock, because that was when his shift ended.

"And Claudia was killed some time between nine, when she left the table, and nine-twenty, when we found the body," I said, "so Daniel couldn't have returned to the hotel in time to kill her."

"Right," Beverly said. "He claimed again that Claudia was meeting a woman—he didn't know who."

"Did he say why?"

"Just that Claudia needed to show her something. That's all I have. Oh, and I finally got through to Dorothy. She answered a few questions before pleading fatigue, but I count it as progress."

I explained about Dorothy's accident.

"Well, the ice has been broken. She and I will be buddies before this is over," Beverly said cheerfully. "I sense a story, something beyond a tenuous connection to a murdered girl."

For the next few days, I buckled down into a routine of cleaning, laundry, shuffling the kids around to their play dates and summer activities, and just generally taking up slack while Gus attended his morning computer course. One afternoon at the end of the week the telephone rang.

"I got the records today." The voice was almost a whisper.

"Dorothy?"

"Yes," she said a little louder. "I got Marguerite Miller's hospital records today."

"That was fast. I thought they were going to take at least a week."

"It has been a week," she reminded me.

"Oh, yeah. I guess it has. Have you read them?"

"Only the first pages—some of the history. My head started hurting and I got so tired that I had to stop." She paused to call out to someone, and then said, "Ellen's in the kitchen, so I can talk. Anyway, you were right: Marguerite's father had her admitted for observation because of despondency."

"Despondency?"

"And melancholy. I guess that means she was depressed."

"How was she found? Where was she?"

"I don't know yet. Every time I start to read, my eyes get blurry and I feel weak." She sighed. "There was something about a fishing village in New Hampshire."

"So she stayed in the area," I mused. "New Hampshire's coastline is less than twenty miles long, so she couldn't have gone far when she ran away from the hotel."

"I put the papers in my bedside table. I could look—" Dorothy offered halfheartedly.

"That's all right," I assured her, although I was a little disappointed that she couldn't tell me more important facts. "What's important now is that you rest."

"I'll call you when I finish the file," she said. "Or maybe you'd like to come and read it yourself."

I said I'd like to if she felt up to having company, and when she suggested the following day, I agreed. By the time I said goodbye, Dorothy's voice sounded weak again, which concerned me. She obviously wasn't doing as well as she said she was.

I knew I should wait a few more days before descending on her, but the urge to see those files was strong. The next morning, figuring that I'd surely redeemed myself by now, and that my errant adventure had dimmed in Gus's memory, I said, "Mayta has been wanting to go up to the outlets. Can you keep an eye on the kids for a couple of hours?"

Gus looked up from organizing his tools or whatever he was doing at his workbench in the garage and gave me the evil eye. "You're not going to participate in another break-in, are you?"

"Funny." I forced a chuckle. Okay, so maybe it would be a while longer before the Danvers episode faded from his memory.

I called Mayta and, just to make an honest woman out of myself, asked if she wanted me to go to the outlets with her. It took a moment's thought, but she said yes and offered to drive. Then I called Dorothy. She sounded tired, even a little disoriented, but insisted that she felt well enough to have company. "I need to return your book," I said.

"Which book?"

"Marguerite's European history book that you loaned to me. Remember?"

"Oh, yes. I shouldn't have forgotten that. Those two books— the history and the poetry—are all I have of hers." Her words faded off.

"Maybe tomorrow would be a better day to visit."

"No!" Her voice was strong again. "I'm sleepy at the moment because I just had my medication. Come in an hour or so. I do want to see you, Andy."

Just after noontime Mayta's old blue Buick pulled into the driveway. I jumped in before she could get out to chat with the kids or to Gus, so she made do with waves. Max and Molly barely noticed her anyway, so engaged were they in some project that involved transporting their entire collection of rubber animals, from dinosaurs to cows and pigs, back and forth between the sandbox and the three-foot-high pool Gus had just put up.

" 'Bye sweeties," I called out the window as we backed out of the driveway, but they ignored me, too. I turned to Mayta, "Thanks for springing me. How badly do you want to go to the outlets?"

"Not very. Why?"

"Dorothy got Marguerite's hospital records from the state. I've been dying to see them, and since the Danvers thing, Gus hasn't exactly been a stronghold of encouragement, so . . ."

"Of course I'll go to Dorothy's with you," she said. "I'm curious to find out what happened to Marguerite, too. It was me who told you about her to begin with."

She merged into traffic on the Gillis Bridge, and we crossed the Merrimack River heading north. The gap between the Buick and the cars in front of us immediately widened, while the cars behind us braked and tightened into a bumper-to-bumper line.

Unable to resist a little ribbing, I said, "This is just a suggestion, but if we drove a bit faster we could make it to Portsmouth before nightfall."

"Better safe than sorry," she chirped.

Smiling, I settled into my seat, anticipating a slow leisurely ride, which is the usual with Mayta driving. We talked about the beautiful stretch of weather we'd been having, and then I mentioned that when I'd called Dorothy she still sounded weak. "I guess it takes a while to recover from something like that when you're older."

"Yeah, I can attest to that," Mayta said dryly, and I wondered which of her age-related ailments was acting up now.

"Take the next exit."

She switched on her blinker. "Do you think Dorothy's up to having two visitors?"

I'd also been having second thoughts about both of us intruding on her. "It's probably fine, but just to make sure why don't you drop me off first, and I'll call to let you know how she is. You can take my cell and I'll use Dorothy's house phone."

"Okay," she said. "I've been wanting to get some more homemade pasta at that shop downtown, anyway." We had gotten to the area where Dorothy lived, and Mayta slowed down. "Which one is it?"

"The next one—the dead end." A few minutes later, we pulled up in front of the house, and I quickly acquainted her with my cell phone.

"Don't forget to listen for it," I said as I got out.

Mayta turned around in the neighbor's driveway and gave a small toot on her way back down the road. I waved from the stoop, and then rang the bell. The door was unlocked, so after knocking and still receiving no answer, I opened it, poked my head in, and called out. Dorothy answered and I followed her voice down the hallway.

"Hi! How are you?" I said, entering her bedroom. She wore a nightgown, but her hair had been combed, and she was alert, sitting propped up by pillows, magazines and newspapers strewn around her on the bed.

"Sorry I didn't answer the door. It wasn't locked, and by the time I got there—"

"You knew I'd have come in anyway. That's okay."

"I've hardly been out of bed at all this past week." She gave a wan smile.

"Well, you need to recuperate. That was a nasty fall." I set Marguerite Miller's Eastern European history book on her nightstand. "Thanks for letting me borrow this."

"Was it interesting?"

"Actually, it was pretty dry stuff, but the fact that Marguerite read it thoroughly is interesting. Do you know why she marked some passages? I assume she was the one who did it."

"Yes, nobody else has touched the book. It was probably a school text. Or perhaps she just had a particular interest in history." Dorothy pushed herself further up, and I helped adjust the pillows behind her. "I don't know why I have to stay in this bed," she said, sounding like her old self. "I feel well enough—just tired. But Ellen says one more day."

"Where is Ellen?"

"She went out food shopping. She'll be back in an hour or so, which gives me time to show you the records." She leaned over, opened the drawer of her nightstand, and removed a large brown envelope. "Ellen gets nosy sometimes and I wanted to keep them to myself for a little while."

"How long has Ellen been with you?"

"Oh, about ten years now. I had an operation and she was my home health aide while I recuperated. I kept her on, partly for companionship, and when she had to leave her apartment some years back, I suggested she move in here since we get along and I have plenty of room. It's worked out nicely. In exchange for room and board she grocery shops, does my bills, cooks, and dotes on me."

"Sounds like a good arrangement."

"Yes. At this point, the house is as much hers as mine. In fact, I might have mentioned that when I'm gone, Ellen will keep the house."

"That's generous."

"Not really. I only pay her for part-time work and she spends full time fussing over me. She hasn't taken on other health aide work for a while now." As Dorothy weighed the envelope in her hand, I wondered if terms like theirs were unusual. It sounded like a good deal for both, especially if Ellen inherited Dorothy's house.

She handed the envelope to me. I opened the flap and drew out a number of loose pages. First, I just leafed through, my eye catching a few words, titles, and dates: Marguerite's admittance on August twentieth, 1902, the treatment notes, and a discharge page that gave the stark fact of her death: March fourteenth, 1903, of influenza. Then I sat down on a chair beside the bed and began reading from the beginning. "Wait a minute. 'Marital status: Widow.' She was married?" I looked up.

Dorothy nodded. I continued, reading aloud, " 'Deceased husband: Lemuel Adams, fisherman, Isles of Shoals.' Isles of Shoals? That's where she went when she ran away?"

Dorothy nodded again, her eyes moist. "Apparently so. Reading about her makes her so real, doesn't it? Poor girl, losing her mother and father, and then her husband."

"Hmm," I agreed. "Did she elope with this fisherman?"

"It sounds like it. Either she didn't tell her family or they kept it quiet, because I never knew she'd married, and I don't think my mother did, either."

"The file is labeled Miller, her maiden name."

Dorothy leaned over and looked at the name typed at the top of the page. "I wonder why they didn't use her married name."

"Maybe because she married below her social class. Or maybe since nobody knew about it, and her husband had died anyway, the family just didn't acknowledge it."

Dorothy thought a moment, then said, "I suppose the family might've ignored a marriage they didn't approve of."

I shuffled through the papers. "Does it say anything about her husband?"

"Not that I saw, but I haven't read the whole file."

"If Marguerite was admitted with 'despondency and melancholy' on August twentieth, 1902," I said, "her husband must have died close to that time. I'll look up obits in Portsmouth for July and August of that year, and see if I can find out more about Lemuel Adams."

A car pulled up outside and Dorothy hurriedly motioned to put the papers away. "Walter's stopping by with his girlfriend, Vivian," she said, wrinkling her nose. "She's a nurse and thinks she knows everything. I don't want her seeing these."

I put the papers inside the envelope and handed it to her, but she thrust it back at me. "Take it home to read." When I hesitated, she said, "Take it! Hurry!"

I tucked the envelope under my bag on the floor, and then remembered Mayta. "I left Mayta outside. Do you mind if I call her?"

"Of course not. The phone's in the front hall. Please invite her in."

On my way to the phone, I glanced in the doorway of the den, which I surmised doubled as a guest room since it had a pullout sofa, probably where Ellen's brother stayed when he visited. Something in a stack of books on the floor under the window caught my attention. I stopped and entered the room to look. Among the modern bindings was one faded red spine. I moved two books off the pile, picked up the slender leather-bound volume with no title, and opened it. What I saw literally made my jaw drop. Scribed in delicate hand in browning ink on the first page was, "My Journal", and underneath, "Marguerite Elise Miller," with an address in Boston. I turned to the first page.

Today, Bess and I attended a consumer fair on the Boston Commons. It was the usual kind of event, with all matter of household conveniences, very interesting. We were brave enough to ride the Ferris wheel—a tremendous view from the top if one is brave enough to open one's eyes, which we were! Something strange happened with a fortuneteller, though, and I must think

about what it means. When she began to read my palm, I became
so frightened! I did not want to hear it so I left abruptly, before
she could say a word. Why did I not want to hear my fortune?

The question mark was made bold, thickened by extra ink strokes. I started to turn the page, but from down the hallway, raised voices—one of them Dorothy's—reminded me that Walter and his girlfriend had arrived. They must have come in through the kitchen, and were now in Dorothy's room. Reluctantly, I slipped the book back in the stack under the windowsill, determined to retrieve it later.

Why wasn't the journal among Marguerite's other books? Dorothy had said that *A History of Eastern Europe* and *Modern Verse* were all she had of Marguerite's. Did that mean she didn't know of the journal's existence? If so, how had it gotten here?

Quickly I made my call to Mayta. There was no answer, which didn't surprise me. She could be some place where my less-than-dependable service was cutting out. Or, lacking cell phone savvy, she probably stuck the phone down in the bottom of her pocketbook and wasn't attuned to its ring—a few bars of Bob Seger's "Old Time Rock & Roll." I didn't leave a message in the mailbox because she wouldn't know how to access it and returned to Dorothy.

The voices broke off when I entered her room. It was not Walter and his girlfriend who had arrived, but Ellen, having returned early from shopping. She sat on the edge of Dorothy's bed.

"Why, hello." Her questioning eyes moved from me to Dorothy. "I didn't see a car out front."

"I got dropped off." I kept my tone casual, noticing the grim set to Dorothy's mouth. What had they been arguing about and why hadn't Dorothy mentioned my being there? "My mother-in-law is picking me up," I said.

Ellen's eyes darted for a scant second beyond my shoulder.

Recalling Dorothy's comment about Walter and his girlfriend, I said, "I should go. You're expecting company."

"Oh, no," Ellen said quickly. "We're not expecting anybody."

"Well, I just stopped by for a short visit."

"You needn't rush off." She stood, though, and I took the hint.

I leaned down and patted Dorothy's arm. "I'll come again soon." She smiled faintly, her excitement over the records gone now.

I slipped the strap of my bag over my shoulder, keeping the large envelope tucked between it and my body as I exited the room. Ellen followed, closing the door behind us.

"She needs her rest," she said. "She has congestive heart failure, you know."

"But she seems so healthy, other than the concussion from the fall, I mean. And on the phone you said she was doing well."

"She's doing well with the concussion. However, problems with her heart have recently gotten worse. You might have noticed that she tires easily."

"Yes, I did notice that." I recalled the sound of her voice on the phone. But she'd said it was the medicine that had made her tired.

"She denies it, of course." Ellen escorted me down the hallway, making it impossible for me to duck into the den and retrieve the journal.

"I'd like to visit again," I said at the door.

"Of course. She likes seeing you."

Outside, I paced back and forth on the sidewalk, wondering if Mayta would wait for a call I now was unable to make, or if she'd eventually just come. Finally, too impatient to wait any longer, I started walking down the road just as Mayta's car appeared.

221

"Why didn't you call?" she asked as I hopped in.

"I did; you didn't answer. But never mind. Something funny's going on in that house."

"What do you mean?" She started to put the car in park.

"No! Go," I said. "I need to go somewhere else to think."

She pulled away from the curb, turned around in the neighbor's driveway again, and proceeded back down the street. "Why do you say something funny is going on?"

"For starters, Ellen wanted me to leave."

"She was like that the last time. She doesn't like Dorothy getting upset."

"Yeah, I know. But she lied about expecting her brother and his girlfriend. Dorothy had just told me they were coming over, and then Ellen said they weren't expecting anybody."

Mayta shrugged. "Plans change."

"And she and Dorothy were arguing about something."

"Probably over Dorothy not resting like she's supposed to be," Mayta said. I thought about the congestive heart failure and Dorothy's independent spirit, and ceded the point.

"Okay, how about this: I found Marguerite Miller's journal in the den. Dorothy never mentioned it; in fact, she said the poetry and history books were all she had that belonged to Marguerite."

"Marguerite's journal?" Mayta glanced over at me.

"Yeah, it's the real thing. Has her name written in it and entries beginning in 1901."

"Did you read it?"

"Just the beginning. Ellen came home and I had to get out of there."

"So, do you have it?" We stopped at the end of the street and Mayta switched on her blinker.

"No, I had to leave it, and I couldn't even ask Dorothy about it because Ellen was there. But," I said brightening, "I do have the hospital records."

"Great!" Mayta said. "Let's find a place to stop. I can't wait until we get home to look at them."

"Watch out!" I warned as a shiny dark SUV turned in front of us, cutting close to our car. Close enough for me to identify the man sitting next to a woman, and to see that the side of his angular, handsome face (what actor did he remind me of?) was bruised and swollen.

"Now what the heck was he in such a hurry for?" Mayta said, annoyed.

"See?" I said. "Ellen did lie about expecting someone. That was Walter and his girlfriend—Vivian, I think her name is."

CHAPTER EIGHTEEN

What better place to stop on a beautiful day, with a mild breeze coming off the ocean and no clouds in the sky, than the Grand Hotel? We felt justified in the indulgence since we hadn't spent much time at Dorothy's—with Ellen all but giving me the bum's rush out the door—and therefore weren't expected home right away.

"One of those fancy drinks on the porch," Mayta suggested as I reached into the backseat for Marguerite's hospital records.

The porch was vacant, so we took the wicker settee in the corner that we'd had both times before. Remembering its fresh summery taste, I ordered a Cosmopolitan, and Mayta did the same. I tried not to wince at the price; we were paying for ambiance, right?

"This is becoming an enjoyable habit." I raised my drink in a salute, clinking glass rims with Mayta. We sipped, taking in the view of the marina, deep blue water still as glass, the islands off in the distance.

"Those must be the Isles of Shoals." I looked at them with renewed interest, reminded of what I'd just learned about Marguerite Miller's whereabouts in 1902.

Mayta nodded. "You can see them really well when it's clear like this."

"I read about them at the Seacoast Historical Research Library. How they were first fishing communities, then resorts. How one—Appledore, I think—was a literary colony for famous writers and thinkers."

"We'll have to take the ferry out one day," Mayta said. "The tour goes around the islands, gives their history, and, if you want, lets you off on Appledore to walk around and see the old houses and such. I did it once years ago."

The waiter came out to ask if we wanted to order food. We declined and he left.

"Did you read about the murders in the late 1800s that took place out on one of the islands?" Mayta set her glass down, ready to tell the tale.

"The guy who rowed all the way out from Portsmouth one night and killed a couple of women for a few bucks?" I said. "Yeah, I read the news account. It was creepy." Then I recalled something else I'd read that day at the library. "There was another tragedy out there, some thirty or forty years after the murders. A number of waitresses from one of the island hotels drowned when their boat capsized."

"Never heard about that one."

"I can't remember the particulars, but I made a copy of the article. I should read it again because I think it happened around the time Marguerite was out there." I leaned down to pick up the envelope at my feet. "Speaking of whom . . ."

"The Isles of Shoals? Marguerite was out there?"

"Yep. Here, see for yourself." I opened the flap, pulled out the hospital file, and set it on the low table in front of us. I was patient while Mayta fumbled in her pocketbook for her glasses, stuck them on her face, and then picked up the top page, the admission form I'd read earlier with Dorothy.

"She married this Lemuel Adams—a fisherman?" She glanced up over the rim of her glasses. "That's what she escaped to? A life as a fisherman's wife out on a little island?"

I shrugged. "Escape from the kind of life she apparently didn't want in Boston."

Mayta flipped to the next page, the patient's history, which I hadn't yet seen, and we put our heads together over it. We read about the young woman's seemingly idyllic life as an attractive, accomplished daughter of a prominent Boston physician. She had belonged to several social organizations, was involved in charities, played the piano, wrote poetry, and had been engaged to a young man of solid character and good social standing.

"So she ditched the fiancé with all his prospects, whom she'd known all her life, to run off with some fisherman," Mayta said, more in wonder than in disapproval.

"Or she ran away from all that first, then met the fisherman and married him. Whichever it was, the marriage was short-lived. About a year later, Lemuel Adams died."

"That's sad. How did he die?"

"Dorothy didn't know." I picked up the top pages—the background information—and handed them to Mayta. "Here, divide and conquer. Tell me when you find anything interesting."

I took the remainder of the stack, sat back against the cushions, and began reading the treatment section. After a few moments, Mayta said, "Listen: *'Miss Miller began to exhibit erratic behavior as her wedding date approached. Her father sent her to New Hampshire for a respite in hopes of calming her nerves. The reverse proved true as Miss Miller became even more distressed. When her father came to see her there, she announced that she did not want to marry her fiancé and, moreover, wanted to stay in New Hampshire, perhaps procure a position as a tutor. Dr. Miller would not approve this. He convinced his daughter not to break off the engagement for the time being, and to return to Boston. That night she disappeared from the hotel.'"*

"The girl had a mind of her own," I said.

"Hmmm," Mayta agreed. Her finger following the words on the page, she continued, " *'At first it was surmised that Miss Mil-*

ler had run away to avoid the marriage, but when no sign of her was found, foul play was suspected as it seemed unlikely she could have disappeared so effectively on her own.' ''

"Ha!" I looked over to see the words for myself. "Apparently, she was smarter than anyone gave her credit for." I stood and crossed to the balustrade, where I leaned against it, and tried to decipher the scrawl of a Dr. Fells: *"Today we talked about Marguerite's childhood . . .''; "Marguerite talked about the importance of studying history today . . .''; "Marguerite read some of her poetry . . ."* The notes were cryptic, without detail; there was little, apparently, of psychiatric interest. The doctor reported that Marguerite had improved significantly over the first month with one detail: she would say little about the year during which she ran away, married, and lived on Appledore Island.

"Okay." Mayta glanced up to make sure she had my attention. "This says that about a year after Marguerite disappeared, her father, Dr. Miller, was contacted by Marguerite's husband's mother. She'd found his address among her daughter-in-law's personal papers—apparently she didn't know much about the woman her son married if she had to search through her belongings. Anyway, this woman—the mother-in-law—said that her son was recently deceased, and that now, without his income, she couldn't support his widow, Margaret."

"Margaret?"

"Yeah, apparently Marguerite changed her name. The mother-in-law asked Dr. Miller to come get his daughter, and he did. He took her back to Boston and, shortly afterward, upon advice from a Dr. Blatz, had her admitted to the state hospital for 'melancholy.' "

"So that was how she was found, and how she came to be at Danvers," I said. "But hospitalized for grief?"

"Yeah. It seems like there should be something more. If she was grieving, wouldn't she be better off with family?"

"I wonder if Lemuel Adams, himself, knew the background of the woman he married." I looked out over the water, thinking that this view of wooded shoreline and ocean would be (if you squinted past the luxury yachts at the marina in the foreground) much the same as Marguerite's was in 1901.

"What are you finding over there?"

"Not a lot. In her therapy sessions, I gather Marguerite discussed only what she wanted to. She wasn't cooperative when it came to talking about running away or her marriage."

"It takes time to come to terms with a loss," Mayta said.

We pored over our respective pages for the next few minutes. Then Mayta said, "Here's what she was finally diagnosed with. They gave her all these examinations, and found her neurologically and physically sound, but diagnosed her with a *'traumatic psychosis.'* " She straightened the pages back into a neat pile on the table. "Well, of course she was traumatized by her husband's death, but how did that make her psychotic?"

"Maybe we're not getting the complete picture." My attention was still on the page in my hand. After a few moments I said, "Listen to this: *'October second, 1902. Today Marguerite was apprised of a tragic event. Two days ago her parents were killed when a train struck their automobile. She was understandably inconsolable. Therapy was canceled and she was given medication and bed rest.'* "

"Poor girl," Mayta murmured.

I ran my finger down the paper. "The dates for therapy sessions are closer together now, and less is written down." I crossed to the settee and sat down next to Mayta. We bent our heads over the last few pages, reading them silently together. Several entries began with, *"Marguerite reluctant to talk . . ."* or *"Marguerite refused to answer . . .",* followed by descriptions of her sitting, looking down at her folded hands, or standing at the window gazing out as if expecting someone. When she did speak, she mentioned a person named Emil, which was reported only as, *"Marguerite spoke of Emil again."* Someone—the doctor?—had written *"childhood friend? lover?"* in the margin.

"Lover?" Mayta scoffed. "Within a few months, the poor girl loses her husband and pretty much her entire family and this shrink thinks she has a lover?"

"It was the Freud era, remember? Everything had sexual undertones." I turned to the next page. " *'Marguerite talked about Emil today,'* " I read aloud. " *'She was, at different times, precise and vague in telling about him. She said that he came from France, that his family had been persecuted, his home burned, and his father put in jail, where he died. She described him as having long dark wavy hair, wearing colorful clothes, and possessing an empathy and intuitiveness unlike anyone she's ever known. But, when asked, she would not give his age or his last name, when she first knew him, or where he lived. When asked what Emil did for a vocation she hesitated, and then mentioned that he once worked in a circus. When asked if he was still alive, she said she didn't know, even though she spoke of him in present tense."*

"Why are they obsessed by some old friend of hers when she's mourning for her husband and parents?" Mayta said.

"Well, apparently, this man is the only person she talks about." I turned to the next page, a discharge form that briefly explained that Marguerite had died of influenza. "Wait a minute—where are the rest of the files?" I shuffled back through the papers, which were not numbered, but ordered by the dates of the therapy sessions. They stopped abruptly with the entry for December eighteenth, 1902, which cut off in the middle of a sentence at the bottom of the page.

Mayta took the discharge page from me. "She died in March of 1903, so there's about three months missing."

I picked up the cover letter from the state records department, which I'd slid to the back of the pile in my haste to get to the interesting stuff. Now I looked at it for the first time. "This explains it. Apparently the files were in such a mess by the time they were retrieved that many were lost. The office had been broken into and everything scattered all over." I recalled the stairwell at Danvers, flooded with paper that we had literally waded through—missing files, perhaps? I put the pages back in order and slid them into the envelope.

"Too bad," Mayta said. "I wonder if her doctor ever figured out who Emil was."

"Yeah, and how she met him. I don't imagine many circus workers ran in her social circle."

"Or fishermen," Mayta pointed out. We picked up our large Y-shaped glasses with their pretty pink beverages and sipped in contemplation.

"We're either going to have to get something to eat, or call Gus to come pick us up," I said. "This drink is going straight to my head."

"Mine too. We missed lunch." Mayta signaled to a waiter who had just stepped out onto the porch. "This is on me. We deserve a treat."

The young man took Mayta's order of two appetizers: clams on the half shell and spiced sesame tuna tartare with jicama-ginger slaw and cilantro oil.

"What's that last one?" I asked after the waiter left.

"I don't know." She lifted one shoulder. "I felt like being adventurous."

We leaned back into the plush flowered cushions and let our surroundings soothe us. An offshore breeze had picked up, teasing wisps of hair out of Mayta's recently styled coiffure so that they stood out around her head like a halo, but Mayta didn't mind. She closed her eyes and smiled. If she were a cat, she'd have been purring.

"I think," I said, "that Marguerite was in so much pain she

couldn't talk about what hurt her the most. While I know next to nothing about psychology, I do think that being so young and losing a husband, and then shortly after, losing both parents so tragically, would make anyone depressed. But psychotic?"

The waiter arrived and set the appetizers down in front of us. We spread linen napkins on our laps and then placed samples of each dish on our small plates.

"I get the feeling from those doctor notes that she wasn't playing their game," Mayta said.

I took a forkful from a shell, my thoughts divided between Mayta's words and the wonderful mix of spices, breading, and clam, which I let sit on my tongue for a moment before chewing and swallowing.

"Maybe they declared her psychotic because she wasn't cooperating. There could be other files or nurse's records that say she was screaming and tearing out her hair back on the ward." She paused to take a small bite of the tuna tartare. "I'd love to hear the story from Marguerite's point of view."

I sat up in sudden inspiration. "Hey! Maybe we can!"

"Can what?"

"Hear it from Marguerite's point of view."

"The journal!" Mayta said, catching on. "You think she had it when she was hospitalized?"

"That journal came from somewhere, and if it wasn't handed down to Dorothy with Marguerite's other books, where has it been?"

"At Danvers all those years?"

"Ellen does Dorothy's bills, so she probably opens the mail. Maybe she opened this package from the state and took the journal out before she gave the records to Dorothy." I looked inside the envelope, visualizing the slim book I'd held in my hands. "Yep, the journal would fit in there alongside the records." Then I turned the envelope over and looked at the

231

front. "Not enough postage, though. It couldn't have come with the records."

"So how did it get to Dorothy's house?"

I took another bite as I thought. "Claudia told Dorothy that she had more proof her grandmother was Marguerite's daughter. I'll bet that proof was the journal—Claudia must have had it." I dropped the fork onto my plate with a clatter. "Oh, why didn't I just take it when I had it? I could have sneaked it out somehow." I reached for my pocketbook and dug for my cell phone.

"What are you doing?"

"I'm going to ask Dorothy about the journal." I tapped in the number. A man answered on the fifth ring. I was surprised until I remembered that Walter and his girlfriend had arrived after we'd left.

"Hello, may I speak to Dorothy, please?"

"Oh, I'm sorry, but she's sleeping right now. May I take a message?"

"No, uh . . ." I was struck dumb with a sensation, then a thought. The sensation was of Walter standing on this porch, a few feet away from where I now sat. I tried to place the voice I'd heard the night of the gala. There, against the white porch rail, just this side of the steps. The conversation between the tennis player and his companion had come from that vicinity. Could it have been Walter and his girlfriend?

"May I ask who's calling?" The voice was deep, a little husky.

"I'll call back," I managed to say before pressing the end call button.

"What's the matter?" Mayta gave me a quizzical look.

"I think Ellen's brother, Walter, was the man I heard talking the night Claudia was killed. They were discussing a tennis match in this show-offy kind of way, like they wanted others to be impressed, then suddenly his voice dropped and he got serious. You know how when someone starts whispering, you tune into it?" Mayta nodded. "Well, that's what I did, and I heard him tell the woman he was with to follow somebody who was wearing a green dress. Remember? I told you about it?" Mayta nodded again.

"Well, it was Walter," I said. "I've been, trying to place him ever since I met him at Dorothy's. I thought he reminded me of some actor, but now I think he and his girlfriend, Vivian, were the couple I heard here on the verandah that night, and then saw later in the dining room."

"So what are you saying? What does it mean if they were here?"

"Maybe Vivian—Walter's girlfriend—was the woman Claudia was supposed to meet."

"But why? What's the connection between her and Claudia?"

"I don't know." Had Claudia known Walter and Vivian before she contacted Dorothy? Or had she met them when she went to Dorothy's house? Or maybe it wasn't until the night of her murder that she met them.

"What are you thinking?" Mayta had devoured an entire stuffed clam while I'd been puzzling over things, and now she was impatient with my silence.

"According to Daniel, Claudia was supposed to meet a woman that night to show her something. Suppose that woman was Vivian, who called and set up the meeting with Claudia, which would account for Claudia saying she was meeting with a woman. But then Walter was there also when she arrived."

"Why go to all that trouble?"

"To knock her off track or because she'd be more likely to go meet a woman, rather than a man."

"But . . . why would she go to meet either of them?" The remainder of the appetizers sat untouched as we pondered possibilities.

"Do you remember that Claudia showed Dorothy a piece of a letter she got from her grandmother, supposedly from Dorothy's mother to Marguerite?" Mayta nodded and I continued, "Well, when Dorothy didn't accept it as proof that Claudia's grandmother was Marguerite's daughter, Claudia said she had something else that would prove it. Suppose that something else was Marguerite's journal."

"The journal you saw at Dorothy's house?"

"Yes. If Claudia's grandmother had one of Marguerite's letters, she might also have had her journal, which she passed on to Claudia. Maybe the journal was the proof Claudia was going to show to Dorothy." I leaned forward, caught up in a reasoning that was becoming more plausible. "Walter found out and, for some reason, didn't want Claudia to give the journal to Dorothy."

"So he planned the meeting to intercept it," Mayta said.

"Yes. Perhaps blackmail was part of the scenario, and somebody didn't follow through on his or her part, and Claudia ended up murdered. That's what Claudia was trying to say when she died: 'Mahg' for 'Marguerite's journal'!"

"But who was blackmailing whom? And why would an old journal be that important?"

"I don't know. The important point now is that Claudia's folder wasn't on her when we found her. If the journal was in the folder in her pocketbook when she went to that arranged meeting, and I found it afterward at Dorothy's, then somebody got it from Claudia at the hotel, which means—"

"—that somebody from Dorothy's house murdered Claudia," Mayta finished. We were now both perched tensely on the edge of the settee. "Maybe it was Ellen, not Walter's girlfriend, who called to set up the meeting with Claudia," she said.

I followed that idea down a road I'd been avoiding. Could Dorothy's own companion be involved? Ellen appeared overly protective, but was it something else? Had it been Ellen and Walter, or all three of them—Ellen, Walter, and Vivian—who'd plotted against Claudia, and were now plotting against Dorothy? I thought of Dorothy's lassitude, of Ellen's comment about congestive heart failure; was she setting the stage for Dorothy's death? "And now," I said soberly, "I think somebody might be trying to kill Dorothy."

"What do you mean?"

"She's always sleeping or tired. I think she's being overmedicated."

"But by whom?"

I recalled Dorothy's pointed comment to Walter: *Off to the track again?;* the strange block-lettered envelope addressed to Walter—a threat?—and his bruised face today. Did he have gambling debts? "Perhaps by Ellen, Walter, and Vivian," I said, the idea chilling me.

We hadn't finished our drinks, had eaten only half of the clams, and had barely touched the spiced sesame tuna tartare with jicama-ginger slaw and cilantro oil, but we stood in unison. "I'll drive," I said.

"No, I'm fine," Mayta insisted, tucking two twenties and a ten under a plate. I didn't argue, and we dashed off the porch, down the driveway, and across the parking lot to the car.

Chapter Nineteen

Mayta turned the car around in a wide arc and we headed back to Dorothy's, neither of us talking on the way. The dark blue SUV was parked out front and a couple stood on the walk.

"Look, there they are," Mayta said. "Is that Vivian, the girlfriend?"

"Must be. Drive past the house but don't slow down," I instructed her. Absorbed in conversation, the couple paid no attention to the passing car, so I took the opportunity to scrutinize them. Walter carried himself like an athlete, a tennis player, perhaps. If I didn't know otherwise, I'd think from his bearing and crisp clothing that he had money and status. The woman was in her mid-thirties—a good ten years younger than Walter—and tall with a slouchy nonchalance, born, I assumed, from years of trying to minimize her height. She was dressed with casual elegance in white slacks and a nautical striped shirt. Both were slim and well coiffed; Walter's dark hair peppered with just the right amount of distinguished gray on the sides, her brown hair pulled back into a sleek ponytail.

With a few alterations of setting and dress, I was able to place them, in my mind's eye, at the Grand Hotel. I was sure they were the couple I'd seen in the dining room the night Claudia was murdered, and that Vivian was the woman in the yellow gown I'd bumped into outside the rest room. I was sure also that Walter and Vivian had been the ones I'd overheard both times that night, first plotting against Claudia on the verandah, and then when he made his escape after the murder.

"Okay, what do we do now?" Mayta said when we reached the street's dead end.

"Pull over." I located my cell phone in the jumble at the bottom of my purse. "I could be wrong—in which case I will apologize profusely—but better safe than sorry."

Mayta pulled over to the side of the road and cut the ignition. I tapped in nine-one-one, only to have it blip at me three times. "Oh, why now?" I wailed, snapping down the cover in exasperation.

"Can't you plug that thing in or something?"

"I could if I had the jack. It's in the glove compartment of my car at home."

"So," Mayta said. "Do we just sit here?"

"For a moment, anyway." I threw the phone back in my purse. Then, from outer space, some seemingly irrelevant thought dropped into my brain. "The kitchen chair Dorothy fell through," I said.

Mayta looked at me as if I'd just turned plaid. "What about it?"

"Dorothy said Walter was supposed to fix it." I paused a moment to order my thoughts. "Which means he knew it was unsafe. Walter knew about Dorothy's habit of standing on chairs to reach things. He turned off the light from the pull string so it wouldn't come on with the wall switch, and threw the string up over the fan blades. Then he put the broken chair handy, knowing Dorothy would get up on it to turn on the light and fall."

I recalled something else: the shocked look on Ellen's face at the door when I told her there'd been a crash from inside the house. "And Ellen suspected her brother of setting it up! She knew immediately that the light had been turned off by the pull string. Damn! I shouldn't have left Dorothy!"

"Are you saying—"

"Yes! Walter's already attempted to hurt Dorothy once. And Ellen must be part of it or at least knows about it. We've got to get to her right away!"

Mayta reached for the keys in the ignition, but I put a hand on her arm. "We'll go back on foot and approach from this side. There's a border along her lot that will shield us."

From the empty driveways, I guessed that most of the residents were working professionals. We kept to the sidewalk until we reached Dorothy's neighbor's property, then cut diagonally across the front lawn to the shaggy hedge that bordered the two yards. Finding a dead patch in the undergrowth where the hedge was less dense, I squeezed through to the other side as stiff twiggy branches scraped my bare arms; half a dozen tiny dots of blood sprouted. I held back as many of the attacking limbs as I could for Mayta, and she made it through unscathed, thanks to my intervention and her long-sleeved blouse.

We found ourselves no more than three feet from the side of Dorothy's house. Ducking below windows, I sidled along the peeling, alligatored clapboarding. At the front of the house I stopped, brushed paint chips off my arm, and peeked around the corner to see if Walter and Vivian were still outside. They were not.

I backed up and Mayta pressed into the hedge to allow me to pass. I pointed toward the rear of the house, and we headed that way, again ducking under windows until we approached the one I figured was Dorothy's bedroom.

Inside, two people, a man and a woman, were speaking softly: Ellen and Walter? Or Walter and Vivian? I flattened myself against the side of the house next to the window, and Mayta did the same on the other side of me. I couldn't make out words, but the inflections of the two voices were argumentative. Slowly, I inclined my head in order to see into the room. Through the window a slice of the scene became visible: the bed with its blue chenille bedspread, and the midsection of Dorothy's body lying inert under it. I leaned out a little further and saw Dorothy's head on the pillow, her face slack and expressionless. A sudden movement and a khakied backside obliterated my view—Ellen. Another movement as Ellen slid once more from view. Footsteps left the room, and a third person spoke for the first time. Although I couldn't understand the words, it was what punctuated them—a high tinkly laugh—that identified the speaker and sent shivers up my spine.

"Go ahead," Walter said in a terse voice. A new picture was framed in my sliver of a view: two bare arms. One—Dorothy's— lying white and still at her side atop the nubby blue spread. The other arm—Vivian's—advancing, a hypodermic needle held aloft in slender tanned fingers with red painted nails. I gasped. The arm halted and Walter said, "Someone's outside."

I shoved Mayta toward the hedge and we pushed through, letting ourselves in for a considerable amount of scratching and poking. On the other side we froze, smarting and holding our breath.

"No one's there," Vivian said at the window. Walter murmured something in a dismissive tone, and then both voices moved back into the room.

I bent down and picked up a hefty rock from underneath an evergreen. I pointed toward the street, indicating with two gestures that Mayta should go there and throw the rock at the house. She frowned. With hand signals, I explained that I would go to Dorothy. Mayta shook her head, but I nodded vigorously. I took her sleeve and pulled her further out of hearing.

"Throw it at the house," I whispered into her ear, "then go get the car. Find a phone somewhere—somebody on this street has to be home—and call nine-one-one."

Frowning her disapproval, she accepted the rock I thrust into her hand. As she headed for the street, I followed along the shrubbery on the neighbor's side until I was even with the rear of Dorothy's house, where I again plunged, grimacing, through to the other side. I took a moment to ensure I hadn't been observed, and then darted across the flagstone patio. Upon reaching the kitchen door, I heard a shatter of glass coming from the living room in the front. I paused in wonder that Mayta's aim was good enough to hit a tiny pane in one of Dorothy's colonial windows. I'd meant for her to target the clapboarding, but a broken window was even better; it wouldn't be ignored. I entered the unlocked screen door as a commotion of feet headed toward the front of the house.

Dorothy appeared to be sleeping, propped up against several pillows, when I slipped into her room. She was pale and breathing unevenly, but looked peaceful. I hesitated a moment; if she really did have congestive heart failure, as Ellen said, would I be putting her in more harm by interfering? But then the gut feeling that had propelled me thus far kicked in, and I knew I had to get her out of there. I shook her shoulder gently, and her eyes popped open in alarm, then softened in relief upon recognizing me. She started to speak, but I put a finger to her mouth.

"Shhh! Do you want me to take you out of here?"

She nodded, quick little bobs of her head, but made no effort to move.

"Right now?" I asked, to be sure we were on the same page. She nodded again. I put my arm behind her shoulders to assist her, but she appeared to have little control of her body. I'd only managed to get her to a sitting position when footsteps sounded in the hallway. Having no choice, I eased Dorothy back onto the pillows. Her eyes widened in a silent plea. I scanned the room for a hiding place. The bed's covering was too short on the sides to shield anyone underneath, and the closet door was on the other side of the room, so I lunged for the open, screenless window.

"I'll be back," I promised in a whisper. Seeing the hypodermic needle on the corner of the dresser, I picked it up and tossed it out the window before sliding over the sash. I barely had time to duck down before footsteps entered the room. I hoped I hadn't been heard, and that I hadn't put Dorothy in an even worse situation with the occupants of the house. At least they couldn't inject her with drugs, I reassured myself as I scanned the ground around me. No needle; I'd have to come back and search later.

"Were you talking with someone?" Ellen's voice moved toward the window, below which I crouched. Just then a car pulled away from the curb—Walter's, I guessed from the impatient spurt of loose gravel—and Ellen must have paused to listen, because no head appeared above me. I held my breath, feeling relief that there was at least one less person to deal with in the house.

Another sound from the street—Walter's car skidding to an abrupt stop—set both Ellen, on the interior, and me, on the exterior, in motion. She dashed out of Dorothy's room as I hurried alongside the house to the front to peek around the corner. Down the block, sitting cockeyed in the middle of the street, was the dark SUV. Through the tinted rear window I made out the silhouette of a passenger—Vivian. Walter stepped out of the driver's-side door. From our respective positions, Ellen on the front lawn and me at the corner of the house, we craned our necks, trying to figure out what had happened. I, at least, was hoping that help had arrived.

But it was no patrol car that had halted Walter's escape. On the other side of the SUV, majestically straddling the dead-end road from one side to the other, blocking the only egress, stood Mayta's big old blue Buick. A squint of the eyes assured me that Mayta had vacated the car, and I gave a brief prayer that she'd gotten herself to a safe place. Then I did an about-face and raced to the rear of the house.

One-on-one were odds I felt I could handle. With a confidence and determination I'd lacked on the first rescue attempt, I charged through the kitchen door, snatching up a broom on my way. Dorothy was alert when I stormed her room, and she struggled to sit up. Before I reached the bed, however, I heard Ellen behind me at the door. I swirled around and fiercely swung the broom, catching the side of her head and knocking off her glasses. After half a dozen or so more swipes with the brush end of the broom I realized it was a dumb choice of weapon. Then Ellen charged me. I grabbed a small electric alarm clock, ripping the cord out of the wall, and flung it. The clock failed to connect with any part of Ellen's anatomy, but it served the purpose of distraction. Ellen flinched, stepped back, and tripped over the rocker behind her, then fell into a sitting position, legs sprawled out in front of her on the floor. I moved quickly, taking advantage of a momentary lull in the action.

Dorothy had managed to push herself upright with her legs over the side of the bed. More responsive than earlier, she helped as I pulled her to her feet and half carried her out of the room past Ellen who, appearing dazed, made no immediate effort to get to her feet. We shuffled down the hall, through the kitchen, and out into the yard. I hesitated at the hedge, then turned and pushed backward into the multitude of sharp tiny branches, shielding Dorothy as I drew her through after me.

On the other side, I paused to look around. Dorothy was calm and trusting as I figured out what the heck I was doing. I had to find a place to hide before Ellen got her senses back and came after us. And there was Walter to consider; he might return to the house, find his sister, and come after us, too. With one arm, I grasped Dorothy around her middle and, resembling an entry in a three-legged race, we hobbled across the lawn.

"Are your neighbors home?"

Dorothy shook her head. "Both work," she managed to say.

"I guess we'll have to do a B & E, then. We've got to get to a phone." I adjusted my grip around Dorothy, and we rounded the back corner of the neighbor's house. She tried to be helpful, but her legs didn't want to move, and our progress was slow. Luckily, the first door we encountered was unlocked, and we stumbled into a garage. I pressed the lock button in the knob, and then steered us along the wall, keeping out of the line of sight from the garage door's window. We reached the entrance to the house to find it locked.

"Crap!" No doubt Ellen, with or without Walter, was out there by now. Our only recourse was to hide, hoping we'd entered unseen and had left no obvious trail. Hoping that, somehow, Mayta had managed to contact help and it was on its way. Dorothy leaned against the wall, catching her breath, as I scanned the garage, looking for a hiding place large enough for both of us.

It was a neat garage; in fact, it was the garage I'd dreamed of having and had pestered Gus into trying to achieve. Along one side, various shiny machines for lawn maintenance and landscaping stood lined up at attention. Behind them, on wall hooks, hung an impressive array of hand tools, arranged by genre and size. On the opposite side of the room cans of paint, turpentine, oil, and the like were arranged in rows on shelves that ran the length of the wall. The result of such organization was that the two stalls were left free—imagine!—for cars. Cars that were, of course, gone at the moment, leaving an expanse of open space. The old adage, a place for everything and everything in its place, ran through my head, but not in admiration. At that moment, I would have given my Bob Seger CD collection to find a cluttered garage like mine back home, where a herd of bison could bed down undetected for a week.

As seconds ticked by, I reassessed the situation. Ellen was undoubtedly angry I'd attacked her, but rather than come after us, wouldn't she be more likely to take off while she had the chance? And Mayta's car wouldn't have waylaid Walter for long; he could have easily just driven up over the sidewalk and lawn and continued on his way. Maybe all Dorothy and I had to do was stay out of sight for a while, give everyone a chance to get away, and come out when it was clear. Relaxed somewhat, I looked around for a place Dorothy could sit. Then she tensed.

"I hear something," she said.

I heard it too: muffled voices from outside. I went back to my fear that Ellen and Walter and possibly even Vivian were after us. *Can you follow tracks in grass?* I thought of the well-groomed lawn of the neatnik who lived here and decided it was possible.

"Oh Andy, we're trapped." Dorothy's voice was a thin dry whisper.

"Shhh, it's okay," I said. But my insides were jumping with alarm. Where was Mayta? Had she been able to call the police? Was she safe?

The only possible shelter from sight was the line of machinery, so I guided Dorothy in that direction. I helped her down into the big canvas grass-clipping basket attached to a lawn mower. Thankfully, her mobility was returning and, being agile for a woman her age, was able to sit with her knees drawn up. As soon as she was safely situated, I climbed into an open wagon attached to a mowing tractor, and curled up as small and inconspicuous as I could. Almost immediately, I heard footsteps at the door and sensed someone peering through the window. Then the knob was tried, and I waited for the glass to be broken, for someone to enter, to find us.

CHAPTER TWENTY

Mr. Neatnik was not spic and span; twigs and small stones dug into my side and pebbles and grit embedded themselves into my cheek. When no glass broke nor door crashed open after about four hours (okay, maybe ten minutes or so), I dared to raise my head a few inches and listen. Silence, then a soft moan nearby.

"Dorothy, are you all right?" I whispered.

Another moan in response. "My back hurts. I can't stay in this position any longer."

"I'm going to look out. Just hold tight another sec, okay?" I unfolded out of my cocoon and slowly climbed out of the wagon, trying to minimize the resulting metallic groaning and squeaking sounds. I moved toward the door, watching for someone to appear in its square of glass. Halfway there, I caught a flash of color out on the periphery of the yard. Before I could process what I'd seen, I dropped to the floor, heart hammering. After a moment, I crawled to the door and raised myself enough to peek outside. Mayta was at the far edge of the lawn, peering around her, one hand at her forehead acting as a visor against the bright sun. Faintly, I heard her call my name.

I scrambled to my feet, pulled open the door, and shouted. She spun around and hurried toward me in a half run.

"Where have you been?" She was breathless and irritated.

"In here, hiding. Where did you go? Did you call nine-one-one?"

Dorothy waved an arm above the canvas mulching bag. "Please, help me."

"I couldn't call on that phone," Mayta said as we hurried over to rescue Dorothy, who, in trying to rise, almost toppled over the edge of the bag. "I kept getting that blipping sound."

"It's dead. I told you to go to a house." One on either side, we hoisted Dorothy to her feet and helped her out. Mayta brushed grass clippings off her nightgown as I retrieved a slipper and put it on her foot.

"Thank you," Dorothy breathed.

"Are you okay?" I asked and she nodded. We paused so she could get her breath and steady herself.

"I remembered about the phone being dead later," Mayta said. "Anyway, I went to get the car instead because I saw those guys head for the SUV. I pulled past and blocked them before they got away from the curb. Then I hightailed it out of the car and up to the neighbor's house on the other side."

"Jenny was home?" Dorothy asked, surprised.

"Yeah, she and her husband took the day off. She'd come to the door to see what was going on, and she let me in."

"Do you think you can walk now?" I said.

"I think so." Dorothy took a tentative step and we tightened our holds on her.

"So where's Walter and Vivian?" I asked as we moved toward the door.

"Oh, they just drove up on the curb and went around me," Mayta said sheepishly. "That blocking thing works on TV, but I guess it wasn't such a great idea in real life."

"So they took off."

"Yeah, but I did call the police from Jenny's and gave them the license number." Mayta lowered her voice and spoke behind Dorothy. "I told them Walter tried to kill somebody—maybe an exaggeration—but it made it seem more urgent."

"Wait," I said. "If Walter and Vivian left, who did we hear walking around?"

"I guess it was Jenny and me looking for you. We peeked in here, but didn't see anything. Good hiding spot, by the way."

"Yeah, if we'd really needed to hide." I felt a bit silly that the drama had been unnecessary. As we started across the lawn, Dorothy's knees began to buckle, so we steered her to a lawn chair.

"I just don't seem to have any energy." Dorothy sank into the chair.

"Of course you don't after all you've been through," Mayta said soothingly. "I'll go get help."

"No." Dorothy put out a hand to stop her. "Just give me a minute to catch my breath."

I drew Mayta away a few steps. "Is Ellen still there?"

"Yes, but she's harmless. She won't be going anywhere on her own."

"Was she hurt?" I said, concerned. "I hit her, but I just wanted her to back off."

"No. She's okay, just feeling pretty down. Jenny's husband is with her."

"I guess I chose the wrong neighbor to go to."

"It would have been hard to get around that side of the house without being seen," Mayta said. "Even if you'd known they were home."

We joined Dorothy again. "Let's get you back to the house," I said. "Can you make it that far?"

Dorothy said she could, so we helped her up and, sandwiching her between us, got her across the yard, this time skirting the hedge at the front. Upon entering the house, we found a policeman and policewoman in the living room. They were talking with a dejected-looking Ellen and a man, whom I guessed was Jenny's husband. They all looked up at us, but we escorted

Dorothy straight down the hallway to her room. She was so beat by that time, I don't think it even registered that there were extra people in her house.

After we got her into bed, an officer came in. She spoke gently and briefly with Dorothy who told her, in abbreviated sentences of mostly single-syllable words, that she had been feeling weak lately, and that Ellen had always taken good care of her, but that she'd begun to have uneasy feelings whenever Ellen's brother Walter and his girlfriend Vivian visited. The officer asked if she had those uneasy feelings about Ellen as well. Dorothy hesitated a moment, then said that she had.

Jenny came in then, introduced herself to me, and, noting Dorothy's physical and emotional exhaustion, shooed everyone out. In the kitchen, I explained to the officer how I'd met Dorothy, her connection to Claudia, my suspicions concerning the chair accident, Dorothy's increasing tiredness and disorientation over the past week or so, and finally the hand I'd seen ready to administer an injection. Then an ambulance arrived, and the officer was summoned to talk with the EMTs. I trailed after her to the living room where Ellen was slumped in a chair, her face in her hands. A short middle-aged man with thinning hair rose from a chair adjacent to Ellen's.

"Al," he said, holding out his hand. "I live next door."

"I'm Andy."

"I've known these two women for a long time." Al glanced at Ellen. "I can't believe Ellen would harm Dorothy. She's devoted to her."

Ellen's head jerked up, her face blotched and red. "I never meant to hurt her," she said to Al. "But I had to help my brother."

"How did you help Walter?" I said.

"He's my only family," Ellen continued, still to Al. "They were going to hurt him if he didn't pay."

"Who was going to hurt him?" I pressed, but she just shook her head.

"I had to make a choice." Her voice dropped.

"So your choice was to go along with your brother's plan to drug Dorothy—perhaps to kill her—for what? Her house?" Ellen didn't answer, and I was suddenly very angry. "This kind woman, who depends on you for her care, who treats you like family, even leaves you her house in her will—you repay her by trying to kill her?" The policewoman frowned and put a hand on my arm, but I ignored her. "What injections were you people giving Dorothy?"

Ellen turned to me then, her look blank. "I didn't give Dorothy injections."

"You both need to leave now," the officer said sternly to Al and me.

"In Dorothy's room, just about twenty minutes ago," I said. "I saw—" The officer took hold of my arm then and escorted me, with Al following, down the hallway to the kitchen.

"Leave the questioning to us," she said before returning to the living room. Al joined Jenny at the table, but I continued through the room and out the back door, too worked up to be contained inside. I followed the brick path around the house and found Mayta sitting on the cement bench in the garden. She moved over to make room for me, but I couldn't sit.

"Ellen denies they were giving Dorothy injections." I paced in front of her. "But I saw—" I broke off, remembering the needle. "Wait a minute." I stopped and then dashed off around the side of the house. Under the bedroom window I dropped to my knees and crawled around, gingerly looking through the grass and under the bushes. After a few minutes, I found the hypodermic needle, propped up against the side of the house, its tip stuck into the ground, where it had bounced and then landed after I threw it out the window. I teepeed three small sticks over it.

The officers were conferring with each other in the entrance-way when I approached. "I have something you should see," I said.

"I'll stay here." The male officer inclined his head toward El-len. His partner nodded and followed me out the main entry and around the house.

"I don't know what's in it, but I'm pretty sure it wasn't legally prescribed for Dorothy." I reiterated that Dorothy had been unusually vague and tired lately, and that I'd seen someone ready to administer an injection. "I believe it was Vivian."

She dug out a bag from her pocket, knelt down, and picked up the needle with great care. We went back into the house where one of the EMTs joined us.

He reported that Dorothy's vital signs were normal and that she refused to go to the hospital, so they were leaving her in Jenny's care. Jenny, a nurse herself, had offered to stay with Dorothy overnight and to call the doctor in the morning.

After the EMTs left and the officers took Ellen to the station for questioning, I joined the others in the kitchen, including Mayta who had come in from the garden. Al rose to offer his seat, but I waved him back down and leaned against the counter.

"There's coffee, if you want." Jenny nodded toward the machine by the sink.

"Thanks, but no. How's Dorothy?"

"She's sleeping," Jenny said. "I think she'll be fine tonight, but I'll stay on the couch in case she wakens."

"Jenny, you're a nurse. Why would someone be giving Doro-thy injections?"

"Well, she's not diabetic." She cocked her head in thought. "And I can't think of any other reason she'd need injections."

"Unless they wanted her out of commission," I said.

"I can't believe Ellen would hurt Dorothy." Al was hunched

over his heavy diner mug, both hands wrapped around it. "It just doesn't make sense."

"How long have you known Ellen?" I said.

"For as long as she's worked for Dorothy." Al looked at Jenny, who pursed her lips, thinking.

"At least ten years," she said. "Dorothy asked me about home health services after her operation, and I recommended the agency that sent out Ellen. Ellen worked out so well that she quit the agency so Dorothy could hire her privately."

"They had some arrangement that included Ellen's room and board," Al said. "I don't know the details, but it's worked well. Ellen has a secure job and a home, and Dorothy has a companion who takes care of her needs."

"And who will inherit a nice house when her employer dies," I said, watching for their reactions.

Al looked up in surprise and Jenny said, "Oh? I didn't know that, but I guess it makes sense. They're very close."

"What about Ellen's brother and his girlfriend?"

"I'd never seen her before today," Jenny said, "but Walter . . ."

"He's a weird one," Al said.

Jenny nodded in agreement. "He's been coming more the last few months. Dorothy didn't like it much. She'd say things about him visiting again and that it was probably to borrow more money from Ellen. I got the feeling Ellen wasn't crazy about having him around either, but had no choice."

"She felt she had to help him," I said, recalling Ellen's comment.

"Yeah, but it was more than that." Jenny rested her elbows on the table and folded one arm over the other. "Ellen and I would talk sometimes out in our backyards about how Dorothy was doing, her garden, and other things, but she was close-lipped about her brother. I'd mention him, and she'd clam up and

251

look worried."

"Why was she worried?" Mayta asked.

Jenny thought a moment and then shook her head. "I don't know. It was like this weight was on her shoulders when he was around. Their parents died when they were young and I had the impression she saw herself as kind of a parent to him, even though she's not much older."

Since there was nothing more we could do for Dorothy, and she was in good hands with Jenny, Mayta and I said our goodbyes. It was almost six-thirty by the time we pulled away in the car.

"I'm starved," Mayta said. "We didn't get to finish those wonderful appetizers at the hotel."

I raked my fingers through the bottom of my pocketbook, culling a reclosable baggie of Goldfish crackers I'd forgotten about and a container of Tic Tacs. We shared the crackers while reviewing the events of the day.

"Al said Walter borrowed money from Ellen," I said. "Do you remember when we first met Walter? He was leaving Dorothy's house and she asked him if he was off to the races?"

"Yeah, she obviously disapproved."

"Right. So I think Walter has gambling debts, and he comes around now and then to hit his sister up for money. Maybe he's after Dorothy's money, too."

"I thought she didn't have any." Mayta put her blinker on and edged into the middle lane.

"She doesn't. At least according to her. Are you actually going to pass another car?"

"You said you needed to get home."

"Yeah, but I didn't mean you had to speed. You're going—what?" I peered at the speedometer. "Sixty-two miles an hour? Whoa! I better tighten my seat belt."

"Oh, shut up."

I parceled out the last of the Goldfish, dropping Mayta's share into her outstretched hand, and then stuffed the empty bag back into my pocketbook. "And who is this Vivian? She seems way too involved in what's going on to just be Walter's girlfriend."

"Hmmm." Mayta popped the crackers into her mouth, replaced her hand on the steering wheel at two o'clock, and hunched over the wheel.

"Okay, let me just ruminate for a minute, for my own sake," I said, aware that my audience was, at best, giving me half an ear. "I first saw Vivian—or rather heard her—at the Grand Hotel gala opening. Walter told her to follow a woman wearing a green dress—presumably Claudia, because that was what she was wearing. Claudia, we know from Daniel's statement, had been contacted by a woman—perhaps Vivian—who wanted something from her—possibly Marguerite's journal." I stopped. "Damn! In all the excitement I forgot to go back and get that journal from the den."

Mayta glanced at me. So she *was* listening. "Is it safe?"

"I think so."

"Go on." Mayta had gradually moved ahead of the slowpoke car, and now crept back into the outside lane. Once there, she decelerated and relaxed her grip on the steering wheel.

"Okay," I said. "Back to the meeting at the hotel: Vivian probably told Claudia that she was representing Dorothy and to bring the journal to the meeting to prove she was the great-granddaughter of Marguerite. Claudia brought the journal, thinking it was going to get her into Dorothy's good graces. Or maybe Walter and Vivian offered to buy it—as a kind of bribe. Whatever the situation was, Walter and Vivian tried to take it, Claudia fought them, and one of them stabbed her."

"That's conjecture," Mayta said.

"Not all. Claudia possessed something important that had to

do with Marguerite—possibly the journal. Walter and Vivian were at the gala when Claudia was murdered, and the journal appeared at Dorothy's house in the room where Walter slept. So, *if* Claudia had the journal at the Grand Hotel, then either Walter, Vivian, Ellen, or some combination of the three took it from her—murdering her in the process—and brought it to Dorothy's house."

"Except we can't place Ellen at the hotel," Mayta said. "And if Walter and Vivian wanted the journal so badly, why didn't they take it with them today when they took off?"

"Because . . ." I slumped back in the seat. "I don't know."

We'd reached our exit and Mayta pulled off onto the ramp. We drove through town in silence. Two blocks from my house, she asked, "Do you think they'd come back to get it?"

I shuddered to think of Walter and Vivian returning to the house in the night with just Dorothy and Jenny there. "I don't think they'd run the risk of that; they must know by now that the police were called." Then it became clear to me why they hadn't taken the journal with them. "I don't think Walter wanted the journal. He just didn't want Claudia to have something that might prove Dorothy has heirs. He didn't want anything to jeopardize Ellen inheriting the house from Dorothy."

Mayta pulled into my driveway, turned off the engine, and we sat for a moment. "I don't know," she said. "There's got to be more."

"Yes, there's still something missing," I agreed. "I haven't figured out that piece yet."

Night
On the Road to Portsmouth
June Twenty-Third, 1901
The dress is thin for the night air, the satin shoes impractical for walking the dirt road, and her gauzy wrap is all but useless. Still, Marguerite is glad she decided to wear her prettiest garments. The admiring look in Emil's eyes when she ran across the lawn, the gossamer skirt flowing about her, to where he was waiting, was worth it. You are beautiful. I love you, *he'd said, taking her into his arms. And then they'd dashed off, exhilarated spirits carrying them like air-filled sails, Marguerite barely feeling the ground beneath her. She was running away, Emil beside her.*

Now the excitement of the escape has settled into purpose: to cover as much ground as quickly as possible. They travel on the road; there is little traffic at this time of night, and they can easily get off in time if a carriage appears. While keeping a steady pace, they talk intermittently in low tones, saying little of immediate plans, nothing about long-term ones. Emil wants them to make it to Portsmouth where they will meet up with members of his group, who may or may not still be with the circus—Marguerite isn't sure about this, but doesn't ask. She also doesn't ask what will happen after they meet the others—where they will go, what they will do. She is following Emil's example, taking things as they come.

They rest periodically under a tree or against a stone fence, Emil holding her, warming her. Her feet become blistered, sore, and she's sure that, if she could see them in the dark, her shoes are dirty and ruined. One time they fall asleep sitting, backs against a tree. Waking suddenly, they find the sky a gradient lighter.

"Hurry," Emil insists. "We must make it to Portsmouth before daylight."

They push on, Marguerite limping. Dawn has broken by the time they cross over a small bridge and reach the outskirts of the city. Now it is harder to avoid people, farmers driving horse-drawn wagons, workmen walking to whatever jobs they have. They leave the road and follow along the river. Most of the fishermen have already put out to sea for the day, but a few are at dories still.

Marguerite carries her shoes and stockings. She walks slowly, letting her painful feet sink into the cool wet sand. The sun is suddenly high and there is no longer anyone to hurry her along. She will need to while away the daylight hours unseen. Portsmouth was not the best choice, she realizes now; she hadn't thought about all the people who would be around during the day, or about how noticeable she might be. It would have been easier to hide in the countryside.

Exhausted, her feet swollen and hurting, she plops down out of sight on dry sand beneath a wharf. It could be the wharf under which she and Emil first stood together, first touched, with the sea washing around their feet. She closes her eyes to bring back that feeling of him close to her. Emil in the moonlight. Emil of the night. She had been sure—no, she had hoped—that this time he wouldn't abandon her in the daylight. Unable to keep her eyes open, Marguerite lies on her side, curls her body into a comma, and falls asleep.

Lemuel Adams broke his stride to veer off the road and jump down the short grassy bluff onto the sandy shore. Hours wasted already because of a busted rudder, now another hour more to be spent waiting for the piece to be repaired so he could install it, which would take even more time. He could go nowhere until he got the part; he'd barely made it into port with the crippled boat. He was too impatient to wait in the shop while the part was being repaired and, even though he'd only been in the city of Portsmouth fewer than a dozen times in his whole twenty-five years, he had no desire to take up time by meandering its streets. He should be out fishing. He had already accepted that it would be a day's loss, for once the rudder was repaired it would be too late to do anything but make it back home to the island. Still, he hurried onward to the boat where there was something worthwhile to do—repair lines, order his tackle. He was not a man to sit idle. In the five years since he'd taken over the boat from his father, Lemuel hadn't missed a day, other than when inclement weather made it foolhardy to put out to sea.

He was almost on top of the swirl of pinkish froth in his path before he realized it was not foam from the sea, but a diaphanous manmade fabric billowing slightly in the breeze, and that it was wrapped around a figure lying in the sand. He did slow down then, and approached with trepidation. It happened occasionally that a drowned body was washed ashore. Lemuel himself had come upon one out on the island—a reckless soul who'd been swimming where he hadn't ought to have been—and he had participated in a rescue effort once when a sailboat overturned, recovering two bodies from the surf.

But as he approached the person—a young woman lying on her side—he saw that her clothes were not sodden and that she was not dead. The gentle rise of her shoulder and the peaceful half smile on her face proved she was only sleeping. He started around her, giving her a wide berth, thinking not to disturb her, and in fact was several yards beyond when he thought better of it and turned back.

Whatever the circumstances, it was not proper to leave a lady lying in the sand. He looked around and, seeing nobody nearby to whom he could appeal, approached her again. He squatted, elbows resting on knees, and cleared his throat. Immediately, her eyes flew open and she pushed herself to a sitting position, gripping a drawstring bag to her chest with one hand. Despite the mussed hair, wild and dark about her face, and the disarray of her clothing, he could see that she was well bred. The rumpled dress and the flimsy tattered shoes, which lay next to her in the sand, were of fine quality and her face was pale from lack of exposure to the harshness of the outdoors.

"Excuse me, ma'am," he said, unsure of how to proceed. "Um, have you . . . met with harm?"

She shook her head, looking at him as if trying to place him among her acquaintances. An intelligent face, he thought, but there was something about the eyes that gazed intently, then lost focus and shifted over his shoulder. Lemuel glanced behind him at the empty expanse of beach.

"Are you in need of help?" he tried again. What was she doing here? Why was there nobody with her?

"Yes, please." She kicked her legs free from the tangle of the skirt and got to her knees, then reached out for him to take her free hand. After a slight hesitation he did, and as he rose himself, pulled her, wincing, to her feet.

"Are you hurt?"

"It's just my feet. They're blistered from walking."

From where had she walked? Why was she out walking in such finery? At a loss for what to offer, Lemuel finally said, "May I escort you somewhere?"

She righted her clothing and picked up her shoes. Then she offered her hand. "I am Margaret."

Awkwardly, he shook her hand, and then dropped it. "Lemuel Adams," he replied in turn, wishing she'd just answered his question with a no so he could continue on his way in good conscience.

"I've arrived late and missed my connection. I was to have met friends here, but . . . it seems they've gone on." She did not seem overly concerned about the fact. "Do you live in Portsmouth?"

"No. Appledore." The name didn't appear to register with her so he gestured downriver. "The Isles of Shoals. Busted my rudder and had to put to shore. Portsmouth was closer and now I'm stuck for at least

another hour."

"Why, that is where I am to go," she said, eyes widening. "Do you suppose you might take me there? So I can catch up with my friends?"

He wrinkled his brow. "Which island?"

"I'm not sure. Which island did you say you lived on?"

"Appledore," he repeated, thinking this a strange conversation.

"What are the names of the other islands?"

"Star Island, Smuttynose—"

"Yes, I think it was Appledore. Will you take me there?" She glanced around her as if afraid someone might come up and catch her unawares.

Lemuel had had little experience talking with young women. His social life outside of his family had consisted mainly of attending a one-room schoolhouse with a teacher who instructed no more than eight children at any time, aged seven to sixteen. There had been, over the years of Lemuel's upbringing, few girls of his age who lived on or visited the island. More visitors came to the larger Star Island, of course, to stay at the hotel there. And there were young people who came out summers to work at the hotel, and Lemuel had met a few of them. But for the most part, hotel employees socialized among themselves, not among the fishermen and their families. Besides, Lemuel spent long days at sea in the summer and had little time or use for empty talk.

He regarded the young woman before him. She had a way of looking at him without completely focusing her eyes that he found unsettling. He suggested taking her to the police station where she could get help in contacting her friends, but she shook her head.

"No! I must get out to Appledore Island. Can you take me, please?"

She was so insistent that he reluctantly agreed. He had already given up on fishing for the day, anyway. He explained that he could not leave until his rudder was repaired, however, so she sat back down in the sand.

"Then I'll wait here." She tucked her skirt under her pulled-up

legs. "Where is your boat?"

"There." He pointed with some pride down the beach. She looked at it, but did not show if she was impressed. "Shall I come get you when I'm ready to leave, then?"

"Yes, please," she said.

Still, it seemed odd to walk off and leave her sitting there all alone. "Are you hungry? Would you like to go up into town?"

"No," she said and that satisfied him. He did not want to have to escort her into town, and now he felt he could leave, having offered everything he could think of. By the time he reached his boat, though, he was worrying about the long trip out to the island with this young woman as company. He was used to being at sea by himself, or in earlier years with only his father; he'd never before had passengers aboard. He might have to talk to her. He fretted about that for a few minutes while he tackled a damaged line, glancing in her direction. Finally, he decided that if she wanted to talk to him that would be fine. But it was his boat, she'd begged for passage, and while he would give her that, he would not be pressured into providing conversation. Thus decided, he bent to his work.

Marguerite watches the young fisherman sitting in his beached boat, his head with its sun-streaked hair bent over lap work. He is well mannered and earnest, like Emil, but more serious, with a slight frown she suspects is his regular countenance. He is strong, too, like Emil, but sinewy—tall and thin. She decides he is someone she can trust.

After an hour, he walks toward her, but passes by with only a nervous smile in her direction. She had stood, thinking he was coming for her, but remembering the broken rudder sits back down. Some time later he passes by again without acknowledgment. In his hand is the repaired piece. He works on his boat with sure and quick hands and is finished within the hour. Marguerite jumps up, anxious to move her stiff limbs, more anxious to get away from the glaring light of day where she could be found at any moment. She reaches the boat before the fisherman can come for her.

"*We must push off.*" *His eyes take in Marguerite's impractical dress and the dainty shoes, bag, and bunched-up wrap she carries.*

"*I can help.*" *She tosses her belongings into the boat and starts to hitch up her skirt. Then, realizing she will need both hands, lets it fall again. The hem spreads out around her on the water, floating film-like on the surface as they push the boat deep enough to support both of them in it. Lemuel clambers over the side and helps Marguerite do the same.*

"*Lucky to be out of here before low tide,*" *he mutters, righting the course with his oars. Marguerite sits opposite him, where he has indicated. She doesn't know what she will find on the island where this boat is taking her, but believes she is directing a necessary course for herself, and feels satisfied. She wonders if Emil will come to her on this island. She smiles at the memory of him as she watches the fisherman opposite her pulling at the oars. She catches him glancing at her, then averting his eyes quickly when they meet hers.*

"*Tell me about your family,*" *she says, and he tells her he has a father, who is unwell, and a mother, but no brothers or sisters. She asks how he spends his days, and he looks at her as if it is an odd question. He explains that he puts out to sea every day that he can, and on those days that he cannot because of the weather, he mends lines and makes ready to go to sea.*

She tries again. "What is the island like? Is it beautiful?" He says that only a handful of people live there full time. He supposes the island is beautiful, but he has been nowhere else—other than Portsmouth and Kittery—and therefore has little with which to compare it. He adds no description, offers no clues as to what the island is like. He bends into his labor, the outline of muscular arms showing through his shirt as he rows, his head ducking down to avoid her inquisitive eyes. His tousled fair hair catches the sun's rays, and Marguerite thinks it must smell like the sea.

She smiles again at the solemn industrious young man before her, deciding that he is, in fact, unlike Emil, who still lingers in her mind. Yes, different but not in a bad way. She finds his spare conversation peaceful, and his nervous way of sneaking looks at her somewhat endearing. She lets Emil fade. He will come to her again—but perhaps not right away.

"Do you believe in destiny?" Her voice was so thin and light it was almost snatched away by the breeze.

Lemuel shook his head, more in confusion than in reply, wishing she would just sit quietly and not pester him with questions. He increased his effort on the oars. The bow of the boat crested a sudden wave and then smacked down in its trough, sending a fine spray of water over them.

"Oh!" she said in surprise, but continued undeterred. "There is a Roma word for it: bart." He felt her eyes focused squarely on him now, looking for a response. "It means that some things are meant to happen, that certain people are meant to meet, to be together, and nothing can get in the way."

He scowled and looked up despite himself, catching her gaze. He felt his ears pink as he immediately dropped his eyes again. Roma? What language was that? What was she talking about? What a strange woman he has saddled himself with.

"I read about it in a book," she explained, though he'd voiced no question. "I like to read."

CHAPTER TWENTY-ONE

Mayta called right after the six a.m. news on Monday. Gus was already downstairs making coffee. I, however, was still abed, floating somewhere between comatose and consciousness, barely aware of a distant ringing that punctuated a steady thrumming on the roof overhead. Saturday's events had been tiring, and then there had been the telling, rehashing, and justifying of Mayta's and my part in them to Gus. I'd hit the bed last night ready to sleep for a month.

"My mother," Gus said, gently shaking my shoulder. I groaned through my torpor. "Walter and Vivian have been arrested."

I came awake then, bounced up, and grabbed the receiver he held out. Quickly, Mayta relayed that Walter and Vivian had stopped for gas somewhere up the coast of Maine, and a policeman in an idling undercover vehicle had recognized the car, run a check on the license plate, and then pulled them in for questioning for attempted murder.

"Attempted murder?"

"Yep. Something must have been found in the car."

"Or the Portsmouth police took those injections I told them about seriously." I squinted through the gloom at the alarm clock. "I'll bet Beverly has more information, but it's too early to call her."

"Let me know if you find out anything more."

"Will do." I lay down the receiver and sat on the edge of the

263

bed listening to the rain intensify. Above the café curtains the sky was as dark as dusk. I considered falling back into my still-warm spot and trying to recapture that wonderful half-sleep state, but I was too awake. With a sigh, I heaved myself up. Then, catching a whiff of freshly brewed coffee, I let it lure me downstairs.

"Whole wheat toast?" Gus was slathering two slices with peanut butter.

"Sure." I plopped down at my usual place at the table where a steaming mug already stood. "Did you catch the news?"

"No, but Mom told me about the arrest. I think that's all they said, that the two of them were arrested."

I sipped my coffee thinking that, for the time being, Dorothy could rest easy, and hoping that whatever the police had on Walter and Vivian, it was enough to keep them away from her for a long time.

Just before eight o'clock I punched in numbers I'd committed to memory. Sure enough, Beverly was already at her desk.

"Good gosh, girl! You're early! I just got in, haven't even gotten up to date on everything yet. Give me some time and I'll call you back, okay?"

Gus took off to get some lumber to repair the back porch in case the rain let up, and I sat waiting for Beverly's call. Twenty minutes, a third cup of coffee, and another piece of toast later, the telephone rang.

"Hello, Andy? Chauncey Brown, here. How are you?"

"Hi, Chauncey. I'm doing well, and you?" Hearing movement upstairs, I started pulling together breakfast things—bowls, spoons, cereal boxes.

"Fine, just fine." He hesitated a moment, as if deciding whether to continue the small talk, then said, "I have some information on Claudia Harrison, if you have time to hear it."

"Oh, yes! Please go ahead."

He cleared his throat. "I looked into the Harrison family and found no biological relationship between them and the Millers, Dorothy's family."

"Oh." Having already come to that conclusion, I wasn't enthused.

"But," his voice rose in promise, "there was a friendship between Claudia's great-grandmother, Sophie, and Marguerite Miller."

"A friendship?" The kids shuffled into the kitchen arguing about something. I put a finger to my lips and waved them to the table.

"Yes," Chauncey said. "I found out that Claudia's great-grandmother, Sophie, was the illegitimate child of a teenager who had been dropped off at the hospital by her disgraced father. Sophie was born at Danvers in—let me see . . . 1893. Sometime shortly afterwards, her young mother left without her, her identity never to be known by Sophie because the records were sealed at that time. However, if her descendants wanted to, they could get that information now."

"You're saying that Claudia's great-grandmother wasn't Marguerite's child, but she was a friend of hers? They knew each other?" I pushed the Cheerios box across the table and Max grabbed it first. Molly pursed her lips in anger. Quickly, I shoved an opened package of mini muffins at her.

"Yes to both questions. Sophie grew up at Danvers, worked in the laundry there, and lived on one of the high-functioning units until she married at age eighteen."

"When did you say she—Sophie—was born?"

"In 1893."

"Marguerite was at Danvers from fall of 1902 until her death in January of 1903," I said, doing some fast figuring.

But Chauncey was faster. "That would make Sophie nine years old when Marguerite was there. There's no way she could have been Marguerite's daughter."

"Then why would Claudia make that claim? She had to have known when her great-grandmother was born, and she had Marguerite's hospital admission information, which would prove that Marguerite's year there didn't jive with Sophie's birth."

Chauncey agreed. "But let me tell you what else I found out." Over the phone I heard a soft rustle of papers. "During the year she was there, Marguerite took Sophie under her wing, treated her as a little sister, gave her small gifts—hair ribbons, trinkets, and the like, even drawings that her own sister, Melinda, had sent in her letters."

"Drawings? Like the stick figure one that Claudia showed Dorothy?"

"Yes, that might really have been part of a letter from Dorothy's mother to Marguerite, just as Claudia claimed." Chauncey's voice quickened in excitement. "Anyway, to continue: the little motherless girl, Sophie, greatly admired the beautiful young Marguerite, and—this is conjecture on my part—probably fantasized about having her as a mother."

"That makes sense." Cradling the receiver between chin and shoulder, I opened the refrigerator, took out the milk and a carton of orange juice, and set them on the table. "Where did you get all of this?"

"I obtained access to some records through a former col-league of mine," he said vaguely. "And I called Claudia's mother, who turned out to be quite helpful after I introduced myself and explained I was representing family members who were interested in Marguerite Miller as part of genealogy re-search."

"Ah," I said, thinking I could have done that—called Claudia's mother. But then it had probably taken Chauncey's charm to elicit the information. "Did she shed any light on why Claudia lied about being a descendant of Marguerite's?"

"I think so." As he paused, I watched Molly uncap the near full gallon of milk and lift it, swaying precariously, aloft. I reached across the table and wrested the container from her. While she pouted, I poured milk on her cereal, and then between Max's spread fingers, which were clamped down over his Cheerios to prevent them from overflowing.

"Claudia was very close to her Grandmother Harrison, who liked to tell stories about her mother Sophie—Claudia's great-grandmother," Chauncey was saying. "As Grandmother Harrison got older, her stories became confused. Claudia's mother tried to point this out, but Claudia preferred her grandmother's romanticized versions even when they didn't make chronological sense. One story was about a rich young woman who ran away with a lover and had a child. Sound familiar?"

"Except for the child, it sounds like Marguerite. A fantasy Sophie might have had when she was in the asylum?"

"That was my thought," Chauncey agreed. "Young Sophie yearned for a mother and Marguerite was the ideal."

I grabbed the carton of juice as Molly was reaching for it and filled their glasses, then checked to make sure both had every conceivable thing they could need for a few minutes before moving into the dining room to escape the slurping and spoon-clinking-in-bowl sounds.

"I don't think Sophie lied so much as told stories she wished had been true," Chauncey continued. "She made up a background story about herself when her child asked, and then that child—Claudia's Grandmother Harrison—added some details, and passed on the revised story to Claudia."

"Who became so obsessed with it that she got her boyfriend to bring her up to New Hampshire to find Dorothy and convince her they were related," I said. "Did she really believe that her great-grandmother was Marguerite Miller's daughter?"

"According to her mother, she did."

"Then she wasn't trying to swindle Dorothy."

"No," Chauncey said. "I don't think so. She just got caught up in a romantic story and deluded herself into believing it true."

"What about the hospital record on Marguerite? How did Claudia get hold of that?"

"I imagine she claimed to be a descendant and requested it from the state."

"Much the way Dorothy got her records," I said. "I don't suppose they get picky on a request for a patient who's been dead for a hundred years."

"That reminds me," Chauncey said, "when her grandmother died, Claudia took her papers, which contained some letters and an old diary, all of which had originally belonged to Sophie."

"A diary—Marguerite's journal! So Claudia did have it."

"You know about it?"

"Dorothy has it, or rather it's at her house—she doesn't know she has it. But that's the connection! If Claudia had the journal, then Walter and Vivian got it from her! And Walter killed Claudia because he feared the journal would prove Claudia was an heir, which would threaten his sister's inheritance."

"Inheritance?"

I'd forgotten that Chauncey wouldn't know the recent developments, so I gave him the nutshell version of Dorothy's near overdose and the arrest of Walter and Vivian. Anxious to get off the phone in case Beverly called, I eased out of the conversation with a promise to keep him updated.

I cleaned up the kitchen, thinking of poor Claudia, wondering how her death had come about: Had Walter planned to kill her and take the journal? Or had he been caught up in a sudden rage—perhaps because she wouldn't give him what he wanted—and killed her in the heat of the moment?

I glanced at the wall clock, surprised to find it was ten already.

I gave up on Beverly for the time being and went upstairs to get ready for the day. I passed by the toy room where Max and Molly had pulled out the Brio train set, all of the Fisher Price farm animals, most of the Play Mobile people, and the entire set of wooden building blocks. I leaned a shoulder against the door, not daring to tread onto the heavily mined floor, but also not wanting to interrupt what had all the earmarks of another marathon play session. Smiling, I watched them interact, speaking only a word now and then, moving around each other, building and arranging with a mutual intuitive understanding of some large plan known only to themselves.

"Hey, guys, how about getting dressed," I suggested halfheartedly.

Deep in concentration, they didn't hear me, so I left them to their play. On a rainy miserable day, why should anyone have to get out of his or her pajamas? I was debating whether to follow their example and flop down on the bed with a book when the telephone sounded again. I sprinted into the bedroom and picked up before the second ring.

CHAPTER TWENTY-TWO

"Okay. Here's what I have." Beverly started right in. "The officer found a bag with vials of an as-yet unidentified drug along with containers of prescription-strength sedatives in the back-seat of Walter's car. Vivian tried some story about why she had the drugs, showing RN credentials, which turned out to be fake because she lost her license some years ago on a conviction for illegal possession of drugs." She paused for a quick breath before continuing, "Then, when questioned about Dorothy, Vivian started blaming Walter for misrepresenting Dorothy's health, saying that she—Vivian—had advised against the injections, but it was Walter who insisted, and even administered them when she would not."

"But I saw Vivian ready to inject Dorothy!"

"Yeah, it sounds like they were all in cahoots together—even Ellen, who, according to Vivian, went along with whatever her brother said to do. Anyway, when she was told they were being held on suspicion of attempted murder, Vivian had a meltdown and vehemently denied they meant to kill Dorothy. They just wanted to keep her mildly sedated."

"But why?"

"She said Walter was afraid Dorothy would change her will and leave the house to somebody other than his sister."

"Did they really mean to kill Dorothy?"

"I wouldn't put it past them because the police found Claudia's missing pocketbook in the trunk of their car." I gave a low whistle as Beverly rushed on, "At first, Vivian denied knowing anything about it. Then she started talking.

"Apparently, Walter was at Dorothy's when Claudia visited her. He caught the gist of their conversation and panicked, thinking that Dorothy might change her will and cut out Ellen, who was, in essence, supporting him. Walter had Vivian—pretending to be Ellen working on behalf of Dorothy—call and set up a meeting with Claudia. The intention being to get hold of whatever papers Claudia had that might prove she was Marguerite's great-granddaughter."

"Why not just have Ellen set up the meeting?"

"I don't think she was involved at that point. Anyway, since Claudia was already coming to the Grand Hotel gala opening, she agreed to meet there."

"And she chose the room in which to meet," I said as clues began to fall into place. "Just as I did, Claudia figured out that Room One-thirteen was originally Marguerite's room. She probably tried to book it for herself, found out it was part of the tour, and so knew would be free. She might even have been suspicious of the meeting and wanted to make sure people would come around at some point."

"Probably."

" 'Follow the green dress,' " I said.

"What?"

"I overheard Walter telling Vivian to follow Claudia. Never mind. Go on."

"So, the three of them met," she continued. "Walter offered to pay for whatever Claudia had, but she refused. She recognized Walter from the house, saw that Vivian was not Ellen, and threatened to tell Dorothy that they were plotting against her. At this point, Walter tried to take the journal and papers. Claudia fought him and began to scream, which is when Walter lost it, grabbed the letter opener, and stabbed her. Vivian claimed she tried to stop him.”

“When Claudia said ‘Mahg,’ she was trying to say ‘Margue-rite’s journal.’ ”

“Maybe,” Beverly said.

“So Walter took the journal and left,” I said, “but didn’t escape right away because I heard him arguing with Vivian below the verandah when the police were questioning everyone. I’m guessing that he wanted to leave, but she thought they’d look suspicious if they did.”

“Right,” Beverly said. “She stayed to give an excuse in case they noticed Walter gone.”

“While Vivian was going on about all this, what did Walter have to say?”

“Nothing. Walter was in another room, refusing to talk. Anyway, that’s when the officer up there, who gave the info to my source down here, had to leave.” Beverly paused for a quick breath. “They’re being held in Maine right now, but they’ll be brought back to Portsmouth to face attempted murder charges on Dorothy, and I’m guessing murder charges as well—Claudia’s.”

“Wow,” I said. “It’s over, then, isn’t it?”

“Or just beginning; there’s the trial. Listen, I’ve got to go. This is a big story and I’m under deadline. Keep what I’ve told you under your hat for the time being, okay? I’ll be in touch soon. I plan on doing a story on the hotel, and on Dorothy and Marguerite and your part in bringing them together.”

I immediately shared what Beverly had told me with Gus—much of it made the evening news, anyway—and he brought up a question that had also bothered me: When and to what extent had Ellen gotten involved? She hadn’t been part of Claudia’s murder, but must have known about it afterward. She hadn’t planned the chair incident—Walter had—but she suspected him and she had apparently allowed Vivian to give Dorothy illegal drugs. Gus tended toward believing Ellen had been part of a grand plot to do away with Dorothy and get hold of her house from the beginning. I wasn't sure about that, but I felt that there was something missing from Vivian's story, and that it had to do with Ellen.

That night I was too restless to settle down with Gus to watch the Red Sox game on television, so I went to the computer in the den and looked up the Portsmouth obituaries for July and August of 1902, something I'd been meaning to do. When I had no luck, I just googled Lemuel Adams, Isles of Shoals, 1902, and hit pay dirt. He was listed in a newspaper article about a drowning incident.

To the accompaniment of moans, groans, and the occasional cry of despair—the Red Sox were apparently falling to the Yankees—I read words that became more and more familiar. I went to get the folder on Marguerite, the Grand Hotel, and other notes and photocopies I'd made at the Seacoast Historical Research Library. I located a detailed newspaper account for the Isles of Shoals drownings.

> *July seventeenth, 1902. A headwaiter, his assistant, and twelve young waitresses from the Oceanic Hotel on Star Island, along with a fisherman attempting to rescue them, were drowned by accident in the most heartrending tragedy in years. The party of fourteen was returning from a sail when a sudden squall came up. An observer who was on the Oceanic Hotel pier when the group set off said, "They were laughing and joking as they boarded. Never a jollier party than these young people."*

I skimmed the next few paragraphs detailing the incident. The skipper, a local fisherman, had been hired to take out sailing parties from the hotel on his whaleboat. On this particular day, there was a brisk breeze from the southeast so he headed northwest, sailing within the lee of the islands. Upon their return, the twelve girls were lined up along the port gunwale to offset the list of the boat. When they entered the harbor between Appledore and Star Island, a steamer was arriving at the hotel pier. As the skipper went on starboard tack in his approach to the harbor, the girls all crowded to the starboard side to see the passengers leaving the steamer, only fifty feet away. The whaleboat entered the lee of the steamer and wind pressure on the sail was suddenly cut off. The boat jerked up and because of the weight on the one side, listed all the way to starboard, and water poured over the gunwale. I read on, looking for a name.

"Being well ballasted to make her stiff on wind, she sank like a plummet," said the skipper, the only survivor of the accident. "She were drawn under by a terrible suction and struck bottom." The squall was in full force now, making it difficult to get help out to the young people. Two fishermen from Appledore launched a dory through the strong breakers. The steamer, having dislodged its passengers, tried to help, but the wind and waves drove it into the rocks, so it had to pull away. Then fishermen from Star and Smuttynose came, their dories bobbing crazily in the tumultuous waters. Eight of the girls were brought to shore, but none survived.

Charles Dawson and Lemuel Adams—there it was!—were the first fishermen on the scene. They were able to bring in two of the girls, but at the cost of Lemuel Adams's life. According to Dawson, "When we got to where the boat went down, the girls were all bunched together. Lem grasped two, trying to keep their heads out of the water, while I rowed as best I could in the rough sea. About fifteen yards from the shore Lem was thrown from the boat. I couldn't reach him, then lost sight of them. By the time I gained land, they had washed ashore, Lem still holding onto the two girls. We tried in vain to resuscitate them."

The bodies were carried to the Appledore Hotel and placed in a row for identification. The next day a diver found the whale-boat intact and, one at a time, discovered the remaining bodies at a depth of about sixty feet. When the seas were calm, the coroner of Kittery and the undertaker of Portsmouth came out to take the fourteen bodies of the hotel workers to Portsmouth to be claimed by relatives. The body of Lemuel Adams remained on the island, and was identified by his wife. Lemuel, son of the late Jonathan Adams, who died of illness last fall, was a third-generation fisherman on Appledore. He leaves behind a wife and a mother.

There was silence in the other room. Gus had either turned off the game in disgust, or followed it through to the bitter end and was now mourning in silence. I put the computer to sleep, but continued sitting at the desk, thinking. I wondered if Marguerite had found her brief time with Lemuel Adams worth what she'd gone through: running away, giving up her family and the creature comforts of wealthy Boston society, then suffering the loss of a husband. I wanted to believe that she'd been happy with her choice. That the day-to-day realities of being a fisherman's wife had in some way measured up to her hopes. Or at the very least, she'd felt satisfaction at having directed the course of her life, if only for one short year.

CHAPTER TWENTY-THREE

I called Jenny on Sunday and received word that, other than being tired and anxious over Saturday's events, Dorothy was recovering nicely. Jenny would continue staying with her nights until the visiting nurses evaluated her and made recommendations for her future. I hoped those recommendations precluded Dorothy moving abruptly from her home, but I couldn't see her functioning on her own there, and it was unlikely she'd find the same kind of arrangement she'd had with Ellen. If Dorothy had as little money as she'd claimed, her options could be limited.

Although anxious to get back to Marguerite's journal, I knew I had to give Dorothy a few days before pestering her, so I forced myself to be patient. Meanwhile, I tried to figure out the extent of Ellen's involvement. She had been giving Walter money to pay off gambling debts that were, according to her, so large his creditors were threatening him (I thought of his bruised face, and that strange envelope addressed to him in block letters). It seemed unlikely that Ellen could make enough money working for Dorothy to pay off big creditors.

Another detail that tickled my brain was what Vivian had told the police, that Walter's motive in drugging Dorothy had been to keep her sedated so she couldn't change her will. Walter had already gotten rid of the supposed threat—Claudia—so why would he still worry about the will? If he needed money, he might want his sister to inherit the house sooner rather than later, but that meant he'd want Dorothy out of the way permanently, not merely sedated. Was there some reason to keep Dorothy alive but submissive?

I called a friend of mine, Angie, who does accounting for a couple of small businesses in town, and picked her brain. She said it would be easy for somebody in Ellen's position to skim off a little money here and there, maybe even larger amounts, but then those could show up as irregularities and the bank would probably call to check them out.

"How else might someone get regular large sums without being noticeable?"

"That's hard to say," Angie said. "You'd have to look at the books. You might find a discrepancy somewhere." She sounded doubtful, so I surmised that the idea of Ellen skimming copious amounts of money from Dorothy's monthly Social Security checks was probably flawed. At best, it was another thing to put on hold until I could visit Dorothy. I thanked Angie and said goodbye.

By the middle of the week, Jenny felt that Dorothy was back to normal and could receive visitors, so one afternoon Mayta and I set off for Portsmouth. Jenny met us at the door and gave a quick whispered update.

"The police analyzed that syringe. It was Diazepam—no way was it prescribed for her!"

"What's that?" Mayta whispered back.

"Anti-anxiety medication. You've probably heard of the brand name, Valium."

We nodded and she went on, "Anyway, they took samples of her other meds and found that one of them—Temazepam, a sedative—was not prescribed either. Temazepam is especially dangerous in combination with Diazepam. Affects the muscles and balance, makes you weak and groggy. No wonder Dorothy was in bed all the time!"

"They wanted to keep her out of commission," I said, "but

could that combination kill her?"

"Probably not. At least not in the regular doses she'd been getting."

I frowned, wondering again about the motive for keeping Dorothy weak and groggy. "Vivian and Walter supplied the drugs, Vivian administered the Diazepam, but it must have been Ellen who gave Dorothy the Te—what was it?"

"Temazepam," Jenny said.

"Yeah, the Temazepam. She gave her that along with her regular meds, so Ellen is as much to blame as the other two. She had to know what it was."

Jenny arched her eyebrows and put a finger to her lips, which I took to mean that she hadn't told this to Dorothy. "I spoke with her doctor, and we've got the prescribed meds separated from the others," she said. "I'll make sure she gets what she's supposed to get until somebody else takes over."

It was good to see Dorothy sitting up, dressed, and alert again when we entered the living room. Jenny offered to make tea, and while she was in the kitchen, Mayta, Dorothy, and I made casual conversation. I was anxious to get to the journal, and was about to bluntly ask about it when Dorothy finally spoke. "You found Marguerite's journal."

"It was in the den," I said quickly. "Did you read it?"

"Actually, I'd forgotten about it until just now." She smiled, knowing my impatience. "I wanted to wait for you, anyway."

I didn't need a formal invitation to scoot down the hallway. The journal wasn't in the pile of books under the window where I remembered leaving it, so I scanned the room. When my glance fell on the small secretary in the corner, I recalled Angie's comment that somebody should go through Dorothy's finances. On a whim, I went to it and unashamedly shuffled through the piles of papers. Most were flyers and Ellen's own bills, which I gave no more than a once-over. Then I noticed a stack of envelopes held together with a yellow plastic clip in one of the secretary's cubbies. I pulled it out, thumbed through, and saw that all were addressed to Dorothy.

I sat on the edge of the bed and spread the envelopes out on the chenille bedspread. Most of the senders were easily identified by their return addresses: an electric bill, a water bill, a couple of local charities, and a decorating magazine—probably a renewal notice. One, however, listed its identity only as LGI, with an address in New York City. It had been opened so I slid out the letter, which gave an accounting of profits and gains for the quarter that had ended in April. I found no explanation for what LGI stood for or who they might be, other than an investment company.

"Ahem." I looked up to see Mayta at the door. "Did you get lost?"

"Come look at this," I waved her into the room.

She took the letter I held out to her, perused it, and handed it back with a shrug. "It's an investment company. Did you find the journal?"

"Not yet." I went over to the secretary again and looked through the contents in the other cubbyholes, then pulled open the top drawer. "According to that letter, Dorothy should be receiving dividend checks. There's no computer around, which means Ellen probably doesn't do bills online, so there must be an accounting book."

Mayta heaved a sigh. "Andy, I don't think we should be doing this."

But I'd already found a red ledger. I pulled it out and opened it. It was neatly filled out month-by-month, beginning in January of the previous year. I read through the accounts in— monthly checks from Social Security—and the accounts out— utilities for the most part.

"Aha! No income from LGI."

Mayta peered over my shoulder. "Maybe the company didn't make a profit, or they don't send out dividends regularly."

"Nope. According to this letter, the company is making a profit, and they have been sending out monthly checks, as 'specially requested.' I skimmed this entire ledger—the last sixteen months—and there are no entries from LGI." I returned to the secretary and began a more thorough search.

"Maybe they go straight into a savings account."

"Then there should be proof somewhere. I have a strong feeling, however, that they don't." I went through the contents of the drawer again.

"I hate it when you do this." Mayta had moved back to the doorway. "Let's just find the journal and get out of here."

In the very back of the drawer, I found a brown leather checkbook and, underneath it, another checkbook with a blue plastic cover. I opened the first and noted the two names imprinted on the lefthand corner of the checks: Dorothy L. Dennis and Ellen Timmons. I flipped through the transaction register, which closely matched records in the ledger book: deposits of Dorothy's monthly Social Security checks, and accountings of checks written to utility companies, the grocery store, the pharmacy, and a few other stores or services that were nominal and appeared legitimate. No large checks had been written or withdrawals made. Nor had any additional income been deposited.

I opened the second checkbook and found the same two names on those checks, the difference being that this account was with another bank. Why different banks? Why two checkbooks? The answer became clear as I looked through the register, which, like the ledger, also began in January of the year before. Here was what I'd been looking for: monthly deposits for $2,200—undoubtedly from LGI—along with five deposits for around $500 and four deposits of between $1,300 and $1,400.

Most telling, though, were the periodic withdrawals for a thousand here, a thousand there, sometimes more, sometimes less. Money taken out had no notations other than "withdrawal," but I could guess where that money went. I skimmed through the pages to the end. The balance, which was up to date, read $890. A quick figuring, give or take a few thousand, gave me a sum of roughly $44,000 that had moved in and out of this account.

"Bingo!" I waved the checkbook in the air. "This is why Walter wanted Dorothy quiet but alive. He needed her investment checks to keep coming so Ellen could deposit them into a secret account and then siphon the money off! They were stealing between $2,000 and $3,000 a month from her!"

Mayta squinted at the register I stuck in front of her nose. "But he tried to kill her. The chair in the kitchen, the drugs."

"No, he didn't. He knew she was getting suspicious. He wanted her injured so they'd have an excuse to slip in medications to keep her weak, out of the way, maybe to make her appear foggy-minded as if dementia was setting in—people with dementia tend to be suspicious and think others are stealing from them, so you don't take them seriously." I grabbed the ledger and letter and strode past Mayta, down the hall to the living room.

"Dorothy," I began, with more force than I meant to. She jumped, and Jenny looked up from the tray she'd just set on the coffee table. I tempered my tone before continuing. "Do you know of an investment, LGI, in your name?"

Dorothy frowned as she considered the question. "No, but then I haven't looked at my finances in years. I inherited some investments from my mother when she died about thirty years ago. Maybe that's one of them."

"*One* of them? That's what the other deposits are, then," I said, more to myself than to her. "Of course there would be more than one investment."

"Yes, there were two or three, but they didn't amount to much."

"Well," I held the paper aloft, "I found a quarterly statement from LGI, one of the companies you have an investment in, which has apparently done quite well. According to this record, you should be receiving monthly dividend checks of about $2,200."

"Oh, my." Dorothy put a hand to one cheek. "I had no idea! That's quite a bit."

"Yes, it's a nice sum." I handed the statement letter to her, along with the ledger and the leather checkbook, all of which she put in her lap. "The problem is there's no accounting of those checks in either of these."

"What does that mean?" Jenny asked, but I could see realization dawning on her face.

Dorothy read the letter and set it down on the sofa next to her. Gingerly, as if it was an unfamiliar object belonging to someone else, she picked up the checkbook, leafed through the transaction register, and put it on top of the letter. The ledger she merely opened to the first page and closed without going any further. "Are you saying that Ellen has been taking those checks for herself?"

Nobody replied.

"Yes," Dorothy answered her own question. "That's it, isn't it?" She averted her gaze to her garden outside the glass door. "I'm a foolish old woman who has stuck her head in the sand. I think I knew that Ellen was taking money from me, but I ignored it."

"I also found this." I held out the other checkbook. "Regular deposits and withdrawals of large sums of money. Although there's no information given other than the amounts, I'm sure we'll find that this is where the missing income from your investments has been going. Ellen has been giving it to her brother to pay off his debts."

Dorothy looked at the checkbook, but made no move to take it. I continued, "I thought it was the house Walter wanted, but he was more concerned about not losing this source of income."

"Yes," she said quietly, "The signs were there: the tension he brought into the house, the way Ellen was worried whenever he was around, the frequent calls on his cell phone that upset him, and that time he showed up looking like somebody had hit him. I knew he was doing more than casual gambling, and that Ellen didn't have much money to give him."

"Who is Vivian?" I asked. "How did she come into the picture?"

"She started coming around with Walter a few months ago. He introduced her as his girlfriend, and then, after my fall, he said she was a registered nurse who could administer medication at the doctor's orders. Except I don't think my doctor would have ordered injections without telling me."

"He didn't," Jenny put in firmly.

Dorothy shook her head. "So needless, the whole thing. I would have loaned Ellen money if she'd asked—maybe not to give to that depraved brother of hers, but if she'd told me what was going on, I would have helped in some way. And she shouldn't have worried that I'd change the will."

"Even now?" I couldn't resist asking. "Ellen stole from you—that's embezzlement."

Dorothy's forehead puckered in thought. "If I don't tell the police about that other account, she can't be charged for stealing, can she?"

"I think they'll find out anyway during their investigation. The police know that she gave you illegal drugs."

"But Ellen wasn't in the room when Vivian administered those injections."

I glanced at Jenny, who gave a slight shake of her head. It wasn't the time to bring up Ellen's obvious abuse of the Temazepam pills.

"But she had to have known what was going on," I gently. "And it was Ellen who told me you had congestive heart failure, which you don't. She wanted you to appear frail."

Dorothy blinked away the tears welling in her eyes. Jenny looked down at her tea mug, and Mayta gave me a disapproving frown. Perhaps I'd been too direct, but Dorothy couldn't have any illusions about Ellen's part in the scheme to harm her, to steal her money. Still, I felt bad for what I'd said. I opened my mouth to try to soften my message, but Dorothy spoke first.

"You're right, Andy." She raised her chin, her eyes meeting mine. Her short hair had been styled, and the simple silver and amethyst earrings and matching necklace she wore complemented her lavender print dress. I realized that I'd never seen her anything other than meticulously attired, even while lying abed in her nightgown. After all she'd been through, she still held her composure, back straight, hands one atop the other primly in her lap.

"I did become suspicious of the injections and the extra pills I began taking after my fall," she said, eyes dry now. "My doctor always explains changes in my medications. Once, I argued with Ellen and refused to take them until she showed me the bottles themselves. I questioned one that didn't have my doctor's name on it, and she gave me an explanation I took at face value. I wanted so badly to believe in Ellen that I wouldn't let any doubts in. I've depended on her for so long. And now, I just don't know what I'm going to do."

"Oh, Dorothy, things will work out." Jenny dropped down next to her and took both of her hands in her own. "Al and I are right next door. We can help you."

"There are choices," Mayta said. "You have an extra $2,200 a month now that you didn't realize you had—even more with those other investments you mentioned. You could hire another home health aide. Or you could move into an assisted-living situation or an independent-living community."

"Yes," Dorothy said, nodding slowly. "I have a lot to think about. Right now, though, let's have a look at that journal you said you found."

CHAPTER TWENTY-FOUR

Jenny had taken advantage of us being there to run some errands. As Dorothy, Mayta, and I walked down the hallway to the den, I worried that the journal might not be there after all. Maybe, being in a hurry that day, I'd read the inside page wrong. Maybe Walter or Ellen had taken it and hidden it elsewhere or, worse, destroyed it. But it had just been my memory playing tricks, because all it took was a little wider search. I located Marguerite Miller's journal almost immediately, two stacks over from where I thought I'd left it.

I picked up the slim book, plain except for the faint gilt lettering, *Journal,* on its front, and held it reverently, sure I felt the pulse of life—Marguerite's—within. The pages, feathery soft with age, no longer lay together, the writing upon them giving the book added volume. When Dorothy reached out to take the journal, I realized I'd been holding it for some moments. I handed it to her, and she lowered herself onto the edge of Ellen's bed. Mayta and I took seats on either side.

"I never imagined this existed." Dorothy ran a hand lightly over the smooth red-fading-to-pink leather and opened to the first page. " *'My Journal, Marguerite Miller':* It's her handwriting. I recognize it from the inscription in her history book."

"What's this?" Mayta tugged at a corner of paper peeping from the pages. Out slid the torn bottom portion of a handwritten letter with two lines of a message: *Papa has promised to bring you home soon. I miss you so much. Love, Melinda.* Below the

286

signature was a drawing of two stick figures, one labeled *me* and the other *you,* with spiral hair and long triangular skirts, arms encircling each other.

"Why, that's the paper Claudia showed me." Dorothy stretched out a tremulous hand to take it. "I didn't think much of it then, but in conjunction with this journal, I think she must have been telling the truth: This was written by my mother to my aunt, Marguerite."

"Chauncey Brown found out that Marguerite befriended a young girl, Sophie, in the asylum," I said, aware that I might have to explain who Chauncey was and why I'd asked him to look into the background of Dorothy's family. But Dorothy was gazing in awe at the scrap of paper in her hand and didn't question my comment. I continued, "Sophie was Claudia's grandmother. Marguerite gave her little gifts like the pictures your mother drew on her letters."

"This journal must be the other thing Claudia promised to show me." Dorothy said, appearing not to hear my words. "How did she come by it, I wonder."

"Maybe Marguerite gave it to Sophie when she became ill," I said. "Or Sophie took it when Marguerite died. Whichever, eventually it was passed down to Claudia—Sophie's granddaughter."

Mayta jiggled the foot on her crossed leg impatiently. "Let's read it!"

Dorothy tucked the paper into the back of the journal and opened to the first entry. " *'May sixth, 1901,'* " she read aloud. " *'I begin this journal, a birthday gift from my friend Bess, at the start of my adult life, my eighteenth year.'* "

"You have no trouble reading her script," Mayta said.

"It's very like my mother's. I feel almost like I'm reading my mother's words." Dorothy fell silent, skimming the next page. "Mostly day-to-day stuff, despite her intent not to tell it—get-togethers with friends, comments on family. Interesting for me, though probably not so much for you two."

"Skip ahead," I urged. "We can read it in detail later, but I'd like to know what her thoughts were at the time of her disappearance."

Dorothy obliged, flipping through the next few pages. "Not at the hotel yet, but this is interesting: *June fifth, 1901. Something strange happened today. Bess and I went to a fair held at the Common. On a whim, we decided to have our fortunes told. Bess went first and was told that she would marry and have three children. When it was my turn an overwhelming feeling came over me: dread and fear. I know I am to marry Timothy, that we will have children, but to hear it foretold by this gypsy woman somehow would have seemed to seal a fate that I realized in that instant I dreaded. I bolted before she could tell me what I didn't want to hear.*'"

"Ah! The seeds of unrest," I said. "When does she get to the hotel?"

Dorothy turned to the next page. "Here it is. She's been there for a couple of days now."

I leaned closer to look at the date. "Is there an entry for the day she arrived?"

"No, this is the first one. *June fifteenth, 1901. How I wish I could live on this small beautiful island and never go back to Boston. I would not need anything so grand as this hotel; one of the pretty little homes along the way to Portsmouth would be perfect.*'" Dorothy's voice suddenly choked and she stopped. "I'm sorry. I don't know why . . ." She fanned fingers in front of her tearing eyes.

"There, there." Mayta patted her knee. "It's understandable. After all that's happened, and now hearing your aunt's own words, of course you'd be emotional."

I reached for the tissue box on the desk and passed it to Dorothy. "Do you want me to continue?" I asked gently.

"Yes, please." Dorothy touched a tissue to her eyes. Mayta scooted over and I took the place in the middle.

I skimmed the next two pages in which Marguerite expounded on the beauty of the ocean, the trees, the rock outcropping along the shore, mentioning people in general—fishermen, hotel workers, other guests—but nobody in particular. I skipped parts that were either repetitive or difficult to read because of the handwriting, and began at an entry a couple of days later. "Here we go. A change of attitude: *June seventeenth, 1901. I will not go back. I have decided that I do not love Timothy and cannot marry him . . .* something, something—can't make it out . . . *It is not fair that I am expected to follow through on decisions I made as a child. How can one know her heart at seventeen?' "*

"I'd agree with that," Mayta said.

" *June eighteenth, 1901,'* the next day," I continued. " *'I went to Portsmouth with others from the hotel. There was another fortune-teller and this time I summoned the courage to have my palm read. She told me what I'd expected, that I would marry and have two children, but I'd already prepared myself to discount her words. Then she told me something that I did take seriously. She said that I should follow my heart's desire. I have been thinking of that advice. I think it means that I should do what I feel is right for me.' "* I held up the page and squinted at it. "I can't read this part. The ink's blurred."

"It's getting interesting," Mayta said. Dorothy nodded as she blew her nose.

"It's clearer at the bottom of the page: *'I believe the perfect companion for me would be someone who lives with nature. He would live and work in the open where there is sunshine and water and trees. He would not wear a businessman's suit, but casual clothing, that of a workman perhaps. He would make his living by his talents or craftsmanship. We would walk in the woods, sit by the sea, and contemplate the mysteries of the universe. We would have need of nobody else, and would never go to the city.'* " I paused, reading ahead to myself.

"Dreams of a young romantic." Dorothy smiled ruefully.

"Yeah, and listen to this: *'June twentieth, 1901. I have found someone who will help me steer the course I have set for myself. He is handsome, mysterious, a little earthy, and, of course, completely devoted to me. I have given him an exotic background—a Roma from Europe, where his family was persecuted—and even a name, Emil. We walk the beach at night, run through the woods under the moon, and talk for hours about nature, feelings, destiny, past lives.'* "

" 'I have given him'?" Mayta said. "What does that mean? She made up a background for somebody she met?"

"It does sound like that," Dorothy said. "What do you think, Andy?"

I didn't answer right away because I remembered something. "Those bracketed phrases," I said, "the ones in Marguerite's Eastern European history book. They had to do with the Roma, the gypsies." I pushed the journal onto Mayta's lap and rose.

"Oh, don't leave," Mayta protested. "Let's continue reading."

"I'll just be a sec." I hurried down the hallway to the bookcase where I remembered Dorothy putting the history text of Marguerite's I'd borrowed. I grabbed it, along with the other one, her poetry book, and returned. I found the spot in *A History of Eastern Europe* where the two passages were marked, then sat back down between Dorothy and Mayta, and read aloud, " *'Beginning in 1834 slaves, including many gypsies, or Roma as they were sometimes called, were freed in Eastern Europe. Ten years later, the Moldavian church liberated their gypsy slaves, and in 1848 Transylvanian serfs were emancipated.'* " I moved my finger over to the opposite page. "Then there's this: *'Following Romania's abolishment of slavery in 1856, large numbers of gypsies emigrated to western Europe, where they set up encampments in the countryside, enduring hostile attacks from villagers and imprisonment from the government.*' " I looked from Mayta to Dorothy.

Dorothy's brow puckered. "You think she made up a background for somebody from information out of a history book?"

"No," I said. "I think she invented a companion using these facts. Like a child makes up an invisible friend."

"But why?" Dorothy asked. "She couldn't have believed he was real."

"Maybe she did," Mayta said. "Maybe that's why she was hospitalized."

I closed the history book, set it on the floor, and picked up the volume of poems. I intended to leaf through it, but it fell open where the spine had broken. I perused the page, noting that Marguerite had underlined the title of a poem. "Listen," I said after a moment. "This may have been another inspiration for Marguerite's imaginary companion. It's called *The Wanderer:*

> '*To the edge of the town from a far exotic land,*
> *Came a wanderer with* kumpa'nia, *his fellow*
> *transient band.*
> *Darkly handsome, brightly adorned, he stepped out*
> *with tambourine,*
> *Struck it once, twice, setting loose a fury the town*
> *had ne'er seen.*
> '*Tis life's own blood, nature and fate, 'tis bart—the*
> *way things are.*
> *Soulful eyes flashing, firelight plashing upon his*
> *angular face,*
> *Blue hair streaming, sinewy limbs striking, stomping*
> *out the pace.*
> *All ringed round, twirling, fiddling, crying out the*
> *lively song,*
> *All but one who watched, with love, her* ves'tacha
> *incite the throng.*

291

> 'Tis life's own blood, nature and fate, 'tis bart—the
> way things are.
> Then came the gadje, brandishing torches, touching
> them to caravans,
> Squeals of horses, cries of children, moans of the devil
> beng.
> 'Til nothing was left of the zest and the beauty of her
> beloved te'sorthene,
> But her wail when she ran to be at his side and lift
> his tambourine.
> 'Tis life's own blood, nature and fate, 'tis bart—the
> way things are.' "

After a moment I said, "Marguerite described her companion as handsome, mysterious, earthy."

"And a gypsy—a Roma—whose family was persecuted," Mayta recalled. "You're right. He did sound a lot like the wanderer. And the part about fate—she talked about that, too."

"A romantic young woman could be affected by that poem," Dorothy said, a smile tugging at the corners of her mouth. "It gave me a few tingles."

I leafed through the rest of the book, but found no other markings. I set it on top of the history book at my feet and took the journal from Mayta, continuing where I'd left off. " *June twenty-second, 1901. The worst has happened. Alice notified my father of my evening walks, which she disapproves of, and now he and Timothy have come to fetch me home. I told Papa of my change of heart concerning Timothy, thinking that I might receive some understanding, but he became very stern, allowing that while I may have a choice in marriage, I have none in deciding whether to return to Boston. Furthermore, he said there would be great disappointment, even disgrace, for all if I broke off the engagement. I cannot marry Timothy, but it seems that neither can I return home without marrying him.*

" *'June twenty-third, 1901. My father has left me with little choice but to defy him. I trust that, in time, he will come to understand why I had to go. I shall leave no letters of my intentions. When I am safely away, I will write to Mama and Papa and Timothy explaining my decision, and also to Melinda, asking that she return Timothy's book and his mother's ring.'* " I looked up. "So she did leave the engagement ring."

Dorothy shook her head. "It was never found. I remember my mother saying there was some strife between the families because the ring wasn't returned."

"Then what happened to it?" I said. "Did she change her mind and take it with her? Was it stolen from the hotel?"

"She planned on giving it to Melinda," Mayta said. "Either she took it with her to send to her sister later, or left it in the room for her to find."

"This could be why Claudia became intrigued with the notion of a missing diamond ring," I said. "Maybe she thought it was still hidden in the hotel room, and that's why she went to that room."

"If it was left in the room, it's long gone," Dorothy said. "Go on. Maybe we'll learn more."

I skimmed the next page. "I don't think so. It takes up again more than a year later. She's writing from the hospital now. *'August twenty-fourth, 1902. I have not written in this journal for so long, but the doctor has suggested that putting down my thoughts and feelings may help me so, although I am not enthusiastic about it, I will endeavor to do as he recommends. They say I cannot be released until I have recovered, so I must find the strength to fight this debilitating melancholy that weighs heavily upon me. My father, who has become my support, assures me that entering treatment is my best hope of recovery.*

It has been one month since a most devastating event took the life of my beloved husband. I did not fully realize the strength of my feel-

ings for Lemuel until his death sapped my desire to live. Ours was not the idyllic union that, in my innocence at the beginning, I'd hoped for. Lemuel was a practical man, while I tend to be a romantic—fanciful, as my father would say. The differences in our personalities, which had first attracted us to each other, made for many misunderstandings. However, we had begun to forge a strong relationship based on mutual respect and sincere fondness. I became more practical in my expectations while he learned to appreciate what he called my 'romantic notions' like wanting to accompany him on his fishing boat, or take walks simply for pleasure's sake. Even his mother had mellowed in her feelings toward me, and was looking upon me more as a daughter. I believe Lemuel and I could have had a happy life together. Then came the terrible accident at the Oceanic Hotel wharf that I find so difficult to think about. Perhaps, in time, I will be able to talk about it with Doctor Lyle but not now.' "

Mayta made a sympathetic sound. "The poor girl was grieving. She should have been home with her family, not put away somewhere."

Dorothy sniffed and I passed her the tissue box again. "Please continue, Andy," she said. "I like listening to your young voice, imagining that it's Marguerite talking."

I ran a finger down the page. "More everyday stuff about some of the other women, her doctor, meals, the gardens, and of course, wanting to go home. She sounds hopeful, but resigned, just waiting to be discharged." I paused at an entry, leafed ahead, and then returned to the beginning. "Here, these are different—more introspective."

State Lunatic Hospital at Danvers
Danvers, Massachusetts
September 1902

Marguerite sat on her single bed, hands on either side of her face, the tips of her fingers covering her ears to dim the pitiful cries from the other end of the dormitory. "Daddy! Daddy! Come get me, Daddy!" the woman wailed in a childish high, thin voice. If they didn't come to subdue her soon, Marguerite knew from experience, the fit would escalate from verbal to physical, with the woman throwing things. Then Marguerite, as the only other occupant of the room, would have to seek shelter or become a target. It was probably better to leave right now, but she waited. Surely someone would come any second.

I do not belong here, she thought, as she did many times each day. Although some of the women were kind, others had odd and even bizarre behaviors. One ranted constantly against her husband, berating him as if he stood right there beside her. Another visited almost every day with a downtrodden-looking man, whom she called "my lawyer," smugly telling everyone that she was going to be released soon, while the attendants smirked behind her back. Marguerite felt sorry for these lost souls, but she believed that if they would cooperate with the nurses and doctors, they could be cured. As for herself, she thought of her illness not as something she had, but as a void within her, a painful emptiness she was powerless to fill. She yearned to leave, to return to her parents' home, but Papa wouldn't allow it until the doctors said she was better. So she must be patient and try to get well. But she did not belong here.

The woman's cries were shrieks now, louder and more insistent and interspersed with curses, but still nobody came. Where were the nurses? Marguerite dared to look in her direction. The middle-aged woman was writhing on her bed, her shapeless dress hoisted up and twisted around thin white legs, her hair a dark wild tangle on the pillow. But she had not yet focused on her surroundings, and Marguerite weighed the chances of tiptoeing past and reaching the hallway without detection. Slowly, so as not to creak the bed springs, she rose. She lifted the mattress, pushed her journal under it, and began to make her way down the aisle between the rows of beds. She was halfway to the door, almost even with the woman's bed, when the woman sat up and fixed her gaze on Marguerite. Her face contorted with rage as she grabbed at the edges of her mattress, catching hold of the sheet and pulling it free. She waved her arms, grabbing at air with her hands, and kicked her legs, her eyes never leaving Marguerite, who froze. Then two attendants hurried in. One gestured Marguerite past as they restrained the woman. Released, she ran from the room and down the deserted hallway.

She was breathing heavily when she reached the stairwell and ducked under it, crawling into the far corner. There, she wrapped her dress around her pulled-up legs, laid her forehead on her knees, and let loose silent tears. "Papa, Mama," she whispered, then clamped her lips shut, realizing how similar her appeal was to the woman's in the dormitory. But she did want her family. She'd realized how much she'd missed them when her parents visited for the first time a couple of weeks before. Mama and Papa still disapproved of her imprudent behavior in running away, but they had forgiven her. Papa said she'd ruined any chance of a respectable life outside their home as she was "not marriageable" now, but she did not believe it. If she wanted to marry again—she couldn't imagine it at this point, but if she did—then she would; if she decided not to marry again, then she would still have a productive life, perhaps in taking up studies of nature or history. Of course, she had not said any of this aloud to Papa. She must first convince him that she was ready to come home.

Thinking of this now, she raised her head, blotted the corners of her eyes dry with the tips of her fingers, and backed out of her hiding spot. She would not gain her release by crawling into corners to cry. Nor could she slip out of a window and just walk away, she told herself firmly. Not this time.

When she thought of it, she was surprised at how easily she had done that: stepped out of a window and into another world, taken herself out of one life and put herself into another one. Whatever power it was that had taken hold of her had been both good and bad. The act itself—leaving on her own accord—had given her a sense of possibilities that, even now, she still possessed. Not marrying Timothy had been a good thing; marriage to Lemuel, even for such a short period, had been good. Being cut off from her family had been a bad thing. And then, of course, there was Lemuel's death, the horrible way he died, his lifeless body so white and strange, laid out among the others on the shore. But she couldn't think of it. Shaking her head against the picture forming in her mind, she replaced it with one that always brought a smile: Lemuel in his boat, his mussed blond hair fluttering in a breeze as he frowned over some aspect of his work—mending fishing gear, untangling nets, judging the sea and sky on the horizon.

With Lemuel gone, it had become unbearable to be on that island, in that house. His mother, despite her selfish motives, had done Marguerite a good turn in writing to her father, something Marguerite had been too proud to do. She'd been sure she'd never again see her family; then suddenly there was Papa, come to get her. Now, she was again separated from her family; but this time she knew that all she need do was behave in a prudent manner and be patient until Papa came again to get her, as he had promised.

Three more weeks passed before Melinda was finally allowed to visit. Marguerite had been reading on a bench in the perennial garden on a warm fall afternoon. It was Sunday, when the public was invited to enjoy the hospital grounds, so she hadn't paid notice to people walking by. While she always hoped for a visit from her parents, she hadn't expected them on that particular day, so it was a wonderful surprise when she looked up to see Mama and Papa stopped in front of her. Then Melinda stepped out from behind Papa, and Marguerite jumped up. With cries of joy, the sisters hugged and began talking simultaneously, Melinda telling of the family's new acquisition—an automobile!—and Marguerite asking a million questions about it. Laughing, their parents left the sisters to themselves.

The girls sank to the bench, holding hands, and continued talking nonstop. Marguerite noticed how much her sister had grown up in the past year. As an equal now, Melinda demanded to know why Marguerite had behaved in the manner she had. Marguerite tried to explain the desperation that had propelled her to run away, but Melinda did not understand. She declared it a mistake for Marguerite to have ended the engagement to Timothy. She told her that Bess no longer counted Marguerite as a friend, which saddened Marguerite, but not as much as it appeared to sadden Melinda. She also said that Timothy was so angry at Marguerite that he had returned her letter unopened, and refused to accept the book Melinda tried to deliver for her. This news served to bring back Marguerite's frustrations that she should have to stay in this place; that she couldn't just go see Timothy herself, and explain things to him the way she should have done to begin with.

All too soon, Mama and Papa returned, and after a short walk around the garden together as a family, it was time for them to leave. Marguerite and Melinda hugged, promising with happy declarations that soon they would be together every day.

Shortly after her family's last visit, Dr. Lyle summoned Marguerite to his office. It was a bright crisp October day, the weather having changed in temperature so that sounds and smells must be shut out, and the lovely countryside experienced through glass. Marguerite, with an uncomfortable feeling that the meeting was not for a happy purpose, focused on the view out the window behind the doctor: the wide expanse of green grass that rolled over the hill and melded with the gold and muted reds of the trees beyond. In gentle terms, Dr. Lyle told her that her parents had met with an unfortunate accident. Marguerite barely heard the details: the car on the tracks, an oncoming train, both instantly killed. She left his office without saying a word and, despite the cold, went out to her favorite place in the gardens, sinking down the path between the rose bushes, now thorny and bare of flowers and foliage. Mama and Papa gone? She tilted her head to the heavens, as if expecting to see them looking down upon her. Dear Mama. Dear Papa. Gone. She stayed until she was chilled through and an attendant came to get her.

Day after day, she could not bear to think of it, yet her mind would focus on nothing else. She had witnessed Lemuel lying lifeless, yet had learned to dash away that horrible picture when it came unbidden to her memory. But she could not do the same with thoughts of Mama and Papa. Although she had not seen the accident, refused even to learn the details of it, scenes of them bleeding and dying haunted her. It had become too cold to escape to the refuge of the garden, so she reverted to the only place she could be alone. Under the staircase, she wept, tried to make sense of the reality that everyone dear, save her beloved sister, was lost to her now.

She was allowed to attend her parents' funeral and there she saw Melinda for only the second time in the past year and a half. They fell into an embrace, soothing each other, and it was some consolation. But then Aunt Adelaide told her she was taking Melinda with her to New York, and that Marguerite was to return to the hospital to continue her treatment.

One evening, weeks, perhaps months, later, Marguerite stood at a window in the dormitory, wishing that she and Melinda could be together, that they might comfort each other. She looked out over the gardens, stark now in their November repose, the lawn silvered by the rising moon. Though she could not see them from here, there were woods beyond the manicured grounds. For the first time in many months she thought of Emil. Could he be out there waiting for her? But that was a dangerous thought because the halls here were well monitored and the outside doors locked. And there could be no climbing out of windows—locked also, and too high, with no convenient porch roof beneath them. It was dangerous, even, to allow Emil into her head. Dr. Lyle seemed to read her mind; what if he found out about Emil?

Deep in thought, Marguerite hadn't noticed the nurse at her side. It was evening medication time and the young woman held out a glass of water and two pills. Irritated at being bothered at that instant, Marguerite pushed her hand away and the glass fell to the floor, breaking. Before Marguerite could apologize, the nurse called and two attendants rushed in from the hallway. One grabbed both of her hands, and Marguerite's natural instinct was to struggle, which made things worse. The other attendant grabbed her hair, jerking her suddenly backward onto the floor, while the first attendant tightened her hold on Marguerite's hands and planted her knees on Marguerite's stomach to hold her down. The nurse, meanwhile, had obtained another glass of water, and now she knelt down and pinched Marguerite's nose. When Marguerite's mouth opened, the nurse forced the pills between her teeth, poured the water in after them, and clamped her mouth closed. Only when Marguerite had swallowed the pills and the water did they let go of her.

Sputtering, half choking on remains of the forced water, she staggered to her feet. She tore past persons standing by, sitting, and lying on beds, some who looked on idly or with interest, and some unaware of the drama or who had turned away from it. Down the hallway she ran, hair flying, face streaming with tears that mixed with the dribble of water and spittle on her chin. When she was as far into the corner under the stairway as she could go, she brought her legs up and hid her face in the dark, comforting recess between knees and chest. The roots of her hair throbbed with pain where they had been pulled; her heart thudded with exertion, but also in anger. These past weeks, she had felt herself changing, and now, she knew it was complete. She no longer believed the circumstances that had brought her here unique. Nor did she think of herself as so different from other inmates. From Millie, for instance, who had witnessed her betrothed shoot and kill her own brother, or from Elena, who had attempted suicide when she became dispirited after the death of her only child. Then there were others whose stories seemingly had no basis in illness at all: the wife who became "insane" because her husband ran away with her savings; the woman whose son-in-law had her committed because he wanted her house for himself and his family; the little girl born out of wedlock. Their behaviors—sadness, anger, distrust—seemed to Marguerite appropriate reactions to their circumstances.

Outwardly, she moaned, her tears soaking the thin dress fabric pulled tight over her knees, but inwardly she railed against the unfairness of it all. Why should a person's tragedy be compounded by being locked away from those—family, friends—who might help her to heal? By having her rights as a citizen taken away? By being labeled insane? Was it wayward for the sad, the hurt, the wronged to desire some measure of control over their lives? But then, the lack of autonomy was the reason many of them, especially the women and children, had ended up there.

Marguerite's only solace was Melinda's affectionate letters with their witty drawings. Aunt Adelaide had deemed it unhealthy for her sister to write Marguerite, so Melinda had to be stealthy in her mailings. And Marguerite could not respond because Aunt Adelaide intercepted all correspondence. Once, she sent a letter to Melinda by way of enclosing it with a note to Aunt Adelaide, but even this did not work. Aunt told Melinda about the contents of the letter, but would not give it to her, saying it would be better for Melinda to forget her insane sister.

As she began the new year of 1903, it became clear to Marguerite that she must hide her feelings of hopelessness and somehow rise above them. She had learned, through other women and her doctor, that the way to win her dismissal was by behaving in a particular way to prove that she was able to "fit herself into her personal environment." To that end, she determined to become industrious, docile, and helpful, so that she and Melinda could be together as soon as possible. In addition to convincing the doctors, she must also win over her aunt, who was now her guardian. This was an equally great task, for Aunt Adelaide had not yet forgiven Marguerite's past actions, which she felt had damaged the family's reputation.

Marguerite made herself useful in the clinic, and it was there that she got to know the little girl, Sophie, who was everyone's pet. Small for her age, with bouncy dark curls and wide blue eyes, Sophie was mischievous and lively. Her abundance of energy was put to work folding bandages, fetching supplies for doctors, and helping orderlies make beds. Still, she was often restless, for there were few other children around, and none with her curiosity and playfulness. She made friends among the adult women, who became doting surrogate mothers, holding her on their laps, brushing her hair, singing to her, and engaging her in finger play.

Sophie's was a sad story, unfortunately not unfamiliar now that Marguerite had learned the histories of many of the women. Sophie's mother had been an unmarried and unprincipled teenager, whose father disowned her upon learning of her pregnancy. He brought her to the hospital, where the child was born and had lived since. Sophie knew no other home, nor was it likely she ever would, for who would claim her? After some years, the little girl's mother had managed to gain her own release but, in hopes of starting a new life, dared not take an illegitimate child with her.

Sophie immediately took to young, beautiful Marguerite, making her her special friend among the women. Marguerite, in turn, assumed much of Sophie's care, seeing to it that the little girl ate well, was clean, and dressed properly. They became inseparable, working

side by side in the clinic, taking their meals together, playing tag in
the garden, and telling stories at bedtime. It became accepted among
the other women, if not among the staff, that Sophie was Marguerite's
charge. Marguerite vowed to herself that when she obtained her
release, Sophie would not be deserted again; she would come with her.
A vague plan began to form, one in which she and Melinda and
Sophie all lived together somewhere. Not Boston, though; it would be
a place with sun and sea and space. She told Sophie about
Portsmouth, about New Island where the Grand Hotel of the Atlantic
stood, and about Appledore Island. Together, they talked about the
things they would do when they were able to go to those places.

In February, the direction of questioning by Doctor Lyle changed.
Marguerite had been careful to appear normal in her daily talks with
the doctor, avoiding topics that caused her grief or anger, feelings that
she found difficult to control. The death of her parents and of Lemuel
were intensely private; to talk aloud of them to a stranger—for she
still considered Doctor Lyle a stranger—was to break open fragile
coverings on wounds desperately trying to heal. But Doctor Lyle
pressed on these topics, and the more he did so, the more unresponsive
she became. Likewise, she refused to react to his provocative comments concerning her future: Was she satisfied to spend her life at the
hospital? How could she ever hope to support herself on the outside if
her aunt would not take her? The doctor's purpose, Marguerite supposed, was to elicit an emotional response, which would then give him
something to address. But Marguerite would not become upset or
angry, believing that if she continued to act calmly, Doctor Lyle
would eventually have to recommend her release, even if Aunt Adelaide wouldn't have her.

But Doctor Lyle continued his prodding. He began asking questions like: Have you experienced a yearning for a dissimilar kind of
life? Do you have an explicit dissatisfaction with reality? Have you
found your happiness in fantasies or daydreams wherein you remold
reality to fit into your heart's desire? Using Marguerite's own words—

heart's desire—was the first clue that he had been reading her journal. Marguerite denied being dissatisfied with reality. She had been happily married, hadn't she? Lemuel most certainly had not been a fantasy and she was quite satisfied with her life on the island. What about Emil? he asked, with a hint of triumphant glint in his eye.

She knew then positively that somebody had sneaked her journal from its hiding place under her mattress. Doctor Lyle had, at last, succeeded in eliciting an emotion from her; she was so incensed at the invasion of the only privacy remaining to her in this place—her journal—that she could barely contain herself. As calmly as she could manage, she told the doctor that yes, Emil had been a fantasy. That she had knowingly invented him when she had needed to, and that when he had served his purpose, she had knowingly allowed him to depart. But what did that have to do with her state now that she was functioning completely in a very real world? Indeed, if ever in her life she had need to escape reality, would it not be now with all that had happened to her these past six months? Didn't the fact that she was not now indulging in fantasies discount her past weakness?

Her circumspect behavior these last months should speak for itself, she argued. She heard her voice rise in pitch and gain in speed, but could neither modulate nor stop her words. She pointed out her recent aid in the clinic. Had she not spent hours assisting the nurses in caring for those ill with the recent influenza? Did this not demonstrate her worth as a contributing citizen? She paused for breath, feeling her face flushed and hot. Doctor Lyle sat in the sturdy oak chair behind his neat desk, legs crossed and hands resting one atop the other on his knee. He was watching her with half-lidded eyes and a small smile.

Marguerite stood, turned, and strode to the door. There, she turned for a last word. "I will not indulge you, Doctor Lyle, in providing more fodder for our sessions," she told him. "There will be no more entries in my journal until I am released from this prison."

CHAPTER TWENTY-FIVE

"February fifteenth," I said. "The last entry. She died a few weeks later."

"From a broken heart," Dorothy said.

"No. She was too much of a fighter for that. She died from what they listed on her death certificate—the influenza. Probably picked up while working in that clinic." I closed Marguerite's journal with its empty pages at the end and handed it to Dorothy. "I guess that completes the story of Marguerite Miller."

Dorothy accepted the journal, nodding, her eyes shiny. "If only she hadn't run away."

"Oh, but she had to!" Mayta said. "She couldn't continue on the course set for her, and the only way to alter it was to do something drastic—to run away."

"But she ran away from the idea of marriage and then ended up getting married immediately anyway," Dorothy said. "Wasn't that the same course?"

"Not at all," Mayta said. "When she ran away, *she* set the course for herself. Granted, she did marry pretty quickly, but it was her choosing, and it was somebody outside her social circle. What she did was quite daring; after all, we're talking about 1902 when, even with money and position, a woman couldn't vote or own land—"

"—or get herself out of an institution her father or husband put her into," I finished. "Are you saying it was worth all she went through?"

"No," Mayta said soberly. "But maybe some of it was."

"The little girl she writes about—Sophie—was Claudia's grandmother, but clearly not Marguerite's child and therefore Marguerite wasn't Claudia's great-grandmother, yet Claudia, after having read this journal, persisted in believing—or pretending—that she was."

"It doesn't matter. At least Marguerite had a friend in that place." There was a catch in Dorothy's throat. "I'm glad of that."

"I thought of something while you were reading," Mayta said. "That part about giving a book to Timothy?"

"Melinda tried to give him a book from Marguerite and he refused it. He also refused her letters—"

"No. What Marguerite wrote about the ring and the book before she ran away."

"Oh, that." I flipped back, found the entry, and read again, " *'When I am safely away, I will write to Mama and Papa and Timothy explaining my decision, and also to Melinda, asking that she return Timothy's book and his mother's ring.'* "

"Was she referring to one of these?" Mayta leaned down and picked up Marguerite's books.

I turned to Dorothy. "Where did they come from? Is it possible that Marguerite had them in her hotel room?"

"I suppose so," she said. "They were among my mother's things, which she got from Great Aunt Adelaide."

I opened the history text again, read *M. Miller* in Marguerite's script, and then inspected the book inside and out.

"What are you looking for?" Dorothy asked.

But Mayta, seeing where I was going, said, "Check out the other one."

The poetry book was small and worn. I opened the cover, read the inscription, *To M. Love, T,* written in an unfamiliar hand: *To Marguerite, Love Timothy.* "This is it."

"Marguerite asked her sister to return it because it had been a gift from Timothy," Mayta explained to Dorothy. "She asked her to return this book *and* the ring."

"Oh," Dorothy said, but she still didn't understand what Mayta and I did. I looked inside the back cover, then closed it and inspected the volume from all angles. Holding it in both hands, I let the book fall open where it had before at the broken binding, which was roughly in the middle. An Emily Dickinson poem was on the right, three shorter ones—*The Wanderer* among them—were on the facing page. With the book still open, I tilted it to look inside the half-inch triangular space created between the bound pages and the gaping spine. I should have seen daylight from the other side, specifically my feet on the floor since that was the direction in which I looked, but something blocked the view.

"Is it there?" Mayta leaned over my shoulder to see.

"What are you looking for?" Dorothy said again.

"Not sure yet." I squeezed a finger into the gap between binding and spine, but it got stuck two inches in. Fearful I'd damage the book, I withdrew my finger and snatched a pencil from Ellen's desk. I poked the eraser end into the space and made contact midway down with something soft. Carefully, I prodded it and, with a little effort, the lodged object moved. Once loosed from its spot, it slid out and fell onto the floor by Dorothy's right foot. She leaned over, picked up a small wad of yellowed tissue paper, and put it in her lap.

Mayta and I watched her fingers pull open the paper and then freeze in the air as she gasped.

"Well, look at that!" Mayta smiled widely.

"So she did leave it behind," I said.

With great care, Dorothy picked up the slender yellow-gold band between thumb and forefinger, and raised the ring to the

307

fading light coming in the window, turning it back and forth so that the round solitaire caught a weak ray and sparkled. "Marguerite's diamond. My, my!" She pushed it over the enlarged knuckle of her little finger and held out her hand for us to admire.

Based on my limited experience with gems, I guessed it to be a very nice stone, not especially large—probably not over one carat—but very white and clear. "It's beautiful. Simple and elegant."

"How could it have been in that book for over a hundred years?" Mayta shook her head in wonder.

"Well," Dorothy said, "my aunt felt so disgraced by Marguerite that she kept her belongings packed away in the attic. When the books came to my mother, she probably never even opened them because she wasn't one to sit and read. And I've only looked through them once or twice in all the time I've had them. If Andy hadn't found it, this ring might have remained stuck there for many more years."

Dorothy hugged the journal to her chest, Marguerite's diamond twinkling on her little finger. "As sad as her story is," she said, her voice husky, "I feel I've been given back a member of my family. This journal has brought Marguerite to life for me."

My hands rested on the two books in my lap and I thought about the power within them, the words that had lured Marguerite into another world. From a few paragraphs in one and the lines of a poem in the other, she had molded an ideal that had helped her bridge the gap between longing and doing.

However crazy it might have been to follow a fantasy, that act had given her the strength and courage to forge the beginnings of a future that, if not what she had dreamed of, had at least been one of her own making for a short period. And in doing so, she had gained the confidence to survive what came afterward: the tragedy of her husband's death and the frustration of being institutionalized.

"You know," I said, "I believe that, given time, Marguerite would have survived it all—the loss of her husband and her parents, the betrayal of her aunt, and her hospitalization. I'm sure she somehow would have obtained her release. The only obstacle her willpower could not match, the thing that ultimately defeated her, was physical illness."

CHAPTER TWENTY-SIX

"Pretty nice." Despite the casual tone, Gus was taking it all in: the uniformed doorman who had just ushered us into the lobby of the Grand Hotel of the Atlantic, the polished parquet floor, and the elegant furnishings, including a gleaming mahogany table that supported a menacing floral arrangement large enough to devour a person who got within striking distance.

"Wait until you see the view," Mayta said under her breath. This was the third time she and I had been there, after all, so we were able to show a little decorum. Still, we paused at the entrance to the dining room to allow Gus the full effect of sky and river, spectacular in gradients of purple in the growing dusk, as viewed through windows.

Beverly had reserved a table, and everyone else was already seated with drinks. Chauncey stood as we approached, took Mayta's hands and kissed her cheek, and then did the same with me, whispering in my ear that he'd finally taken care of his bill from the gala and that from here on out, he was going to be aboveboard with all of his transactions. But he had the same mischievous twinkle in his eyes, so I laughed and said I doubted it, and he laughed in response.

Then Beverly gave a "Hey, Andy," and a wave from the opposite side of the table. It was hard to believe this was only the second time Beverly, Chauncey, and I had gotten together. But then, I'd spoken with both of them often enough by telephone that it seemed we were friends. I guessed the urgency of the experience we'd shared had something to do with it, also.

I introduced Gus to everyone, noting to myself that the last time I'd been in this dining room—the night Claudia was murdered—there had been the same number of people seated around the table. Gus and Dorothy now replaced Claudia and Daniel.

Dorothy, looking stylish in a pretty lavender print dress and matching cardigan, waved me into the seat next to her. She held out her right hand. On it twinkled Marguerite's diamond. As I bent to admire the ring, she glanced at Chauncey and said, "Your friend—Mr. Brown—told me he looked up Marguerite's fiancé's descendants. You asked him to do that?"

I nodded, smiling. "Even though he assured me that 'possession is nine-tenths of the law,' I knew you'd feel guilty keeping the ring if you felt it wasn't legally yours."

"I did think of returning it to the family, if I could find them," she admitted. "But Mr. Brown said there aren't any left. Timothy Farley married, but died fairly young and never had children, and his sister Bess unfortunately died in childbirth." She looked down with fondness at the ring on her finger. "I had it appraised when I took it in to be sized and cleaned. At first, after I found out its worth, I wasn't going to wear it, but then I thought, what am I saving it for?" She laughed. "I think these recent events have taught me how important it is to enjoy life while you can, and I intend to do that!"

I leaned over and hugged her. When I straightened, I realized the waiter was at my side, so I gave him my drink order—a Cosmopolitan, of course. Mayta said she wanted one also, and Gus ordered a beer. Then we were all talking at once, Mayta with Chauncey beside her, Gus with Beverly across the table, and me with Dorothy, who told me of her plans to continue living in her house for the time being.

"I realize now that I gave up my independence too easily,"

she said. "I let Ellen take over more and more things I could have continued doing for myself."

"So what will you do?"

"I've advertised for a part-time home health care worker, but this time she'll not live with me, nor pay my bills. I may not be the best physically, but I can maintain my books like I used to."

I had no argument with her. Dorothy was as sharp mentally as anyone I knew, and I told her so.

"But I'm not going to stick my head in the sand," she said. "I intend to find out about assisted-living places in the area and plan for the future."

When our drinks came, Beverly stood and raised her martini glass. "I'd like to propose a toast. To Dorothy, for the strength she's shown these past weeks, for her discovering a fascinating part of her family history, and," she paused for effect, "for sharing it all with me."

We laughed, thinking of how long it had taken for Dorothy to warm up to Beverly, and how, with perseverance, Beverly had finally gotten her "scoop." She had, of course, covered Claudia's murder, the surrender of Daniel Shropsgrove (alias Dean) and then the arrest of Walter and Vivian. But the real story had come—as Beverly had known all along it would—from Dorothy herself.

"When does your series begin?" Mayta asked after the last clink of glasses.

"Next week," Beverly said. "The *Monitor* will publish the first in a three-part, in-depth series about a woman," she inclined her head toward Dorothy, "tracing an ancestor back to a mental hospital. The week after, part two delves into the history of institutions in our country and the stigma still associated with mental illness, and then finally—thanks to Andy, her friend Sandy, and again to Dorothy—part three investigates the movement to categorize and clean up institutional cemeteries.

"Andy arranged for Sandy to show us the cemeteries there," Beverly said, "and now Andy and Dorothy have joined the restoration committee."

"At first, I just wanted to find Marguerite's grave and have her reburied in the family plot in Boston," Dorothy said. "But when I saw the work the memorial committee was doing, I wanted to help out. I can sit at a table and search through files as well as anyone else." She turned to me. "Andy's been wonderful, picking me up at the bus from Portsmouth and driving me down."

"I wanted to do it," I protested. "The project intrigued me also."

"Anyway," Dorothy continued, "my focus has shifted from just finding Marguerite to wanting the cemetery restored to proper respectability with names on individual markers for as many of the graves as possible—there are about seven hundred and fifty. I may never find out which grave is Marguerite's, but I can make sure that, at the very least, her name is included with others on a monument. She was a beautiful and kind young woman whose life affected others, and she deserves to be acknowledged as more than a number.

"Which," she said, holding up her wine glass again, "brings me to another toast." She waited until we'd all followed suit. "To Marguerite," she said. "It was her death, and subsequently the discovery of her life, that has brought us all together today." We touched glasses once more in the middle of the table. Then our waitress returned to take our orders and I picked up the menu.

As I vacillated between the pan-seared salmon and the roasted breast of chicken with mashed potato cake, I thought about Dorothy's words. Often, throughout my teaching years especially, students or others have asked why we should study history; how does something that happened in the past affect us in the present? I'm always surprised at the question, for it seems so clear to me; yet, each time it forces me to reevaluate and articulate my answer in a slightly different way. Everything accomplished in the present has basis in the past, I say. Would we have skyscrapers if we hadn't first had the pyramids of Giza? If we don't keep alive the awful knowledge of events like the Holocaust, can we be assured they won't be repeated?

Now, as I watched Dorothy, her physical presence expanded with a new connection to a life in the past, her face lit with a sense of purpose for the present, I wondered again at how powerful an experience reaching back into history can be. Just the act of acquainting herself with one young woman who died more than a century ago had prompted Dorothy to reengage in life. As if reading my mind, Dorothy caught my eye and winked.

"You're deep in thought." Gus's voice was low in my ear. "Care to share it?"

Before I could answer, the waitress arrived, pencil poised. Once more I skimmed the mouth-watering descriptions of two entrees, did a quick eenie, meenie, minie, mo, and said, "The salmon."

"Oh, look!" Mayta said in quiet awe. The sun had slid down beyond the horizon, draining all color from the sky. Now, across the expanse of the Piscataqua's black velvety surface streaked the shimmering reflection of a rising full moon.

ABOUT THE AUTHOR

Tempa Pagel was born in Pontiac, Michigan. She is a middle school teacher, currently residing with her husband in the historic city of Newburyport. She has two grown children, whose early antics often find their way onto the pages of her books. *They Danced by the Light of the Moon* is her second Andy Gammon mystery.